caroline kepnes

YOU

**SIMON &
SCHUSTER**

London · New York · Sydney · Toronto · New Delhi

A CBS COMPANY

First published in the United States by Simon & Schuster, Inc., 2014
First published in Great Britain by Simon & Schuster UK Ltd, 2014
A CBS COMPANY

This paperback first published in 2015

1 3 5 7 9 10 8 6 4 2

Simon & Schuster UK Ltd
1st Floor
222 Gray's Inn Road
London WC1X 8HB

www.simonandschuster.co.uk

Simon & Schuster Australia, Sydney
Simon & Schuster India, New Delhi

A CIP catalogue record for this book
is available from the British Library

Paperback ISBN: 978-1-47113-737-2
eBook ISBN: 978-1-47113-738-9

This book is a work of fiction. Names,characters, places and
incidents are either a product of the author's imagination or are
used fictitiously. Any resemblance to actual people living or
dead, events or locales is entirely coincidental.

Printed and bound by CPI Group (UK) Ltd, Croydon, CR0 4YY

For you, Dad

"First of the day, God willing, see you tomorrow."
—Harold Samuel Kepnes,
January 29, 1947–November 13, 2012

1

YOU walk into the bookstore and you keep your hand on the door to make sure it doesn't slam. You smile, embarrassed to be a nice girl, and your nails are bare and your V-neck sweater is beige and it's impossible to know if you're wearing a bra but I don't think that you are. You're so clean that you're dirty and you murmur your first word to me—*hello*—when most people would just pass by, but not you, in your loose pink jeans, a pink spun from *Charlotte's Web* and where did you come from?

You are classic and compact, my own little Natalie Portman circa the end of the movie *Closer*, when she's fresh-faced and done with the bad British guys and going home to America. You've come home to me, delivered at last, on a Tuesday, 10:06 A.M. Every day I commute to this shop on the Lower East Side from my place in Bed-Stuy. Every day I close up without finding anyone like you. Look at you, born into my world today. I'm shaking and I'd pop an Ativan but they're downstairs and I don't want to pop an Ativan. I don't want to come down. I want to be here, fully, watching you bite your unpainted nails and turn your head to the left, no, bite that pinky, widen those eyes, to the right, no, reject biographies, self-help (thank God), and slow down when you make it to fiction.

Yes.

I let you disappear into the stacks—Fiction F–K—and you're not the standard insecure nymph hunting for Faulkner you'll never finish, never start; Faulkner that will harden and calcify, if books could calcify, on your nightstand; Faulkner meant only to convince one-night stands that you mean it when you swear you never do this kind of thing. No, you're not like those girls. You don't stage Faulkner and your jeans hang loose and you're too sun-kissed for Stephen King and too untrendy for Heidi Julavits and who, who will you buy? You sneeze, loudly, and I imagine how loud you are when you climax. "God bless you!" I call out.

You giggle and holler back, you horny girl, "You too, buddy."

Buddy. You're flirting and if I was the kind of asshole who Instagrams, I would photograph the F–K placard and filter the shit out of that baby and caption it:

F—K yes, I found her.

Calm down, Joe. They don't like it when a guy comes on too strong, I remind myself. Thank God for a customer and it's hard to scan his predictable Salinger—then again, it's always hard to do that. This guy is, what, thirty-six and he's only now reading *Franny and Zooey*? And let's get real. He's not reading it. It's just a front for the Dan Browns in the bottom of his basket. Work in a bookstore and learn that most people in this world feel guilty about being who they are. I bag the Dan Brown first like it's kiddie porn and tell him *Franny and Zooey* is the shit and he nods and you're still in F–K because I can see your beige sweater through the stacks, barely. If you reach any higher, I'll see your belly. But you won't. You grab a book and sit down in the aisle and maybe you'll stay here all night. Maybe it'll be like the Natalie Portman movie *Where the Heart Is*, adapted faithlessly from the Billie Letts book—above par for that kind of crud—and I'll find you in the middle of the night. Only you won't be pregnant and I won't be the meek man in the movie. I'll lean over and say, *"Excuse me, miss, but we're closed"* and you'll look up and smile. *"Well, I'm not closed."* A breath. *"I'm wide open.* Buddy.*"*

"Hey." Salinger-Brown bites. He's still here? He's still here. "Can I get a receipt?"

"Sorry about that."

He grabs it out of my hand. He doesn't hate me. He hates himself. If people could handle their self-loathing, customer service would be smoother.

"You know what, kid? You need to get over yourself. You work in a bookstore. You don't make the books. You don't write the books and if you were any good at reading the books, you probably wouldn't work in a bookstore. So wipe that judgmental look off your face and tell me to have a nice day."

This man could say anything in the world to me and he'd still be the one shame-buying Dan Brown. You appear now with your intimate Portman smile, having heard the motherfucker. I look at you. You look at him and he's still looking at me, waiting.

"Have a nice day, sir," I say and he knows I don't mean it, hates that he craves platitudes from a stranger. When he's gone, I call out again because you're listening, "You enjoy that Dan Brown, motherfucker!"

You walk over, laughing, and thank God it's morning, and we're dead in the morning and nobody is gonna get in our way. You put your basket of books down on the counter and you sass, "You gonna judge me too?"

"What an asshole, right?"

"Eh, probably just in a mood."

You're a sweetheart. You see the best in people. You complement me.

"Well," I say and I should shut up and I want to shut up but you make me want to talk. "That guy is the reason that Blockbuster shouldn't have gone under."

You look at me. You're curious and I want to know about you but I can't ask so I just keep talking.

"Everybody is always striving to be better, lose five pounds, read five books, go to a museum, buy a classical record and listen to it and like it. What they really want to do is eat doughnuts, read magazines, buy pop albums. And books? Fuck books. Get a Kindle. You know why Kindles are so successful?"

You laugh and you shake your head and you're listening to me at the point when most people drift, go into their phone. And you're pretty and you ask, "Why?"

"I'll tell you why. The Internet put porn in your home—"

I just said *porn*, what a dummy, but you're still listening, what a doll.

"And you didn't have to go out and get it. You didn't have to make eye contact with the guy at the store who now knows you like watching girls get spanked. Eye contact is what keeps us civilized."

Your eyes are almonds and I go on. "Revealed."

You don't wear a wedding ring and I go on. "Human."

You are patient and I need to shut up but I can't. "And the Kindle, the Kindle takes all the integrity out of reading, which is exactly what the Internet did to porn. The checks and balances are gone. You can read your Dan Brown in public and in private all at once. It's the end of civilization. But—"

"There's always a but," you say and I bet you come from a big family of healthy, loving people who hug a lot and sing songs around a campfire.

"But with no places to buy movies or albums, it's come down to books. There are no more video stores so there are no more nerds who work in video stores and quote Tarantino and fight about Dario Argento and hate on people who rent Meg Ryan movies. That act, the interaction between seller and buyer, is the most important two-way street we got. And you can't just eradicate two-way streets like that and not expect a fallout, you know?"

I don't know if you know but you don't tell me to stop talking the way people sometimes do and you nod. "Hmm."

"See, the record store was the great equalizer. It gave the nerds power—'*You're* really *buying Taylor Swift?*'—even though all those nerds went home and jerked it to Taylor Swift."

Stop saying Taylor Swift. Are you laughing at me or with me?

"Anyway," I say, and I'll stop if you tell me to.

"Anyway," you say, and you want me to finish.

"The point is, buying stuff is one of the only honest things we do. That guy didn't come in here for Dan Brown *or* Salinger. That guy came in here to confess."

"Are you a priest?"

"No. I'm a church."

"Amen."

You look at your basket and I sound like a deranged loner and I look in your basket. Your phone. You don't see it, but I do. It's cracked. It's in a yellow case. This means that you only take care of yourself when you're beyond redemption. I bet you take zinc the third day of a cold. I pick up your phone and try to make a joke.

"You steal this off that guy?"

You take your phone and you redden. "Me and this phone . . ." you say. "I'm a bad mommy."

Mommy. You're dirty, you are.

"Nah."

You smile and you're definitely not wearing a bra. You take the books out of the basket and put the basket on the floor and look at me like it wouldn't be remotely possible for me to criticize anything you ever did. Your nipples pop. You don't cover them. You notice the Twizzlers I keep by the register. You point, hungry. "Can I?"

"Yes," I say, and I am feeding you already. I pick up your first book, *Impossible Vacation* by Spalding Gray. "Interesting," I say. "Most people get his monologues. This is a great book, but it's not a book that people go around buying, particularly young women who don't appear to be contemplating suicide, given the fate of the author."

"Well, sometimes you just want to go where it's dark, you know?"

"Yeah," I say. "Yeah."

If we were teenagers, I could kiss you. But I'm on a platform behind a counter wearing a name tag and we're too old to be young. Night moves don't work in the morning, and the light pours in through the windows. Aren't bookstores supposed to be dark?

Note to self: Tell Mr. Mooney to get blinds. Curtains. Anything.

I pick up your second book, *Desperate Characters* by one of my favorite authors, Paula Fox. This is a good sign, but you could be buying it because you read on some stupid blog that she's Courtney Love's biological grandmother. I can't be sure that you're buying Paula Fox because you came to her the right way, from a Jonathan Franzen essay.

You reach into your wallet. "She's the best, right? Kills me that she's not more famous, even with Franzen gushing about her, you know?"

Thank God. I smile. *"The Western Coast."*

You look away. "I haven't gone there yet." I look at you and you put your hands up, surrender. "Don't shoot." You giggle and I wish your nipples were still hard. "I'm gonna read *The Western Coast* someday and *Desperate Characters* I've read a zillion times. This one's for a friend."

"Uh-huh," I say and the red lights flash danger. *For a friend.*

"It's probably a waste of time. He won't even read it. But at least she sells a book, right?"

"True." Maybe he's your brother or your dad or a gay neighbor, but I know he's a *friend* and I stab at the calculator.

"It's thirty-one fifty-one."

"Holy money. See, *that's* why Kindles rule," you say as you reach into your Zuckerman's pig-pink wallet and hand me your credit card even though you have enough cash in there to cover it. You want me to know your name and I'm no nut job and I swipe your card and the quiet between us is getting louder and why didn't I put on music today and I can't think of anything to say.

"Here we go." And I offer you the receipt.

"Thanks," you murmur. "This is a great shop."

You're signing and you are Guinevere Beck. Your name is a poem and your parents are assholes, probably, like most parents. *Guinevere.* Come on.

"Thank you, Guinevere."

"I really just go by Beck. Guinevere's kinda long and ridiculous, you know?"

"Well, Beck, you look different in person. Also, *Midnite Vultures* is awesome."

You take your bag of books and you don't break eye contact because you want me to see you seeing me. "Right on, Goldberg."

"Nah, I just go by Joe. Goldberg is kind of long and ridiculous, ya know?"

We're laughing and you wanted to know my name as much as I wanted to know yours or you wouldn't have read my name tag. "Sure you don't wanna grab *The Western Coast* while you're here?"

"This will sound crazy, but I'm saving it. For my nursing home list."

"You mean bucket list."

"Oh no, that's totally different. A nursing home list is a list of things you plan on reading and watching in a nursing home. A bucket list is more like . . . visit Nigeria, jump out of an airplane. A nursing home list is like, read *The Western Coast* and watch *Pulp Fiction* and listen to the latest Daft Punk album."

"I can't picture you in a nursing home."

You blush. You are *Charlotte's Web* and I could love you. "Aren't you gonna tell me to have a nice day?"

"Have a nice day, Beck."

You smile. "Thanks, Joe."

You didn't walk in here for books, Beck. You didn't have to say my name. You didn't have to smile or listen or take me in. But you did. Your signature is on the receipt. This wasn't a cash transaction and it wasn't a coded debit. This was real. I press my thumb into the wet ink on your receipt and the ink of Guinevere Beck stains my skin.

2

I came to know e. e. cummings the way most sensitive, intelligent men my age came to e. e. cummings, via one of the most romantic scenes in one of the most romantic love stories of all time, *Hannah and Her Sisters*, wherein an intelligent, sophisticated, married New Yorker named Elliot (Michael Caine) falls in love with his sister-in-law (Barbara Hershey). He has to be careful. He can't casually make a move. He waits near her apartment and stages a run-in. Brilliant, romantic. Love takes work. She is surprised to run into him and she takes him to the Pageant Bookstore—are you catching a theme here?—where he buys a book of e. e. cummings poems for her and sends her to the poem on page 112.

She sits alone in bed, reading the poem, and he, meanwhile, stands alone in his bathroom thinking of her as we hear her reading. My favorite part of the poem:

Nobody, not even the rain, has such small hands.

Except for you, Beck. These past few days, I've learned so much.

You put your tiny hands to work on yourself when the mood strikes, which it does, often, which reminds me of another joke in *Hannah*, where Mia Farrow teases Woody Allen that he ruined himself with excessive masturbation. You're okay, I hope.

The trouble with society is that if the average person knew about us—you, alone, orgasming three times a night, and me, across the street, watching you orgasm, alone—most people would say I'm the fuckup. Well, it's no secret that most people are fucking idiots. Most people like cheap mysteries and most people have never heard of Paula Fox or *Hannah* so honestly, Beck, fuck most people, right?

Besides, I like that you take care of yourself instead of filling your home and your pussy with a string of inadequate men. You're the answer to every banal and reductive article about "hook-up culture." You have standards and you *are* Guinevere, a love story waiting for the one, and I bet you capitalize The One when you dream of him. Of me. Everyone wants everything right now but you are able to wait with

Such small hands.

Your name was a glorious place to start. Lucky for us, there aren't a lot of Guinevere Becks in the world—just the one. The first thing I had to find was your home and the Internet was designed with love in mind. It gave me so much of you, Beck, your Twitter profile:

Guinevere Beck

@TheUnRealBeck

I've never had an unspoken thought. I write stories. I read stories. I talk to strangers. Nantucket is my homeboy but New York is my homebitch.

Your revealing bios at various online journals that publish your blogs (unless you want to call them essays), and your thinly veiled diary entries (unless you want to call them short stories), and the poems you write sometimes have fleshed you out. You are a writer born and raised on Nantucket and you joke about island inbreeding (but you aren't inbred), and sailing (you are petrified of boats), and alcoholism (you lost your father to the bottle and write about it a lot). Your family is as tight as it is loose. You don't know how to be here, in the city where nobody knows anybody, even though you had four years of practice as an undergrad at Brown. You got in off the wait list and you remain convinced that there was some sort of mistake. You like polenta and cherry pie Lärabars. You don't take pictures of food or concerts but you do Instagram (but really only old things, pictures of your dead father, pictures of beach days you can't possibly remember). You have a brother, Clyde. Your parents really were assholes about the names. You have a sister, Anya (serious assholes, but not the kind I thought). Real estate records show that your house has been in your family forever. You hail from farmers and you're fond of saying that you don't have "a place" on Nantucket, but that your family made a *home* there. Full of disclaimers, you're like a warning label on a pack of cigarettes.

Anya is an islander and she'll never leave. She's the baby who wants nothing more than walks on the beach and the clear division of summer and the desolation endemic to a seasonal tourist trap. Anya is fucked in the head over your dad. You write about her in your stories and you turn her into a young boy or an aging blind woman or, once, a lost squirrel, but it's clear that you're writing about your sister. You envy her. How come she doesn't have the weight of ambition? You pity her. How come she has no ambition?

Clyde is the oldest, and he gets to run the family's taxi business on the island. He's married with two kids and he's the paint-by-numbers parent of the family. That much is clear from his picture in the local paper: a volunteer fireman, leather-skinned, standard-issue American man. Your dad has the record of any small-town boozer and he's not above a DUI or a public intoxication and your brother responded by being the opposite—sober, extremely sober. If you had been born first, running the family business might have been an option. But you were a classic middle child and you did well in school and your whole life you were labeled "the hope," the one who would get away.

The Internet is a beautiful thing and you sent a tweet an hour after we met that day:

I smell cheeseburgers. #CornerBistroIsMakingMeFat

And let me tell you, for a moment there, I was concerned. Maybe I wasn't special. You didn't even mention me, our conversation. Also: *I talk to strangers* is a line in your Twitter bio. *I talk to strangers.* What the fuck *is* that, Beck? Children are not supposed to talk to strangers but you are an adult. Or is our conversation nothing to you? Am I just another *stranger*? Is your Twitter bio your subtle way of announcing that you're an attention whore who has no standards and will give audience to any poor schmuck who says hello? Was I nothing to you? You don't even mention the guy in the bookstore? *Fuck*, I thought, *maybe I was wrong.* Maybe we had nothing. But then I started to explore you and you don't write about what really matters. You wouldn't share me with your *followers.* Your online life is a variety show, so if anything, the fact that you didn't put me in your stand-up act means that you covet me. Maybe even more than I realize, since right now your hand is heading down to your cunt yet again.

The next thing the Internet gave me was your address. Fifty-One Bank Street. Are you fucking kidding me? This isn't a frenzied Midtown block where harried worker bees storm to and from the office. This is tony, sleepy, ridiculously safe and expensive West Village real estate. I can't just hang out on your block; I have to fit in with the la-di-da folk. I hit up the thrift store. I buy a suit (businessman and/or driver and/or kept man), carpenter pants and some kind of tool belt (handyman on a break), and a bullshit tracksuit (asshole taking care of his precious body). I wear the suit for my first visit and I love it here, Beck. It's quintessential Old New York and I expect Edith Wharton and Truman Capote to cross the street hand in hand, each carrying a Greek paper cup of coffee, looking as they did in their heyday, as if they'd been preserved in formaldehyde. Princesses live on this block and Sid Vicious died on this block a long time ago, when the princesses were gestating, when Manhattan was still cool. I stand across the street and your windows are open (no curtains) and I watch you pour instant oatmeal into a Tupperware bowl. You are not a princess. Your Twitter confirms that you won some kind of real estate lottery:

Um, not to sound like @AnnaKendrick47, but I love you awesome nerds of the @BrownBiasedNYC and I can't wait to move to Bank St.

I sit down on the stoop and Google. The Brownstone Biased Lottery is an essay contest for Brown University graduates who need housing for graduate school in New York. The apartment has stayed in *the Brown family* (whatever that means exactly) for years. You're an MFA candidate in fiction writing, so it's no surprise that you won a lottery that's actually an essay contest. And Anna Kendrick is an actress in this movie *Pitch Perfect*, which is about college girls who sing in a cappella competitions. You see yourself in this girl, which makes no sense. I watched that *Pitch* movie. That girl would never live the way you do.

People pass by your *parlor level* apartment, ever so slightly above ground level, and they don't stop to stare even though you're on display. Your two windows are wide open and you are lucky this is not a well-trafficked street. This must explain the deluded sense of privacy you have. I return the next evening (same suit, can't help it) and you walk around *naked* in front of the open windows. Naked! I hang out again across the street on the stoop and you don't notice me and nobody notices you *or* me and is everyone here fucking blind?

Days pass and I grow anxious. You parade too much and it's unsafe and it only takes *one* weirdo to spot you inside and decide to go and get you. A few days later I wear my carpenter costume and I fantasize about putting bars on your windows, protecting this display case you call a *home*. I think of this neighborhood as safe, and it is, but there's deathliness to the quiet here. I could probably strangle some old man in the middle of the street and nobody would come outside to stop me.

I return in my suit (so much better than carpenter garb) and I wear a Yankees cap I found at another thrift shop (I'm *that* asshole!) to mix it up, just in case you were to notice, which you don't. A man who lives in your building climbs the very small staircase (just three steps) that leads to an exterior door (it's not locked!) and that door is so close to your apartment. If he wanted to (and who wouldn't want to?), he could lean over the railing and rap his knuckles on your screen and call your name.

I come in the day, in the night, and whenever I am here, your windows are always open. It's like you've never seen the nightly news or a horror movie and I sit on the steps of the brownstone across the tiny, clean street that faces your building and I pretend to read Paula Fox's *Poor George* or pretend to text my business associates (ha!) or pretend to call a friend who's late and loudly agree to wait another twenty minutes. (That's for the neighbor who always might be hidden away, suspicious of the man on the stoop; I've seen a lot of movies.) With your open-door policy, I am allowed into your world. I smell your Lean Cuisines if the wind is right and I hear your Vampire Weekend and if I pretend to yawn and look up, I can see you loaf, yawn, breathe. Were you always like this? I wonder if you were this way in Providence, parading around as if you want your rarified neighbors to know you naked, half-naked, addicted to microwave foods, and masturbating at the top of your lungs. Hopefully not, hopefully there is logic to this that you'll explain to me when it's time. And you with your computer, as if you need to remind your imaginary audience that you're a writer when we (I) know what you truly are: a performer, an exhibitionist.

And all the while, I have to be vigilant. I slick my hair back one day and wear it shaggy the next. I must go unnoticed by the people who don't notice people. After all, if the average person was told about an often nude girl prancing around in front of an open window and a love-struck guy across the street watching, discreetly, most people would say I'm the nut. But you're the nut. You're just not called a nut because your pussy is a thing that all these people want to know about, whereas my whole being is abhorrent to your neighbors. I live in a sixth-floor walk-up in Bed-Stuy. I didn't allow my nut sack to be raided by the College Loan Society of Bullshit. I get paid under the table and own a TV with an antenna. These people don't want to touch my dick with a ten-foot pole. Your pussy, on the other hand, is gold.

I sip my coffee on the stoop across the street and grip my rolled-up *Wall Street Journal* and I breathe and I look at you. I never wear the tracksuit because you make me want to dress up, Beck. Two weeks pass and a portly dowager emerges from her quarters. I stand, fucked, but a gentleman.

"Hello, madam," I say and I offer my assistance.

She accepts. "It's about time you young men learned how to behave," she rasps.

"Couldn't agree more," I say and the driver of her town car opens the door. He nods to me, brothers. I could do this forever and I settle back onto my stoop.

Is this why people like reality TV? Your world is a wonder to me, seeing where you lounge (in cotton panties bought in bulk online from Victoria's Secret; I saw you tear into the package the other day) and where you don't sleep (you sit on that couch and read crap online). You make me think; maybe you're searching for that hot guy in the bookstore, maybe. This is where you write, sitting so erect with your hair in a bun and typing at bunny-rabbit speed until you can't take it anymore and you grab that lime-green pillow, the same pillow you prop your head against when you nap, and you mount that thing like an animal. Release. This is where you sleep, at last.

Also, your apartment is small as hell. You were right when you tweeted:

I live in a shoebox. Which is ok bc I don't blow Benjamins on Manolos.
@BrownBiasedNYC #Rebel

My #BrownUniversity mug is bigger than my apartment. @BrownBiasedNYC #realestate #NYC

There's no kitchen, just an area where appliances are shoved together like clearance floor samples at Bed Bath & Beyond. But there's truth buried in your tweet. You hate it here. You grew up in a big house with a backyard and a front yard. You like space. That's why you leave the windows open. You don't know how to be alone with yourself. And if you block out the world, there you'd be.

Your neighbors go on, like children—town cars pick them up from their enormous nearby homes and redeposit them at day's end—while you fester in a space meant for a maid or a golden retriever with a sprained ankle. But I don't blame you for staying here. You and I share a love of the West Village and if I could move into this place, I would too, even if it meant slowly going insane from claustrophobia. You made the right choice, Beck. Your mother was wrong:

Mom says no "lady" should live in a shoebox. @BrownBiasedNYC #momlogic #notalady

You tweet more often than you write and this could be why you're getting your MFA from the New School and not from Columbia. Columbia rejected you:

Rejection is a dish best served in a paper envelope because then at least you can tear it up or burn it. #notintoColumbia #lifegoeson

And you were right. Life did go on. Though the New School isn't as prestigious, the teachers and students like you well enough. A lot of their workshops are accessible online. A lot of college is accessible online, which is yet another strike against the increasingly irrelevant elitist system that they call "college." Your writing is coming along, and if you spent a little less time tweeting and spanking the kitty . . . But honestly, Beck, if I were in your skin, I'd never even put clothes on.

You like to name things and I wonder what you'll name me. You are attempting to have a Twitter contest for the name of your apartment:

How about #Boxsmallerthanmybox

Or #PitchPerfectWatchingPad

Or #Yogamatclosetmistakenforapartment

Or #Placewhereyoulookoutthewindowandseetheguyfromthebookstore-watchingyouandyousmileandwaveand

A cabbie lays on his horn because some freshly showered asshole who crawled out of a Bret Easton Ellis rough draft that never saw the light of day is crossing the street without looking. He says *sorry* but he doesn't mean it and he's running his hand through his blond hair.

He has too much hair.

And he's walking up those steps like he owns them, like they were built for him and the door opens before he's there and that's *you* opening the door and now you're there, guiding him inside and kissing him before the door slows to a close and now your hands

Such small hands

are in his hair and I can't see either of you until you're in the living room and he sits on the couch and you tear off your tank top and climb on top of him and you grind like a stripper, and this is all wrong, Beck. He tears off your cotton panties and he's spanking you and you're yelping and I cross the street and lean against your building door because I need to hear it.

Sorry, Daddy! Sorry!

Say it again, little girl.

I'm sorry, Daddy.

You're a bad girl.

I'm a bad girl.

You want a spanking, don't you?

Yes, Daddy, I want a spanking.

He's in your mouth. He barks at you. He slaps at you. Once in a while Truman Capote walks by and looks, reacts, then looks away. Nobody will report this to the police because nobody wants to admit to watching. This is Bank Street for fuck's sake. And now you're fucking him and I return to my side of the street where I see that he's not making love to you. You're grabbing his hair—too much hair—like it might save you and your stories. You deserve better and it can't feel good, the way he grips you, big weak hands that never worked, the way he smacks your ass when he's done. You hop off and you lean against him and he pushes you away and you let him smoke in your apartment and he ashes in your Brown mug—bigger than your apartment—and you watch your *Pitch Perfect* while he smokes and texts and pushes you away when you lean into him. You look sad and

Nobody in the world has such small hands

except for you and me. Why am I so sure? Three months ago, before you knew me you wrote this tweet:

Can we all be honest and admit we know #eecummings because of #Hannahandhersisters? Okay phew. #nomoreBS #endofpretension

See how you were talking to me before you even knew me? When he leaves, he isn't holding *Desperate Characters* by Paula Fox. He is a blond misogynist popping his collar and blowing hair out of his eyes. He just used you and he is not your *friend* and I have to leave. You need a shower.

3

BEFORE you, there was Candace. She was stubborn too, so I'm gonna be patient with you, same way I was patient with her. I am not gonna hold it against you that in that old, bulky laptop computer of yours you write about every fucking thing in the world except me. I am no idiot, Beck. I know how to search a hard drive and I know I'm not in there and I know you don't even own anything resembling a notebook or a diary.

One possible theory: You write about me in the notepad on your phone. Hope remains.

But, I'm not gonna pull away from you. Sure, you are uniquely sexual. Case in point: You devour the "Casual Encounters" section on Craigslist, copying and pasting your favorite posts into a giant file on your computer. Why, Beck, why? Fortunately, you don't participate in "Casual Encounters." And I suppose that girls like to collect things, be it kale soup recipes or poorly worded, grammatically offensive daddy fantasies composed by desperate loners. Hey, I'm still here;

I accept you. And, okay. So you do let this blond creep do things to you that you read about in these Craigslist ads. But at least you have boundaries. That perv is not your boyfriend; you sent him into the street, where he belongs, as if you are disgusted with him, which you should be. And I have read all your recent e-mails and it's official: You did not tell anyone that he was in your apartment, inside of you. He is not your boyfriend. That's all that matters and I am ready to find you and I am able to find you and I owe that to Candace. Dear Candace.

I first saw Candace at the Glasslands in Brooklyn. She played flute in a band with her brother and sister. You would like their music. They were called Martyr and I wanted to know her right away. I was patient. I followed them all over Brooklyn and lower Manhattan. They were good. They weren't ever going to be top forty, but sometimes they'd have a song featured in a wretched show for teenagers on the CW and their website would explode. They didn't have a label because they couldn't agree on anything. Anyway, Candace was the prettiest, the lead of the band. Her brother was your standard drummer fuckup douche bag and her sister was homely and talented.

You can't just bum-rush a girl after a concert, especially when the band's music is ambient techno electro shit and when her psycho controlling brother (who, by the way, would never be in a band were it not for his sisters) is always hanging around. I had to get Candace alone. And I couldn't be some guy hitting on her, because of her "protective" brother. And I was going to die if I didn't get to hold her, or at least make a step toward holding her. So I improvised.

One night, outside of the Glasslands where it all began, I introduced myself to Martyr as the new assistant at Stop It Records.

I told them I was scouting. Well, bands like being scouted and there I was, minutes later, in a booth drinking whiskey with Candace and her irritating siblings. Her sister left; good girl. But her brother was a problem. I couldn't kiss Candace or ask for her number. "E-mail me," she said. "I can take a picture of it and put it on Instagram. We love it when labels reach out."

So I did what any Elliot in *Hannah* would do. I staked out Stop It Records, a sad little joint, and noticed this kid they call *Peters* come and go every day. Before and after work, he'd duck into an alley and smoke a little pot. You couldn't blame him, what with the shit he put up with at work. Peters was the assistant to all the record label pricks in tight jeans who call their glasses *eyewear* and call out for *Splenda* and *extra Parmigiano-Reggiano*. So I camped out with a joint in the alley one day and asked Peters for a light. It was easy to make friends; people at the bottom of the totem pole are hungry for other people. I told him all about the dilemma with Candace, how I told her I work for Stop It and it was *his* idea to e-mail her from his account (asst1@stopitrecords.com) and pretend to be me. Candace wrote back, giddy, hot. And of course, she gave me (asst1) her number.

I didn't feel bad about using Peters; if anything, he finally felt like he had something resembling power. And sometimes you have to play around with the facts to get the girl. I have seen enough romantic comedies to know that romantic guys like me are always getting into jams like this. Kate Hudson's entire career exists because people who fall in love sometimes tell lies about where they work. And Candace believed that I was a scout. I waited until we'd been together for a month before I told her the truth. She was mad at first (girls get mad sometimes, even when the guy is Matthew McConaughey) but I reminded her of the comedic, romantic truth at heart: The world is an unfair place. I know music. I'm smart. I think Martyr deserves to be scouted and worshipped. Had I gone to some liberal arts college and worn vintage socks and subscribed to the notion that a bachelor of arts qualifies someone as employable and intelligent, I could have gotten a nonpaying internship at a shitty record label and parlayed it into a shitty job too. But as it happens, I don't subscribe to that antiquated notion. I'm my own person. She understood, at first, but her brother was another story, one of the reasons it didn't work out between Candace and me.

The good news is that I have no regrets. My troubles with Candace were training for this moment. I had to get into your place, Beck. And I knew what to do.

I called the gas company and reported a leak at your apartment when I knew you would be at your dance class and you always have coffee after class with a friend in the class and this is the only guaranteed time that you're away from your computer. I waited on my stoop across the way for the gas man to arrive. When he did I told him I was your boyfriend and that you sent me to help out.

The law requires that all gas leaks be investigated and the law of guys indicates that a guy like me, having dropped out of high school, has a certain way of dealing with guys who work for the gas company. What can I say? I knew he'd buy that I was your boyfriend and let me in. And I knew that even if he thought I was a lying nut job, he'd let me in. You can't just call in the gas man and not show up, Beck. Seriously.

He leaves, and the first thing I do is take your computer and sit on your couch and smell your green pillow and drink water out of your Brown mug. I washed it because his ashes lingered (you don't know how to wash a dish). I read your story called "What Wylie Was Thinking When He Bought His Kia." It's about an old dude in California buying a shitty import car and feeling like that's the last vestige of his life as a cowboy. The twist is that he wasn't an actual cowboy. He just played cowboys in Westerns. But they don't make Westerns anymore and Wylie never adapted. He never had a car because he spent most of his days at a coffee shop where guys like him sat around talking about the good old days. But they recently outlawed smoking—you italicize *outlawed*, which is cute—and so now the gang has no local place to smoke their cigarettes and tell their stories. The story ends with Wylie in his Kia and he can't remember how to start it. He's holding his key that's just a miniature computer and he realizes he doesn't know where to go so he buys an e-cigarette and returns to the coffee shop and sits alone smoking his e-cigarette.

I'm no genius MFA candidate in your workshops—seriously, Beck, they don't understand you or your stories—but you yearn for what was. You're a dead guy's daughter, thoroughly. You understand Paula Fox and you aspire to make sense of all things Old West, which makes your settling, even temporarily, in New York a self-destructive move. You're compassionate; you wrote about old actors because of the photography books in your apartment, so many pictures of places you can't go because they aren't there anymore. You're a romantic, searching for a Coney Island minus the drug dealers and the gum wrappers and an innocent California where real cowboys and fake cowboys traded stories over tin cups of coffee they called *joe*. You want to go places you can't go.

In your bathroom, when the door is closed and you sit on the toilet, you stare at a photograph of Einstein. You like to look into his eyes while you struggle against your bowels. (And believe me, Beck, when we're together, your stomach issues will be over because I won't allow you to live on frozen shit and cans of sodium water labeled "soup.") You like Einstein because he saw what nobody saw. Also, not a writer. He's not the competition, now or ever.

I turn on the TV and *Pitch Perfect* is your most watched thing, which makes sense now that I can see your college life on your Facebook. I'm finally inside, studying the history of you in pictures. You did not sing a cappella or find passion or true love. You and your best friends Chana and Lynn got drunk a lot. There is a third friend who is very tall and very thin. She dwarfs you and your little friends. This outsider friend isn't tagged in any of the pictures and there must be something redeeming about her because you appear very proud of this friendship, which has lasted since your childhood. The untagged girl looks unhappy in every shot. Her nonsmiling smile will haunt me and it's time to move on.

You dated two guys. Charlie looked like he was always recovering from a Dave Matthews concert. When you were with him you sat on lawns and did club-kid drugs. You escaped that drug-addled dullard and fell into the pin-thin arms of a spoiled punk named Hesher. On a side note, I *know* Hesher, not personally, but he's a graphic novelist and we sell his books in the shop. At least, we do right now, but obviously, the first order of business on my next shift will be burying Hesher's books in the basement.

You've been to Paris and Rome and I've never been out of the country and you never found what you were looking for in Hesher or Paris or Charlie or Rome or college. You left Charlie for Hesher.

And you were cold; Charlie never got over you. He looks permanently drunk to this day in his pictures. You worshipped Hesher and he never reciprocated, at least not on Facebook. There are lots of posts where you praise him and he never responds. Then one day, you became single and your friends "liked" your status in a way that leaves no doubt that you were the one dumped.

Pitch Perfect has ended and I go to your bedroom and I am on your bed, unmade, and I hear the sound of a key entering a keyhole and turning, and a blitzkrieg in my mind, the landlord bitching to the gas man earlier today—

Smallest unit in the building, smallest fucking keyhole, always sticks

—and I hear you put a key into your keyhole and the door opens and the apartment is small and you are inside of it.

You're right, Beck. It is a fucking shoebox.

4

I never go to Greenpoint, where people chase whiskey with pickle juice, but I'm doing this for you, Beck. Just like I hurt my back for you when I fell out of your window so you wouldn't see me when I was trying to see you, trying to know you. And I hate that you could see me here now and think that I'm some dick who overestimates the cultural value of *Vice* and drinks whatever fucking *Vice* tells me to drink. I didn't go to college, Beck, so I don't waste my adulthood trying to recapture my time in college. I'm not a soft motherfucker who never had the guts to live life right now, as is. I live for living and I'd order another vodka soda but that would mean speaking to the bartender in the Bukowski T-shirt and he'd ask me again what kind of club soda I want.

I'm in a mood and you're up there reading in yellow stockings and there are holes in them and you're trying too hard. You left *Charlotte's Web* but I don't look so hot, either. I had to climb out your window and it's a short fall, but a fall is a fall and my back stings and if I hear the word *pickleback* one more time, I swear.

Your best friends are at the table next to mine, loud and disloyal, real F-train types with the boots and the overprocessed hair that quietly insults all the Jersey girls that do that shit on purpose. The three of you were at Brown together and now you're in New York together and you all hate *Girls* and complain about it incessantly but isn't that exactly what you're all trying to do with your lives? Brooklyn, boys, and *picklebacks*?

You sit with the other quote unquote *writers*, which allows your friends to go on about you and unfortunately, they're right: You're so much more invested in being a writer—accepting compliments and drinking whiskey—than you are at writing. But fortunately, they're also wrong: Everyone in this room is too full of pickle juice to understand your cowboy story.

Your friends are jealous. Chana's the big critic, a girl version of Adam Levine with beady eyes and unwarranted self-confidence. "Explain to me again what this fucking MFA shit does for you if you're not Lena Dunham?"

"I think maybe you can teach?" says Lynn, and Lynn is dead inside, like a corpse. She Instagrams methodically, clinically, as if she's gathering evidence for defense, like her entire life is dedicated to proving that she has a life. She loudly mocks your *reading at Lulu's* as she tweets about how *psyched* she is to be at a *#readingatLulus*, and I'm telling you, Beck, I swear.

Lynn again: "Do you think this is like an art opening where you go once and you're good or is this gonna be like . . . an every week thing?"

"Do I set up a fucking runway every time I finish a design?" Chana vents. "No. I work on it and work on it more until I have a *collection*. And then I work on it again."

"Is Peach coming?"

"Don't put that in the universe."

They might be talking about the unsmiling tall girl but it's not like I can ask them.

"Sorry." Lynn sighs. "At least at art openings you get free wine."

"At least at art openings you get art. I'm sorry, but a *fucking cowboy?*"

Lynn shrugs and it just goes on, a machine gun that won't stop, can't stop.

"And can we talk about her costume?"

"She's trying too hard. It's kinda sad."

"What the fuck are those tights?"

Lynn sighs and tweets and sighs and the machine-gun fire quickens for the last round.

"No wonder she didn't get into Columbia," Chana snipes.

"I feel like this is all cuz of Benji," says Lynn. "I feel bad for her."

Benji?

"Well, this is what happens when you fall for a sociopathic party boy."

All I hear is *fall for* and you love him and you lie to them, to your computer, to yourself and you think they don't know it and they do know it and oh no. *Benji.* No.

I have to stay tuned, present, and Lynn sighs. "You're being mean."

"I'm being real." Chana huffs. "Benji is a snobby little prick. All he does is get fucked up on overpriced drugs and launch pretend businesses."

"What did he major in?" Lynn wants to know.

"Who cares?" Chana snaps and I care and I want to know more and I want to cry and I don't want you to *fall for* anyone but me.

"Well, I still wish he'd be nicer to her," Lynn says.

Chana rolls her eyes and crunches on ice cubes and disagrees. "You know what it is? Beck is full of herself. And Benji is full of himself. I don't feel bad for either one of them. She's got us here pretending she's a writer and he's got the world pretending he's a freaking *artisan*. What a joke. They both just love themselves. We're not talking about overly sensitive, tortured souls writing poems about the bleakness of it all or whatever."

Lynn is bored and I am too. She tries to steer Chana away from her diatribe. "I feel so fat right now."

Chana grunts. Girls are mean. "You see all this crap about his organic soda company?" she asks. "Brooklyn makes me want to move to LA and buy a case of Red Bull and rock out to Mariah Carey."

"You should tweet that," Lynn says. "But not in a mean way."

You are hugging the other *writers* and this means you will come here next and Lynn is relentlessly kind. She simpers. "I feel bad for her."

Chana sniffs. "I just feel bad for the cowboys. They deserve better."

You are sauntering over to the table, which means they have to stop talking about you and I am so happy when you finally arrive and hug your two-faced friends. They make golf claps and sing false praise and you guzzle your whiskey as if you can drink yourself into a Pulitzer Prize.

"Ladies, please," you say, and you're tipsier than I realized. "A girl can only tolerate so many compliments and cocktails."

Chana puts a hand on your arm. "Honey, maybe no more cocktails?"

You pull your arm away. This is you postpartum. You birthed a story, and now what? "I'm fine."

Lynn motions to the waitress. "Can we snag three picklebacks? This girl needs her liquid courage."

"I don't need any courage, Lynn. I just got up there and read a fucking story."

Chana kisses your forehead. "And you read the shit out of that fucking story."

You don't buy it and you push her away. "Fuck both of you."

It's good that I see this side of you, the nasty drunk. It's good to know all sides if you're gonna love someone and I hate your friends a little less now. They exchange a look and you glance at the bar. "Did Benji already leave?"

"Sweetie, was he supposed to come?"

You sigh like you've been here before, like you don't have the patience now, and you pick up your cracked phone. Lynn grabs it.

"Beck, no."

"Gimme my phone."

"Beck," says Chana. "You invited him and he didn't show. Leave it alone. Leave him alone."

"You guys hate Benji," you say. "What if he got hurt?"

Lynn looks away and Chana snorts. "What if he's . . . *an asshole?*"

You can tell Lynn never wants to talk about any of this ever again. Of the three girls, she is the one who will eventually leave New York for a smaller, more manageable city where there are no fiction readings, where girls drink wine, and Maroon 5 plays in the local jukebox on Saturday nights. She will photograph her eventual, inevitable babies with the same gusto with which she photographs the shot glasses, the empty goblets, her shoes.

But Chana's a lifer, our third wheel for the long haul. "Beck, listen to me. Benji is an asshole. Okay?"

I want to scream YES but I sit. Still. *Benji*.

"Listen, Beck," Chana rails on. "Some guys are assholes and you have to accept that. You can buy him all the books in the world and he's still gonna be *Benji*. He'll never be *Benjamin* or, God forbid, *Ben* because he doesn't have to, because he's a permanent man-baby, okay? He and his club soda can fuck off and so can his stupid ass name. I mean seriously, *Benji*? Is he kidding? And the way he says it. Like it's Asian or French. *Ben Geeee*. Dude, just fuck *off*."

Lynn sighs. "I never thought about it that much. Benji. Ben Gee. Gee, Ben."

There's a little laughter now and I am learning things about *Benji*. I don't like it but I have to accept it. Benji is real and I get another vodka soda. *Benji*.

You cross your arms and the waitress returns with your picklebacks and the mood has shifted. "So, you guys really liked my story?"

Lynn is quick. "I never knew you knew so much about cowboys."

"I don't," you say and you are in a dark place and you pick up your shot and you knock it back and the girls exchange another look.

"You need to never speak to that fucker ever again," Chana says.

"Okay," you agree.

Lynn picks up her shot. Chana picks up her shot. You pick up your empty shot glass.

Chana makes a toast: "To never speaking to that fucker and his bullshit club soda and his fucking haircut and his no-show ass ever again."

You all clink glasses but those girls have something to drink and your cup runneth empty. I go outside so I'll know when you leave. Some asshole emerges, vomits.

Pickle juice, I swear.

5

THERE are three of us waiting in the Greenpoint Avenue subway station at 2:45 in the morning and I want to tie your shoelaces. They're undone. And you're too drunk to be standing so close to the tracks. You're leaning with your back against the green pole with your legs extended so that your feet are planted on the yellow warning zone, the edge of the platform. The pole has four sides but you have to stand on the side facing the tracks. Why?

You've got me to protect you and the only other person in this hellhole is a homeless dude and he's on another planet, on a bench, singing: *Engine, engine, number nine on the New York transit line, if my train runs off the tracks pick it up pick it up pick it up.*

He sings that part of the song on a loop, loudly, and your head is buried in your phone and you can't type and stand and listen to his musical assault all at the same time. You keep slipping—your shoes are old, no tread—and I keep flinching and it's starting to get old. We don't belong in this dump; it's a minefield of empty cans, wrappers, things nobody wanted, not even the homeless singing dude. The kids you run with live to ride the G train, like it proves they're down, "real," but what your friends don't realize is that this line was better off without them and their cans of Miller High Life and their pickle-scented vomit.

Your foot slips. Again.

You drop your phone and it lands in the yellow zone and you're lucky it didn't fall onto the tracks and I get goose bumps and I wish I could grab you by the arm and escort you to the other side of that pole. You're too close to the tracks, Beck, and you're lucky I'm here, because if you fell or if some sicko had followed you down, some derelict rapist, you wouldn't be able to do anything. You're too drunk. Your laces in your little sneakers are too long, too loose, and the attacker would press you down on the floor or against that pole and he'd tear those already torn tights off and slash those cotton panties from Victoria's Secret and cover your pink mouth with his oily hand and there'd be nothing you could do and your life would never be the same. You would live in fear of subways, run back to Nantucket, avoid the "Casual Encounters" section of Craigslist, get tested for STDs on a monthly basis for a year, maybe two.

The homeless dude, meanwhile, doesn't stop singing *engine engine* and he's urinated twice and he hasn't gotten up to do it, either. He's sitting in his piss and if some sicko followed you down here to finish what you started with those torn stockings, this dude would just keep singing and pissing and pissing and singing.

You slip.

Again.

And you narrow your eyes at the homeless dude and growl but he's on another planet, Beck. And it's not his fault you're wasted.

Did I mention that you're lucky to have me? You are. I am a Bed-Stuy man by birth, sober, collected, and well aware of my whereabouts and yours. A protector.

And the bullshit thing is, if someone saw the three of us, well, most people would think I'm the weird one just because I followed you here. And that's the problem with this world, with women.

You see Elliot in *Hannah* scam his way to be near his sister-in-law and you call that romantic but if you knew what I went through to get into your home, that I messed up my back trying to know you, inside and out, you'd judge me for it. The world fell out of love with love at some point and I know what you're doing with that phone. You're trying to talk to *Benji*, the club soda, too-much-hair, no-show motherfucker with whom you have encounters that are not casual, at least not to you. You seek him. You want him. But this will pass.

And part of the problem is that phone. You have that function on that fucking phone that enables you to know when your texts are opened and ignored. And Benji, he ignores the fuck out of you. He is more passionate about blowing you off than he is about being inside of you and this is what you want? You stab at your phone. Your phone. Enough with this phone, Beck. It's gonna do you in, waste your voice, and cripple your fingers.

Fuck that phone.

I'd like to throw it on the tracks and hold you as we wait for the train to run it down. There's a reason it's cracked and there's a reason you left it in your basket at the bookshop that day. Deep down, you know you'd be better off without it. Nothing good comes from that phone. Don't you see? You do see. Otherwise you'd treat that phone well. You'd have put it in a case before it cracked. You wouldn't stand here fumbling with it and letting it dictate your life. I really do wish you'd throw it onto the tracks and go offline and turn your head and look over at me and say, *"Don't I know you?"* And I'd play along and we'd talk and our song would be *engine, engine, number nine on the New York transit line, if my train runs off the tracks—*

"Can you please stop singing?" You growl, but the dude can't even hear you over the singing and pissing and singing and pissing and you whip your head around too fast and damn it you need to not lean back like that but you do.

It happens so fast.

You reach out your arms but you're wobbling. You drop your phone and you lunge to grab it and in the process you misstep—"Aaah!"— and you slip and trip on that damn shoelace and you fall splat and somehow you land the wrong way and you roll off the yellow danger zone and down into the actual danger zone. You scream. It's the fastest slowest fall I've ever seen and you're only a voice down on the tracks now, a shriek and his singing doesn't stop, *engine engine number nine*, and it's the wrong soundtrack for what I have to do now, bad back and all. I run across the platform, look down at you.

"HELP!"

"It's okay, I got you. Gimme your hand."

But you just scream again and you look like that girl in the well in *The Silence of the Lambs* and you don't need to look so freaked out because I'm here, offering my hand, ready to pull you up. You're shivering and staring down the tunnel and your head's filling with fear when you need to just *take my hand.*

"Omigod, omigod I could die."

"Don't look that way, just look at me."

"I'm gonna die."

You take a step forward and you know nothing of railroads. "Stay still, half the shit down there can electrocute you."

"What?" And your teeth chatter and you scream.

"You're not dying. Take my hand."

"He's making me crazy," you say and you block your ears because you don't want to hear *if my train runs off the tracks* anymore. "That singing, that's why I fell."

"I'm trying to help you," I insist and your eyes pop. You look down the tunnel and then up, right into my eyes.

"I hear a train."

"Nah, you'd feel it. Gimme your hand."

"I'm gonna die." You despair.

"Take my hand!"

The homeless dude croons as if we're a nuisance he's got to outsing *pick it up pick it up pick it up* and you cover your ears and scream.

I'm getting impatient and an engine *will* come on these tracks eventually and why are you making this so hard?

"You wanna get killed? Because if you stay down here you will get run over. Take my hand!"

You look up and now I see a part of you that's new to me, a part that does want to be killed and I don't think you've ever been loved the right way and you don't say anything and I don't say anything and we both know that you're testing me, testing the world. You didn't get off that stage tonight until the last person stopped clapping and you didn't tie your shoelaces and you blamed the world when you tripped.

Pick it up pick it up! Engine, engine, number nine

I nod. "Okay." I reach down with my arms, palms up. "Come on. I got you."

You want to fight. You are not easily rescued but I am patient and when you are ready, you wrap your hands around my shoulders and allow me to save you. I hoist you, loose sneakers and all, onto the yellow danger zone and then roll you onto the dirty gray danger-free concrete and you're shaking and you hold your knees to your chest as you scoot backward into the part of the green pole that faces inward, the safe place to sit, to wait.

You still don't tie your shoelaces and your teeth chatter more than ever and I scoot closer to you and I point at your useless, flat, nonathletic sneakers. "May I?" I ask and you nod.

I pull the laces tight and tie them in double knots the way my cousin taught me a hundred years ago. When the train sounds down the way, your teeth stop chattering, and you don't look so scared anymore. I don't have to tell you that I saved your life. I can see in your eyes and your glistening, grimy skin that you know it. We don't get on the train when the doors open. That's a given.

6

THE cab driver was reluctant at first. I guess I would be too. We look crazy from the near death of it all. You're a fucking mess. I'm so clean that it's almost disturbing, pimp-clean to your whore-dirty. We're a true pair.

"But the thing is," you say, going over the recent events for the umpteenth time, your legs folded under, your arms flailing as you speak. "The thing is, at the end of the day, I couldn't live if that guy wasn't gonna stop singing. I mean I know I must have seemed crazy."

"Nuts."

"But I had a bad night, and at some point you have to set rules, you know? You have to say, I will not put up with this. I will die before I continue to live in a world where this guy will *not* stop singing and polluting a shared environment."

You sigh and I love you for trying to spin this into some sort of strike against complacency and what fun it is to play with you. "Still, you were pretty drunk."

"Well, I think I would have done the same thing sober."

"What if he'd been singing the Roger Miller version?"

You laugh and you don't know who Roger Miller is but most of the people in our generation don't know and your eyes narrow and you stroke your chin and here you go again, for the fourth time. Yes, I'm counting.

"Okay, did you ever spend a summer working on a ferry?"

"Nope," I say. You are convinced you know me somehow. You have said you know me from college, from grad school, from a bar in Williamsburg, and now, from the ferry.

"But, I swear I know you. I know I know you from somewhere."

I shrug and you examine me and it feels so good, your eyes hunting me.

"You just feel close to me because you fell and I was there."

"You were there, weren't you? I'm lucky."

I shouldn't look away but I do and I can't think of anything to say and I wish the cab driver were the kind to babble intermittently.

"So what were you up to tonight?" you ask me.

"Working."

"Are you a bartender?"

"Yeah."

"That must be so much fun. Getting people's stories."

"It is," I say, careful not to reveal that I know you write stories. "It's fun."

"Tell me the best story you heard this week."

"The best?"

You nod and I want to kiss you. I want to take you onto the tracks before *engine engine number nine* grinds to a halt and swallows you whole and fuck the drunk out of you until *the New York transit line* swallows us both. It's too hot in here and it's too cold out there and it smells like burritos and blow jobs, middle-of-the-night New York. *I love you* is all I want to say so I scratch my head. "Hard to pick one, ya know?"

"Okay, look," you say and you swallow, bite your lip, redden. "I didn't want to freak you out and be, like, this psycho who remembers every tiny little social situation she gets herself into or whatever, but I was lying. I *do* know how I know you."

"You do?"

"The bookstore." And you smile that Portman smile and I pretend not to recognize you and you wave those hands. *Such small hands.* "We talked about Dan Brown."

"That's most days."

"Paula Fox," you say and you nod, proud, and graze my arm with your hand.

"Aah," I say. "Paula Fox and Spalding Gray."

You clap and you almost kiss me but you don't and you recover and sit back and cross your legs. "You must think I'm a fucking lunatic, right? You must talk to like fifty girls a day."

"God, no."

"Thanks," you say.

"I talk to at least seventy girls a day."

"Ha." And you roll your eyes. "So you don't think I'm, like, stalker-crazy."

"No, not at all."

My middle school health teacher told us that you can hold eye contact for ten seconds before scaring or seducing someone. I am counting and I think you can tell.

"So true. Which bar do you work at down there? Maybe I'll come by for a drink."

I won't judge you for trying to reduce me to someone who services you, who rings up your books and delivers your picklebacks.

"I just fill in there. Mostly I'm at the bookstore."

"A bar and a bookstore. Cool."

The cab rolls to a stop on West Fourth Street.

"Is this you?" I ask and you like me for being deferential.

"Actually," you say and you lean forward. "I'm just around the corner."

You sit back and look at me and I smile. "Bank Street. Not too shabby."

You play. "I'm an heiress."

"What kind?"

"Bacon," you sass and a lot of girls would have gone blank.

We are here, at your place. You are looking in your purse for your phone that is on the seat between us, closer to me than you, and the driver shifts. We're in park.

"Here we go again with me and the always disappearing phone."

Someone raps on the car door. I jolt. The motherfucker actually knocks on the window. *Benji.* You reach across me and roll down the window. I smell you. Pickles and tits.

"Benji, omigod, this is the saint who saved my life."

"Good job, dude. Fucking Greenpoint, right? Nothing good happens there."

He raises his hand for a high five and I meet his hand and you are sliding away from me and everything is wrong.

"I can't believe this but I think I lost my phone."

"Again?" he says and he walks away and he lights a cigarette and you sigh.

"He seems like a jerk but, you have to understand, I lose my phone all the time."

"What's your number?" I blurt and you look out the window at *Benji* and then look back at me. He's not your boyfriend but you're acting like he's your boyfriend.

I'm good, calm. "Beck," I say. "I need your number or your e-mail or something in case I find your phone."

"Sorry," you say. "I just spaced. I think I'm still kind of freaked out. Do you have a pen?"

"No," I say and thank God that when I pull a phone out of my pocket it's mine and not yours. You give me your e-mail address. You're mine now and *Benji* calls, "You coming or what?"

You sigh.

"Thank you *so* much."

"Every time."

"I like that. Every time. Instead of 'anytime.' It's pointed."

"Well, I mean it."

Our first date ends and you're going upstairs and fucking the shit out of *Benji* but it doesn't matter, Beck. Our phones are together and you know that I know where you live and I know that you know where to find me.

7

MY thoughts are firing too fast (you, me, your tights, your phone, *Benji*) and when I get like this there's only one place for me to go. I walk to the shop, go to the way back and unlock the basement door. I close it behind me and stand in the vestibule that looks to Curtis, to anyone, like a storage closet. I fish in my pocket for the true key, the key that unlocks the next door, the final barricade between the shop and the soundproof basement. I lock the door behind me and by the time I reach the bottom of the stairs I am smiling because there it is, our beautiful, enormous, beastly enclosure: the cage.

"Cage" really isn't the right word, Beck. For one thing, it's huge, almost as big as the entire fiction section upstairs. It's not a clunky metal trap you'd find in a prison cell or a pet shop. It's more like a chapel than a cage and I wouldn't be surprised if Frank Lloyd Wright had a hand in the design, what with the stark mahogany beams as smooth as they are heavy. The walls are genius acrylic, unbreakable yet breathable. It's mystical, Beck, you'll see. Half the time, when collectors write fat checks for old books, I think they're under the spell of the cage. And it's practical too. There's a bathroom, a tiny stall with a tiny toilet because Mr. Mooney would never go upstairs for "something as banal as a bowel movement." The books are on high shelves accessible only by climbing a ladder. (Good luck, thieves.) There's a small sliding drawer in the front wall, the kind they use at a gas station in a sketchy neighborhood. I unlock the door and go inside. I'm inside and I look up at the books and I smile. "Hi, guys."

I take off my shoes and lie back on the bench. I fold my hands under my head and tell the books all about you. They listen, Beck. I know it sounds crazy, but they do. I close my eyes. I remember the day we got this cage. I was fifteen and I'd been working for Mr. Mooney for a few months. He told me to come in to meet the truck at eight sharp. I was on time but the delivery guys from Custom Acrylics didn't show up until ten. The guy behind the wheel beeped and waved for us to come outside. Mr. Mooney told me to observe as the driver yelled over the roar of the engine, "Is this Mooney Books?"

Mr. Mooney looked at me, disgusted by *Philistines* who can't be bothered to read the sign above the shop. He looked at the driver. "Do you have my cage?"

The driver spat. "I can't get this cage in that shop. Everything's in parts, guy. The beams are fifteen feet long and the walls are too friggin' wide to get through that door."

"Both doors open," said Mr. Mooney. "And we have all the time in the world."

"It ain't about time." He sniffed and he looked at the other dude in the truck and I knew that they weren't on our side. "With all due respect, we usually put these babies together in backyards, mansions, big open spaces, ya know?"

"The basement is both big and open," said Mr. Mooney.

"You think we're getting this fucking beast into a *basement*?"

Mr. Mooney was stern. "Don't swear in front of the boy."

The guys had to make at least two dozen trips, lugging beams and walls out of the truck, through the shop, and down the stairs. Mr. Mooney said not to feel bad for them. "They're working," he told me. "Labor is good for people, Joseph. Just watch."

I couldn't imagine what the cage would look like when it was done, if it was ever done. The beams were so dark and old-fashioned and the walls were so transparent and modern. I couldn't imagine them coming together until Mr. Mooney finally called me downstairs. I was in awe. So were the delivery guys. "Biggest one ever," said the sweaty driver. "You keeping African grays? I friggin' love those birds. They talk, so cool."

Mr. Mooney didn't answer him. Neither did I.

He tried again. "Your shelves are wicked high, mister. You sure you don't want us to move 'em down? Most people want the shelves, like, in the middle."

Mr. Mooney spoke, "The boy and I have a lot of work to do."

The driver nodded. "You can get a shit ton of birds in here. Pardon my French."

After they left, Mr. Mooney locked the shop and told me the delivery dolts were no better than the wealthy sadists who keep birds in cages. "There's no such thing as a *flying cage*, Joseph," he said. "The only thing crueler than a cage so small that a bird can't fly is a cage so large that a bird *thinks* it *can* fly. Only a monster would lock a *bird* in here and call himself an animal lover."

Our cage was only for books and Mr. Mooney wasn't kidding. We did have a lot of work to do. Workmen installed sealant in the walls that rendered the entire basement soundproof. More workmen came and built and expanded the back wall of the shop so that the door to the basement opened first into a vestibule that contained the *real* door to the basement. We were building a top secret, soundproof clubhouse in the earth and I woke up so excited every day. I assisted Mr. Mooney as he wrapped dust jackets in custom-fit acrylic cases (*gently, Joseph*), before placing the jacketed books into acrylic boxes with air holes (*gently, Joseph*). Then he put that box into a slightly larger metal box (*gently, Joseph*), with a label and a lock. When we had ten books or so, he would climb a ladder in the cage and I would pass him the books one at a time (*gently, Joseph*), and he would set them on those *wicked high* shelves. I asked him why we had to go through so much trouble for books. "Books can't fly away," I said. "They're not birds."

The next day, he brought me a set of Russian nesting dolls. "Open," he said. "Gently, Joseph."

I popped one doll in half and got another doll and popped that doll in half and got another doll and so on until the final doll that could not be popped in half, the only whole doll in the bunch. "Everything valuable must be hidden," he said. "Or else."

And now you *pop* into my head and you're more beautiful than a doll and you'll love it in here, Beck. You'll see it as a refuge for sacred books, the authors you love. You'll be in awe of me, the key master and I'll show you my remote control that operates the air conditioners and humidifiers. You'll want to hold it and I'll let you and I'll explain that if I wanted to, I could jack up the heat and cook these books and they'd turn to mold and dust and be gone, forever. If there's any girl on Earth who would appreciate my power, it's lovely, unpublished you in your little yellow stockings with your dream of writing something good enough to get you inside this cage. You'd drop your panties to get in here, to live in here, forever. I drop my own drawers and cum so hard that I go deaf.

Fuck. You are good. I try to stand. I am dizzy. *Gently, Joseph.*

It's almost time to open and I catch my breath and I go upstairs. There are only two of us who work here now that Mr. Mooney is retired. There's Curtis, a high school kid, kinda like I was back in the day. He does stupid stuff just like I did. Heck, when I was sixteen years old, Mr. Mooney gave me a key, and of course, one night I forgot to close the cage.

"You failed, Joseph," said Mooney when he was younger but still old, the kind of guy who was never young, not really. "You failed me and you failed the books."

"I'm sorry," I said. "But we never shut cabinets or doors in my house."

"That's because your father is a pig, Joseph," he said. "Are you a pig?"

I said no.

A few days later, I snuck into the cage and took out a new, old *Franny and Zooey*, a signed first edition. I decided to like it more than *Catcher in the Rye* just to be unique. And I loved it, Beck. What a book! Sometimes I flipped back to the beginning just to rub my finger on Salinger's signature. You had to pay $1,250 to do what I did. But I didn't pay. And neither did the woman who stole it from the desk at the register.

I would recognize her anywhere. She had reddish hair and a

49

paisley scarf, and was thirty, maybe thirty-five. She paid cash. I told Mr. Mooney I'd work extra to make up for it and I promised I would find her. I cut school and skulked the streets until my toes were bleeding. But it's hard to find a woman when you don't know her name or where she lives. Mr. Mooney ordered me to go into the cage and close my eyes. I was scared. When I heard him lock the door I knew I was locked inside.

I didn't have a ladder so I couldn't reach any of the books; you can't walk into the Louvre and kiss the *Mona Lisa*. I had no phone, no sunlight, no darkness. All I had was my brain and the buzz of the AC unit and the daily slice of pizza (cold because steam is no good for old books), and coffee (lukewarm in a cup from the Greek diner), both of which Mr. Mooney slipped to me through the drawer. The days and nights got lost. Mr. Mooney cared enough about me to teach me a lesson. I learned.

He let me out of the cage on September 14, 2001, three days after September 11. The whole world was different then and Mr. Mooney said my father had never called; he probably thought I was dead. "You are free, Joseph," he said. "Be wise."

I didn't spend as much time at home after that. It wasn't hard to slowly disappear. My mom left when I was in second grade so I grew up knowing that it was possible to leave people, especially my dad. I don't feel sorry for myself, Beck. Lots of people have shitty parents and roaches in the cabinets and stale, raw Pop-Tarts for dinner and a TV that barely works and a dad who doesn't care when his son doesn't come home during a national disaster. The thing is, I'm lucky. I had the bookstore.

It doesn't take a fucking village to raise a child. Mr. Mooney was the boss now, the dad I wanted to do right by. I kept hunting for the *Franny and Zooey* thief and right after 9/11, I wasn't alone. Everyone was like me, searching the streets. People wanted to find their families; I wanted to find the thief. There were flyers for missing people all over the city. I thought about learning to draw and plastering the city with drawings of the thief. I could pretend she was my mother. I didn't go through with it and sometimes I think the thief died in one of the Towers, karma. But most of the time I think she's probably out there, alive, reading.

I am in the L–R Fiction stacks when the doorbell chimes and I am ready. You told your girlfriends you would come by around this time. I know this because I have your phone and you are not the kind of girl who locks her phone with the four-digit password. I have been reading your e-mails. I have taken pictures of the passwords you keep in your password folder. This way, when you change your password, if you change your password, I'll know the possibilities. You are not the kind of girl who comes up with new passwords. You have three in rotation:

ackbeck1027

1027meME

1027BECK$Ale

It gets better. You don't want to tell your mother that you lost another phone. You went and got a *new* phone with a *new* number and a *new* plan. I know all this because your *old* phone is still active. So I read the mass e-mail you sent to your friends announcing your new phone number because I can read all your e-mail! Chana was mortified:

WTF? Tell your mother you lost your phone and get that shit

shut down. Identity theft! Perverts! Beck, seriously. Tell your
mom you fucked up. She'll get over it. People lose phones. Get
the phone shut off. It's not that dramatic.

You wrote back:

Phone is probably in gutter; so yes, it's really not dramatic. If
someone does have it, I'm a poor MFA candidate with debt.
Who's stealing that identity? And if someone thinks I'm pretty
enough to put my selfies all over the Internet, well then I'll feel
pretty. ☺ Just kidding. But seriously, it's all good. I wanted a
new phone anyway! I love my new number!

Chana would not relent:

YOU GET A NEW PHONE WHEN YOU TELL THEM
YOU LOST YOUR OLD PHONE. Your mother will know you
lost your phone because of your NEW PHONE NUMBER.
Also: $$$$$

You were stubborn:

Please calm down, C. I told my mom I changed numbers
because I wanted a New York one. She doesn't even know
how to text, let alone read the bill. It's fiiiiine. And money?
Whatever. One more little bill isn't going to kill me at this
point, you know?

Chana didn't reply and I love your mom (Thanks!) and I love
you, you little hypocrite! Your old (but still working!) phone is an
encyclopedia of your life and it will be open to me as long as your
mother pays the bill. Score one for the good guy! Oh, Beck, I love
reading your e-mail, learning your life. And I am careful; I always mark
new messages unread so that you won't get alarmed. My good fortune
doesn't stop there: You prefer e-mail. You don't like texting. So this

means that I am not missing out on all that much communication. You wrote an "essay" for some blog in which you stated that "e-mails last forever. You can search for any word at any time and see everything you ever said to anyone about that one word. Texts go away." I love you for wanting a record. I love your records for being so accessible and I'm so full of you, your calendar of caloric intake and hookups and menstrual moments, your self-portraits you don't publish, your recipes and exercises. You will know me soon too, I promise.

Starting today.

You're here.

"Hang on," I call out, as if I don't know it's you up there and I'm so full of shit. I trot up the stairs and into the stacks and you're here in a plaid jumper and kneesocks and you dressed up for me, I know you did, and you're holding a pink reusable bag.

"Engine, engine, number nine," I say and you laugh and I am so good when I have time to prepare. "What's up?"

I go in for the hug and you let me hug you and we fit well together. My arms take you. I could squeeze you to death and to life and I pull away first because I know how you girls can be about this stuff, your basic instincts ruined by magazines and TV.

"I brought you something," you coo.

"You didn't."

You respond, "I did."

"You didn't have to."

"Actually, I didn't die." You laugh. "So I kinda did."

We're walking up to the front and I know why we're walking up there. You want me. You want me here. You know that if we stay in these stacks I'm gonna press you against the F–K placard and give you a present and I'm behind the counter and I sit as I planned—with my hands intertwined behind my head as I lean back and put my feet up and my navy T-shirt lifts just enough so that you can see my midsection—you need something to dream about—and I smile.

"Show me what you got, kid."

You lay it on the counter and I lower my legs and move forward and I'm hunching over the counter. I could touch you I'm so close and I know you like my cologne because you and Chana lust after a bartender who wears this cologne which is why I bought it and I open my present, my present from you.

It's *The Da Vinci Code* in Italian and you clap and you laugh and I love your enthusiasm and this is something that comes more naturally to you than writing, giving. You are a giver.

"Open it up," you say.

"But I don't speak Italian."

"The whole book's not in Italian."

I flip through and you are wrong and you grab the book and drop it on the counter.

"I know for a fact that the first page is in English. Open."

I open. "Ah."

"Yeah," you say. "Read up."

There you are, in black ink. You wrote to me:

Engine, Engine, Number Nine
On the New York transit line
If some drunk girl falls on the tracks
Pick her up pick her up pick her up

I read it out loud; I know you get off on your writing and you clap at the end and there it is in writing. You are literally asking me to pick you up and you nod and your name is there so it's not freaky when I say it.

"Thank you, Guinevere."

"It's Beck."

I lift up the book. "But it's also Guinevere."

You concede, you nod. "You are welcome. . . ."

I took off my name tag in the cage. You are pretending you don't remember my name and I help you out. "Joe. Goldberg."

"You are welcome, Joe Goldberg," you say and you sigh and on you go. "But that's kind of fucked, right, because I came here to thank you and now I'm saying, 'You're welcome.'"

"Tell you what," I say and this is it, just how I practiced. "Now that we're both alive and nobody's singing and you got me this sweet-ass present, which is great because of all the books we have in this place, Italian Dan Brown is not one of them . . ."

"I noticed," you sing and you blink and smile and you're rocking a little.

I breathe. This is it, the next step. "Let's get a drink sometime."

"Sure," you say and you cross your arms and you're not looking at me or saying a specific time or date or place and now there are elements of our dynamic coming slowly into view, like a photograph in a darkroom—you didn't write your number in the book and you got me the joke part of our thing—Dan Brown—instead of the shared serious part of our thing—Paula Fox—and I think you have a hickey. A small one, but still. You bought Paula Fox for *Benji*. You bought *Dan Brown* for me.

"The thing is," you say, "I still can't find my phone and I don't have a new one yet so I'm not making a lot of plans, you know?"

"Yeah."

I pretend I have to check something on the computer and I think of the way you e-mailed your friends about me, the way you talked more about the fact that I rescued you than the fact that you're obsessed with me, so obsessed that you had to pretend you didn't remember me. You didn't tell Chana and Lynn about the way you think about me when you mount your green pillow, about how nervous and intimidated you were with me. You were so nervous and distracted by me that you lost your phone, Beck. Remember? Instead, you e-mail your friends about *Benji* and I have to speak or I'll blow it.

"So, you never found your phone?"

"No, I mean, yeah, I mean, I think I left it in the subway station."

"You had it in the cab."

"Oh right, I did, but I mean who remembers the name of the cab company, right?"

Premiere Taxi of Lower Manhattan.

"Nobody ever remembers the name of the cab company," I agree.

You ask me for a pen and I give you a pen and you grab one of our bookmarks and flip it over and write down your e-mail address that I already know. "Tell you what," you say as you scribble. "I'm really busy with school and stuff, but why don't you e-mail me and we'll make a plan."

"I hope you know those bookmarks are for paying customers only."

You laugh and you are awkward without a phone to dive into and you look around, waiting to be excused. You really do have a daddy complex, Beck.

"Not for nothing, but these books aren't gonna sell themselves, so why don't you skedaddle and let me, you know, get back to work."

You smile, relieved, and you almost curtsy as you back away. "Thanks again."

"Every time," I say. And I planned that and you smile, no teeth, and you don't say good-bye and I don't say "Have a nice day" because we are beyond pleasantries and you gave me your e-mail address and now I have to choose which draft to send to you. I knew you'd come in and I knew you'd give me your e-mail so last night I wrote different versions of my first e-mail to you. I was up all night writing, Beck. Just like you. I was in my cage, Beck. Just like you.

I put your bookmark with your e-mail in the Italian Dan Brown. It fits perfectly.

8

I hope that most people at this point in time realize that Prince is one of the great poets of our time. I didn't say *songwriter*— I said *poet*. Prince is the closest thing we have to e. e. cummings and people are so stupid because they don't come in here and buy books of Prince poems.

It's been seven hours and fifteen days since you took your love away.

That is one of the greatest first lines of a poem in all time for a number of reasons, primarily because of the reversal of hours and days. A nonpoetic person would cite days and hours. A poet is different. A poet transforms the world with

Such small hands.

You haven't written back to me yet. You have forwarded my e-mail to Chana and Lynn. You have giggled over photo-booth pictures of the three of you—*ChanaLynn . . . us!*—and exchanged dozens of idiotic e-mails about nothing. You have found the time to read and respond to your classmates' short stories and beg the bosses at

WORD in Brooklyn to let you read but you haven't written back to the guy who saved your life. You are still in pursuit of *Benji* and it has not been *seven hours and fifteen days* but we are getting there, Beck. It's not funny anymore.

You wrote to *ChanaLynn*:

> *How come I have to be a stereotypical chick that meets a nice guy and is like, thanks but no thanks? I don't read* Cosmo *or do cleanses or post selfies, which means I don't fit the profile for lame-girl-who-hates-nice-guys. I mean Benji is married to his business and this guy is the total opposite, works at a business, you know? Also, rooftop at the Wythe on Friday?*

Chana wrote back first:

> *Beck, is this the guy you met at KGB? Wythe maybe.*

And this tells me that you meet too many guys. You have this hunger for strangers. That's why you read Craigslist "Casual Encounters." No, you don't have casual encounters (thank Christ), but at the same time you treat life like a giant fucking casual encounter, wasting time with Benji, with random guys from places like KGB.

Lynn wrote back:

> *They got shrinks on campus that can answer that question, girl. ☺ Also, KGB guy was super cute. Also, Wythe yes unless maybe UES for a change? Just a thought . . .*

These girls don't know about our Italian Dan Brown and the extent of your crush because you don't tell them and finally in the middle of the night after *five hours and eight days* you write back to me:

> *How about happy hour on Thursday?*

I wait *three hours and one day* to write back:

That works. Where?

You didn't earn my humor this time. You don't write back right away. *Four minutes three hours and two days* pass before this bullshit stinks up my inbox:

Sorry omigod one of those weeks. Whatever you do, do NOT go
to grad school. Anyway. How about next week?

Like Prince, I have a poetic nature and I know how to shift my perspective. Driving you into my arms isn't working out, clearly. You are scattered and you flirt and you crack phones and you don't delete anything and you use your period to get extensions at school and a lot of your e-mails have more creative vitality than your stories and you're talking to like nine dudes on nine different sites. You flirt. With everything. Do you realize how much crap you have in your shopping basket at Anthropologie.com? Christ, Beck, you need to learn some decision-making skills. In the meantime, I see that you are sick. Sick like your father was. You're hooked on *Benji*. And I can't get you off *Benji* until I know about Benji.

Which takes all of about thirty-five seconds.

Benjamin "Benji" Baird Keyes III is a friggin' joke. He's been to rehab, which is a travesty; you can tell by his smug face that he's not capable of genuine addiction. He owns an organic club soda company that symbolizes everything bad about right now. His business is called Home Soda, a superior alternative to commonplace club soda because "while a club is exclusive, a home is the most exclusive place in the world. You can get into a club if you pay a cover. The same cannot be said of a home."

Beck, you can't tell me you buy into this, not really. Benji's little start-up is a runaway, underground Whole Foods–style success, and his pastel-laden website includes a diatribe on Monsanto (as if this kid's parents don't profit directly from Monsanto, as if this kid wasn't fucking raised on Monsanto—literally, his dad worked for fucking *Nestlé* when Benji was a kid), and yet Benji rants. A photo essay (otherwise known as a fucking slide show) reveals that Benji came up with Home Soda while camping with friends on Nantucket. *Camping* is a bullshit term; Nantucket is not New Hampshire and Benji was staying at a friend's waterfront summer home. I blow up the photo and see the untagged girl from your Facebook profile. *Aha*. So you know Benji through that miserable odd girl, who does have a legitimate smile, reserved for wealthy friends in staged propaganda photos. But did you go camping with them? Nope. You probably weren't invited. Your friend probably fed you some bullshit excuse about there not being enough room on the beach. You are the townie and Benji is the tourist who literally enters you and uses you as a vacation from the wear and tear of the artisanal club soda business only to dump you before Labor Day. He is the daddy you try desperately to please, the daddy who leaves, no matter what you do.

Your emotional livelihood is a demented seasonal economy where Labor Day is every other fucking day. He rents you out, the same way he rents loft space in SoBro (South Bronx to those of us who don't need to make up bullshit pet names for neighborhoods where we're not wanted). And he cheats on you, Beck. A lot. Compulsively. He is in intense pursuit of a performance artist who fucks with his head the way he fucks with yours. It has been *six minutes and three hours and one day* when you e-mail me:

> *This is random, but I am in Greenpoint. Are you maybe*
> *bartending right now?*

I respond:

I'm not, but I could meet you at Lulu's.

You respond:

IT IS ON BABY! Sorry for all caps. I am just excited!

I wait *twelve seconds nine minutes and no hours* before writing back:

Haha. On my way. 5?

You don't write back but I have to take two trains to get there and the *Hannah and Her Sisters* soundtrack is playing in my head, all the songs at once, so loud that I can't listen to the music on my phone or the music on your phone and all I can think about is our first kiss, which will likely take place in *eighteen seconds nineteen minutes and three hours* when we are both drunk in a cab on Bank Street and I get it now, why dudes jerk off on trains sometimes. But I don't. I have you in my future. The train can't go fast enough and *engine engine number nine* and look how much we share already and we haven't even fucked and I got you a present too. I'm bringing you *The Western Coast.* And it's inscribed:

Engine, Engine, Number Nine

On the New York transit line

If you go in a nursing home

This here book will be your tome

It's not perfect but it's close and I had to buy you something, reward you for stepping up, and the train is here and I hope that Prince eventually got to be where I am, pounding up the *sixteen steps and two blocks and one avenue* toward the rest of his life. But I'm only halfway up the subway stop stairs when your phone beeps. There is a lot of information to process and I have to sit down and I do. Things have changed. Quickly, too quickly. Nearly two weeks after your mass e-mail announcing your new phone number, Benji has e-mailed you back:

Hi.

And you wrote back:

Come over.

And he wrote back:

☺

And then you e-mailed me:

Ack, I had to go to a school thing. Reschedule for next week? Sorry. Sorry!

And then Benji wrote to you:

Give me an hour, work thing came up.

And you wrote back:

☺

You're smiling because you want life to be like it was before your father messed up on Nantucket, without secrets, without danger. You write about how safe it is there, how claustrophobia and comfort go hand in hand. Your family never locked the doors to the house or the cars and they left the car keys in the ignition but come March, you'd give anything to see a stranger. You tweeted a few weeks ago:

The island of #Manhattan is like the island of #Nantucket: Groceries are expensive, drinks are expensive & in winter, everyone goes nuts.

That's cute, Beck, but the island of Manhattan is nothing like your precious Nantucket. Let me tell you what I did last Tuesday.

On the island of Manhattan, you have to lock your shit up or some streetwise guy might just stop by a friggin' club soda factory for a tour on a Tuesday when he knows the boss isn't around (special thanks to Benji's Twitter feed) and excuse himself to use the bathroom and bypass the bathroom for Benji's office (which is unlocked), and bypass the rest of the club soda tour for a private tour of Benji's computer (which is also unlocked), and learn that Benji keeps a calendar with links to @lotsamonica's performance schedule. She's on today, live-doodling at a converted fire station in Astoria (bite me). As a verified fan of hers on all social media platforms (oh the things I do for you, Beck), I am granted access to the live coverage and though I don't see Benji the man (the place is too crowded), I see bottles of Home Soda in all the filtered pictures. He's there. A comment from some chick with bangs and pink glasses proves it:

Benji rocks for bringing club soda. #organicforlife #homesoda #drinkfreeordie

So there it is. Your precious Benji doesn't show up at your reading but he treks all the way to Astoria in the middle of the day because he thinks Monica is superior, because she's tall and blond and he mistakes her doodles for art. I have to calm down. You don't know about this. You're not a fan of Monica's because you're not an imbecile. But you need to know and I can't get out of that bloated factory fast enough. I need to save you.

I am the kind of guy who prepares for emergencies like this, so I already have an e-mail account called HerzogNathaniel@gmail.com. You don't do your research so you don't know that Nathan Herzog is the food critic at Vulture's new *Eats* section who sucks the tit of pretentious beasts like *Benji* and his Home Soda. I read the guy's stuff; I'm not impressed. But Benji kisses his ass, tweeting his reviews in a flagrant effort to get his own puff piece on the site. And over at the exhilarating news blog on HomeSoda.com, "fans" of Benji's pussy water grumble incessantly about why Home Soda has yet to be featured on *Vulture*.

Until now.

Obviously, I use my new e-mail account to impersonate food fuckwad Nathan Herzog. And soon, Benji will receive an e-mail from Nathan Herzog, who just sipped the most fantastic club soda of his life and realizes he is late to the party but remains desperate to meet Benji. He writes:

> *Is there any way you could meet now? There's a bookstore on the*
> *Lower East Side, Mooney Rare and Used, and it's a great place*
> *to start. There's a café downstairs; nobody knows about it.*
> *Sincerely,*
> *N.*

It takes Benji only nanoseconds to reply:

> *Absolutely, Nathan. I'm flattered and I'm en route.*

I don't respond. What kind of an asshole says *en route*?

I am on the subway thinking about you when I realize that I have fucked up. Something is missing.

The Western Coast.

With my signed inscription.

I left it on the sidewalk when I took a minute to recover after realizing you blew me off and Mr. Mooney was right. I will never be fully capable of running the bookstore. I am not a multitasking businessman at heart. I am a poet, which is why I know that I am *four stops, one transfer, three blocks, two avenues, and one flight of stairs* away from stopping at my apartment to pick up some treats for Benji. I text Curtis:

> *No need to come in today, I got it covered.*

He writes back: *Sweet.*

9

I round the corner and see Benji yanking on the door to the shop and I caught him too, even better. I smile broad. I own this fuck. "There he is," I call. "The Home Soda man!"

"Mr. Herzog, it is a true honor," he coos, that fucking kiss-ass in a Brooks Brothers blazer and for what?

"Sorry I'm late," I say and I fake a fumble for the keys. Food critics who are part owners of café-book hybrid places are, by nature, a clumsy folk. "But it's worth the wait. I promise."

I unlock the door and we're in and Benji is too nervous to notice that I lock the door behind me.

"This place is a gem," he marvels. "They serve coffee here?"

"Now and then," I say and I could work for *New York Magazine*'s bullshit website. I watch *Mad Men* and know about Jay Z and overpriced ramen. "For now though, would water do?"

"Excellent, Nathan."

Excellent, Nathan. So while Benji prattles nervously about how much he loves books and bookstores and people who read books I am pouring a baggie of crushed Xanax into a glass of water. He'll gulp. He's nervous. He takes the water. He thanks me. He can't even say thank you without sounding like a phony. I let him go on and say I've just got to tend to something behind the counter and he is all apologies and *that's perfect, Nathan* and *I cleared my calendar for this* and I'm moving papers around and listening to the Xanax overtake him. Did I put enough in? He's woozy and he wants to sit down.

He almost wobbles toward the counter. "Do you mind? Is there somewhere I could sit a minute?"

Punching him is gratuitous. But then, he did use the word *excellent* a dozen times in twenty fucking minutes. He's out cold and on the ground and I walk into the main floor and lift his feet. Here he goes, down the stairs. He doesn't wake up while I drag him into the cage and I lock him in there and smile. *Excellent.*

His Brooks Brothers blazer provides a wealth of goods. There's his drug purse, packets of heroin or coke or Ritalin or whatever the kids are doing these days and a plastic key card (I leave that). There's his wallet (I take that). And then there's the grand prize that is his phone (I don't have to tell you that I take that). Benji is as fearless as you, Beck, and within seconds I have access to his Twitter, his e-mail, and the Home Soda blog on the website. Naturally, his phone is full of pictures of the Monica performance artist person. She is nauseating, splayed, always posing. I pick a "sexy" one and tweet it from Benji's account. Two words accompany the photograph:

#Beautifulovely #Yes

You are meant to interpret this as Benji's way of calling you

#Inadequate #No

And you do. Oh, Beck, it hurts to see you cry, feel so rejected. Don't you know how much I'd like to go hug you and prop you against that green pillow and fill you with love and mass-produced club soda? I want all that. But I can't intervene. You need your space to detach from this asshole and I wait for your sadness to turn into anger. And then it does and you write like a snake, you slither:

I am not your fucking plaything, Benji. I am not a no-hearted phony piece of shit performance artist cum Dumpster. I am a human being. A real human being, just like the song, and you do not blow me off. Do you hear me? This is not how my life goes. Treat me like you treat your soda. Or you know what? Better yet, fuck your soda. Give that a shot. Stick it right in there into that glass bottle and fuck your soda because that's what you love. You don't love me. You don't love anyone.

Your e-mails are true and beautiful. But there's a problem. They all get stored in drafts. You don't have it in you to send them. You're still holding on to this townie fantasy that this shaggy-haired *camping* tourist will throw away his ideals for you. You want that. There is not a lot I can do. So I stand by. I read your e-mails.

Chana is right: *Honestly, Beck. It would be nice if Benji loved you, but he doesn't. So it's not surprising when he bails on you and cheats on you and pulls that weird Daddy shit. You know? This will sound weird, but I am happy for you. Let this end already.*

Lynn chimes in: *I think there are no good guys in New York. It's not like I'm in some rush to get married, I love it at the UN. And I would rather go work in Prague than get married, but honestly, I don't think there are good men here. They're all Benjis.*

Chana writes back: *Get off eHarmony, Lynn. Seriously.*

I am optimistic until you have a separate private e-mail exchange with this Peach person. You're different with her.

You: *I sound like such a girl, but I haven't heard from Benji. He kind of bailed on me. He's probably just busy but what if . . .*

Peach: *What if you got so busy writing something awesome that you forgot about him. It's like in yoga when you put all your energy into one sacred place: you.*

You: *You are soooo right. Thank you, wise one!*

But it doesn't matter what your friends think. You're still drafting e-mails to him. And now you want to know where he is and when you're going to see him. You want him. *Still.* You need my help and I forge an entry in Benji's Home Soda blog:

Spontaneous trek to the ACK. New inspiration, new flavors with the help of a lovely companion.

He is the kind of asshole who would refer to Nantucket by its airport code, ACK, and of course he didn't invite you. He didn't tell you he was going. He just left. He's no good. And he used the word *lovely* and you're supposed to think he's with Monica and write him off once and for all. *Still,* you send the link to Peach, and you are sad, not mad. She writes back:

Sweetie, he's an entrepreneur. And he's probably referring to Rascal, his family's Lab. Don't jump . . . to conclusions!

We are at an impasse. None of this has worked. You forgive this fucker who tweets a filtered photo of the come-fuck-me soda cunt. There were no cases of gratis Home Soda at your reading, Beck, but you *still* want him and I *still* have to fix this. I send you an e-mail from Benji:

Long story. Be well, kid.

You open the e-mail seconds after I send it. You don't forward it to your friends and you don't draft another violent fuck-you e-mail. Now you are *still* and I am not surprised when my phone alerts me that I have a new e-mail an hour later. It's you:

Thursday instead?

I did it. Finally. I have only one word for you:

Yes.

WHEN the little pansy wakes up, I don't know how much time has passed but he's yawning like it's been a century. He doesn't seem to get it at first and he makes awkward small talk about the cage—*is this mahogany?*—and then he talks about parrots. Finally, it dawns on him that there are bars separating us. He reaches for the door and for the second time today, I watch this prick yank a door handle.

"You don't need to do that," I say. I try to keep him calm. I am kind.

"Let me out," he snaps. "Now."

"Benji," I say. "You need to settle down."

He looks at me. He is puzzled. Candace's brother was also puzzled. The assholes are always puzzled when the order of the universe is restored, when they are held accountable for their cowardly, pretentious, loveless ways.

10

IT'S Thursday morning and our date tonight is my reward for the past three days. Babysitting Benji is no joke, Beck. I don't even know how many times I've locked and unlocked and locked the basement doors as I've come up and down. Curtis knows he isn't allowed in the basement and he doesn't have a key. My hand is cramped from gripping the key like it's my lifeline. And it is.

And I'm tired, Beck. It took me a solid hour to pry up the false-bottom floorboard where I keep my machete. I had to take a train all the way to New Haven to use his ATM without raising any flags. I'm not saying it's not worth it and I did come up with a good plan. I decided to use Benji's phone to construct a narrative. I know, it's a fucking brilliant plan. Because you *follow* him on Twitter, you will now bear witness to his descent into drugs and idiocy. It all started in New Haven, where I got two grand out of his account and tweeted a photo of the bullshit Yale bulldog mascot:

The original #bulldog is back. #whatupnewhaven #meandmolly

So now everyone (you) will think Benji's gone back to his alma mater for a bender. If there's one thing I've learned about Ivy League people, Beck, it's that you all really like going back to school for reunions. This is a good plan and I can't let his fancy-boy bellyaching get to me. It's like you know I'm at my wit's end and you text me:

Hey you. Up early. No idea why. So what are we doing tonight? ☺

Benji barks: "Is that Beck? Joe, if that's what you want, she's all yours."

We've been through this. About an hour after he came to, the fucker recognized me from the cab. So now he thinks he's figured me out. He thinks I'm obsessed with you. He thinks I trapped him in here because of you. The truth is so much more complicated and self-satisfied chirpers like him don't know that it's always wiser to be quiet in lockup. He laid his cards out and he talks about you like you're his. But you're not a beat-up BMW, you're not his to give away. I bark, "Do your test."

"Joe," he says, which is dumb because every time he says my name I'm reminded of the fact that he knows my name, an obvious complication going forward. I compose myself and I write to you:

Morning, sleepyhead. Hope you had sweet dreams. See you at 8:30 on the steps at Union Square. When it gets dark we'll go somewhere else.

I hit SEND and I can't wait to see you and I pick up the list of Benji's five favorite books because we've got work to do:

Gravity's Rainbow by Thomas Pynchon. He's a pretentious fuck and a liar.

Underworld by Don DeLillo. He's a snob.

On the Road by Jack Kerouac. He's a spoiled passport-carrying fuck stunted in eighth grade.

Brief Interviews with Hideous Men by David Foster Wallace. Enough already.

The Red Badge of Courage by Stephen Crane. He's got Mayflowers in his blood.

Benji has already failed tests on *Gravity's Rainbow* (duh) and *Underworld*. He keeps saying he would have made a different list of books if he knew there was a test coming. That's how privileged people think: Lie unless you know that you can't get away with lying. You're nothing like him and you write again:

There's no fucking way I'm responding to a smiley face and I can't anyway because Princess Benji wants a soy latte and a *New York Times* and some Kiehl's and his fucking Evian and his Tom's toothpaste. I tell him to make do with what I gave him: coffee from the Greek diner, a *New York Post*, a small tub of Vaseline, and a scoop of baking soda from the centuries-old box in our employee restroom.

You write again:

Where are we gonna go after it gets dark?

I can't be mad at you because you're obviously just hot for me. You wouldn't be mirroring my words if you weren't excited and I write back to you:

You'll know when you need to know. Wink-wink.

The wink-wink might have been a mistake and I feel sick.

"Look, Joe, I can't take a test on a book I haven't picked up since high school without being amply caffeinated."

I make an executive decision because I can't listen to him anymore. "Forget *On the Road*. Tear up the test. We're done today."

He lifts his head up and looks at me like I'm God. "Thank you, Joe. I never read *On the Road* and, well, thank you."

He's thanking me for making him admit to being a complete, total liar. Even while fighting for his life, he's lying. I want this kid to understand and I try.

"You didn't read *On the Road*?"

"Not exactly."

"But you put it on your list."

"I know."

"I told you to make a list of your favorite books."

"I know."

"Unbelievable. Don't you realize you're in the bottom of a bookstore? That you're in a *cage*? You don't come in my store and lie. You don't do that."

"Don't be mad."

His eyes shift for just a second. He's aware of the machete. There's no choice. I gotta pick it up. I cross over, slowly. I reach for it. And I hold it. And I don't face him.

"You don't wanna do this," he whimpers.

Before I speak, I spread my feet a little bit farther apart. I occupy as much space as I can. "I spend my time making tests for you to take, tests on books that you say you read. And you didn't read any of these fucking books. Which means you wasted my time. And you don't want me to be mad. You think the world works like that?"

"I'm a fraud, okay?"

I turn around. He crosses his legs and hangs his head and runs his hand through his too-long blond hair. He is nimble and weak and he might disintegrate at any moment. I'm still holding the machete, which feels so unnecessary, given his condition. I nod at him, like: *Go on, shithead. Go on.*

It's amazing how you can see money in people. His chick-smooth hands have been softening for centuries before he was born and his thick hair never thinned from nights in the wind, days bent over shoveling snow or sand or ash. Something about that hair, something about the slope of his nose proves that life is unfair.

"In my defense, I love the book in a postmodern kind of way where I've always sensed that it contains something that I relate to. I think it's the kind of book that echoes my beliefs and my sentiments and I've always related well to people who have read the book and I've written about the book. You know, I majored in comp lit and it's possible, it's very possible to read a book without reading it in the traditional straightforward manner. You can read about a book, Joe. Do you know what I mean? Do you understand?"

"Yeah, Benji. I understand."

"See, I thought you might, Joe."

"Yeah, I don't have a Yale degree but my bullshit detector is *excellent*. Top drawer, even."

I start to walk up the stairs and he rants about what an asshole I am and what his father's gonna do to me and then he's begging, "Gimme a copy of the David Foster Wallace! I'll read it! I'll read it and then you can make a test I swear! Joe! Joe!" The basement is insulated. Mr. Mooney put his money into making this place a private place. Benji can scream all he wants and nobody's gonna hear him, just like nobody heard me, and you text:

You're funny, Joe.

The wink-wink didn't put me on your dork list and the sun is shining and I lock the basement doors and I text you:

I got books to sell. Be on the south steps of Union Square. Center. 8:30 sharp.

And I shut off my phone. I told you where to be and when and if you think you're gonna get any more from me today when you get me all night, you got another thing coming.

THE day is against me. I forgot that Stephen King has a new book out, *Doctor Sleep,* the long-awaited follow-up to *The Shining.* New King means crowds, even a week or two after the book's release— people are lazy—and hordes of shoppers giddy to be reunited with Danny Torrance. But I want *you,* Beck. *Doctor Sleep* turns my shop into a fucking Church of Stephen and I have no room to think about you, prepare for you. We are inundated with Kingophiles, couples trying to save their marriage with a *book club,* older fans who have waited forever, young punks who want to check into an independent bookstore on Facebook, freaks who highlight the bad parts and yearn to reeanact, withdrawn dullards longing for the companionship promised by a page-turner, women who want more out of a book than a feisty fuck with a commitmentphobic banker. Everyone loves King and I love *you* and today I should be thinking about how I'm going to part my hair and whether or not you're going to lick your fingers when we eat. Instead I talk about Danny Fucking Torrance, *all growed up*! I love Stephen King as much as any red rum drinking American, but I resent the fact that I, the bookseller, am his bitch.

You're an *MFA candidate* and we might talk literature tonight. For all I know, you could be so nervous that you collapse into a fog of pretension and praise a crap-infested *chapbook of experimental narrative*. And what am I going to say in return? *Can you believe Danny Torrance is all growed up?* Books don't get any more commercial and anti-chap than Stephen Fucking King (unless you want to talk about Dan Brown, but you can't compare the two because Dan Brown's not literary). And if Mr. King were here, he would be on my side; he knows that first dates require effort. He also likes books other than his own and he'd be proud of these folks if they read something they didn't hear about on *Good Morning America* (but not a *chapbook of experimental narrative*). Plus, Mr. King owes me; I sell his fucking books! Of course, he's not here and the sun loiters, still, and the register is tired and I've had the same conversation eighty-five thousand times today.

"Did you see that review in the *New York Times*?"

"I sure did."

"Can you just wait to read it? Jack Nicholson was so scary in the first!"

Philistines and I smash the register when it gets stuck—again—and I hit it because time is moving too slowly. I miss you and I want you and finally here's a woman who's *not* buying Stephen King. She's buying Rachael Ray cookbooks and she acts like I hit her, not the register. She does the passive-aggressive sigh and starts pounding at her Twitter app on her phone:

Bad customer service is the worst! #mooneyrare

She wants me to see and she lets the cursor blink and okay, lady, okay. I apologize for my ill manner and tell her that Rachael Ray is underrated and she deletes her tweet, which is good. There comes a point when the universe needs to get on your side or go fuck itself and the universe gets in line. I take a moment to send a tweet from Benji's account:

Home Soda and absinthe? Yes. #fiveoclocksomewhere

The next asshole is rummaging through his wallet for his credit card to buy his Stephen King so he can (fingers crossed) read about a sicko doing sick things because he's too much of a pussy to do all the sick things he wants to do, things he's probably wanted to do since he was a kid.

That's the problem with this never-ending centipede of lemmings, Beck. You know they're all pussies, each and every one of 'em. They buy these books to get scared because their lives are too easy. How pathetic is that?

"They say the ending is amazing and you can't see it coming."

"Yes, they do. Is that cash or charge?"

You think Benji was a tough dude to date? Well, try having the same conversation over and over while Benji's in the cage trying to dig his way to China. Yeah, you put up with his bullshit, Beck, but did you ever lock him in a cage and listen to him bellyache 24/7? The kid is allergic to gluten and peanuts and yeast and dust and sugar and Visine. I got him a Reese's Peanut Butter Cup and he went batshit on me and said the mere *smell* of peanut butter could kill him.

Please.

You know what the fucker is really allergic to? Real life. I'm doing the kid a favor. When he gets outta here, he's gonna be pissed about being locked up but he's also gonna thank me for making him into a man.

"I own every book Stephen King has ever written."

"That's great. That's something to be proud of."

But did you read them, fuckface?

And, honestly, Beck, do you know how hard it is, sleeping at the shop just in case Mr. Mooney does a late-night drop-by to look at the seventies porn in the basement? Answering questions about Stephen Fucking King while knowing that I gotta buy apples and honey for the pansy in the cage—I gotta pray the whole time I'm out with you tonight that Curtis is too stoned to be curious and try and get downstairs, that Mooney's too old and lazy to want his porn. Beck, I love you, I do, but you don't know about problems. I gotta be aware of the distant possibility that I leave and Curtis takes over and *one random old dude* with bank decides that today is the day he coughs up six grand for a signed Hemingway and Curtis calls Mooney and Mooney limps over here and the three of them go downstairs and make the worst day of Benji's life into the best day. I have problems. Real ones.

"Can you believe all these people? I thought I was the only one who buys paper books anymore!"

"Nobody buys paper books anymore," I say to customer number 4,356 who is a carbon copy of number 4,343 and all the others. "Unless they're by Stephen King."

You think you have problems. I know what you got. Even with Benji in the cage, I know. You've got deadlines and you gotta read the shitty stories by the other wannabes in your classes and you think your hairdresser fucked up your hair and Chana thinks she's pregnant even though the dude barely got it in and Lynn says if she got pregnant she'd move home and have the baby and you say if you got pregnant you'd name it *#anythingbutBenji* and your friends are sick of you bitching about Benji, using any excuse to bring up his name. I mean really, Beck. Girls. Somehow it takes you fifty-two e-mails to figure out the most basic, simple shit:

Chana is not pregnant, which makes sense, given that she didn't full-throttle fuck anyone.

Lynn is dead inside.

You are not over Benji, but you will be once you go out with me.

Okay, you have one legitimate problem. Your mom e-mails you drunk at night, sad, wants to talk, wants to yell, but, Beck, if you knew what I put up with for you, you wouldn't spend so much time moaning about your problems and you'd read the stories you gotta read for grad school and cuddle up with your green pillow and thank God that you don't have a 160-pound princess locked in your basement asking if the chicken in a fucking sandwich is free range.

I mean he was kidding, right?

"Don't you just love Stephen King?"

"Who doesn't?"

He's not stupid. I'll give him that. He read my face and he didn't like it but he ate the chicken sandwich. And you know what? He didn't puke after. But he's a nervous wreck and a slob and he misses the toilet when he pisses and twice he *has* vomited all over the toilet. And twice I've had to cuff him to the cage and clean up his mess. Labor is cleaning up a pansy's fluids after you just restocked the shelves and the window display with the new Stephen King for the third time in one fucking day while dealing with all the people who worship Stephen King bombarding the store for the Big New Stephen King Book that they all need on the same fucking day because God forbid they opened their eyes to a lesser-known author. People. What can you do, right?

My phone buzzes and it's 6:00 P.M. and it's official. The only books I sold today besides Stephen King are those Rachael Ray cookbooks and no wonder Benji never read any of his favorite books because most people don't read anymore and this is not the way I want to be when I'm less than three hours away from sitting with you on the steps.

"They say this is his best book yet."

"Let's hope so."

Curtis will be here in ten minutes because he's supposed to get here at six and he's never been on time because he's part of Generation Benji, all busy with his fake life in his fucking gadgets, tinderokcupidinstagramtwitterfacebookvinebullshitnarcissism incorporatedonlinepetitionsfantasyfuckingfootball. I'd love to fire him, but he respects me so I let him stay even though he asked me to hold a Stephen King book for him and listens to Eminem through unnecessarily giant headphones and takes like a year to read a single fucking book.

"Did you read this yet?"

"It just came out today."

"Well, they must ship them a day early, though. You can't tell me you didn't read the first chapter."

"No, I didn't read the first chapter. Is this gonna be cash or charge?"

I wait. The after-work depressed book buyers are coming steady, going home to their dungeons to let Stephen King distract them from their pathetic, lonely lives. We're so lucky, Beck. So much of

America—Benji included, cuz I'm a nice guy and I gave him one before I took off—is gonna be hunkered down reading Stephen King tonight but you and I are gonna be out living our own lives together. I pity these people.

"Do you mind if I run over and grab another book?"

"Actually, we've got a line and I already ran your card."

And there's no way I'm pissing off everyone so this broad can buy some Candace Bushnell because she is so slow to realize that she doesn't like Stephen King. She's only buying it because of the crowds. It's the original virus, this kind of shit.

6:06 now and I know what you're doing. You're smearing on eyeliner to get that Olsen-twin eye you think you need to look hot, which you don't. You're blasting your Bowie, *Rare and Well Done*—the music you play before you go on a date, music that makes you feel cool, crutch music you can talk about when you feel insecure—and you're deciding which little tank top best accompanies which little bra and eventually all of it gets to you and you're on your green pillow because the only way to get bed head is to get in the bed and fuck yourself. It's true what they say about you chicks being dirtier than us dudes, you are. I'm still keeping up with your e-mails as I wait for credit cards to run and you girls e-mail each other about your bodily events. It's all so un-Victorian. You are a Bowie girl, futuristic in your clinical control of your skin and your eyelashes you get sewn on in Chinatown, so crass that you tell your friends you're gonna rub one out before our date.

Rub one out.

"Excuse me?"

"Are you all set?"

"Yes. Can I have a bag for the book or are you gonna charge me extra?"

6:08 and the next dude in line is buying the new King and *The Shining* just to be bold—he calls *The Shining* a *prequel* and I want to cut his face—and what an awful world it is out there, Beck. What a miracle that you came in here, so happy, when most of the people who come in are so miserable, everyone except for you and me and Curtis, who holds the door for Mr. Shining and starts with his bullshit.

"Dude the L train is wacked."

"Take over the register."

"Fifteen minutes I stood there. Nothing."

"It's nothing but Stephen King tonight so you can close when the last copy goes."

"Cool. But, like, I just really need the hours."

6:11 and the punk wants hours and it's a waste of my time and I gotta get hot for you and clean for you and close my paper cuts and brush my teeth with my new Tom's natural toothpaste (thanks, Benji!) and I clench my jaw but Curtis is dense and not good at reading faces because of the way his head is shoved in his phone most of the time.

"Just close up after the King is done."

"Yeah, this city can blow me if it can't even get a train to run on time, you know, brother?"

"Just try and text if you're gonna be late next time."

"You look beat, son. Go on. I got this."

The little Beastie Boy motherfucker was late and I'm his boss and he is calling me *son* and the last thing in the world I need is this little shit telling me I look tired.

"You got a line, Curtis," I say and when I walk outside, away from the basement, away from the books, I smile at nothing, at the idea of you, like me, *preparing*. You're probably on your green pillow because it's almost time and for the first time in a long time I head home with drippy Simon & Garfunkel in my head because it's not Stephen King Book Day anymore, Beck. This night is ours.

11

I don't get home until seven and I'm not out of the shower until 7:15 and I stub my fucking toe on one of my typewriters and there's blood but I won't see this as an omen. The typewriter—Hector, an '82 Smith Corona I found in an alley off Bushwick—was in the way, but I'm nervous and maybe a little bloodshed's good for the nerves and fuck, maybe Hector's nervous too. You'll meet them all soon, Beck, all the typewriters I collect because one day, the computers will all blow up and I'll be the man with twenty-nine (and counting) beat-up machines and everyone will be standing in line to get into my apartment and buy one. Because obviously, one day, the world is gonna reverse and I'm just waiting.

You like that movie with that guy who pulls a rickshaw around Canada and that dude's mostly about the white T-shirt so I'm going for a classic white V-neck tee and jeans and the belt I found at the Army Navy store. The buckle is big, but not in a bullshit Ryan Adams kind of way. It's the real deal and it's old and dented and you're gonna wanna touch it when you see it because it's just like the one the cowboy in your story wears.

I get onto the subway and I text you:

Running a little late.

You text me right back:

Me too.

The road goes by in a slow flash because I'm not really on this train. I'm so excited to see you that the world doesn't even exist right now. I get off the train and send a tweet from Benji:

I'd fuck Miley Cyrus. For the record. #deepthoughts

And I'm done with my work and the air is perfect and when I arrive in Union Square I hide behind a kiosk and watch you arrive at the steps and look around for me and sit down and wait for me. It's 8:35 and you were lying, you weren't running late. You were just as excited as me. I text you:

Sorry. Be there by 8:45.

And I watch you text me back:

No worries. Me too! See you at 8:45.

You care what I think and you're nervous and I'm nervous and at 8:52 I take my first step toward you and I can hear my heart in my throat, I can't believe it's happening, us, together. You see me coming and you smile and wave and you stand up to greet me and you look so fresh and clear-eyed and ready and you bite your lower lip and you smile with every part of your body and you play. "You're late, mister."

"Sorry about that."

You can't stop smiling and I let you wait the right amount of time where you think I'm cool, not rude, and you take a deep breath and look up and then down. "You also said we'd go somewhere when it got dark and, well, it's already dark out."

"I know," I say and I sit down and pat the concrete and you plant your sweet little buns beside me. This is nice. This is it and I deliberately waited until it was dark to walk up to you. You are a woman and I am a man and we belong in the dark together and you smell good, pure. I like this.

"You really should try cleaning your shoes once in a while," you say and you tap your ballet flat into my brand-new white Adidas.

"That's why I was late," I say. "Had to shine these puppies for an hour."

You laugh and we fall into talking so easily, about Paula Fox and sneakers and the weirdo homeless dude who's talking to a trash can. There is chemistry. We win! We've been on the steps I don't know how long but there's no rush to go. You like it here.

You like to be on display. And whenever there's an unexpected silence, we joke about my sneakers.

"Now those are seriously white, like Ben Stiller white." You laugh.

"Yeah, I'm gonna tell my shoe-shine man you said so."

"Well, I should hope so. He did a bang-up job, Joe."

You said *bang* and you said *Joe* and that has to mean something, it does.

"I tipped him," I say and you start telling a story about accidentally stealing shoes from an outlet and we've been on the steps for almost twenty minutes and you're so nervous and excited that you keep talking about shoes as if you have to keep talking about shoes or you might jump me right here, on the steps. I chose this spot because my whole fucking life I've walked by these steps and seen couples that make me feel alone, rejected. And now there are loners passing by you and me, jealous, and you're still talking and fuck, it's hard to listen when I can smell your body wash.

"So I'm like, I didn't steal these. I accidentally kept them on. I mean who steals from a shoe store on an island, right?"

"A very brave and lovely lady who goes by the name Beck, apparently."

I said *lovely* and you smile and it was just right. You think I get you and all my reading was not for nothing.

"You must think I'm a psycho," you say. "Why did I even tell that story?"

"Because it's a first date. Everybody has an anecdote they tell on a first date. It's always funny and it's always based in truth, but it's always a half-truth."

"So I'm a lying bitch," you say, and then you smile and you cross your legs and even though you're in jeans two motherfuckers check you out as if they can see through denim. New York.

"No," I say. "You're a thieving, lying bitch."

You laugh and you blush and I laugh and you stretch and you're in your red bra and your white tank and your Thursday-night jeans and your pink cotton panties teasing me as you reach for the sky and uncross your legs and lay back and rest your little head on the cement and I want to mount you right here on these steps, at this inappropriate hour, in front of the motherfuckers checking you out and the Rasta hawking hemp bracelets and the angry bitches going home to read *Doctor Sleep* on their iPads. I want you here, now, and I can't get up when I'm this hard.

"You seem young," you say and just like that I'm soft.

"Huh?"

"No, no, no. Don't get upset, Joe. That came out wrong."

"Good, because I just turned seventeen and I'd hate to think I look sixteen because then you'd look like a pedophile and that's no good."

You slap my leg and you like me more all the time and you hunch, you bite your lip the way you did at your reading, when you're about to make a little revelation. "I just mean that a lot of my friends are in a rush to be settled," you say. "They seem old to me sometimes, like they lost that thing, that openness that makes a person seem young."

"How much weed did you smoke before you got here?"

I get what I wanted, another light slap and I love to make you laugh and I love you for giving me what I want without losing your focus. Like a laser beam, you go on. "See, I started to feel old my junior year of college. I was gonna go to Prague and I backed out at the last minute and a lot of my friends, they made me feel old, like I'd missed out on something I could never get back, as if Prague was going out of business. As if that was it, forever, as if you have to be in college to go abroad."

"We could go now," I say and my joke isn't funny and please stop talking about college because it makes me lose my game.

"Anyway, my point was that you have a young vibe. It's good. Like anything is possible and we could still theoretically run for president or learn sign language or visit every castle in Bruges."

All I heard was *we* and I smile. "You want me to gas up my NetJet?"

"I'm serious," you say and you move your body closer to mine. "What about you? What did you want to be when you were little?"

"A rock star," I say and I follow your lead and lean back, closer to you and now we're both looking up at the sky. I bet we look great from above, lit by stars, in love.

"When I was little, I wanted to be a singer." You sigh.

"Is that why you like *Pitch Perfect* so much?"

You turn your head and sit up. I fucked up.

"How do you know I like that movie?"

"I was just guessing." Fuck. "I know it's really popular."

"Huh," you say and fuck. "Do *you* like that movie, Joe?"

"I don't know," I say and I'm beet red and fucked. "I haven't seen it. But if you like it, I mean, it's probably good."

"Note to self," you say and you're not looking at me. "Become less predictable."

You don't say anything and I don't know what to say and fuck that Anna Kendrick, it's on her. I can't tell if you feel bad about yourself or creeped out by me. How could I be so careless? I worked so hard to prepare and I blow it on a *movie* when you finally look at me there's new sadness in your eyes and it's my fault. I did that. And there's only one way to fix it.

"You're not predictable, Beck. You're just on Facebook."

"So you're stalking me," you say without a trace of sadness and you smack my leg, you like me, you do.

"Well, I wouldn't call it stalking." I smile. "It's not like it's private or anything."

You laugh and smack me—again!—and you stand up and stretch your arms above your head. I see your belly button and I like looking up at you and we both know that you liked being looked at and you stretch this way and that way and slap your hands on your hips.

"Did you look at all my pictures?"

"Only a couple hundred, you know, just the ones from last weekend."

You hang your head and wave your arms. "No. No. I don't want to be predictable Facebook girl with her whole life out there."

"That's not your whole life."

"It's really not."

"You save a lotta that shit for Twitter."

You slap my knee and you like it and I like it and skaters pass by and a toddler screams about chocolate ice cream and a hippie plays a banjo and a gainfully employed cunt in heels is talking too loudly on her phone. All of it is for us and your voice lowers.

"I looked for you."

"Yeah?"

"I was gonna look at your pictures, but you're not on Facebook."

"I used to be," I lie. "But I burnt out on it. Some people, it's like they care more about their status updates than their actual lives."

"So true," you say. "One of my best friends is like you, big time anti-Facebook."

"I'm not real anti."

"Well, you're not on it."

I know that you're talking about Peach and now you think I'm like Peach and nobody likes this Peach so this is a bad thing. I panic. I get quiet. The toddler is silenced by chocolate ice cream and the wind is picking up and it's getting darker, darker by the second, and the skateboards land hard and you want to look at your phone, I can feel you wanting to tell your friends, *This guy I'm with just announced that he stalked me on Facebook. That is all.*

"So, you wanna eat something or what?" I say. I stretch and remind you that I got biceps and I'm ready to kill anyone who'd dare to look at you.

"Or what?"

"I figured you'd wanna eat something. I don't have an 'or what' lined up."

"Do you ever notice how many words we waste?"

"Yeah," I say and I almost mention you and Chana and Lynn's bullshit talk about hate-watching *New Girl* but I catch myself.

"I want to be more careful with my words and only say what I mean. Cut the fat out."

"Yeah," I say. "I get that."

"So yes. I want to eat something."

I stand up and offer my hand even though you don't need it and you take it. "You first," I say and you know I want to watch your ass as you walk down the steps. "What are you in the mood for?"

"I'm flexible," you say and you look back. "As long as it's near my place because I have to be up early tomorrow."

WE'VE had Corner Bistro burgers and fries and the vodka and the whiskey and I let you steer the conversation. You did tell me about Benji, "my druggie ex, I push him away but he always comes back. But let's not talk about that." I agreed (I'm agreeable!) and we moved on to your childhood (yours on Nantucket, mine in Bed-Stuy, your defensiveness about being a townie, my prepared knowledge of your island, which impresses you because I've never actually been there). You exclaim, "Joe, you're so smart, you'd almost think you work in a bookstore!" You reference college often, "Ivy League bullshit" and

"Yale guys." Finally, you're lit enough to ask me what you really want to know.

"When did you graduate?"

"I didn't," I say. "I didn't even start."

You nod. You are never around guys like me. I start to laugh. You start to laugh. I am never around girls like you and I start another round of who's-read-more-books.

I win again and you are flabbergasted. "S-sorry," you stutter. "I feel almost rude saying this, but, you didn't go to college and you're probably more well read than half the people in my workshop. It's insane."

I darken. "Don't tell the kids at school."

You smile and wink and we have a secret. I know how to talk to you and I fucking killed it, and the proof is that we're the last ones here and you understand why I insisted we sit in the way back. We've got the room to ourselves. We're at a four-top and the other tables are cleaned up and the chairs are stacked on the tables. You sit against the wall and I face you. You look to the left, to the right, and then at me. You ask me for permission to lie down on the bench but I have a better idea.

"You could do that," I say. "Or I could just take you home."

You slow blink on purpose and you sass, "And then what?"

"Whatever you want, Beck."

You grin. "So, you're a gentleman?"

I don't answer that and you're shy and drunk at the same time. The irony of your intentionally chalky eyes is that the more you drink, the more you rub your eyes and the more you rub your eyes, the less you look like a brunette Olsen twin and the more you look like you.

"Lie down," I command.

"Yes, sir," you say and your cheeks flush and your nipples harden and your panties are soaked right now. You lie down. I want to grab on to you but there's no way I'm even kissing you tonight.

"Put your hands on your head."

"Are we playing Simon Says?"

"No," I say and imagine if we fucked in here. Imagine. The air smells like beer and bacon and Murphy's Oil and I breathe it in and you put your hands on your head and there is a God because a little old Bowie plays now and you smile and I watch you smile and think about you naked and because I'm a little drunk I stand up and you hear my chair move and you open your eyes.

"Close your eyes, Beck."

You do what I say and you speak. "I was just gonna tell you about this album."

"I don't wanna know about this album," I say. This is me training you to treat me special. I'm not some Ivy League asshole who's gonna respect you because you know about an obscure David Bowie album and I sure as hell ain't gonna let you tell stories you told *Yale guys*. You're mine now and you'll do as I say and Bowie sings about strangers coming, staying, and you murmur along to prove that you know the words. What a horrible time you've had with the Benjis of the world who care about shit like that.

I walk around the table and sit right next to your head. You giggle and keep your eyes closed and you're not murmuring anymore and you're throbbing with want. I slouch and kick my feet up on a chair. My cock is inches from your head and your mouth and you can smell it and your little nostrils flare and you swallow, nervous, and I look down at you with your eyes closed and your mouth just slightly open as Bowie crows as if humans are a letdown. He sure wasn't singing about us, Beck.

"This is nice," you say before the song is over. "Maybe they'll forget we're here and lock us in."

"Yeah," I say and fuck it if my brain doesn't go right to Benji. I want to stay with you forever and yet I have to feed my new pet. Even locked up he's getting in the way of us.

"Hey," you say. Your eyes are wide open and the song ended and it's Led Zeppelin now, too loud for where we are and you know how to give an order. You learned from friends who grew up with maids. "Walk me home."

"Yes, miss."

We walk two blocks without a word and both of us have our hands in our pockets as if they have to stay there, or else. We're both too turned on to make small talk and the night is quiet down here and there's nobody around and we reach your stoop and you walk up two steps so that we're standing face-to-face. But I would know that you've done this before even if I hadn't seen you do this with my own eyes. This is your bullshit game. I'm not gonna kiss you, Beck. You're not gonna tell me what to do with your body.

"This was nice." You purr.

"Yeah," I say. No purr. "You got an early morning so you better get in there."

Conflict suits you, Beck. You see a high school graduate who, in theory, should be trying to jump your bones. You also see a guy who's *read more books* than everyone in your workshop. I rock your world and I won't kiss you and you nod, what choice do you have?

You're pissed and your green pillow's gonna take a fucking beating tonight and you're gonna think about me and you're gonna wait for it, and get sick with want for it, for me, the same way that toddler screamed and waited for his ice cream, the same way America waited for Stephen King and I waited for Curtis, and Benji's across town waiting on me. You're gonna wait.

"Sweet dreams, Beck."

"You want a water for the road?" you say while you're standing at the door and holding it open, your invitation to come inside, your last attempt.

"I'm all right," I say, and I don't look back. You are fucking obsessed with me and honestly, I'm kind of relieved that I gotta deal with Benji and his organic apples and club soda right now or I might follow you inside and wait for you to unlock the door and throw you onto the couch and give you what you want, what I want. But no. You will give me water, but not a fucking plastic bottle as I'm hitting the road. When you quench my thirst, it will be after our first fuck, in your bed and you will bring me a glass of water and we will share the glass and it will be the first of many. I don't have the strength to turn you down when I want you so bad, but I do have a pansy in the cage.

Fucking Benji: a savior. Who knew, right?

I smile all the way home and at home I tell my typewriters about the night and I *rub one out* in your honor and shower and slather up in Kiehl's and download Bowie's *Rare and Well Done* so I can listen to it on my way to the shop. I have to go out again. How the fuck am I supposed to sleep when I'm waiting for you to e-mail your little friends about our date? I stop at the deli and pick up Cheerios and milk because Benji deserves a treat too. I'd whistle if I knew how and I enter the shop and trot down the stairs and find Princess Benji pouting and picking at his fingernails. I can tell by one glance at *Doctor Sleep* that he hasn't even opened it. I am a professional. I slide the Cheerios to him through the drawer along with a pillow. How nice am I, right?

But the princess sniffs the bowl and backs off. "Is that almond milk?"

"Just read your book and eat," I say. "The test will be on the first hundred pages. Go."

I trot upstairs and sit down for a nice long Beck sesh, which consists of listening to *Rare and Well Done*, looking at pictures of you I stole from Facebook, watching scenes of *Pitch Perfect* on mute. I get so lost in you that it gets bright in the shop and I should be tired given all the drinks, all the excitement, but I'm high on you and I want to take you to the London that Bowie sings about in the album you love. But what I have to do right now is go back downstairs to see if Benji learned to follow the directions.

What a sight, Beck. He isn't just reading King. He's devouring the new book like a chubby kid with a candy bar. I start to applaud and of course he drops it and fakes a yawn. I tell him it's time for a test and he doesn't want a test—no duh—and I tell him it's time for a Club Soda Test.

"But you said to read the King."

"That's right. And you did. Congratulations."

And now comes the sissy rant. He doesn't want a club soda test because he has a stomachache and a headache and he thinks he's allergic to something in the books and he needs a Band-Aid (is this camp, asshole?) and a B vitamin and a cream for his eczema, which is aggravated by the "cheap" coffee (of course the milk is from a cow tit, Benji) and he's tired and he doesn't want to be tested anymore.

"It's time to get started, Benji."

"I need more time. I'm telling you I'm intolerant of dairy. This cereal is like poison," he tells me.

"Club soda will settle your stomach."

"Please," he begs.

"You never read *Brief Interviews* either, did you?"

He doesn't say anything and I'm shaking my head and I feel like calling Yale Fucking University and telling them that their product is bullshit.

"I'm not a bad person," he says.

"Of course you're not."

And you know, Beck, he's not an asshole. He's just so fucking insecure he has to drop the King he loves. I give him another shot.

"So, how's that King?"

"Eh," he says and he still hasn't learned a thing.

I line up three identical red Solo cups, each full of club fucking soda, on a tray.

"You didn't read *Brief Interviews* and every day there's a test."

"I have serious money, Joe, family money. I have a car, a mint Alfa Romeo. Do you want a car? Because I can get you a car."

I pull the drawer open and lift the cups off the tray and into the drawer, *gently, Joseph*, one by one.

"All right, Benji, it's time to get started."

"Joe, wait. Don't do this." He falls to his knees. "I mean it. I have *money*."

He really is an idiot and can't read a situation and I almost feel sorry for him and I motion for him to stand and he stands. Good dog.

"Benji, I'm not drugging you."

"Thank God."

"This is a test. Each cup contains club soda," I explain. "And you're gonna take a sip from each cup and then you're going to tell me which cup has Home Soda. We're going to see if you recognize your own product."

He crosses his arms. "I need something to cleanse my palate."

I'm a step ahead and I reach into my bag and pull out a stale bagel.

"Were all three bottles opened at the same time? Club soda changes as it's exposed to air."

"They were, Benji."

"I need glass cups because plastic interferes with the chemistry."

"Drink."

I hand him the first cup and he takes it and closes his eyes and gargles and swishes and I want to smash his head into the cup. He spits it in the piss pot and stretches and walks around.

"You know my father has access to a jet. I can get you anywhere in the world. I can get you anywhere and then we forget this ever happened. He'd never even know it was gone. He expects me to blow money, I mean that wouldn't raise a red flag at all."

"Bite the bagel, Benji."

"Thailand. France. Ireland. You could go anywhere. Everywhere."

"Bite the bagel."

He bites the bagel and I pick up the second cup.

"Joe, please. Think about what you want here."

"Take the cup."

"The test still isn't valid because the yeast from the bagel compromises my taste buds and I should gargle with salt water."

I never raise my voice so it scares him pretty good when I do. "Take the fucking cup."

He falls on his knees, the fucker, and he's probably overidentified with the title character in *Doctor Sleep*. Ignorant Benji probably doesn't even realize that Dr. Dan Torrance is a character that originated in *The Shining*, a character that struggled, and Benji's never worked a day in his life, not really, probably made it halfway through *The Shining* and turned on the movie and never even held an ax. Benji is not a real man. You can't call what he does work.

"Stand up."

"Salt water. I'm begging you."

"They don't give salt water out in those Coke and Pepsi tests."

"Do you know what distinguishes club soda from seltzer and sparkling water?"

I groan.

"It's salt, Joe. Sometimes it's sodium bicarbonate. Other times it's sodium citrate or disodium phosphate."

"Just drink it, Benji. You're not bullshitting your way out of a test."

"I'm not bullshitting you," he says. "No bullshit this time. This is what I know."

"Drink it."

He sips from the third cup. He gargles. "This isn't my product."

I ignore his calls to find out if he passed or failed and walk up the stairs. Suspense is good for people. It makes us stronger. This is why America loves Stephen King so much; he keeps us on the edge of our seats until it hurts. He also knows that all people, whether groundskeepers at Fenway or privileged young fucks, are capable of going insane if placed under the right circumstances. Stephen King would appreciate my work with Benji and I smile as I lock the door.

THE deli around the corner has salt and they have Mason jars, and I stock up on both. The guy at the deli is cool and gives me a box, which makes the walk back to the shop easier. The more time I spend on this club soda project, the less surprised I am to know that a few idiots buy into Home Soda. And the more time I spend with Benji, the more I understand why a million other rich idiots *don't* buy into it. Home Soda will never be as popular as Stephen King. You win over consumers by showing you understand them. And you can't market a product if you don't understand the potential buyer for said product.

Benji doesn't know shit about marketing. Coke has tried every marketing strategy known to mankind. That's why Coke is hip and classic, original and new, and dietetic and caloric. Coke is wild-eyed J. Lo's favorite and it's also the whitest, blandest American drink we got. It's a contradiction. It's fucking genius. And Coke spent a shitload of money to be everything to everyone. Your boyfriend Benji's got it all wrong. He thinks it's all about being special, scientific, but you don't get anywhere in this world unless you know how to blend in.

"Gargle," I tell Benji when I get downstairs.

He gargles like he's at the dentist and it's not like I'm not trying to give him a chance. I think most pricks deserve a shot at being something other than a prick. For instance, I know that Benji was, quite literally, spoiled by his family, raised by a mother who never said no and a father who never said boo and a series of nannies who quietly let the little fucker do whatever he wanted. He told me all this shit the second night in here, the night he failed the quiz on *Gravity's Rainbow* and admitted to paying for every essay he ever wrote at Yale. He said he read the first five pages of the book and loved it so much that he couldn't read any more. He said he's too sensitive to read, too moved, that he's built for small doses. For someone so fucking sensitive he sure does take a long time to gargle the salt water.

"Drink it, Benji," I command.

He pinches his nostrils and sips and I don't know what I'm gonna do with him. This kid who was never grounded or beaten or locked up for any sin he ever committed. He cheated his way through college and he's trying to make a living by cheating pretentious fucks with his upmarket soda. Now, for the first time in his life, Benji is being held accountable. Accountability suits him. He's got wrinkles and he doesn't look like such a pansy. He's not perfect, obviously. He still crosses his legs like he's Woody Fucking Allen. He blows his hair out of his eyes, still a pansy after all these tests.

"Which cup was Home Soda?"

"It doesn't fucking matter because I'm selling a vibe. I'm selling health and wealth."

"It always matters. Any idiot can tell Coke from Pepsi."

"That's different."

"Which cup was Home Soda?"

"How do I even know you're telling me the truth?"

"Because I'm not a fucking liar."

"You'd never actually kill me," he says, trying again to have the authority. He thinks I'm the kind of sap who wants to be *seen* by the all-knowing wealthy pussy.

I'm not having it. I make that clear and I continue, "Which cup was Home Soda?"

"You're too smart to kill me," he says, belligerent. "You know someone like me, I have parents that are gonna find out what happened. You'd never really do that to yourself."

I don't say anything. I know the power of silence. I remember my dad saying nothing and I remember his silences more vividly than I remember the things he said.

Benji starts to shake and he picks up Cup One again. But his hand is shaking and when he brings the cup to his mouth, most of it rolls down his chin and onto his Brooks Brothers shirt. I can't get over how many people miss this guy, how many people love him. You should see his e-mail, Beck. He disappears for three days and everyone in the world acts like he's Ferris Fucking Bueller. The e-mails pour in, *where are you how are you are you okay, guy*? I don't respond to any of these people; they need to understand that Benji has gone off the rails. Don't they see his tweets? In any case, it's an indictment of our society, this outpouring of curiosity for this liar's whereabouts. Whoever distributes love in this world is doing a bad job. The beloved Benji bites the bagel and I scroll through your phone to calm my nerves. You didn't e-mail anyone about our night yet, which means you're still busy with your pillow or passed out wasted, and he sips from Cup Two and he gargles and he spits.

"Definitely not Cup Two," he says, and he's so obviously trying to cheat, trying to get a hint out of me. I ignore him. You gotta ignore people until they get in line, especially spoiled rich kids. When I was in this cage, I was good. I didn't fuss and shake like a little girl.

He picks up Cup Three. *"Salute,"* he says, and somehow that's the most offensive thing he's ever said. He's not Italian. What right does he have to say *salute*? He takes a sip and licks his lip and strokes his chin and paces around the cage.

"Well?"

"You know these aren't ideal circumstances for a taste test."

"Life isn't always ideal, not for most people."

"The air is dank. Musty."

"Which cup was Home Soda? One. Two. Or Three."

He clings to the bars and shakes his head and he's crying. Again. I check your sent mail. It's nine in the morning after our date and you are awake. I know this because you have just written to some dude in your class about how much you liked his story. I breathe. You have to do that kind of thing. That's just about school.

"Benji. Which fucking cup?"

He lifts his head and backs away as if he's gonna pass out—yeah right—and he wipes his eyes and crosses his arms and spits out, "None of 'em."

"That's your answer?"

He grabs at his shaggy blond hair that's darker every day—sweat.

"Wait."

"Either that's your answer or it's not."

"They all tasted like shit. Okay? They all tasted like bottom of the barrel ninety-nine cent store chemically enhanced club fucking soda. You're setting me up to fail. This is wrong. This is injustice."

"Is that your answer?"

"Yes."

"Sorry, Benji," I say and his lower lip shakes. "But you're wrong. They're all Home Soda."

You get an e-mail. The asshole in your class:

Thanks, Beck. I'm reading you right now, this is your best yet, nice, very nice.

Benji flares. "No."

And who is this pretentious asshole? *I'm reading you.* The fuck he is, Beck. Come on. Write to Chana. Write to Lynn. You had the best date ever and you're gonna e-mail with some hack from class?

"Joe, there's no way that those were mine."

"Well, they were," I say and now Benji isn't just Benji, he's everyone bad, all the educated liars. "It's called quality control and if you knew anything about business, you'd know that if you don't have quality control, you don't have anything."

He sits down and crosses his legs and I can't help but feel bad for the kid. The world failed him and didn't prepare him for adulthood. Now he's jammed up with a tear-stained shirt and a bellyful of club soda and cow milk. His blond hair and his vocabulary have finally let him down. He speaks. "So, what now?"

But he doesn't deserve an answer. He failed his test. I shut off the lights and walk up the stairs and he rants about needing light and it's obvious he's hooked on King and you're firing e-mails at this dude and all I want is a Coke in a can and a text from you. I turn around and give him his fucking light. He's gonna read a whole book for once in his life.

12

THERE is this girl I fired a couple of years ago. Her name was Sare, which was irritating. Her birth name was Sarah but she wanted to be original and all that bullshit. Sare was a nightmare. She acted like she was doing us a favor by showing up. She suggested Meg Wolitzer books to everyone, even old Asian men. When she had to give change, she reluctantly offered a light fist of coins and made the customer reach over the counter to get it. People hated Sare. She ordered lattes extra hot and left at least three times a week to go back to Starbucks and complain even though an extra-hot latte is obviously not going to be extra hot after a ten-minute walk in the cold. She had dreadlocks even though she was white. She kept a book on the counter to make sure that everyone knew that she was reading Edwidge Danticat or whatever of-the-moment minority woman everyone was supposed to be so jazzed up about. And she read the *New Yorker*, which meant 98.9 percent of her small talk while cleaning up started with "Did you see that piece in the *New*

Yorker..." She never flushed the toilet when she peed, claiming that her parents taught her to conserve. But her pee reeked because she was a vegetarian who lived mostly on asparagus. She wore bullshit eyeglasses and had a boyfriend in med school and when she was at the counter she always curled up and wrapped her body in a shapeless wool cardigan, which made customers feel that they were imposing on her.

When I fired her, I left her a note that her last check was in the bathroom. And I left her check in the toilet full of her asparagus-scented piss. She never came around again. She works for a nonprofit and married the doctor who must be the second-most annoying person on planet Earth simply because he married her. In terms of sheer annoyance, nobody I have ever known has compared to Sare Worthington, saver of the environment, native of Portland, Maine, forever wishing that she were from Portland, Oregon. Bitch should have just moved there.

But I envied her, I did. She was so cool, so unflappable. She was never impressed by anything. We'd get a signed James Joyce and she'd shrug. She made me too aware of myself. I hated that I wanted to impress her and I hated that I was so easily impressed, sniffing the dead ink on the James Joyce. I'm impressed right now, in this cab with you. I couldn't believe it when you wanted to take me to a party at your friend's house. It feels early for friends, but you insisted. And I'd be nervous no matter what because I'm not a party person, but I'm doubly anxious because we're not just going to some random house. We're riding uptown to your friend Peach *Salinger*'s house. The cab jostles us and we're not used to cabbing together and I'm trying to relax but you're not the girl from the Corner Bistro. I'm also damn proud of my work with Benji (Mr. Mooney and Curtis have no idea!) and I don't want to accidentally start bragging about what a good manager I am. So I gush, like some starry-eyed loser. "Salinger. That's something."

"Yeah," you say, too cool. "She's related to him. It's like that."

Sare wouldn't be nervous about going to a Salinger party, but I'm rattled with nerves. I can't believe I'm about to meet one of J. D. Salinger's relatives, on our second date, no less. When I called you to set up a second date, I planned on whisking you uptown to the planetarium where we'd make out in the back row. But you cut me off. "I have a party," you said. "Want to come?"

I said yes. I'd go anywhere with you. But the closer we get, the more nervous I am. I'm scared everyone will hate me and you are scared everyone will hate me. I can tell, Beck. You're fidgeting. A lot. And when I'm nervous, I get nasty. It's a problem.

"So is J. D. her uncle?"

"Nobody calls him that," you say. When you are nervous you get nasty too.

"So how are they related?"

"It's just a known thing." You sigh. "We don't ask. He was so private."

I breathe and I have to remember how you described me in an e-mail to this Peach today:

Different. Hot.

You invited me to a party because I'm

Different. Hot.

But what if I fuck it all up? I feel more insecure with every passing block. We are going to Woody Allen land, where I've always wanted to live. I sell Salinger and your friend *is* Salinger and you are still putting on makeup even though I have already seen you. You've been smearing black shit under your eyes since Fourteenth Street and I'm the one who should be gearing up for a battle. I have a tough time with college people, let alone "Brown people." You scowl at the driver. "I said Upper *West* Side not Upper *East* Side."

You have a Prada bag and a glare and I feel like I picked up the wrong Beck. You must be psychic because you blush, defensive. "I'm sorry. I don't mean to sound bitchy. I'm just nervous."

Phew. I tease you. "Me too. I'm worried your friends won't like you."

You get a kick out of me and you give up on whatever it was you were searching for in your purse and start talking to me. You don't just tell a story, you live it. When you tell me about your favorite birthday party ever, which was when your dad let you and two friends take the ferry to the mainland to see *Love Actually* and you met a guy, I learn that I am capable of envying a *thirteen-year-old boy*. Talking to you is like traveling through time and you sigh. "He meant a lot to me."

"You still know him?"

You smile at me. "I was referring to Hugh Grant."

I'll fucking kill Hugh Grant. "Ah."

"You know, Joe. Hugh Grant works in a bookstore in one of his movies."

"No shit?" I say and I won't kill Hugh Grant. We're about to kiss, I can feel it, but your phone buzzes with a text.

"It's Peach," you say. "If I don't respond right away, she freaks out."

"Is she as crazy as Uncle J. D.?"

You don't laugh at my joke and Peach better know how lucky she is to have you. Now she's calling, as if you had time to respond to her text. "We're almost there," you tell her and then I hear her scream into the phone, "You are not a *we*, Beck."

You get off the phone and our vibe is off. You don't laugh when I say that J. D.'s niece seems like a piece of work. *No, Joe. She's not his niece.* I don't like the way you say my name and I should shut up but I don't; my instinctive hatred of Peach is winning. "I just don't get it. You're such good friends and she doesn't tell you how she's related to one of the most famous writers in the world?"

"It's a boundaries thing."

You're pushing me away on our second date even though I'm *Different. Hot.*

You're afraid of love and it's sad and I don't want to walk into a roomful of strangers. But we are here and I am your escort. The doorman opens the cab door and you let him help you out. I wanted to do that. "Come on," you say. "I don't want to be late."

If Peach hadn't called, you would have said, *we* don't want to be late.

THE elevator is like a reset button and we agree that it smells like lavender. The walls are papered with flowers. Violets, I think. It's an old elevator and there's a small bench and we stand side by side and watch the buttons light up as we pass each floor.

"Penthouse, huh?"

"Yeah," you say and you shift your Prada to your right shoulder, between us. "I'm so happy I remembered to switch bags. Peach gave me this bag for my birthday last year. I would have felt terrible if I forgot to bring it."

There is no way we are going to talk about purses before we have sex so I pretend to be curious. "Did Peaches go to Brown too?"

"It's Peach," you say and you lick your finger and smudge your eyeliner. You're nervous and the elevator is slow and why can't we just hit the red button and stay?

"Ah."

"It's never Peaches," you say in a tone so serious you'd think we were talking about politics. "Well, actually, that's not true. Her middle name is Isabella so sometimes we joke around, you know, Peach Is."

"Uh-huh."

"You get it? 'Is' being short for Isabella?"

I look at you because I know that you think I'm

Different. Hot.

I don't ask permission to touch you, but I raise my hand to your cheek and rub off a speck of eye makeup with my thumb. You swallow. You smile. Your pupils are fat with desire. I look away first. I got you.

"Anyway," you say. "She's an old friend. Her family summered on Nantucket and we met when we were kids. She's a genius."

"That's cool."

"She prepped with Chana at Nightingale and she knew me from summers and Lynn was her freshman roommate. She's like the connector."

I laugh and you blush. "What?"

"You just used prepped as a verb."

"Fuck off."

"That's a demerit, young lady."

111

"And what happens when I get another?" you say and I'm this close to throwing you against the wall and you're this close to grabbing me. The closer we get to the party, the more you want to slap the red emergency button and go at it right here, right now.

I should kiss you but we're almost to the floor marked *P* for Penthouse. You move your purse to your other shoulder; you want me. I graze the palm of my left hand over the small of your back and you almost whinny. Your fingertips brush my leg as the elevator shimmies. I lower my hand slowly. You anticipate. You dangle your fingers, ready. And when my hand finally nears yours, you gasp, lightly, as you open your fingers and latch on to mine. We are holding hands and your sweat is mixing into mine. Wow.

It's time to kiss and I want to kiss but the doors open up and we're here. And I'm speechless. Are we on the set of *Hannah and Her Sisters*? Desire for you is mixed up with jealousy of all this and people know your name but not mine. Your world is bigger than my world and you hug Brown people and some of them have *instruments*— are you kidding with a fucking drum circle, like it's 1995? They're covering "Jane Says" and singing as if they know about lust and weakness. You squeeze my hand.

"Joe," you say. "This is Peach."

Yes it is. She's even taller than I expected with enormous frizzy hair swept into a tornado above her head. She makes you look too little and you make her look too big. You're from two different planets and you're not meant to be standing together. She claps as if she's meeting a five-year-old and I don't like it when girls are taller than me. "Hello, Joseph," she says, overenunciating. "I am Peach and this is my home."

"Nice to meet you," I say and she looks me up and down. Cunt.

"I love you already for not being pretentious," she says. "And thank you for not bringing any wine or anything. This girl is family to me. No gifts allowed."

You are, of course, aghast. "Omigod, Peach, I completely flaked."

She looks down on you literally. "Sweetie, I just said I love it. And besides, the last thing we need is more cheap wine."

You are acting like you committed a felony and she looks at me like I'm the delivery guy waiting for a tip. "I'm stealing our girl for two minutes, Joseph."

You allow her to steal you and I really must look like the fucking delivery guy as I stand here, not knowing anyone, not being known. No girls are coming on to me and maybe I don't look good in here. The only certainty is that I hate this Peach as much as I knew I would, and she hates me right back. She knows how to work you, Beck. You are apologizing for no wine, for not bringing Lynn and Chana, for not taking better care of your purse. And she is forgiving, stroking your back, telling you not to worry. I'm invisible to you in her presence, just like everyone else. *Peach Is* . . . in the way. I look around but nobody wants to say hi to me. It's like they can smell the public school on me. A skinny Indian chick mad dogs me before she nosedives into a line of Adderall or coke and I get out my phone and send a tweet from Benji:

Everything in moderation especially moderation. #homesoda #gobulldogs #smokecrackeveryday

I look up this address on Zillow. This place is worth *twenty-four million* dollars and I find an article about the decor in a fucking society blog. Peach's mother looks even meaner and taller than

Peach and who knows? Maybe it's tough to come into this world and crawl on rugs that cost a hundred grand. Peach learned piano on a mint black Steinway and went to the planetarium whenever she wanted. Of course she takes the glories of the Upper West Side for granted. Of course she loves you for fawning over the Prada. I see a hand-carved credenza and I move in for a closer look. It's an excellent piece, one of a kind. One door has a Jewish star and one door has a cross and maybe I have a shot in this scene. Peach is like me, half Jewish and half Catholic. I grew up with *no* religion and she had *all* religion. She celebrates everything and I celebrate nothing and you've come back to me, with her.

"Isn't this piece cool?" you say and you lean against the credenza.

"It's great," I agree. "You know, Peach, I'm also Jewish and Catholic."

"Oh, Joseph." She is correcting me. I can feel it. "I'm not Catholic. I'm *Methodist*, but you're sweet."

"That's cool," I say and I want to go home. I also want to tell her I'm *Joe*, not Joseph, bastard spawn of Alma Goldberg and Ronnie Passero.

You fake a cough and you look from me to her and back again and your voice is high. "You guys are also both New Yorkers."

Peach speaks slowly, like I'm ESL. "Which borough are you from?"

Cunt. "Bed-Stuy."

"I read that people are starting to move there," she says. "I hope the gentrification doesn't destroy all the local color."

The only reason I do not bash her head in is that you seem so nervous about us meeting that you don't notice her dissing me. I didn't ask her what she does for a living but for some reason she is talking about her job. "I'm an architect," she says. "I design buildings."

I know what a fucking architect is and nobody is ever an architect in real life, only in movies. And did you tell her I am dumb? I try to stay afloat. "That's cool."

"No, what's cool is the fact that you didn't go to college," she gushes. "I'm such a follower. My parents went to Brown, so I went to Brown."

I smile. "My parents didn't go to Brown, so I didn't go to Brown."

She looks at you. "He's funny, Beck. No wonder you're so into him."

You smile. You blush. I'm okay. "He's pretty good, yep."

She raves about how *amazing* it is that I *eschewed formal education entirely*.

It is not a compliment but I thank her anyway. She tightens the scarf around her neck and chastises you for lighting a cigarette as some asshole packs a bong a foot away.

She is done with me, for now, and she asks if you've heard from Lynn and Chana. You apologize. You're nervous about what she thinks of you and I wish I could pull you out of here and take you to my *borough*. She's a hypocrite, a fucking nightmare of a person, worse than I imagined. You are soft and she is hard in skintight red skinny jeans you would never wear. She's anorexic and slightly tattooed with thick frayed hair and a big red blow-job mouth and a Joker's smile and long, spindly, hairy arms that end in sharp, unpainted nails bitten to the quick. You ooze joy and she is an open wound, shrill and wan, unfucked and unloved. She clearly wants you to herself and I don't want to make life difficult for you so I interject, "Sorry, girls. Is there a bathroom nearby?"

You point me toward the bathroom and I flee. No wonder Lynn

and Chana didn't come. If she were a dog, shooting her would be the humane thing to do. But I can't very well shoot her. What I can do is walk around to find the library I saw in the blog. I gasp when I turn on the lights in the library. It's that fucking great. The Salinger family doesn't fuck around and I reach for a first edition of Saul Bellow's second novel, *The Victim*. The poor Bellow's dust jacket is torn. Peach's parents know how to buy books and make babies but they clearly aren't very good at caring for their purchases and their products. Brown people are singing "Hey Jude" again (how original!) and I miss you. I return the broken Bellow to its home and you and Peach walk into the library. I freeze. I hope I'm not in trouble.

"We figured we'd find you here." Peach laughs, as if you two are the *we* and I am just *me*. "I would let you borrow a book but my parents are *so* possessive of their babies."

"I'm all right," I say and I never asked to borrow a fucking book. "But thanks."

You link your arm through mine and it feels good and you sigh. "Isn't this amazing, Joe?"

"Yeah," I say. "You could spend a year in here."

Peach again: "Sometimes I feel like college ruined reading for me, you know?"

"I *do* know," you say and your arm is not linked through mine anymore. "Joe, I bet you've read more books in this room than me."

Peach approves. "A good salesman has to know his product, right?"

I hate Peach more than Sare. She called me a *salesman* and in the living room, the Brown people applaud themselves for knowing the words to "Hey Jude," as if it's not one of the most famous songs in the world. Peach sneezes and pulls a handkerchief out of her pocket. She's probably allergic to me and you leave me and run to her, lovingly. "Do you have a cold?"

"I bet you're reacting to the dust in here," I say. "You're probably not used to it."

"Good point," you say and Peach is silenced, temporarily, as you lead us back to the party. I've never needed a drink so badly in my life and we pass the Brown people as they maul "Sweet Virginia." You get a text from Chana. She's not coming. Peach huffs. "You know, if I were Chana, I might be embarrassed to show my face here too. Is there any guy in this house that she *didn't* sleep with at school? Pardon my crassness, Joseph."

I hate that I am so grateful to be acknowledged and you smile at me (hooray!) and Peach pulls us both into the dining room to greet some *guests*. It's more high ceilings and high Brown people holding court and kicking back at the longest table I've ever seen in my life. They're blowing lines off mismatched candy-colored plates. And the *booze*. There's tons of it. "What's your poison, Joe?" Peach wants to know. "Beer?"

"Vodka," I answer and I smile but she doesn't.

"Rocks?"

"If they're little ones," I say.

She looks at me and then at you and then at me and she guffaws. "Excuse me?"

"Crushed ice does better with vodka than cubes."

I learned that from Benji and Peach crosses her arms and you're fumbling in your purse for something to say, for a tunnel away from

117

me, and I gotta fix this and get rid of her and I try: "Whatever ice you got will work."

"That's awfully kind of you, Joseph. Sweetness, what do you want?"

"Vodka soda."

"Nice and easy," says Peach and she's gone.

Some dude appears with a bag of coke and there's clapping as more Brown people flood the dining room. I feel like Ben Stiller in *Greenberg*, misplaced in the bad way. Too many guys have slept with you. I know because they look past you; you're a restaurant that's easy to get into. And all of these people talk. Constantly:

Remember that spring break in Turks? You have to listen to Tom Waits when you're sober. Remember spring weekend when you got locked out of Pembroke? You have to listen to Tom Waits when you're stoned. Remember that class we took, that graveyard class and we took that field trip and we had those mushrooms? You have to come to Turks with us. Everyone is going.

I don't speak the language and it's a relief to get a drink. Peach simpers. "So Joseph, are the rocks small enough for you?"

"Yeah, yeah, I was just playing."

She moves us into the kitchen and it's the biggest kitchen I've ever been in and I'm trying so hard not to look around like it's the biggest kitchen I've ever been in. It's like the kitchen in that movie where evil rich Michael Douglas tries to have Gwyneth Paltrow murdered because she falls for a poor artist. Everything is stainless steel or marble and the island in the center is the size of a small car. I can't remember if the poor guy gets Gwyneth in the end of the movie and it feels like it matters a lot right now. I can't seem to find a place to put my eyes. I'm either staring at Peach, which is no good, or staring at you, which is worse. A CD juts out from under the *Times* Book Review. It's the soundtrack to *Hannah and Her Sisters*, thank God.

"Nice tunes, Peaches," I say. I can't control the tone of my voice, not in a room this noisy, this smelly, and she looks at me like I just asked her for spare change.

"Peach," she says.

"Peach," you say and sometimes I understand why Mr. Mooney gave up on women.

"Sorry."

"So you're a big fan, Joseph?"

I pick up her fucking CD. "This is one of my favorite movies. It's his best movie."

Peach ignores my proclamation in favor of a Brown girl she hasn't seen in *forever*. It's not fun to share you with all these people and you're drinking really fast, too fast. Do you like me? Do you want me to be more like those flattened cokeheads in the dining room with the Arcade Fire T-shirts and high cheekbones? Is that what you want? God, I hope not and I am holding the *Hannah* CD so hard that it cracks. I put it down. Peach picks it up. You smile at me, and you *do* like me and I'm going nuts.

"I love *Hannah* too, Joseph." Peach sighs. "I've seen it a thousand times."

"I've seen it a million times," I say and why am I competing?

She says I win and she looks at you like she approves. You're happy to see that rich kids and poor kids can get along after all and I almost want to spit in Peach's pointed face to prove a fucking point. She could have been nice to me from the get-go. She didn't have to put you through all this anxiety. But she still wants to talk about *Hannah*.

"Best Woody Allen movie ever," she says. "Scene for scene."

"Song for song," I say and I reach for the CD. Peach holds onto it like I'm inherently dangerous and we're back to square one and you're touching my arm again. "What's your favorite scene, Joe?"

"Oh the end. You know, when Dianne Wiest tells him she's pregnant," I say. "I'm a romantic and I'll own up to that all day long."

I like you tipsy and gazing at me. Peach is disgusted. "You're kidding right?"

She laughs at me and you're not looking up at me anymore. She's acid, this Peach. There's no fuzzy warmth, unless you count the tiny little hairs all over her narrow body. "Joseph, you can't be serious."

"Very much so. I love that shot of them in the mirror. The way they kiss when she tells him she's pregnant."

But Peach is poking at the newly cracked jewel case of the CD with her starved fingers and shaking her head. You touch me in the bad way, like you want me to stop and the Brown singers know the words to "My Sweet Lord" and someone found a fucking tambourine and somewhere in my head I remember that George Harrison's son went to Brown and I hate knowing that at this particular moment.

"Well, Joseph, it's funny you mention that scene because you know that's the one scene that Woody didn't want in," she lectures.

Woody.

"There's no way that's true."

"Actually, it is true. It's the truth."

"No offense, but I kind of doubt it. I think they let him do his thing, you know?"

"My grandfather worked at the studio and he told Woody he

wanted a happier ending. And Woody being Woody objected, but my grandfather, well, he was the guy, you know? *The* guy."

"So your grandfather's *not* J. D. Salinger," I say, because fuck her and she shoots you a look and you sigh and she's not done.

"Anyway," she says. "It's funny that your favorite scene in the movie is the one scene that he didn't want."

"Peach," says Beck. "Do you have any club soda?"

"There's a case of Home in the fridge," she says, smirking, eyeing me, knowing exactly what the fuck she's doing.

I raise my glass. "To your grandfather."

She doesn't raise her glass. "The Hollywood monster who slapped sappy, happy endings on every movie you ever saw and avoided his children like the plague and single-handedly ruined the tone of some of the most iconic pictures in America? No. No, Joseph. You don't want to toast that man."

You've practically crawled into the Subzero and I bet you're thinking about Benji and it's not in the way that I'm thinking about Benji and you emerge with your glass—red now, you chose cranberry juice, you choose me. And at long last, you correct her, you tell her I am *Joe, not Joseph* and I thank you as I raise my glass even higher because I can give her what she wants now that you've corrected her, now that you've picked sides.

"To you, Peach," I say in the deferent voice I reserve for persnickety older ladies. "For schooling me on my favorite movie."

She looks at you. You shrug like, *yeah he's that good*, and she looks at me. I sweeten the deal. "In all seriousness, Peach, I could pick your brain for hours. I love Woody Allen."

She doesn't sip after the toast and she sighs. "Okay that's *one* good thing about college. Staying up all night and talking about movies. You would have loved it, Joseph."

Instead of punching her in the face, I raise my glass for another toast. She stares down into her asshole sangria and asks you if you told Chana that some guy Leonard is here. You step away from me to hunt for your phone. You're sorry again and Peach forgives and this party is never going to end, ever. You are too tipsy to text and you growl in frustration.

Peach raises one eyebrow and she probably learned how to do that the summer her parents undoubtedly shipped her off to Stagedoor Manor Acting Camp, hoping that she might flower into Gwyneth Paltrow, the same summer she perfected the art of bulimia and learned how to insult people like me.

And then I look at you and what's this? You're cradling your phone in your hands and smiling. I have to know what has captivated you and Peach doesn't exist anymore. Nobody does. When I stand behind you and look down into your phone, I see a clip from *Hannah and Her Sisters*, the part where *Woody*'s character goes to a Marx Brothers movie. It was all worth it and I put my hands on your shoulders. We watch the rest of the scene together and God bless Groucho Marx.

WHEN we get into the elevator at the end of the night that threatens to never end, you don't wait until the doors are closed. Ever since I caught you watching my *Hannah*, you have wanted to be closer to me. And now, you are. I haven't even pushed the button when you drop your purse to the floor. You pull my face to yours and hold me. You pause. You drive me crazy and then. And *then*. Your lips were made for mine, Beck. You are the reason I have a mouth, a heart.

You kiss me when people can still see us, when we can still hear Bobby Short—*I'm in love again, and I love, love, love it*—because you made Peach play the soundtrack from *Hannah and Her Sisters* because you want to know what I know and hear what I like to hear. Your tongue tastes like cranberries, not like club soda, not anymore anyway. When the elevator doors close and we're alone, you start to pull away. But I pull your hair and bring your mouth to mine. I know how to leave you wanting more. And I do.

13

I fucked up. The day after our date, I left you a voice mail asking to take you to a movie at the Angelika. Fucking amateur. You responded with a text two hours later:

Already saw it actually and still hungover kind of ☹ and have so much writing to do. But see you soon! ☺

In truth, you hadn't seen the movie and you weren't hungover and you weren't writing, unless by "writing" you mean e-mailing your friends about Benji.

Fucking Benji.

I look at my phone and it's been *fifteen hours and two long days* since we kissed. You told Chana and Lynn that you're not "ready" for me because you have "Benji Brain." I can't kill Benji until *you* kill Benji and I try to stay calm. I've spent two days selling books, minding Benji, and remembering our kiss, *our kiss*. You described it to Lynn and Chana:

Joe is really intense. I don't know, he's a maybe. . . . Anyway, do you guys think I should write to Benji?

Your *maybe* hurt worse than *Benji* and there was nothing *maybe* about our kiss. I win the case every time I go over it in my head: You like my hair. You said so in the cab. You grabbed on to me, Beck. You weren't drunk. You find me *intense* and that's a compliment. It is. I try to be calm. I won't achieve definite status until you have the honor of receiving my cock. But this morning I woke up to this tweet from you:

That day when you can't not go to IKEA anymore. #procrastinationation #brokenbed

I kicked one of my typewriters. How could you send *#brokenbed* into the world knowing that I would see it? Are you trying to drive me nuts? Chana wrote to you right away:

Broken bed. WTF?

You wrote back:

Not broken, just old and creaky. I figure some dude is more likely to help me if it's broken, right? Would you want to help if I made you dinner or something?

Chana didn't respond. You e-mailed a few guys on Craigslist who assemble furniture for cash:

Do you go to IKEA and bring stuff back to NYC or do you only assemble stuff?

Upon learning that assemblymen do not double as slaves, you reached out to me:

Do you like Ikea? Hint hint.

It goes without saying that I don't like IKEA. But of course I wrote back:

Love it actually. Go there every day. Why?

It's not romantic and it's a daylight date but I understand that your attraction to me is so *intense* that you need to keep a safe distance. That's why you wrote back:

125

Want to get on the boat with me? There will be meatballs. ☺

Meatballs is a sexless word and the *boat* is actually a ferry that goes to IKEA. Furniture shopping is a thankless task but you murmured *I like you* about a thousand times in the cab after Peach's party and those murmurings trump whatever bullshit you spew to your friends on Twitter. I wrote back:

No meatballs required, but I'll get on a boat with you.

So this afternoon, you and I will go to IKEA, where there will be no chance of us having sex. I know how you girls operate and I know the three-date rule and all that shit. But I also know for a fact that we have a bigger obstacle between us: Benji. After you invited me to IKEA, you e-mailed Lynn and Chana and told them to look at Benji's Twitter:

Scary, right? I'm worried about him. ☹

I'm obviously not doing a good job with the Benji tweets. They're supposed to turn you *off* but you still care and Lynn and Chana tell you to stop:

Lynn: *Beck . . . it's okay to get dumped. It happens.*

Chana: *I'm sure he's on a yacht in St. Barts with some art whore telling her how worried he is about you. Honestly, B, you're starting to make me think that Peach is right. And it's awful to think that Peach is right. But you need to let. Him. Go.*

They're right, but you love hard and it's my fault that you're jammed up like this and I promise to do better with the tweets. You deserve to cut the cord with Benji. And you can't very well fall for me if you're worrying about him.

I have a heart just like you, so I splurge. I gather some of Princess Benji's favorite things: a vegan burrito, a soy latte, a pint of fake ice cream, and the *New York Observer*. He responds well, grateful, and he's inhaling that burrito like an animal and mourning the loss of Lou Reed.

"He's the reason I did so many good things and so many bad things."

"What's your favorite song?"

"They're all equally vital, Joe," he lectures. "You can't break down an artist's impact on the culture by citing specific songs or lyrics. It isn't about favorites. It's about the value of his entire oeuvre."

Typical, and I'm ready to send his last tweet as he licks the lid of the pint. He's perpetually ravenous. There's emptiness in him that can never be filled, emptiness that dresses up well at prep school, where a lack of willpower is called *creativity*. I tune him out and tweet for him:

Smoked it to the filter, licked it to the bone. #gotcrack #gotmeth #aintgotnothingatall #LouReedRIP

I hit TWEET. It's too quiet. I look into the cage and fuck me if Benji didn't get into his stash while I had my head buried in his phone. His packets are on the floor next to his card. I call out, "Benji."

Nothing. This isn't a part of my plan. I walk up to the cage. I call again but he doesn't move. There's powder on his upper lip and drugs have never looked so unglamorous. I know he's been taking a line here and there. But I've ignored it all because I hate drugs. I have never done drugs. Is this my punishment for being drug free? I wish I could take a picture and send it to you so that you could see what Benji boils down to, but I can't. Finally, he comes to and I'm so relieved that he's alive that I could kill him, which feels clichéd as all fuck and I raise a fist.

"Okay," he says and he shakes. "Benji out. Kill Benji."

"Quit the dramatics," I say. "I'm not in the mood."

And I'm not. It's not like I enjoy having to put somebody to sleep, even when said somebody is so lacking in courage and imagination that he needs to fill himself up with drugs at the very moment when he should be fighting for his life.

"Did you kill me yet?"

"Eat your fucking ice cream."

"It's not ice cream." He laughs. "It's nondairy."

I roar, "Shut up and eat!"

He laughs and it's called *smack* because I want to *smack* him, with his arms flailing. He's licking the pint of not-ice-cream like the junkie he is. And this is what you love, Beck? He picks up the *Observer* and tries to tear it in half but he's too fucked up and he staggers to his feet.

"Sit down, Benji."

"Did you kill me yet?"

He is a zombie and a cripple and he is talking again. "Joe, my man. Come on. You don't think it's funny? This girl stalks me for like a hundred years and now here I sit. Dead! Because you're stalking *her*!"

"Nobody's a stalker."

"Except you, Joe," he snips. "You know, I have nothing to do in here but think. And I get it. You didn't happen upon her in the subway that night. And honestly, if you want her that bad, if you really, really don't want to believe me when I tell you that she's crazy. Fine."

"Fine."

He groans, again, and it's typical of a guy like Benji to accuse you of being a stalker. I hear pinheads all over the city bragging about being "stalked" by girls and what a joke, right, Beck? Like any man could ever be troubled by your interest, let alone threatened. *Stalker.* What bullshit. What infantilism. I turn to go. But he calls out, "Wait."

He crawls to the cage and drops his plastic key card from his drug kit. "Take it."

"Why?"

"Storage locker," he says. "I'm a klepto, Joe."

"I've got things to do."

"That key opens the locker," he says, desperate. "The address is on the back. And nobody knows about it. I'm Stephen Crane."

"You're not Stephen Crane."

"I am to the guy who rented me the locker." He smiles, fucking heroin. "*The Red Badge of Courage.* That's the one book on that list that I read."

Of course that's the only book he read. Guys like Benji do all their homework in middle school so they never have to try again.

"Take all of it, Joe. Sell it. Pawn it. Do it." He's whimpering and I can imagine him at Disneyland, throwing a fit about the heat. "Please, Joe. There's a ton, Joe. I started stealing when I could walk. Just ask my parents. Hi, Mummy."

He nods off and he better not die. I care about him because *you* care about him and I want him to die honorably, when the time is right. I don't want him to die high, pissing his pants, giving his shit away. There are two more bags that flew out of the blazer and I have to go in and get them so he doesn't overdose while we're at IKEA. He starts to sing again, *and the colored girls go do do do.* I hit the cage with my machete. "Stop."

"Joe Joe mad." He drools and his words are melted butter, like his brain.

You text:

You ready soon?

I don't know what to say to you and he is eyeing me, amused. "She's not worth it."

I text you:

I need an hour, work is tough.

He pulls an electronic cigarette from that fucking blazer and whistles and somehow I'm the one caged. "She's crazy, Joe."

I tell him he's high, but my voice is weak. He pulls hard on that fake cigarette, an addict to the bone. He is the storyteller and I am the listener and I could smash my machete into my foot and that wouldn't change things.

"Wanna know about Beck?" he says and he doesn't make me say *yes*. "I'll tell you about Beck. All she wants is money. A rich dude, anyone. My senior year, she showed up at my place and pretended she was a maid. I knew she wasn't the maid, obviously, but I let her in. And I didn't ask her to suck my dick, Joe. Same way I didn't ask her to scrub the toilet. But she did."

"You're high," I say but I sound even less convinced, pathetic.

He cackles. "Well, shit, Joe. Of course I'm high."

I try to erase the image of you sucking his dick and I can't. "If she cares about money so much then why is she all over me to go out today?"

"Today?" He laughs again. Fuck. "That's cold, Joe. She won't even give you a *night.*"

He's a bird soaring in the cage and Mr. Mooney was wrong. The bird that thinks it's flying really *is* happy. He hates you and you love him and everything is wrong. I'm standing and I don't mean to be and he's still flat on his back, the fucker.

"The date is today because we're going to IKEA to get her a new bed," I say and fuck him once and for all.

He stares at me. Nothing. But then he writhes like a dog in the sun and laughs. "She did the same thing to me, rode my dick all night. Then she went off about the stupid fucking red ladle and tried to get me to go to IKEA."

I don't know about a *stupid ladle* and you're texting:

See you in forty-five ☺

You didn't ride my dick all night and Benji is imitating you: *"Take me to IKEEEEEAAA, Benji. Pretty please with red ladles on top."* He laughs and groans and he's not imitating you anymore. "If she wants to get spanked with a ladle, she should find some creep on the Internet, you know?"

No matter what I do or how hard I try I will always wind up like this, trapped by a guy who has more, knows more. I will not let him win. I unlock the cage and he tries to escape. I kick him into the corner like the dog that he is, pick up his leftover drugs off the floor, and flush them down the toilet. I thank him for the crap in his locker and he cries and I feel better already. I was wrong. I am the one in charge. He may have the red ladle, but I have the key.

14

YOU haven't been able to wipe the shit-eating grin off your face since you put your hand on mine to insist on paying for the IKEA ferry tickets. You look prissy in white jeans I've never seen before, jeans that tell me you're not breaking a sweat today. You're in flip-flops and your toenails sparkle and your hair is in a bun and you don't have any hickeys, so there's that. You are "thrilled" that I am "up for a jaunt" and you promise to make it fun and you better try your damnedest because the whole time you're talking to me, I'm just seeing your mouth as an orifice for Benji's cock and I'm thinking of the way you joked with your friends in your e-mail:

You: *Joe is a go. Slave for a day. Score one for Beck!*

Chana: *LOL you know you have to blow him or give him a handy.*

You: *No no he's not assembling, just going with.*

Lynn: *Do you think if you asked him he would install my AC unit?*

Chana: *Lynn, are you offering to blow Joe?*
Lynn: *You're disgusting.*
You: *Nobody is blowing anybody. Trust me.*

WE meet at the docks and kiss hello like platonic European friends or some shit. At least once we get on the boat and sit down we are close. You wrap your arm through mine. I can't tell if you're cold or hot and you smile.

"I can't believe you've never been to IKEA," you say.

"And I can't believe you have."

"Oh, I love it there," you say and you're leaning into me more. "Wait until you see it, all these little staged rooms. You just walk from one living room to another living room and you can't leave without going through the entire store. There's something magical about it. Do I sound crazy?"

"No," I say and you don't. "I'm the same way about the bookshop. You know, I walk around and I feel like the whole world is in there, the most important stories of all time. And then downstairs, in the cage."

"Excuse me. Did you say, *the cage*?"

"Rare books, Beck. Gotta keep 'em safe."

"I guess I hear *cage* and I think animal."

Benji's probably awake by now and the air feels good out here. "Nah, it's like a casino. They keep the money in a cage."

"What is it about stores?"

"Huh."

"You like selling stuff and I am full on addicted to buying stuff in the most stereotypically girly way. I love to shop. I mean I can be in the worst mood and I go to IKEA and come out of there with . . ." You pause and is this it? Red ladle red ladle red ladle. "I come out of there with a couple of place mats, and I feel renewed."

Fuck. "That's good, that's a good way to feel."

Maybe if I share an object with you, maybe then you'll share the ladle with me. I take the AC remote out of my pocket and I remember fantasizing about this moment before I had you. You look at it and you don't touch it and I tell you that you can touch it and you take it out of my hand. You smile. "This is high-tech."

"It's the most important thing I have. It controls the humidifiers and the AC units in the cage," I say. "If I were to jack up the heat and let those books get moist, they'd be gone, forever. Gertrude Stein is dead and she's not coming back to life to sign books."

"I just got the chills," you say and you smile. Ladle? "You would be a good writer, Joe."

"How do you know that I'm not?" I say and you like it and I try again: "Your folks must be proud of you, getting your MFA."

You're entertained and you look out at the water and I follow your eyes and you're still touching me and I wish I could kiss you to get Benji's cock out of your mouth and you play with your hair instead of holding my hand.

"I don't have folks," you say. "I have my mom but she's alone."

I glance around at the other IKEA ferry riders. None of them are like us. They're all talking about end tables and Swedish foods. We are special. We are falling in love.

"I'm sorry," I say, and I am.

"My dad died," you say.

"I'm sorry," I say, and I am.

"I don't know," you say and your eyes are wet but it could be the wind and you know so many guys you could have asked, guys in class, guys online. You asked me. "I guess sometimes I cry for no reason. Death is just so final, you know? He's gone. There's no coming back. He's gone."

You wipe your eyes and I won't let you laugh your way out of this one. "When did he pass?"

"Almost a year ago."

"Beck."

You look at me and I nod and you crumble in my arms, and it looks like we're hugging, another young couple off to IKEA to get feathers for the nest and eat hyped-up meatballs, and nobody can hear you crying except for me. You try to wiggle away but I hold you, and your big Portman eyes are glossy and your cheeks are red and there's an old couple across the way and the dude nods at me like I'm Captain America and we're almost there and you're wiping your eyes.

I want more. I try: "So, what was he like, your dad?"

You shrug and I wish there were a way for me to ask about a red ladle but it's not a normal question and you sigh. "He loved to cook. That was one good thing."

"I like to cook too," I say and I will learn how to cook. Red ladle red ladle red ladle.

"Good to know," you say and you cross your legs. "My shrink would say that I'm not respecting boundaries."

"You see a shrink?"

"Dr. Nicky," you say and I nod.

"Omigod, Joe. Why am I telling you this? What's wrong with me?"

"Don't you think that's a question for Dr. Nicky?" I say. You smile. I am funny.

Now I understand the meaning of Angevine on Tuesdays at three marked in the calendar in your phone. Dr. Nicky Angevine. Bing! And I mean it when I tell you not to be embarrassed. "Seriously, Beck," I say, all comforting. "I think shrinks are great."

"Most guys don't wanna know stuff," you say. "Most guys would freak out at me right now. The crying and the shrinking and the shopping."

"You know too many guys," I say and you smile and you know you need me and you nod like you agree, like you're agreeing to *us*, seeing the light, and the captain blows the horn. You kiss me.

IN the movie *500 Days of Summer*, IKEA is the most romantic place on earth. Joseph Gordon-Levitt and the girl start out in one kitchen and she's sweet on him and pretending to feed him dinner and when the faucet doesn't work—the joke being that all the appliances are props—Joseph jumps out of his chair and walks through a doorway into another kitchen and she is in awe of him and he says, "That's why we bought a home with two kitchens." I watched the clip right after you tweeted about going to IKEA and it's not like I'm some moron who expects life to be like the movies, but it has to be said.

Life at IKEA is not like life at IKEA in the movies.

In real life, I am not Joseph Gordon-Levitt and I have to push a giant metal shopping cart, weaving through the masses while you point out sofas you don't need, wall units you don't have room for, and ovens that are made of cardboard. There are a million people crowding this gargantuan converted warehouse. It's a dystopian nightmare come true where all furniture is cut from the same hunk of cheap-ass wood, where all rooms were furnished with items that came out of the exact same factory at the exact same time. It smells like body odor and Febreze and baby shit and farts and meatballs and nail polish and more baby shit—doesn't anyone get a babysitter anymore?—and it is loud, Beck, and I miss half the things you say because I can't hear you over the other humans. And all the while, I am consciously not thinking about where the red ladles might be in this hellacious sprawl of new shit.

In *500 Days of Summer*, the chick challenges Joseph to a race from the kitchen to the bedroom and the camera follows them as they run through an aisle. The chick flies onto the mattress and Joseph comes next, at a slow crawl. He mounts her and she wants him, you can see it. He whispers, "Darling, I don't know how to tell you this, but there's a Chinese family in our bedroom."

In real life, there is also a Chinese family in IKEA with us, but they are nothing like the quiet family in the movie. There is a small boy who screams and a small girl who poops in a diaper and drools. It feels like they're following us, Beck, and I'm going to lose it if they don't stop fighting. They're so fucking loud that I can't hear what you're saying. You pick up a yellow, fringed pillow and I am sick of missing out on your words. What if you said something important? What if you revealed something to me and I missed it?

You excuse yourself as you squeeze by the Chinese woman, who has stopped abruptly to examine an unremarkable round table. She could get out of the way but she doesn't. You practically have to boost yourself onto the back side of the hunk of junk they call a sofa in order to get closer to me. That woman has nerve and I want to tell her but you hold my hand and maybe it's not so bad after all.

"Feel this," you say. You push the pillow into my hand. I look down and I can see your black panties just below the belt of your white jeans. They've stretched out from all your monkeying around and you're holding my hand and breathing and you don't smell like IKEA and just like that, I'm hard.

"It's soft, right?"

"Yeah," I say. The Chinese dad slams his fist on the table. Bam! We're both startled and the moment ends as you drop the pillow. If this were *500 Days of Summer*, we wouldn't be able to hear him over the Hall & Oates that would be playing just for us. You pick up another pillow, pink. You press it into my palm.

"Well, what about this one?"

I'm your putty and you've got your hair in a bun and you're not looking at me even though you know I'm looking at you and you smile and keep your eyes on my hand on the pillow and you whisper, "I think this is good."

"Me too," I murmur. I've barely been able to hear you speaking for the past couple of hours and your voice is heaven. I missed it.

You look up at me with sweet eyes. "It just feels good, you know?"

"Yeah," I say and it does.

"You can tell when something is right because most things are just plain wrong."

"Yeah," I say and you have to be talking about us, not some twelve-dollar piece of Swedish *chazerai*, but you won't look at me, you won't let me all the way in yet. So fuck it. This is all too good and I'm gonna break in.

"Hey, Beck," I say.

"Yeah?" you say but your eyes are on the pillow, not me.

"I like you."

You smile. "Yeah?"

"Yeah," I say and I put my other hand on your shoulder and now you're looking at me. We're so close that I can see the pores you're always trying to shrink and I can see the eyebrows you didn't pluck this morning, because this morning you didn't know you were gonna want me. This morning I watched you get ready in five minutes flat.

"So we'll get the pillow?" you say.

"Yeah," I say and it won't be long until I'm inside of you. We've just made a pact and we know it and I don't know who grabs whose hand. I just know that we're holding hands and you're holding the pillow and we're weaving in and out of bedrooms and now you're helping me, you've got a hand on the front of the cart. We are in this together, side by side, navigating like an old couple, like a new couple, and you know what, Beck?

It turns out IKEA is pretty fucking awesome.

You grab onto the base of something called the *HEMNES bed* and you look up at me. "Does this work?"

"Yep," I say and you nod. You want me to like your bed. You know it's gonna be *our* bed and you take the little pencil out of your back pocket and scribble down the numbers and letters.

You hand me the slip and smile. "Sold!"

Some girls would take all day and go back and forth but you are gloriously decisive and I am crazy about you. You peck me on the cheek and tell me to have a seat "on my new bed" and you skip off to the ladies' room and maybe you pee and maybe you don't. But you do send an e-mail to the guy you hired off Craigslist to assemble your new shit:

Hey Brian, this is Beck from the ad. I'm so sorry but I have
to cancel today. My boyfriend got the day off so he can do it.
Sorry! Beck

Boyfriend. When you come out of the bathroom, your eyelids are
a little red from the quick job you just did on your brows and your
lips are glossed and your tits are a little higher and you're smiling
and I almost think you rubbed one out in there and you take a deep
breath and clap your hands.

"So can I buy you some meatballs?"

"No," I say. "But I can buy you some meatballs."

You smile because I'm your *boyfriend.* You just said so, Beck. You
did. We park the shopping cart outside of the café area and the noise
level in here is too much and there's a line but you say it's worth the
wait. You are prattling on about meatballs and that damn Chinese
family is in front of us and how did they get here first? They are taking
forever and they are ahead of us, in line and in life—married, with
kids. The clouds are forming in my head because you didn't say
boyfriend to a friend, just to some dude on Craigslist. What if you don't
mean it? What if you were quick to pick out a bed because you looked
at beds online? What if you don't care what I think? What if you're not
thinking it would be nice to go to bed with me, to make a family with
me? The Chinese dad is taking too long and I can't take it anymore
and I reach over his arm and grab the other meatball ladle. *Ladle.* He
shoots me a dirty look and you apologize to him, as if I'm the bad guy
in the buffet line, in the world, and you still haven't told me about the
red ladle. You look at me. "Is something wrong, Joe?"

"They were rude."

"It's just crowded," you say and you think I'm harsh and I am.

"I'm sorry," I say.

Your jaw drops and your mouth opens and then it closes and your eyes are wide and you are dazzled. You purr. "He says he's sorry when he's wrong and he lets me spend two hours looking at couches I don't need? Joe, are you for real?"

I beam. I am. When the Chinese mother shoves my hand out of the way to reach a napkin, I don't even react. I don't have to withhold my anger because I'm not angry. You pick out the meatballs and I pay (I'm your boyfriend!) and you choose a table and I follow you. We sit, at last.

"You know, Joe, I am totally going to help you put the bed together."

"You bet you are, missy."

You split a meatball down the middle and pop half into your mouth and you chomp, *mmmmm*. Now it's my turn and you pick up the other half and I open my mouth. I'm your seal, open, and you pop the half ball into my mouth and I chomp, *mmm*. The Chinese family interrupts, again, when the boy rams a spatula into the white table, which reminds me that you still haven't told me about the red ladle and suddenly these meatballs taste like shit. You told Benji about that ladle. Why not me?

"Are you okay, Joe?"

"Yeah," I lie. "Just realized I gotta take care of some online orders at the shop."

"Well, that's actually good," you say. "I can shower and clean up and you can come over when you're done."

Everything about what you just said is ideal but you still haven't mentioned the red ladle and for all I know you never will. I take charge.

"I just gotta pick up something."

"Really?" you say like it's so hard to believe. "What do you need?"

I can't say ladle. "A spatula."

"A spatula for Joe," you say. "Sounds like a kids' book or something."

The Chinese family sails past us, hightailing it to their next destination in this plastic zoo. You look longingly at them and their full cart and we're on the move again. I search the signs for COOKING UTENSILS and you sigh. "I'm beat."

"Just gotta get the spatula and then we're out of here."

You're done, lazy. "I can stay here with the cart."

"Do you mind coming?" I say. "The last one I got was a piece of shit."

You follow me into COOKING UTENSILS and I walk slowly and hope that the spatulas will be right next to the ladles. I see red ladles and my heart leaps. You don't react to them. You need a push. I pick one up. "Maybe I'll get all red things," I say. "Is that lame?"

You look at the red ladle. "This is really weird."

"What?"

And now, at last, you pet the red ladle in my hand and tell me the story of your red ladle. You were a little girl in a little bed, and the smell of pancakes woke you up on Sunday mornings. Your dad used a special red ladle on Sundays, just Sundays. He would sing along to the top-forty countdown, screw up the lyrics, and make you and your brother and your sister laugh, winter, spring, summer, fall and you couldn't fall asleep Saturday nights, you were so excited for Sunday mornings. And then, he started hitting the bottle. And the Sundays went away and the red ladle stayed in a drawer and your mother's pancakes were greasy and burnt or wet and undercooked and your father was gone but the ladle was still there and bad pancakes smell like good pancakes and he's dead now so there will never be pancakes again. There's nothing dirty about your sweet, sad story and fuck Benji for making you feel bad.

"That ladle is still in our house to this day, as if he's coming," you say. "Life is mean."

I put my hands on your shoulders and you look at me, expectant.

I speak, "I'm getting this for you."

"Joe."

"No ifs, ands, or buts."

The world stops and your eyes gloss over. The Benjis of the world don't understand what you want, someone to make you pancakes. You don't care about money. You don't want to be spanked. You want love. Your father had a red ladle and now I have a red ladle and I will make you the pancakes you want so badly, the pancakes you haven't tasted since he died. Your mouth waters and you submit, softly. "Okay, Joe."

You pick up a silver ladle. "Fresh start," you say and you are right.

I am your boyfriend.

15

I cross Seventh Avenue and smile at every single person who passes by. I am happy. I don't even think I'm walking right now. It's just a dream and if I started to sing and dance, I wouldn't be surprised if all the strangers got in line and followed along. What a magical day with you and now to think of you in your place, showering and shaving those legs so they're nice and smooth for me, brushing the meatball gristle out of your fine little teeth. I can't wait to touch all of you and I am carefree as a guy in a beer commercial as I make my way down Bank Street.

It's actually possible that we can have sex tonight and I really didn't think we would get here this fast. But Benji is still out cold and I put a twenty-dollar salad and a bottle of Home Soda in the drawer for him, so he'll be fine for hours. I am free and I am literally walking up the stairs to your stoop and pressing the buzzer and waiting for you to come jogging to the door, which you do.

"Entrez vous." You giggle and I walk into your lobby and it's

happening, we're going to fuck. Your hair is damp and your pores are gone and there's no bra under that tank top and there are no panties under those low-slung, threadbare sweatpants and you're not wearing any socks.

"I'm kind of a slob," you say as you open the door and I want to tell you that I know but I don't.

"This isn't so bad," I say and I'm not sure where to go. It's an awkward space with you in it and it's so small that it really is meant for one. You stand in front of me with your hands on your hips looking around at all the girl stuff strewn about, magazines and matchbooks, empty vitaminwater bottles, and coupons and receipts, brand-new books, unread, mixed with beloved books, torn and frayed. It's a minefield of shit and maybe that's why you're just staring at all of it. There's a galley kitchen ahead to the left and there's a new toaster and the box from the new toaster on the floor and you really do like new things. The bathroom door is to the direct left and the light is on and the fan is blowing and I reach in and turn off the switch. It was a strange thing to do, and I know it and you are freaked out but thank God you like me so you make a joke of it and laugh.

"Well, yes, Joe, go ahead and make yourself at home," you say and you make your way across the minefield, past the TV and into the bedroom.

I take off my jacket and hang it on the standing coatrack. You turn around and scrunch your pretty little nose at me.

"Get in here," you say.

"Yes, miss," I say and I step on a fucking hanger and it snaps but I just keep going.

Your room. There's a bottle of vodka on the floor and two brand-new glasses (not IKEA), and a paper cup of ice that you pick up and show to me.

"Pretty ghetto, right?" You laugh.

"Nah, ghetto would be if it was in a paper towel."

You giggle and pour ice and vodka into both cups and sit down on the floor by the box of bed. There is music on, the Bowie from our date, and you pat the floor and I sit down across from you.

"Someday I'll be the kind of girl who always has mixers in the fridge," you say.

"Good to have goals."

You smile at me and get on your knees and move closer to me and I lean forward to meet you and when I take my glass I very deliberately feel your hand against mine.

"Thanks."

"No problem," you murmur and somehow, like a ballerina, like a pretzel, your legs relax and spread and you are sitting like a yogi with your bare feet pressed together. You sip your vodka and look up at the ceiling. "I hate all those marks."

"No, Beck, this is an old building. Those marks are the history."

"When I was a kid, I wanted glass box walls. You know those frosted glass boxes? Like from the eighties?"

"You like new things," I say.

You are quick to come back. "You like old things, Joe."

"I like it here," I say and I look around the room. It's smaller than I remember or maybe it's just hot. I want you. "You think your new bed's gonna fit in here?"

"I had a queen before."

You're wrong, because your old bed was a double and it barely fit but I can't correct you. You lick your lips. "So, can I be your assistant?"

"No," I say. "But you *can* be my apprentice."

I always say the right thing to you and it was like that right off the bat. You like words and I know words and we toast for no reason and throw back our drinks and I stand first. I offer a hand to help you up and I'm holding one of your hands, and now both of your hands. This time you're not letting go and I'm getting hard and you've got me with my back against your window and I can hear leaves rustle on trees. Cars swoosh up West Fourth, right through my gut. My senses, Beck, you turn me on, literally, and the wind nips at my back through the screen on the window. You take my hands and you slide them onto your hips, guiding. You maneuver my fingers one by one beneath the elastic waist of your threadbare sweatpants and anyone outside walking by could see us and you bring my hands lower and your butt is soft and yet hard and round and I'm cupping your ass and you let go of my hands and reach up and wrap them around my head and it's on.

You leap up and straddle me and I could walk from here to China with you wrapped around me and I walk across the tiny room and I have you against the wall and I'm kissing you and owning your ass and I like your heels in my back and your bed in a box and there's a horrible sound at the door, metal on metal and a whistle and your legs drop to the floor and you straighten my hair and there is someone at the door.

"Is your mom here?" I say and you lick your hand and tame my eyebrow.

"Nope," you say. "It's Peach!"

So it's like that and you slide away. This is all wrong and this was our time and you run to the door and let Peach inside and I can't hear you but I sure can hear her.

"What is wrong with your hair?"

You say something.

She balks. "You're not fucking the assemblyman from *Craigslist?*"

You say something again.

She groans. "Beck, dessert is supposed to come *after* dinner. What are you thinking when he hasn't even built your bed?"

Now you are loud and clear. "Joe!"

I come when I am called and I nod hello to Peach and she fakes a smile.

"Hi, Joseph," she says. "Sorry to crash your party but our little friend here had originally *hired* someone to make her bed and, as her best friend, it was my duty to join just in case the worker was a *luuuunatic.*"

"Well, surprise!" I exclaim and you laugh but Peach doesn't and man, that vodka was strong.

She looks at you. "Can I pee?"

"Of course," you say. "Are you having a flare?"

"I *am*," she says and she kicks off her sneakers and the smell of her self-indulgent, sweaty feet overwhelms the apartment and now she pulls her hot pink fleece over her birdy little head and throws it on the floor, not on the coatrack. She looks at me.

"Joseph," she says. "I know this is more than you want to know but I have a rare condition with my bladder called interstitial cystitis and when I have to pee, I have to pee."

"Be my guest," I say and she stomps into the tiny bathroom and she doesn't turn on the light. She knows your place. She knows that if she turns on the light, the fan will come on and she won't be able to hear us. She doesn't trust me. But she probably doesn't trust anyone.

I crack up a little but you *shh* me and motion for me to follow you into the bedroom and you are different now. "I am so sorry, Joseph," you slip. "Joe."

"That's okay. Is she all right?"

"Have you ever heard of IC?"

"I what?"

"Interstitial cystitis," you say and you are all best friend business now, tying your hair back with an elastic band and opening a scissor and tearing into the box. I take the scissor and finish the job and you pour more vodka for you, not me, and we're not having sex and you're not my apprentice anymore. Instead, I am hauling the bed frame and the bolts and the Allen wrench and all the little pieces out of the box and you are leaning against the window and smoking a cigarette the way you do sometimes. You're telling me more than I ever wanted to know about interstitial cystitis and this is not how this was supposed to go down.

"So it's awful for her," you say. "She can't drink regular water, only Evian water. Almost all foods irritate her bladder and it's impossible to predict when or what or why or how. She can't eat *any* fast food and if she drinks alcohol, it has to be high pH like Ketel One or Goose, and ideally pear, because pears are soothing to the bladder. Anyway, the poor girl suffers. People think she's being uppity but if she eats cheap stuff, her bladder can literally, like, break."

"She was doing shots of Jäger at her party," I say.

"Joe, don't be like that."

"I'm sorry, I'm just confused."

"It's a complicated disease," you say and I apologize again and you forgive me and you come over and rub my head and kiss my head but then you go back to the windowsill and I didn't sign up to assemble this bed alone. I miss you. My hands were down your pants and now you don't even look at me when you talk.

"Sometimes, if she takes this special pill and she pads her bladder with a lot of goat cheese or milk or pressed pear juice, she can, you know, she can eat other things like Jäger or wheat."

"Sucks to be her," I say and the instructions for the bed are in pictures. The only word in the whole eight-page brochure is IKEA. I am not a visual learner and your cigarette is making me sick.

"It really does," you say. "And I love Lynn and Chana, but they can be so rude with her. I mean they always want to go to pizza or whiskey places and they know Peach can't eat that stuff but they still make these plans. It's not very nice."

"She can't eat *anything* at a pizza place?" I say and I never would have had that vodka if I knew I was gonna be handling a wrench. I thought I'd put this bed together in the morning, after I woke up with you naked in my arms on the couch in your living room.

"Beck!" Peach calls. And she's crying and it's bullshit and I'm sure of it but you stub out your cigarette (and you don't put it out completely, I have to finish the job), and you run away without so much as saying good-bye.

The rich are difficult. You are drawn to their idiosyncrasies and their dramatics. I assemble your bed slowly and sing along quietly to your Bowie and it takes a long time, a long, lonely time and you're out there with her and I can't hear the two of you talking and I have never felt more alone in my life than I do when I tighten the last bolt on your bed. It is way too big for this room and I was right. I take the mattress leaning against the wall and drop it onto the new bed frame instead of sliding it on. I want you to come out here and clap and admire my work. But instead, you text me from the bathroom:

I am SO sorry Joe. Peach is super sick and I don't want to leave her alone. Is there any way you could do us a favor?

What can I do but write back:

Anything.

Now you call for me to come so I walk over to the bathroom door. I don't open it. And neither do you. I knock on the door. "At your service, ladies."

You open the door the tiniest bit and you smile. "Would you mind running to the deli and getting a bottle of Evian and a pear and some more ice?"

"Of course," I say. "Should I grab your keys?"

You start to say yes but she nudges you, I think, and you tell me to buzz when I get back. I don't kiss you good-bye.

It's clear to me as I walk past Graydon Carter's house and breathe in the West Village air. Benji's got to go. Peach is your best friend, so you're allowed to be excessively tolerant of her bullshit, but you've got this thing in you, Beck. And it's not your fault, because everybody has something. Dennis Lehane would call it a *misguided Ivy League omertà* and he would be right. You will always choose the Peaches and Benjis of the world over me because you're loyal to the gentry. I pick up the smallest bottle of Evian and the worst pear in the bucket and a two-buck bag of ice and a pair of rubber gloves I'm gonna need.

I haul my sweaty, sore ass back to your place and you don't buzz me in. You come to the door and take the plastic bag.

"She's really not up for company," you say.

"I get it," I say. "You okay?"

"Oh I'm fine. And so is my bed."

You smile and peck me on the lips and Peach is calling so you run back to her and as I walk cross town to the shop, all the good of our day, all the *boyfriend* joy is obliterated by how much I hate this fucking city for being owned by people like Benji and Peach. It's not until I reach the shop that I realize I left the rubber gloves in the bag. If you ask, I'll tell you that I was going to clean your bathroom. You'll believe me. I know how to do stuff like that, I do.

I go to my corner store that's not as nice as your corner store and pick up more rubber gloves and peanut oil and then I hit up Dean & DeLuca for a soy latte. I get back to the shop and I pour a healthy tablespoon of peanut oil into the soy latte. Benji lies about everything. He's probably lying about his peanut allergy but who knows? Maybe I'll get lucky.

16

MOST people think that Stephen Crane wrote *The Red Badge of Courage* about war. But he didn't. He based his battle descriptions on his experiences on the football field in school. Crane was somewhat of a pussy in his youth, perpetually sick and not a jock. He'd never been to war; he'd only been sacked by the early American equivalent of Clay Fucking Matthews. You should have seen Benji's face when I told him this, Beck. He knew the book inside and out but he knew nothing about Crane, had no idea that Crane was full of self-loathing over the fact that veterans bought his bullshit. He pretty much spent the rest of his days killing himself slowly, enlisting in war after war and trying to make up for the fact that he'd been young, clever, and lucky.

"That's unreal," Benji marveled, shaking his head.

"What's unreal is that you love the book so much but never learned about him."

THIS much is true: Benji wasn't lying; he is, was, allergic to peanuts. He died educated. He died with new confidence and new pride and who says a life has to take eighty years to be lived? He learned, you know? How many people get to go out feeling like they're just hitting their stride? Most people die old, full of pain and regret. Or young and full of drugs and self-indulgence—or sheer bad luck. But Benji had the ultimate privilege; he died with an opening heart, an improving mind. Benji wasn't any good at being Benji, Beck. You know that, above all people. Look at the way he treated you and look at the way he treated his body. The trap I set for him was a relief from the trap he was born into. I created a world where he couldn't steal, where his counterfeit words didn't count. I took his drugs away.

I look out over the water at IKEA on the horizon. It's the craziest thing, Beck. The storage locker Benji told me about, the one with the key card? It's right near IKEA. You gotta get a kick out of the little things and I wonder what Paul Thomas Anderson would make of this "coincidence."

It's easier to make sense of things at sea, in a river that could kick your ass if it wanted to. You remember that we really are nothing compared to the elements, ashes to ashes, Beck, dust to dust. Benji's ashes are in an IKEA box, one leftover from our trip. I tell a deckhand that there were parts missing, that the product looks nothing like the picture. In truth, this box contains Benji's ashes. And you wouldn't believe what I had to go through; a person doesn't just disintegrate to dust.

Two days ago, you started stressing about Halloween. You were going to be Princess Leia (you really are a flirt), and you were taking pictures of yourself and your friends and getting drunk a lot. You did not ask me to be Luke Skywalker, and going forward, we are gonna have some fun fights about how to celebrate Halloween.

And two days ago I started stressing about what do with Benji's body. I had to get Curtis to work crazy hours during Halloween and I had to learn to cremate a corpse. Curtis was amenable; potheads need to buy pot and respond well to overtime. And I figured out what to do with Benji thanks to the instructions on fiscally practical backyard cremation readily available online. It wasn't something I could do in the city so I took Mr. Mooney's car out by Jones Beach and found a good hiding spot. Cremation takes time. You have to keep that fire going for ages and it's not a perfect job. Benji's ashes are definitely bony so you wouldn't want to go pouring them into a colander! A proper cremation requires time and chemicals, but I think I did well, given the circumstances. And I care enough to box him up and bring him home, and most people in my position would leave him out on the island. I crack a smile because when you think about it, you're not really Princess Leia (your buns were much smaller), and I'm not really an undertaker. There's a symmetry of some kind, and I like it.

"How much was it?" says the friendly deckhand.

"Eighty bucks, if you can believe that."

He shakes his head and hoists the box of Benji into the hold. "They rip people off. But the girls love it."

"That's how I got into this mess," I quip, and we laugh and I tip him ten bucks and he is genuinely happy to get that kind of a tip and you know nobody ever tips him.

We're easing into the slip and he's got a cigarette tucked behind his ear and he's holding the line and gathering it and preparing to toss it and he tells me he'll help me lug the Benji box to IKEA but I tell him I got it.

"Enjoy your smoke, guy." I say. "You only go around once."

"Or back and forth six times a day." He laughs.

THE key card works. Benji was right. The storage locker is where he said it would be and there was no trouble getting in because nobody wants to employ humans anymore. Back in the day, there would have been a security guard and a pit bull and there would have been questions.

Who are you?

What's in the box?

Who authorized your access to this locker?

Where is your authorization?

Can you get Mr. Crane on the phone?

Can you get him to come down here?

And my answers wouldn't have been good enough and I wouldn't have known what to do with the box of Benji. But he was generous toward the end of his time on earth. He knew I'd get in here no problem and I think he wanted to rest here. I think he wanted to be reunited with the stolen Rolexes and suits and silver, the stuff he was trained to respect and the stuff that he didn't have the balls to break away from. He was always gonna be an unhappy materialist. I spared him years of pain.

I pop open two bottles of Home Soda, one for me and one for Benji, and I set his bottle by the box. Tell you this, Beck, the shit tastes like heaven once in a while, if you catch the right batch. I glove up and clean up and listen to the carbonation fade. I notice a Mount Gay Rum Figawi Sailing hat from 2006 with the name Spencer Hewitt stitched under the lid. Rich kids have their names stitched into their clothes, because of rooming with klepto brats like Benji and nannies who need help remembering names. I try on the hat. It fits and I decide to keep it. I need it, Beck. It's Nantucket red, faded to a dusty rose hue, sensitive to the elements, regal somehow in spite of being damaged, just like you.

17

YOU don't know that you're in mourning. You don't know that Benji is dead. You couldn't know. But you're off, Beck. You've spent the whole week loafing around having virtual movie screenings with Peach. You can't even leave the apartment to get coffee without debating the merits of Starbucks, Dunkin' Donuts, and the "sweet workers" at your deli. I've tried to get in with you, but right now, you're all mixed up in Peach.

You can't even keep your head straight about a fucking movie. When we went to the Corner Bistro, you told me you love *Magnolia* and you went off on your love/hate relationship with California and your dreams of meeting Paul Thomas Anderson and telling him how fucking smart he is. And I agreed. But Peach tells you his movies are *bloated and judgy* and you agree with her! And judgy isn't even a fucking word and you're supposed to be a writer. I try. I ask you what you're up to and you tell me you're watching *Magnolia* and what do you do? You tell me that you think it's *judgy*. You don't think that.

Peach thinks that. And I try to get together with you but you tell me you're sick.

You're not sick, Beck. You ask Peach to go shopping, to get lunch. She says no. She says she's sick. But I tracked her down. I have to know why she has this hold on you so I've been watching her walk to her *architecture* firm and walk to *lunch* and kiss people hello and pick at Cobb salads all fucking week, Beck. She's not sick. I ask you to go out for a walk, for coffee, soup, for anything. It's always the same:

I'm still sick. ☹

I sleep. Six days since Benji's passing and still I haven't seen you. I don't dream, at least, not that I remember.

THE world is a better place when I wake up because at long last, you got into a fight with Peach. She told you she thinks your shrink is no good and you stood up for your shrink and for yourself. I'm proud of you. And the best part is, now that you've got your head on straight again, you are the you I know and love. You wrote to me in the middle of the night:

> *Okay, this is way too many words and it's way too late but do you ever just feel like telling everyone in your life to fuck off? I don't want to be that girl bitching about her friends but right now, may I just say . . . my friends are bitches! I try so hard to get them together, you see that, and they all bicker and make my life impossible and Chana won't go somewhere if Peach is gonna be there and Peach won't go somewhere if they have happy hour specials because she thinks drink specials bring out the riffraff. The point is . . . And now it's five A.M. and I haven't finished my piece and I have to be workshopped today*

*and just plain ugh, you know? And there's this Blythe girl, this
monster, she hates me, and she's gonna attack this cowboy story
and okay. I am so babbling. But basically, the sun is coming
up and I am thinking of you. See you soon, assuming you don't
decide I'm a crazy person after reading this e-mail? Night.* ☺

And just like that, you've made my day. I wrote back to you short
and sweet:

Dear Beck, I'm buying you six drinks tonight. Joe

You loved it and I got a smiley face and we have a date tonight—
yes!—and I've made all the right moves—yes!—and I put the
typewriter I took to bed back in its place and my hair looks good
today—yes!—and Curtis is working tonight so I don't even have to
close up—yes!—and Peach is out of the picture—yes!—and I cum so
fucking hard for you, Beck. Who knows? Maybe tonight, it happens.
I go all the way to your neighborhood and buy two cupcakes from
Magnolia Bakery. They smell fucking good and I want them but I am
a good boy, Beck, and I have ideas about what to do with all this icing.

BUT then . . . *then.* We're supposed to meet at nine and you call me
at 9:04 and you are breathless, on your way uptown. It's a long story,
you say, but Peach is alone at home, and she thinks someone broke
in because the furniture on the *terrace* has been moved around. You
sound like her in this state of panic. "Joe, listen to me." You persist.
"Whoever broke in shifted her *chaise.*"

I interrupt. "But they didn't steal the chair?"

"No," you say and you sigh. "But someone broke in, Joe. She's
scared."

"Of course," I say and you go on but it's not as dramatic as you're making it out to be. I didn't *break in* and I didn't move her *chaise*. I used a service key I found at the party. And I didn't steal anything. I'm more like Santa Claus because I brought an acrylic jacket for that Bellow, so the bitch should say *thank you.*

"Peach says sorry," you swear to me. "She feels horrible but she is just terrified of having a stalker again."

I won't even dignify the word *again* and I can only imagine the horror stories Peach has spun in years past.

"Don't worry about it," I say and I sound like I mean it and I tell you to be safe and you like me. I forgive you. I do. You're a loyal friend and *chaise* is not your word, it belongs to Peach. I eat both cupcakes and the icing is stale and it would taste so much better if I were licking it off your tits. You tweet a photo a little while later. There are mini cupcakes much smaller than my big Magnolia cupcakes on those bright plates and a giant bottle of bullshit candy cane vodka. You write:

#Girlsnightin

There's no way you could know about my cupcakes. But sometimes, I wonder.

18

YOU do make it up to me the next day. But it's not over six drinks and two cupcakes in a dark bar. Instead, we meet for *lunch* and you tell me all about Peach's depression, her loneliness. We're in sexless Sarabeth's drinking water (also nonsexual), and sampling artisanal jams (supremely nonsexual), and all you want to talk about is Peach (fully asexual). You feel responsible for her because she doesn't have any family around and we're only supposed to go to places like this *after* we have sex and I can't figure the logic in any of it.

"She's perpetually an orphan," you tell me.

"But, you don't have family around either, Beck," I try.

"I know," you say and you pick at a popover. "But I *left* home. It's natural. Her family left *her*. It's sick. They literally all moved to San Francisco the second we graduated."

I'm not surprised and you move on to bitching about *Blythe* and I listen and I nod and I listen and I nod and I eat a fucking popover and you go in the bathroom and e-mail Peach:

I just have to say, Joe is an insanely good listener. Don't lose faith in people!

Peach writes back a lot, suspiciously fast:

That's so sweet! Don't be hard on him, Beck. He sounds like he has potential. I was telling my yoga teacher about your Joseph and she compared him to Good Will Hunting. Is he any good at math? Anyway have fun at lunch! I hope you took him somewhere nice! You are a doll for checking in and please rest assured, my faith in humanity is completely restored. I love being single. We are too young to be tied down, for sure. Have fun with Joseph! I bet he's learning so much from you and that's awesome!

You come back to the table and ask me if I liked math when I was little. I tell you no and when I ask you why you are asking me about math, you shake it off and go back to bitching about Blythe. We get more coffee and I'd like this all so much more if it was happening after we sealed the deal. I can't kiss you good-bye in the middle of the day and what if this is your way of putting me in the friend zone? Is there a friend zone or is that a myth? Does the smart chick end up with Good Will Hunting? I can't remember.

When we part ways outside of Sarabeth's, we hug like cousins and you're not as close to me as you were the night we almost built the bed together.

"This was fun," you say.

"What are you up to later?"

"Girls' night."

"But you had cupcakes with the girls last night."

You caught me and you're cute. "Joe, have you been stalking my Twitter?"

"A little," I say and maybe I could kiss you. It is kind of cloudy, like fall in *Hannah*.

"Well, the thing is, last night was Peach night and tonight is Lynn and Chana night."

"Maybe tomorrow night?" I say and begging you is the opposite of kissing you. I should have let it go.

"I really have to write tomorrow night, but we could get together earlier. Lunch?"

I agree to *lunch* and you're gone and it's a long walk to the shop and I'd like to hate Tucker Max and *Maxim* magazine and Tom Cruise's character in *Magnolia* and think that women aren't as simple as they'd all have you believe. But right now, I almost have to steal a move from the Frank T.J. Mackey playbook *Seduce and Destroy* because I am screwing up. Not fucking you that night I built your bed, not, at the very least, trying to fuck you was clearly a mistake. I am screwing this up, and it's the greatest mistake of my adult life. I didn't even kiss you after I listened to you overanalyze your life for five hours. I suck, royally, and you might think I'm putting *you* in the friend zone.

And it's the worst kind of domino effect because we do have lunch the next day at some new place you say "is supposed to be as yummy as Sarabeth's." Again I don't kiss you afterward and what do you want the day after that? You want brunch. What's the only thing more sexless than lunch? Brunch, a meal invented by rich white chicks to rationalize day drinking and bingeing on French toast. And you don't even drink when we get brunch and pretty soon we're going to places where they don't even have waiters. You're into this fucking deli where you stand in line with nine-to-fivers who read Stephen King on their iPads while they wait for their turn to order their sexless green salads, fucking beans and dressings and scallions and onions (Red or white? Grilled or raw?), for fuck's sake people, it's a SALAD. Stop overthinking it.

You're not on the outs with Peach but you're not under her spell the way you were and I get it now that you like her because she's obsessed with you. Lynn and Chana love you, but they don't think your shit smells like roses. You like to be rocked and lullabied and sedated and our conversations about your short stories and your classmates always end with me telling you how special you are, how talented, how jealous they all are, how clearly better than them you are and you get taller as the clear disposable plastic salad bowl gets emptier and I mean it when I say it and you're lucky that what you want to hear is what I actually think:

"Beck, you're really talented. If you weren't they'd all just shrug."

"Sometimes the best writers get hated before they get loved. Look at Nabokov."

"I'm not competing with you, so I'm comfortable telling you I think you got it."

And you do. When I lie on my couch listening to you go on about Blythe, I feel like I'm living inside of you, through you. I know what it's like to be you and you're right. Blythe does hate you. But hate suits you, inspires you. You rage, "She's a little ball of anger and antidepressants who doesn't speak to her mother, her sister, her father, his wife, or her roommate or her fucking cat or any of the many guys she fucked last week." You break, you breathe. "I mean, Blythe calls herself a *performance artist*—a *prostitute* is what we call that in the real world. She has a webcam service that she calls *art*."

"In other words she's a ho."

"Thank you, Joe."

"You're welcome, Beck."

You go on. "And she hates me for being from Nantucket and liking poetry."

"So fuck her, then."

I try to help you move on, but you don't know why she hates you and it's all you want to talk about.

Every.

Fucking.

Night.

And it would be easier if these talks were happening on a park bench or your stoop or your sofa or your bed that I assembled but they're happening over the phone. And I can't smell you over the phone and I feel like a 1-900-Build-Me-Up hotline you call to feel good about yourself. You don't treat me like I'm your guy; you go to drinks with people from school and call me *after* the drinks and you don't act like there's anything weird about the fact that you didn't invite me to go along. I'm your phone bitch and I don't like it. You don't want to know about my day. You always ask me in the polite obligatory way.

"So how was the shop?"

"You know, shop's the shop. It was okay."

"Yeah?"

"Yeah."

And then I wait for you to want to know more about me and my day but I always cave and say, "So about you? How was school?"

But I can't do it anymore. It's time to save us and it's my job to keep us afloat.

"Hey, Beck."

"Yeah?"

"Let's go out?"

"Oh, I'm in my pajamas and I have class."

"No, no. Let me take you out next week."

There's a pause and you forgot how much you want to fuck me and you're trying to live by Peach Laws: no guys, just stories, but you do want me or you would have made an excuse by now.

"Well, when did you want to get together?"

"Friday night," I say. "No parties. I want to take you out."

I can hear you smiling somehow and you say yes and then you say yes again and it's okay for me to tell you that I read your story "Dust Bunnies" about the summer you worked as a maid. It's okay for me to tell you my favorite parts—of course I liked it when the daddy of the house tried to get with you in the laundry room.

"Oh, you know that's not me in the story."

"But you told me you worked as a maid one summer."

"True, but I didn't throw myself at the men in the house," you say and no wonder Blythe resents you. You are not a stalker and Benji will always be wrong, but you do covet, innocently, only because you're not comfortable in your skin, not yet, but I'm going to help you. You continue, "Joe, I can't say it enough, the level to which I would never have gotten myself into that situation. It's fiction."

"I know." I don't know.

"I'm not some townie whore. It's a made-up story."

"I know."

"I don't go after married rich guys."

"I know."

"So where are you gonna take me, Joe?"

167

YOU'RE happy I refused to tell you because it's not often in life that you get all dressed up and have some place to go without knowing what that place is exactly. You're in a long pale pink skirt with two giant slits and you're wearing high-heeled brown boots—new, for me—the slits are so high I can almost see your panties and you have on a loose brown sweater that will be so easy for me to peel off of you. Your body is an offering, a payment for all those hands-off phone calls, those lunches. Your bra is pink, hot pink, so that I don't forget about your tits under your sweater, not for one second. When I hug you I smell flowers and laundry detergent and pussy juice and I wonder how hard you had to go at your pillow and I'm proud of myself for not checking your e-mail for two solid hours so that I could give us all the suspense we need and you're about to tell me fuck this date, come upstairs and I pull away. It has been so long, Beck. And while you are always adorable, you've never gotten this dressed up for *me*. Tonight you care what I think. We aren't going to see your friends and nobody's taking your picture and posting it on Facebook. Your body and your hair and your lips and your thighs, everything, is for me. Ever since that night I built your bed, you have forced us into asexual, sunlit spaces. I finally have you in the dark and you're not hiding from me anymore and I'm gonna make this last as long as I can. I love this. I love you.

"Let's go," I say, and I take your hand and your hand is good in mine and we walk in silence and it turns out that there is something to all those fucking talks on the phone because there's glue here now, between you and me, and we're both surprised at how well we know each other and I squeeze your hand and you look at me and I hail a cab and one arrives because this is the way it's gonna be for us from now on.

"Where to?"

"Central Park," I say.

"Omigod, Joe. Really?"

"Where they keep the carriages."

You squeal and clap and I did well and I wasn't sure because part of me thought you don't get cheesier than a horse-drawn carriage but in the end, it's been almost two weeks since our IKEA night and I wanted our nocturnal reunion to be as hot as possible. The cab sails uptown and we're there faster than I thought possible and this time, I get out of the cab first. And this time, I run around to your side of the car and open the door for you. I offer my hand. You take it. The cabbie checks you out. I tip him. And before you know it, you and I are side by side in the horse-drawn carriage, nestled like lovebirds.

"This is bold, Joe," you say and you move closer to me, again.

"Those slits are bold," I say and you spread your legs the tiniest bit and you want my help and I'm sliding my hand over your thigh and you're turned on (the trot of the horse, the color of the leaves, me) and you whimper slightly and I get there. Lace panties, dewy with you and you whimper again and push just a bit toward my hand and I get under your panties and you're a pillow-soft warm pond just for me and you say my name and I hold my hand there, just taking you in and you kiss me on the neck.

"Thank you."

"No, no," I say because I can't make words right now. I'm too fucking happy to talk. The talking portion of the story of you and me is done and I use my other hand to move up and take your shoulder in my palm and we stay like that with eyes closed, taking each other in—your hand moving up my leg, painfully, beautifully slow—and you don't even know what comes next and this is the best two hundred bucks I ever spent in my life. Thank you, horse.

SO Benji was right. You do like your luxury. And I realize that I do too. We're tucked into the darkest corner of Bemelmans Bar at the Carlyle and I own you and I'm torturing you, being so close to all these empty rooms, all these soft beds, and I'm not taking you to bed, not just yet.

"Oh come on," you say. "We'll steal a key from the maid. I've never done anything like that."

"What is it you want to do in there, young lady?"

"You know what we're gonna do in there, Joe."

"Yeah?"

You nod and you're nibbling my ear and if I asked, you would get down under the table, here, now. But I don't ask because I want your mouth on my ear. Your hands are on the move, prowling over my belt, that's right, there's room under there, that's right, that's your hand, that's my shirt. Pull it out, yes. You're reaching and you're wanting and you've got me in your hand, home, and they need a new word for hand job because this

Is.

Magic.

You're a ball of want and I have to open my eyes and see something unsexy or I'm gonna blow it and the room feels bright in the dark. I've never felt so safe as I do in your hands. I kiss you and you kiss me and this was well worth the wait and your magnolia is gonna take me in, won't be long now, you're sopping wet, ready.

Nobody is watching us. Nobody is mad at us. Nothing is wrong with us. The waiter in the red jacket who brought us two tall glasses of ice and two cocktail napkins and two small glasses of cold vodka was respectful and good. The drawings on the walls are good, just like they were when I saw them online when I was figuring out where to take you on my golden chariot to train your brain into thinking of me as your passport to money and leather banquettes. I make less than every dude in here, including the waiter.

"Joe."

"Beck."

"I want you. Now." You sound all gooey and warm.

But a fucking waiter approaches, slow, mannered. "Excuse me, sir."

"Huh?"

You pull away and cross your legs and bite your lip. Are we getting busted for PDA? He bows, slightly. "Miss, are you Miss Beck?"

"I'm Beck," you say and the waiter is confused. "Yes, I'm Miss Beck. What's wrong?"

Everything.

"I'm so sorry to interrupt but you've received a rather urgent phone call from Miss Peach."

"Oh God." You cover your throat and it's over. You're not safe anymore.

He looks at me and I nod. He goes and you're tearing into your purse and all that we just did is melting faster than the leftover ice cubes.

"That's weird," I say and you're still rummaging. You carry too much shit around.

"I can't find my phone."

"How did she know you were here?"

You blush. "I may have tweeted."

Beck, Beck, this was supposed to be our night, alone. I did this for you. Those slits were for me and that bra was for me and your panties were for me. How is this going to work if you can't get through a few hours without looking for an audience? There's a pact you make when you slide into a booth and shove your hand down a man's pants, Beck. There's no tweeting when you're fucking and what am I gonna do with you? I want to scream and get more ice but I have to breathe and drink and say nothing.

"Joe, you're not mad, right?"

"No."

"I've never been here. When you were in the bathroom, I dunno," you say and you got your phone and you use it to tap me on the arm and I turn to you. "Joe, I'm so happy to be here. I've always wanted to go here and I was just excited."

"It's fine."

"I should call Peach."

"Okay, Miss Beck. You go call Peach."

Every guy in here watches you slip out and two dudes look at you like they have a shot with you and I would like nothing more than to kick some ass. We were supposed to walk out of this bar together. You're not meant to glide alone in your slutty pink skirt all wrinkled. You unnecessarily lay a hand on the doorman's arm asking what, I do not know and that skirt is a little too see-through, if you want to know the truth. It's gonna be hard to break you, this hungry public part of you that wants to be noticed and observed. You need an escort, Beck, especially if you want to dress like a fucking whore.

"The fuck you looking at?" I say to the primary offender, a shithead at the bar who's still staring at the door you walked out of like he's planning on which part of your little whore body he's gonna fuck first. He's about a hundred years old, not scared, but I'll put the fear in him if he doesn't get in line.

You call from the lobby, "Joe! We have to go. We have to go *now*."

The old guy laughs at me and you shiver, impatient. "I'll get a cab."

"I gotta pay."

"I grabbed the waiter on the way in," you say, all newly dismissive. "It's fine. That horse taxi thingy must have cost a fortune."

And just like that you turned all my good work at making you feel like a princess into shit. You paid and I'm not the man and Tucker Max is somewhere laughing at me with the geezer at the bar and the cartoons are laughing at me and the waiter who makes more than me is laughing at me and you open the door to the cab—you strip all the man out of me piece by piece and I'm your phone bitch and your skirt is a mess—and it can't get worse but it does.

"Where you headed?"

"Seventy-First and Central Park West."

"Peach okay?" I say, surprised that I'm capable of talking out loud.

"No," you say as you tie your hair back with an elastic in that big fucking sexless purse you brought as if you knew it was gonna wind up like this. "You'll never believe what happened."

19

EVERYTHING peaks. It's just the nature of all life.

As we cab over to Peach's, I feel more and more certain that I peaked in the carriage (not a "horse taxi thingy" as you said), and I know I will never be that great of a man ever again. I will never be in that precise place, having picked you up and literally swept you off your feet with your skin fresh and your skirt clean and the night still ahead of us. It's like Michael Cunningham says in *The Hours*: Happiness is believing that you're gonna be happy. It's hope.

Peach took my hope away. You're reading e-mails and sending texts and how do you hold on to me for the first time in our life together and shut it off? You're a million miles away from me, talking to people who have nothing to do with us.

"Hey, um, Beck," I try.

You don't look at me, you are blunt. "What?"

"Want to tell me what's going on?"

"A lot," you say and finally, you look at me. "Oh, you're mad."

"No," I say and it's not my fault that your friends are such assholes and it's not my fault that you couldn't stay off Twitter for one fucking night. These things are out of my control and I am better than you and you know it or you wouldn't be holding my hand and droning on about Peach and the fact that she thinks someone broke into her place and stole shit again, which is ridiculous because I only broke in once and I never stole a damn thing.

"Huh," I say.

You cross your arms. "Look, Joe. She's alone. She's scared. And she's my friend."

"I know," I say.

You snap, "Then don't go *huh*."

You don't have the guts to stand up to Lynn and Chana and I'll gladly be your whipping post tonight. "I'm sorry, Beck. I really am."

You nod. You are loyal.

"But let me just say this. That building is tight. It would be seriously hard to break in."

But you aren't moved and you huff. "Well, it doesn't matter if it happened. She feels like it happened."

I let you win; you're a girl. You're allowed. We ride in silence and I privately note that Lynn and Chana don't call you up on our date and claim that Bigfoot is trying to drown them in the fountain of youth. You're out of the door before the driver has the car in park and I pay, sad.

When I get out of the cab you throw your arms around me, hard and you whisper, "This was the best date ever."

"Define *ever*," I say and I know you want a kiss and so I kiss you. When we walk into the building, we are very much a couple and we get into the elevator and your phone buzzes and you answer and it's Peach.

She screams, "Where the hell are you?"

"I'm sorry, we're in the elevator!"

She groans. *"We?"*

The signal goes and you sigh. "This is gonna be a long night."

"Do you want me to leave?"

I can tell that you wish I was gone, but you link your arm through mine. "Please go easy on Peach. Look, I know she's a lot to handle. But, she's tried to commit suicide, a couple of times. She's weak. She's sad."

"I just don't like to hear you get yelled at."

You smile and squeeze my arm. "You're a protector."

"I am." I pick up your hand that was on my dick. I kiss it and promise you that you're safe.

You coo, "My knight in shining armor."

The elevator yawns and shimmies and the bell chimes and the doors slide open to an ugly sight. It's loud, Elton John is blasting and Peach looks electrocuted, with frizzy hair and sleepless eyes. She's armed with a fucking paring knife, of all things. "What took you so long?" She growls.

She storms through the living room, which is even more vacuous without Brown people. You squeeze my hand, *sorry*. I squeeze your hand, *it's okay*. We follow the angry Peach through her home and if I lived alone in a place this huge, I'd be crazy too.

IT'S been less than ten minutes and already I'm getting that unpaid delivery guy feeling. Peach speaks only to you and when I dare to interject, she waits for me to finish before droning, *as I was saying....* I don't take it personally and I honestly think she'd be just as pissed if you brought Lynn or Chana. But it's not fun, Beck.

I sit back in the sofa with my arms outstretched and you are beside me, but forward, on the edge of your seat. I can't tell you that Peach is poison. Listening to her lie and listening to you get hooked is too much but I can't say a word.

You grab your phone. "I think we should call the police."

She shakes you off and I can't take it anymore and I stand up. "I think I should check things out. You mind?"

Peach shrugs. "Knock yourself out, Joseph."

"Are there any suspects?" I ask and you wrap an arm around my leg. I pat your head.

Peach looks out the window, a classic liar's move. "There's a sad, incompetent delivery boy from this juice place. But I can't fathom him having the wherewithal to break into this building. I mean, no offense, Joseph, but I doubt this kid even graduated from high school."

"None taken."

She squirms. "That came out wrong."

"It's fine," I say and she's lucky I don't care what she thinks. I lean over and lift your chin and kiss you on the lips, wet, open mouth, full on. I pull away and salute Peach on my way out of the room.

I wander into the library-ish room to check on poor Mr. Bellow. No wonder you don't get enough writing done. Peach is an albatross, constantly dragging you down with her troubles, her invented dramas. Right now that Blythe girl in your class is hunkered down over a pot of fuckface tea with a red pen and a tenth draft of a story.

She's listening to Mozart and lost in her *work*. You prefer life. You like the melodrama of this penthouse. I pick up the Bellow (now in a case; you're welcome, Salingers), and I listen to you girls walk into the kitchen. Peach tells you to put a pizza in the oven and you object. "I thought you can't eat tomatoes with IC?"

"Honestly, when I'm flaring and stressed like I am right now, it makes no difference."

"Sweetie." You purr.

"I know," she says. "This is *so. Not. Fair.*"

That's it for me and I bid poor Mr. Bellow good-bye and head upstairs. My first stop is, of course, Peach's bedroom. Last time I was here, I thought it was bigger than the bookstore and upon reentering I realize that to my dismay, I'm right. You could have eight games of Twister going at once in here. And it's well designed, of course. The rich know how to make their walls work for them. French doors abound. Some open into the twenty-foot closet. And some open onto the terrace. I feel the most beautiful piece in here, a bleached mahogany dresser, antique, eighteen, maybe twenty feet long.

I want to relax so I lock the door behind me. I kick off my shoes and peel off my socks and the mink area rugs—*fucking mink*—feel like heaven. The bed is a beauty, an ornate four-poster California king that sits center stage. Ralph Lauren sheets—I check—and mountains of Virginia Woolf books in the built-in bookcase, hardbacks, paperbacks, new, old. She's run a million marathons. The ribbons are the proof, stuffed like bookmarks into the books at random. I run my hand over the bleached mahogany dresser and this is good stuff. What a shame. You can barely see the top because of the plastic forest of hair products. There's a giant TV, but that's a given in a joint like this.

I want to go out on the terrace but the door jams. I yank it, *come on you bitch, open up*, and it does. But I lose my balance and I'm grasping at plastic bottles of hair goo trying to break my fall. It doesn't work and I'm splat on the floor. I knocked over a bunch of bottles and a well-worn copy of *A Room of One's Own* and a bunch of photographs fall out onto the mink. I can't believe my luck as I flip through all sixteen beautiful, revealing photographs, all pictures of you. Peach is quite the photographer, as it turns out.

But the mark of a true great photographer is an independent eye. A great photographer can photograph a gutter and find the right angle and turn that gutter into a steel prism. These pictures are lovely, but these pictures are not art, Beck. No. These pictures are fucking porn and I have to sit down because this is a lot to take in, to know. Peach loves you. Peach wants you. My senses are riled; an enemy lives here and now I realize that these pictures are smeared, loved, and sticky. Some of them have fingerprints. She doesn't just love you, Beck; she's fucking deranged with obsession. I look closely and see streaky layers of lady juice and that's why they all have this filtered look. She touches herself and then you, herself and then you. It's been eons and no wonder the girl is so angry, so pent. The pictures offer the history of your body (thank you, Peach), and I see you at eighteen, maybe seventeen, in a loose tank top, no panties, asleep on your back, in a bed. Light pours in from the beach in the background and you are an angel, eyes shut, legs spread. I see you in a bikini dipping one toe into the water. Your ass is, ironically, a ripe, delicious peach. I see you on a beach at night, mounting some dude, naked. Peach has a good camera because I can see into your eyes and your nipples pop like buttons.

I have to get onto the California king. These photos, Beck.

These.

Fucking.

Photos.

There is a lump under the comforter and I lift the comforter and find a mess of Peach's soiled, dank workout clothes and bloody socks. I climb over the mess and toss another one of her *shawls*, great for hiding her invisible erections I now understand. I spread out these photos and thank Christ the bed is big. I want to fuck every single picture. The one of you in high school, with bangs and the one of you in college, with hips and the one of you mid-fuck, the black-and-white version of you riding some guy. That's not me in that picture but it will be me and I'll grab your neck the way you like, and you'll cry for me and moan, *Joe*. I spew a tankload of hot cum into the nearest fucking thing I can find: a musty sports bra.

Peach won't miss it and I have no choice but to shove it down my pants and tuck it into my boxers. I take pictures of the pictures before I tuck them away into their little Beck box and I smile.

When I calm down and clean up I head downstairs and find you both on the terrace. Everything looks different now and it's a problem. Peach is in love with you and you're mine and life is never going to be easy with her playing sick, playing victim, playing taken, playing anything to get your attention. And I'm different too now, afraid to look at you with the pictures so fresh in my mind. Peach is drunk and babbling about being *stalked*. I sit down on the arm of a chair the way a detective might sit and hold my chin in my hand.

"If I may, Peach. I notice that you've run a lot of marathons. Do you run every day?"

"Why?" she snipes. She wishes I were dead. It's not because I didn't go to college. It's because of the way you look at me.

"Well," I begin. "If you run every day, it's very easy for some creep to figure that out and stalk you."

You wave your hands and the shawl falls onto your lap. "Omigod omigod Joe! Peach runs every day before daybreak through the park."

"Not *every* day." Peach corrects you, but she lowers the volume on Elton, all the better to hear you sing her praise.

"Yes you do, Peach. You're amazing, fearless, I mean you run in the *woods*."

Peach shrugs but you can see her committing those words to memory: *amazing, fearless.*

"That's not safe," I say.

"Well, I live outside of the box, Joseph," says Peach. "That's just who I am."

You pick up the list of men you girls have been working on and I can't listen because of the slide show in my head of you and you and you and you.

"Peach," you say. "Can you think of anyone else? Some guy you dated?"

She shrugs. "Maybe that Jasper guy. We had lunch the other day and I could see that I dented his heart. Who knows? Maybe I broke it and didn't realize."

It's a fucking lie but I have to be strong. "This Jasper guy, did he lose his shit?"

If I said the sky were navy blue, Peach would correct me and call it midnight blue, so of course, she objects. "In *my* experience, men like Jasper handle rejection quite well, actually. Men like Jasper have such rich lives that they don't tend to be overly *emotional* about their personal lives."

"So, you have a lot of ex-boyfriends?" I say and I know I should step off.

"We're all still *friends*," she snaps. "We're not seventh graders, there's no *drama*."

"Good for you," I say and I want to choke her. "I'm not friends with any of my exes, too much passion. I can't just toss that passion aside and go out to lunch."

She doesn't have a comeback and I lean over to kiss you. "Be safe," I say.

"Oh Joe," you say and you don't need to be so dramatic. "Thank you for understanding. I do need to stay here."

Look at all the love in your heart. You are loyal, sweet, and you rise up to walk me to the door and thank me again for being so understanding. We kiss good night as Elton John sings louder, *sitting like a princess perched in her electric chair*. I tell you to go back to your friend. You do.

20

A 2008 study in Germany did pretty much prove that a "runner's high" is an actual medical condition. Unfortunately, for me, I must be only part human because I have been tracking Peach for eight days now and I have yet to experience the "runner's high" that she talks about incessantly. It's been almost two weeks with you staying at her house, just in case the bogeyman stalker returns. Ha. I've only seen you twice.

The first time, seven days ago: You invited me over because you'd gone back to your apartment to gather your things. You packed and asked me about my Thanksgiving plans. I told you I eat with Mr. Mooney and his family and you believed me. You said you are staying with Peach's family because Peach gets depressed when they're around.

We started to fool around and you stopped me and rubbed your hand on your forehead. I thought my life was over but you put your hand on me.

"This is my shit, Joe," you said. "I get weird around the holidays because of my dad. It's not the same since he died."

I told you I understood and I did and then we watched *Pitch Perfect* and you hit pause when Peach called and you took the call and apologized to me and sent me home.

I hid outside your window and lucky for me, you put the phone on speaker. The small talk ended and Peach sighed. "So my mom had lunch with Benji's mom."

"Uh-huh," you said.

"Well, don't you want to know what she said?"

"Benji is a brat," you said, in the calm way that means you don't like him anymore. "And obviously, he's kind of a druggie."

Peach went for an override: "Well, a lot of artists are weak that way, Beck."

You weren't having it and you told her, "By now, he's probably in China full of top-shelf heroin and drowning in Chinese pussy. I mean he's definitely on something. His tweets are lame."

No, Beck. My Benji tweets are not *lame*. They're disarming. They're dark.

And you just kept talking about him. "Honestly, Peach, the last thing I'm gonna do is worry about Benji," you declared. "Did he worry about me?"

"Down, girl."

"Sorry, I'm just packing and it's never easy, packing."

"I have nightgowns you can borrow. You can wear all my stuff."

Man, she wants you and you said you had to go and then you wrote to me to apologize for the abrupt ending and I wrote back to you and told you not to worry and then you went to town on one of your pillows and I listened. And I liked it.

Then again, three days ago: You and me and Peach met at *Serenfuckingdipity* because their chocolate is the only chocolate that she can eat and she *really* needed chocolate what with all the drama over the stalker. We sat at a table meant for children or people who have children and I watched Peach inhale an oversized bowl of frozen hot chocolate and I know from reading about interstitial cystitis that you can't do that if you have that condition (not disease, Peach, *condition*), and she talked more than both of us combined and when I tried to hold your hand under the table you patted my leg, *no*. Then afterward we kissed good-bye on the street and your lips were pursed so tight, they were puckered.

It has not been a happy Thanksgiving. The holiday comes like it always does. Peach's family comes home and you are busy with them and I am not your boyfriend right now and you do not invite me to eat turkey with her family. Curtis wants extra days off and I work all the time. The first time I run, it's because I might fucking kill Peach. I go for walks when everyone else is busy with their family and I find myself drawn to her building because you're there. I run because Peach comes smashing out the door and almost sees me. And if she saw me hanging out around her building, she'd go all nuts and start thinking that I'm a stalker. So yes, for a second there, I ran as fast as I could into the woods after her because I was going to grab her by the neck and make her stop running once and for all.

And I kept running the next day and the day after that because I was disgusted by the fact that I couldn't fucking keep up with her. It's cold in the morning and my thrift store high-tops don't cut it and I bought special running sneakers at a sporting goods store (shoot me, please), and now *my* feet are covered in blood just like Peach's and by the time I get to the shop every day, I am beat. Whoever said running in the morning *gives* you energy never had a day job that involves customer service.

By day ten, I miss your face so much that the pictures of the pictures don't do it anymore. We talk every day, but you are different now that you pretty much live at Peach's. I miss you and me at Bemelmans Bar and I go there one night alone and feel sorry for myself and get a nasty waiter who keeps asking me if I have a friend coming. It's a dark lonely time and I really can't go on like this, Beck.

On day eleven, I look like a real runner in my new sweats and kicks. I even have a freaking *sweatband* wrapped around my head. Peach gets a late start because you girls did some drinking last night, as I saw on your Twitter:

Vodka or Gin? Vodka and Gin is more like it. #girlsnightin

She's slow and off and definitely hungover. She bends over like she's gonna vomit and most people avoid high-impact exercise. It is cold and my legs are humming and I am sick of running through the woods every day. But one thing about running that I will agree to: It is fucking addictive. Less than two weeks into my life as a runner, and I don't need to set an alarm clock.

She always starts out slow before sunrise with Elton John singing *it's four o'clock in the morning damn it, listen to me good* and I know the song so well by now—*someone saved my life tonight, tonight*—and it's not the kind of music that makes you want to work up a sweat. The reason I can hear her Elton John is that she has no regard for shared public space. Dignified respectful citizens of the world use earbuds or headphones to privatize their music. But not Peach. She tucks her iPhone into a band that she wraps around her upper arm. She has a special speaker attached and the music *blasts*. When people sneer at her or object to this, which has happened (I fucking love New Yorkers), she doesn't apologize. She tells them to *deal with it*. And the music! The Elton John is slow and thus contrary and the exercise is a punishment to her body. She is joyless and ugly when she huffs and puffs and most girls run on well-lit paths, but Peach runs where she doesn't belong, alone, save Elton John (*you're a butterfly and butterflies are free to fly, fly away, high away, bye-bye*), and I follow her each day because you are not a butterfly as long as she exists. You are not *free to fly, fly away* because she is a dangerous fucking pervert, photographing you, coveting you. Is there anything sicker than photographing someone while she's *sleeping*?

I have to stop her and I have to save you and I run faster and I am gaining on her, I can smell her now, sweaty, and Elton is louder now (*someone saved my life tonight, toniiiiiight*), and I am your someone and I will save your life. This is it. I summon all my strength and I charge at her and slam her bony body into the ground. She screams but the sound cuts off as her head thuds against a rock. She's out, cold. Elton is *sleeping with myself tonight, saved in time, thank God my music's still alive.* If only Peach could have been more like him: honest, grateful, true.

The music is still going and I'm breathing so heavily and shaking and I want to make the music stop but fingerprints are dangerous. But now that her defenses are gone I understand her music. It's a security system. She was preparing for a moment like this. And while it's annoying, shoving your music on other people, there is something intelligent and bold about it too. It's a shame that Peach's parents are such motherfuckers because there was potential for her to be a good person, an innovator. I let her music play on as a tribute, the irony, of course, being that the music did *not* save her life. But hey, she tried.

Nobody will be that surprised to hear about a dead girl in Central Park. Women who run alone in the dark deprive themselves of their senses. It's a dangerous thing to do, running alone, and as the reality of her body in the woods sinks in, I quicken my pace. I have never run this fast, never known the depth of my lungs and I make it onto the street and disappear into the subway and now I might throw up and I heave and I smile.

Those Germans were right after all. There really *is* such a thing as a runner's high.

And it's a good thing that I'm a bit high on life because a little while later, I get a rather upsetting text from you:

Can't get together tonight. Am at NY Presbyterian. Peach ☹

She is supposed to be in a morgue, not a hospital. Because I have no idea what happened, because I am not a stalker I respond surprised and inquire about details. You tell me that she got attacked in the park. But there's good news too, according to you:

She's lucky. A girl found her right after it happened. Otherwise she might be, you know . . .

I write back:

But she's gonna be okay?

You write back:

Well, physically yes. But emotionally, this is hard. She'll be in the hospital for a while.

You'd never be talking to me if Peach got a glimpse of me, so at least I can be grateful for that. I offer to help and you insist that you don't need me but I will show you that I am a good boyfriend and I will look beyond the injustice of her getting a bed in a hospital. She only gets to stay because her dad is on the board of the hospital. And it's not fair to think of all the genuinely sick people turned away. But nothing is fair.

21

I'M not mad. Really. I'm not mad. You're a good friend. I know that Peach's parents have already gone back to San Francisco. And I know that you have to be there for her. I am not going to challenge you like Lynn and Chana who throw around words like *codependent* and refuse to visit Peach in the hospital. I'm not mad. I'm not! I prove that I'm not mad by sending flowers to her in the hospital. I even pay extra for a big yellow balloon with a smiley face.

Does a guy who's mad buy the balloon? No, he doesn't.

And I'm not being a dick to customers, either. You can tell I'm not mad because I'm more patient than ever. I don't lay into Curtis about being late and I don't bitch him out when he forgets to order more *Doctor Sleep* (the only book we're moving, aside from the *prequel*, of course) and watching that book settle in at the top of the *Times* bestseller list makes me more and more aware of the fact that we're not progressing. Our first real date was the day that book came out and now that book's breaking records and having its *third fucking month* on the bestseller list and I'm reading about the inevitable movie adaptation on the Internet for no reason at all—and I am not mad at you or at King or at the customers or Peach or anything. I am not mad she's a liar. I feel for the poor girl. She's obviously a product of her family's sociopathic tendencies and she's tragically obsessed with you and honestly, if anything, I'm just worried for you.

And I can wait. Some good shit happens fast (a bestselling book), and some good shit happens slow (love). I get it. You are busy. You got class—I get it—and you got Peach—I get it—and you're not avoiding me—I get it—and you have pages due—I get it—and Peach just can't deal with being around guys—I get it—and you can't e-mail as much with all that's going on—I get it—and you think of me when you get into your bed that I made for you—I get it. You see, Beck, I am not a narcissistic asshole who expects his needs to come first at all times. I wake up and run to the water and back and my legs are firmer all the time—you'll see, eventually—and I sell King and I read King and I eat lunch, alone, and dinner, alone, and not once do I bitch at you about blowing me off. Not once.

The balloon, Beck, it was almost ten more dollars with the tax and when I asked you if it got there, I could hear the Peach in you.

"Yeah," you said. "It did."

"Is something wrong?"

"Well, Joe, forget it. I mean for her everything is wrong right now, you know?"

"Beck, what the fuck?"

And I didn't say that in an asshole way. I just wanted you to be straight with me.

"Joe, never mind. It's fine."

"Obviously, it's not."

You let out a sigh and you're the one who's mad and you sound different, like you've been drinking the green juice delivered to Peach's each morning, like you're starting to like this way of life, sleeping uptown, waking up without a single piece of IKEA in the room.

"Don't get mad."

"I'm not mad, Beck."

"We both just felt like the balloon was a little insensitive."

"Insensitive."

"I mean . . . it's a smiley face."

"It's a get-well balloon."

"Yes, but, Joe, it's not that simple."

"On the website it's right there in the Get Well section."

"Yes, but it's not like she got hurt playing tennis."

Tennis.

"Beck, be reasonable."

"I am reasonable."

"I meant no harm."

"I know, Joe. It's just that a giant yellow smiley face is kind of the last thing in the world you want to see when there's some creep out there who broke into your home and attacked you. I mean, it's a smile. This is just, like . . ."

"Jesus," I said.

"It's not a smiling kind of time."

"I'm sorry."

"You don't have to be sorry."

"Beck, can we get coffee or something?"

"I really can't right now."

You never sounded farther away from me and I will take that balloon and stab the fuck out of it and at the same time I will take that balloon and tie it around Peach's neck because WHO THE FUCK CAN CUNT OUT OVER A BALLOON?

WELL, it's been *seven hours and six whole days* since Peach got home from the hospital. You are busy with school and busy with Peach, still living at her house. But you are not too busy to exchange e-mails with a stranger named CaptainNedAck@gmail.com.

You: *Hey, can you call me??*

Captain: *Not right now. Are you still coming this weekend?*

You: *I'm really busy. Can't you just call me?*

Captain: *I want to see you.*

You: *I don't have a car.*

Captain: *Get one and I'll take care of it. You're still size small, right?*

You: *Yes.*

When your plans with the Captain are finalized, you leave Peach's place and get into a cab. I call you. I get voice mail and I do not leave a message. I am not the Captain and you ignore Peach's call and she e-mails you, all caps:

WHERE ARE YOU?

You write back curt, swift:

Writing Emergency. Long story. I'm off to my "writing retreat"
(haha) at Silver Seahorse in Bridgeport. You be good to you
and lock the doors. Love love love Beck

And now Peach is mad at you, and honestly, I don't blame her. It is a bitch to drive to Bridgeport. You rent a car because, as we all know, the Captain is paying. I am stuck in Mr. Mooney's enormous, old Buick. I do a lot for you, Beck. You'd think I'd be the Captain by now and I don't listen to any music for the entire drive to Bridgeport. I'm too sad for music, too sad for Elton John and my head aches.

O Captain, my Captain

I cry.

I get to Bridgeport first. The Silver Seahorse is a small motel near the water, one of those joints where all the rooms are off exposed walkways. Peach wouldn't even set foot in a place like this but this must be the place because it's the only Silver Seahorse in Bridgeport. I listen to local news and eat a gas station burrito. I am so scared for you, for me, for us, that I can't finish the burrito. The Captain. Who is this Captain?

You pull into the lot and I slink down in the seat and watch you in the rearview mirror. You pop the trunk and walk around back but you don't get out the bags because the Captain moseys out of a motel room. He's at least forty-five, maybe fifty with Clooney gray hair—is this what you're into?—and he flicks his cigarette out—fuck you, Captain, I hope you die of cancer—and he picks you up and spins you around and you know what, Beck?

Now I am mad.

Captain AARP Asshole gets into your car. I follow the two of you as he drives, the fucker (and you've never been in a car with me), and you two pull up to an ATM at a Cumberland Farms. You jump out of the car and come back with a wad of twenties. He makes you count the money (I hope he dies *now*), and you are angry and you count slowly, like a third grader practicing and I am reminded of your Craigslist "Casual Encounters" and I fear the worst. I follow you and the Captain back to the Silver Seahorse, and this is me, Beck. The Captain gets out first and opens the door for you and you walk around back and get your bags out of the trunk, and he already has a key and I am close enough to hear.

"Hey, can I have a smoke?"

He shakes his head. "Honey, I can't do that."

"So it's fine for you but not me?"

"Did you bring a costume?"

Costume? Jesus.

"Do you think I brought a costume?" You groan. "Just one smoke, please."

"Hell if I'm gonna give one to ya."

"Are you kidding me right now? This is when you decide to be a fucking father?"

You said *father* and I might collapse as my brain waves sizzle and my heart stops. *Father.* You told me he was dead. You told everyone he was dead. Oh, Beck, why? I don't know if I'm mad or sad because in the present moment I'm just so relieved that you're not paying (or being paid?) to put on a schoolgirl outfit and get banged in a motel room. I breathe. The Captain is your *father* and your father has the key and you groan and follow him into Room 213. I want to know him and I want to follow you in there and I want him to shake my hand and tell me how happy he is to see that his daughter has got such a good man in her life. But you told me he is *dead* so maybe you'd be happier if I went in there and made that happen? I am confused and it is colder by the second.

It's off-season in the shithole that is Bridgeport and the activity of checking into the room helps me steady myself. It's a lot to take in, but I'm relieved. I spout off some bullshit about lucky numbers and request the room adjacent to yours. They give it to me and it smells like bleach and Newports and the walls are thin and after I shower I throw one of the extra towels on the floor and sit down and listen to you fight with your dad (something about money, kids, you sound like adults in *Peanuts* cartoons). He slams the door and you're alone. After you finish crying you shower and now you're wet and clean, like I am, and I hear the door lock. You tear the blanket off the bed—it hits the floor, it's heavy, I hear it—and you start to work away at yourself and you moan—you're loud, I hear it—and now I'm working and you're working and in my mind, there is no wall because I'm fucking you on that bed and you're bent over begging for it and we're in Bridgeport because we want to fuck in a motel and I'm pulling your hair and you're screaming—you are, Beck, you're loud and there's no green pillow for you to cry into—and when it's all done you turn on the TV and light a cigarette. I can hear it and I can smell it and I'm so heavy from doing it with you and not doing it with you that it takes a minute before it hits me.

You know the smiley-face balloon was fine and your father isn't a dead junkie.

You're a fucking liar.

22

MY, you have a way of making me do things I don't normally do. I haven't dressed up for Halloween since the third grade (Spiderman), and though it's gotten harder over the years, I've managed to silently protest that whore of a holiday for the bulk of my life. Yet here I am in a mothball-scented dressing room at Bridgeport Costumes. The dressing room is so small that a fucking Smurf would be sweating. Celine Dion is singing about her fucking heart through the worst sound system in existence while the well-intentioned Irish shopkeeper prattles on a few feet from the dressing room.

"Have you got those pantaloons on yet, son?"

"No," I say and I look in the mirror and I want to die. But I can't die, because you need me. Your father is dragging you to the Charles Fucking Dickens Festival across the sound in Port Jefferson. You don't want to go, but he rented you a costume and after the two of you finished arguing this morning, you agreed to go spend time with his family.

While you and your dad were getting ready for the festival, I hunkered down in my motel room and read up on this fucking *festival*. When you stepped out for a cigarette, I looked out at you and I knew I had no choice. You were a vision in your costume, drowning in red velour as your hair poured out from under a little red bonnet. You were smoking and pouting in the parking lot of the Silver Seahorse Motel. You are the only girl in the world who could look so serious and so silly at the same. Your dad stepped outside to join you, in a top hat and tails. He gave you a white furry muff.

"What am I supposed to do with this?" you asked.

"Put your hands in, keep warm."

"But, I have gloves."

"Beck, can you just give me a break here?"

You sighed and put your hands in that lucky muff and I want to put my hands in you. I'm taking too long to get dressed and the Irish shopkeeper taps her knuckles on the door. She wants a sneak peek, of course. "It's so nice to see young people like you getting into the spirit," she calls. "If you don't mind my saying so, I think those pantaloons are going to suit you quite well, you know."

"Yep, in a second."

"And I'm not sure if I mentioned," she says for the third time. "Rentals must be returned within one week of rental date. Otherwise you might have an old Irish slag knocking at your door in the wee hours. Are you ready?"

"In a second," I say and maybe Irish women don't speak English. Celine Dion is still screaming about her goddamned heart and I'm choking on mothballs and self-loathing and if you would have told your dad about me, he could have rented costumes for both of us. Then you'd be in here with me and I wouldn't even notice the mothballs or the schmaltzy Canadian crap. But, you lied to me. And now I have to walk out of the dressing room and tell the Irish lady that I'm attending the festival on my own.

"Handsome chap like you won't go very long without finding a nice lass, I'm sure." She chortles. And there's a mirror behind her and fuck. This costume certainly does look good on me—my top hat is taller than your father's top hat—but this costume is not a disguise.

"Do you have any beards?"

She objects jokingly, "Are you quite serious, young man?"

"It's cold out there."

"We have beards but they're not at all Dickensian."

"I don't care," I say and she grips my twenties and fumes. Small towns are scarier to me than cities. This woman, who seems all kindly and obsequious a minute ago, is melting down because I want a beard.

"I'm in kind of a rush," I say, the slightest bit of an Irish affect.

She lowers the volume on the ancient tape player. Celine Dion on *cassette* isn't very Dickensian either, but she concedes and points me toward the non-Dickensian, nonrefundable beards, which are in a box in the back marked JOHNNY DEPP/DUCK DYNASTY.

Fucking America, Beck. I just don't know sometimes.

LIFE is aggravating when you're alone in a costume on a party boat with people who are all together, in costumes, on a party boat. We're not even close to docking at *Port Jeff* yet and I shouldn't have boarded the ferry. I didn't think it through. What if you recognize me? You're not gonna want to introduce me to your father while I'm in pantafuckingloons.

I should have gone back to New York but there's no turning this festive boat around so I'm trying to focus on the good: You haven't tweeted once since you've been here or sent one e-mail. But bad thoughts creep in. Your father is back in the picture. What if this means that you tell your mother to shut off your phone? Calm down, Joe. I know your passwords and I will always find a way into you, but I like having your phone. I like thinking of your mother paying for me to protect you. It's hard to be rational in a costume and I try again to think good thoughts. You are capable of going offline and you're lying to everyone, not just me. And in a way, I'm having an easier go of it than you. You and your old man sit on bucket seats in the main cabin. You look gorgeous, of course, the Rose on our Titanic vessel to my crafty, upbeat Jack, and if we were in this together, oh Beck, I'd find my way under that skirt of yours.

But neither you nor your father appears very excited for the Festival and I gather that he drives this boat. Deckhands give him shit for being in costume and the Captain of this particular trip steps out of the wheelhouse and insists on getting a picture of you and your old man. You don't want a picture but your old man insists and I'm tempted to storm across the deck and start a mutiny. But I have to let you and your dad work this out on your own. I know when you need your space. That's why I got the beard.

Your dad asks you if you want a drink and you shrug.

"You want to make this as hard as can be?"

"I just said, I don't know." You sulk and you turn into a teenage girl around your father, which makes a lot of sense.

"Well, Guinevere, do you or do you not want something to drink?"

"Coffee," you snap. "Fine."

He called you *Guinevere* and a group of semidrunk Chuck Dickens fans are starting to sing Christmas carols and some fat guy in a Ben Franklin getup (oh, America) is trying to pass by and loses half of his beer on me. And the air is thick with mothballs and salt water and Coors and I do not like it here one bit. Because you ran away to see your dad who is alive (alive!), and because I want to be there in case you need me, I am gonna have to *sell* a fucking Dickens on eBay to cover the expenses of the motel, the costume, and the psychotherapy I'll no doubt need when I realize I am permanently fucked up from that day I froze my ass off in pantaloons and stood on a deck with a bunch of quarter-wits. The half-wits are at home watching *Great Expectations*, the movie.

THE only thing worse than the boat trip to the festival is the festival itself. The Public Rape of Charles Dickens is an atrocity, Beck. Who knew such crap existed? You knew. You stay away from your half brother and your half sister, both of them kids, little ones, six and eight I'd guess, in costume, everyone in costume, and Charles Dickens would be disgusted that his entire life's work is celebrated by rich old retirees who have nothing better to do than blow money on rented knickers and petticoats and wigs and cross Long Island Sound only to gather with other like-minded nitwits and stroll about the village of *Port Jeff*, where they compliment one another on their fucking costumes and gorge on candied apples and act like it's fun to tour old homes and listen to eighteenth-century guitar and gorge again on caramel popcorn and get their faces painted (as if painted faces have anything to do with Dickens) and listen to chamber music. Honestly, Beck, of all these white motherfuckers on this boat right now (seriously, no black person would ever do this), how many do you think could pass a test on *Oliver Twist*? How many do you think read his lesser-known works?

But there was no way for me to not follow you into this town. And it's a good thing I'm always here, the Kevin Costner to your Whitney Houston, because people get weird in costumes, even old white dullards from Connecticut. They're slightly soused on beers (day drinking is allowed when you're celebrating Dickens), and more than a couple of dudes have gotten a little too cheerful with you and I've got a list in my head of everyone who needs a beatdown. I'd never hit a woman, but your stepmother doesn't like you and she's jealous of the attention you get and her kids aren't all *that* and our kids will be cuter and how does my anger with you always soften into love?

"Guinevere," your stepmother says. Your dad calls her *Ronnie* and she's fighting forty with Botox and bronzing powder and Spanx. You'll embrace your age and you'll be beautiful unlike Ronnie, who barks, "Did you give me change from that vendor with the candy apples?"

"You gave me a twenty."

Your father looks like he's gonna explode and he turns his attention to the shitty little kids, as if they need him right now, which they don't.

You pout. "The candy apples were like five fucking dollars a pop."

Now your dad gives a fuck and he chastises you. "Guinevere, honey, come on."

"Fine," you say, so brittle you might break. You pull both your hands out of your muff and the muff hits the pavement and you start fishing around in that giant Prada bag and your stepmother picks up one of her unimpressive children and lodges the kid on her hip.

"Prada," she says. "Did you get that on eBay?"

"It was a gift," you say, and sometimes you do tell the truth. You hand her two dollars and she takes it and you look up at your dad.

"Can we go?"

THE Dramamine I bought in the gift shop isn't working and the ride back is worse than the ride out. I've spent the bulk of it in this tin can of a bathroom and the colonial Connecticunts are all banging down the door because they're all sick from too much food and fun. And this beard itches and this boat rocks and this toilet won't flush. I jiggle the handle. Some asshole fists the door.

"Some of us got colons too, buddy!"

I don't dignify him with a response but the goddamned boat breaches—is the Captain drunk too?—and I get slammed against the wall and when I throw up I try to move my nonrefundable beard and it drops into the mess in the toilet.

Plop.

There's no way out of this one and the faucet gives barely more than a trickle. If I don't get out of here soon, I'm only going to draw more attention to myself. There is nothing for me to do but bow my head and pray like hell that you aren't part of the lynch mob forming outside of the door to the latrine. If there is a God, you are holding it until you are back in the safe confines of the Silver Seahorse.

And there is a God. There are only four people waiting and it sounded like a dozen and I make a run for the stern. The wind bites back there and hopefully I will be alone and hopefully I can ride out the rest of this trip without ruining your day. I think you would be scared if you saw me and I think it would sound like bullshit if I told you that I went to meet family and there are tears streaked across my cheeks and I can't tell if I'm crying or if it's the wind. I miss my warm, scratchy beard and the pantaloons are made of paper and my legs are fucking freezing.

Finally, the boat slows as we ease into the harbor and then something unimaginably horrible happens to me, something so bad that I might jump off the boat. If it was summer, I would already be in the water because your little half brother and half sister are playing hide-and-seek (great game to let your kids play on a boat, *Ronnie*), and I hear Ronnie calling for the little tykes, who are hiding behind a box right in front of me.

Breathe, Joe. Breathe.

I hear Ronnie running and she gets here fast and grabs each kid by the hand and looks at me. "What a day, right?"

She's flirting with me because she's jealous of you and I'm on team Beck and I know how to get back at her. "Yes, ma'am."

She didn't like that and my *ma'am* had a two-fold purpose. It was supposed to make her feel old (done), and it was also supposed to make her go away. But then two deckhands come out of nowhere and the boat is turning ever so slightly and the deckhands are unraveling rope and the tired, drunk Connecticuts are coming this way because it's just my fucking luck that this boat docks and offloads from the stern.

And if there is a God, then you are fighting with your father and you are lost in conversation. If there is a God, I will be the first one off this boat. If there is a God, this slow-moving steel beast will get there already so your stepmother can take her kids home and feed them the mac and cheese they're screaming about. And if there is a God, then we are docking right now, we are, and there is a kid on land hoisting a ramp, there is. We are getting there and I will be third, maybe fourth off this boat and people are starting to get pushy.

And if there is a God, that is not you I hear behind me. And if there is a God, Ronnie will not ask me (me!) to move out of the way.

"My *husband* is trying to get through," she says and she knows how to exact her revenge as well. Your father squeezes by me and apologizes for the close quarters. He turns his head and whistles for you, just as the boat finally settles and the deckhand releases the ramp that connects the boat to the land.

"Coming!" you say. "Jesus Christ, people this isn't Ellis Fucking Island."

And I love your sense of humor and disgust and I love you and that's why, like a flower to the sun, I turn my head a millimeter, just enough to see your beautiful face and long enough for you to see mine, before the deckhand slaps the ramp down and locks it into place and I shove my way through that crowd and get off that fucking boat.

23

EVERY time I approach an exit, I want to pull off and find a gas station and change out of this musty costume. But I don't. I am paralyzed behind the wheel. I am so panicked that I can only go forward. And the reason is horrifyingly simple: You have called me four times in the last hour since the ferry docked and this can only mean one thing: You saw me.

"No!" I shout and I feel like I've been driving forever and I punch the steering wheel and the Buick veers into the right lane and I cut off a truck and the trucker blows his horn and I open my window and I roar, "Go fuck your mother!"

If he responds, I don't hear it and I roll the window up by hand (Mr. Mooney is a cheap old bastard), and I gotta slow down because it would suck to get pulled over right now. And it's not like this is my fault, you know. You lied to me. Your father is not dead. I was on that boat because you lied to me.

Maybe I don't know you as well as I think I do. But that's ridiculous;

we have a connection. It's just that you messed up. You were supposed to tell me all about your dad, no matter how ashamed you were. And I was supposed to listen and love you and tell you that you were good. And then you would ask me about my life and I would tell you and you would listen to me the way I listened to you and then we would have been closer.

I ride up on a girl going too slow and she flips me off hard. She has a bumper sticker TAILGATERS FLUNKED PHYSICS, and a Boston College sticker and I hate driving and I would like to ram this car into her Volvo and watch her bleed out but no, Joe, no. She's not the bad guy and she won't pay for your mistakes.

This is on you, Beck. You messed up big time and you know I followed you and you know. *You know.* I lay on my horn and tailgate that bitch until she puts on her blinker. When I pass her I slow down so I ride right next to her with one hand on the wheel and one hand giving her the bird. The bitch laughs and I move on. Fuck her. Fuck you.

You will never forgive me and I need to never see you again and I need this family in the Land Rover to fuck off with their skis and their brand-new tires and I ride up on them too, hard, and my phone rings.

You.

The kid in the backseat disobeys his father and turns around and you know what I know about that kid? That kid will wind up at Choate Rosemary Hall (alumni sticker in the rear window), and that kid will be smoking dope and popping pills before his thirteenth birthday and everyone will think it's so fucking glamorous because he's popping pills in the woods off in Connecticut. I give him the finger. I give him a memory. I know what that kid will become and I know he won't pay for his bad choices. He'll get sympathy and respect and I veer around them and jump in front and slam on my brakes and the father beeps, pissed now, alive now, and I rev up and I'm out of there, fuck them and their skis and their snow boots. The heat in this car is broken and I'll never get over the cold from the ferry. I'll never be able to look at Dickens without going back to this day and I pull over to a rest stop and I shut off the engine. It's so fucking quiet. It's so December and it's so over.

My phone rings, again. Loud. *You.*

I ignore (again), and I delete the message because I can't bear the idea of you screaming in fear at me and accusing me of being a stalker. No. This is all wrong and I punch the wheel again and my knuckles are bruised and the bruises will heal but you will never forget the time that guy followed you to Connecticut and put on a costume (a costume!) and stalked you at a festival.

I am probably already an anecdote in the hopper in your head, fodder for a story, a thing of the past, just another suitor. I cry. You call. I shut off my phone. I shut off your phone before your mommy shuts it off, which she probably will, eventually. It is a dark day. Literally.

I drop off Mr. Mooney's keys and he's got his oxygen tank and his bowie knife and someday I'll have a oxygen tank and a bowie knife because you're never speaking to me again and I know it. He means so well and he's such a stand-up guy, a veteran in overalls and here I am and I can't look him in the eye right now because it's so hard to admit that as much as I admire him, respect him, well, I don't want to be like him. I'm a terrible person and he's a good man and he's holding the door open and old people are painfully lonely when they're alone. It breaks my heart how obviously, badly he wants me to come in and have a Pabst with him. A good guy would go in, but we all know I'm a fucking tool.

He tries to joke around. "What's with that outfit, Joseph?"

I forgot about my costume and I think. "I went to a costume party."

He doesn't want to know about the party. "Shop's good?"

"Yeah, real good, Mr. Mooney, real good."

I offer him the keys but he shakes me off. He's still holding the door open. He's not the kind of man who would ever verbalize the fact that he wants company. But he gets it, the way I tuck the keys into my pocket and step back. He retreats into his dank molding home.

"You hang on to those keys," he tells me. "I never use the car anyway."

"You sure, Mr. Mooney?"

"Where am I going?"

"Well, I can take you there if you need."

He waves me off and he won't need to go anywhere. There's a dude from church who takes him to the doctor. And at this point in his life, there is nowhere else to go. I should go inside. But I just can't right now.

He turns around. "I'll bump into ya, kid."

"Thanks, Mr. Mooney."

The door shuts, quietly, and I walk, aimlessly, but somehow I reach my place. One of my typewriters is laughing at me, I swear, because of my costume. I pick it up and I throw it at the wall. Fuck it. It's not like the landlord's ever fixing anything anyway. I strip out of my costume and I want to burn it but I put it in a shoebox and tape it up. I don't want to look at it anymore and I write the address and when I have to put *Bridgeport*, I lose my grip on the pen. I throw on my worst comfort clothes: a raggedy Nirvana T-shirt that my mother left behind and nasty fleece pants from a rummage sale on Houston a hundred years ago. I want to look as miserable as I feel and I tear into the Twizzlers I bought at the Korean deli by Mr. Mooney's place. The new hole in my wall says it all.

There are two Twizzlers left and I've lost time like I sometimes do in here, and I am listening to Eric Carmen's "Make Me Lose Control" on repeat, self-destructing, cutting myself with sappy lyrics about a time in history that I'm too old to remember, about summer love and convertibles with huge backseats. There is a knock at the door and there is never a knock at the door or a hole in the wall and there is another knock. I stop the music. There is another knock.

24

WHEN I open the door, I die. You are here, in my building, in powder-blue corduroys and a little furry jacket. You want to come inside and this is dangerous. All the pieces of you that I've collected are here with me and you are not meant to see them. You still smell like you, like heaven, and you look like you've been crying. You move toward me and I clench the doorknob. "Beck."

You sigh. "I get it, okay? You don't hear from me for a while and then I call you fifty times and show up at your doorstep like some fucking crazy stalker."

And now I know. It's safe to let go of the doorknob. You didn't see me on the ferry. You are soft in your eyes and safe. You want to come in.

I play with you. "You're not some crazy stalker."

"Well, a little crazy," you say. "I had to force the kid at your shop to give me your address."

You are too small to force anyone to do anything and I will kill him and you are frazzled and there's nothing for me to do but get out of the way and let you in. You hesitate once you're inside, as if you've walked into the worst of the bathroom stalls at a movie theater and I wish I had cleaned. There is an open can of sardines in the sink that wouldn't be there if I'd known you were coming. But if I draw attention to the fucking fish, well, that's not good, either.

"I like your shirt," you say. "Nirvana."

"Thanks," I blurt. "It was my mom's."

You nod because what the fuck are you supposed to say to that? "D-do you want me to open a window?" I stammer.

"No," you say. "I'll get used to it."

Fucking Curtis and I scan the living room for bras or panties or e-mails. Nothing. Miracle. You are slipping out of your furry jacket and unzipping your boots and settling onto my sofa like you own the place. One good thing: You are so all about you that you don't seem to notice my apartment. You are blowing your nose and squirming and I sit in my chair that I found in the alley by the bookshop a few weeks ago. When I dragged that chair home on the subway, I assumed nobody would ever see it again, that it was like the chair's last day of being seen.

"So, I know it's been a while," you say. "But I needed someone and I thought of you and . . . you didn't answer my calls."

"I'm sorry," I say and I should have given you a chance. If I were a brave man, this conversation would be happening in your apartment.

You hug your knees and rock. "Anyway, I just don't even know right now. I'm a mess."

"Are you okay?"

You shake your head no.

"Did someone hurt you?"

Your eyes well up and you look at me like you've been protecting someone for so long, like you've always said no when the answer is yes and you squeak out an answer. "Yes."

And you're bawling. I go to you and let you cry and you don't say anything for a while. I scoop you into my arms and let you cry. Your tears soak my T-shirt and I feel like some stalker who will never wash his clothes again and your whole body is shaking from unhappiness and I will make you rattle with joy soon, soon. You pat me on the back. "Okay. I'm okay."

I understand that you need your space and I return to my chair and you let out a big sigh. "Have you ever carried a secret around? I mean, a secret as in a lie. And one day you just fucking can't do it anymore. And you have to let it out?"

I see Candace's musical fucking brother on TV sometimes and I want to smash the screen and tell him that his sister did not *drown* while *body surfing*. I nod. "Yeah, I get it."

Your eyes skate around and they finally land on me. "Well, it's a long story but, Joe, here's the thing. I lied to you and to everyone. My dad is not dead. He's very alive and very well and living on Long Island."

"Whoa," I say. You chose *me*.

"I couldn't hold it in anymore," you say. "I had to tell someone, or else."

"I get it," I say. And I do. And I think that you didn't choose *someone*, you chose *me*. And that means something, Beck. You hunted me down, *me*.

"And you know how girls are," you say. "If I told Peach or Chana or

Lynn or anyone like that, then they'd tell someone and that person would tell someone and someone would send out some cryptic tweet about it and *ugh*. That's why I thought of you. I knew you'd let it stay here."

"I get it," I say. And I do. I keep many secrets and now I have yours.

"And honestly, you know, in a way I'm *not* lying because in every way he *is dead* to me, Joe," you rail on. "But the thing is, he married a *lawyer* and she's rich and he has money and I'm broke. And of course he won't just *give* me money, no. I have to troll around in a fucking Charles Dickens dress with his spoiled offspring in order to get anything out of him."

"That was a lot of information," I say. *"Charles Dickens?"*

You laugh and tell me about the festival. I have to be careful here and I act like I've never heard of such a thing and I let you share the details and I'm methodical in my reactions and then I shake my head. "This is a lot," I say. "Is it worth it? Putting up with all that for a few bucks?"

"Well, life costs money," you say and you cross your arms. "If he can pay for his *new* kids to eat organic candy apples then he should have to pay for his *old* kid too."

"I get it," I say. And I do. Your dad and his wife probably blew four hundred bucks on Dickens costumes, hot cocoa, and candy apples. And you're not the kind of girl to wait tables. Your friends don't worry about money; why should you?

You finish sending a text and relax your arms and lower your legs and when animals open up like that, they want to fuck. You're my animal on my sofa and you look around my home. "Wow," you say. "You really do like old things."

"I found every single thing in here on the street," I say, proud.

"I see that," you say, disgusted. You prefer new, sterile IKEA, yet you tuck your dirty tissues into your mangy purse. Ah, women. You wiggle your toes and start in about your dad again: "Divorce is different when you're from a poor-ish family, you know? My dad met Ronnie on the island when she was on *vacation*. Literally, Joe, he met her at a bar where my *sister* was working. And it was hard enough to start college as the girl who grew up where everyone else goes to *vacation*. I didn't want to tell people that my townie dad ran off with a *tourist*. Enough already, you know?"

"It's not fair," I say.

"It's not," you say and I've never seen you so worked up. "Being an Ivy League townie is one thing, but a townie with an absentee *father*? Fuck that. It's a cliché."

"I get it," I say. And I do. I love you for being the prideful, scrappy little fighter that you are. You're powerful; you kill people. You're brutal.

"I figured when I moved here I'd start all over but I didn't think it through." You sigh and shake your head. "Everyone from school is here and if I told my friends about my dad now, I'd have to deal with it, you know?"

"I know," I say. "People can be judgmental about stuff like this. You have to watch out."

"Nobody knows," you say and your eyes are big, mine. "Nobody."

"Except me," I say and you blush.

"Except you," you repeat and you smile, almost, and then you sadden. "And I know I shouldn't be so insecure, but he didn't just leave, you know? He built a whole new family with a younger, cuter wife and younger, cuter kids."

"Those kids are not cuter than you, Beck."

You're not in a suspicious mind-set, thank God, and you laugh, assuming that I'm making an assumption. "*All* kids are cuter than adults, Joe." You sigh. "That's just the evil nature of Mother Nature."

"Well, fuck her," I say and I get a laugh out of you. "You did your part. You saw him and his family. Did he help you out with some dough?"

You stretch your arms up toward the ceiling and stretch to the right and notice the hole in the wall right behind you. "Jesus," you say. "That's a big fucking hole."

I swallow. "A pipe burst upstairs and they had to get in there."

"And apparently they did," you say and now you're tuning into your environment. You notice Larry, my broken typewriter on the coffee table. You look at me for permission to touch him. I nod. You tell lies. I hoard typewriters. We are *different, hot.*

"His name is Larry," I say. I'm gonna be honest like you.

"Do you name all your typewriters?" you ask.

"No," I say. "I don't name them. They tell me their names when I bring them home."

It is fun to fuck with you and you can't decide if I'm pretentious or insane and I can't tell if you're being sweet or patronizing when you laugh. "Right."

"Beck," I say. "Of course I name them. I'm just kidding."

"Well, Larry is handsome," you say and you lean forward to say hello to him and tinker with his keys. I can see your panties. You ask me a question: "Can I hold him?"

"He's heavy, Beck."

"You can put him on my lap," you say and you're wearing pink seamless bikinis, size small, from the Victoria's Secret Angels collection. I pick up Larry and set him on your lap and pray that you don't notice that your panties are identical to the panties shoved in between the cushions of the sofa. I tell you that Larry is broken because he fell (hahaha), and you pet him, sweet.

"Well, Larry may be broken, but he's a handsome beast, Joe."

"He's a one of a kind," I say.

You study Larry. "He's missing an L."

I have to lie because I can't have you looking around for the L. "Since the day I brought him home."

You look at me. "Do you have anything to drink?"

I don't have anything to drink. *Fucking Curtis.* You return your attention to the typewriter and you want to look between the cushions and make sure the L isn't lost but if you do that, you will find your panties, which you will know are yours if you have a keen sense of smell, which I think you do. You're like a toddler that needs distraction and I take a Twizzler and you grab the last one.

"Do you have any more of these?" you say.

"Afraid not," I say and now I'm worried because you stop chewing and your eyes lock on something in my bedroom.

You squint. "Is that the Italian Dan Brown I gave you?"

I want to close my bedroom door but that would be weird so I turn around and follow your gaze and realize you are looking at the special shelf I built for the Italian Dan Brown. It could be worse; I could have put the *Book of Beck* on that shelf.

"I think that's your book," I lie.

You pet Larry and you grin. "That's sweet, Joe."

I swallow the rest of my Twizzler and I have to get you out of here. "You wanna go get some more Twizzlers?"

"Hell yes," you say and I walk over to you and you look even smaller with Larry on your lap and you pat him. "Lift, please."

I lift him off your lap and your powder-blue cords have new dark scuff marks and I put him in his normal spot on the floor and you step back into your boots and slip into your little furry jacket and walk across the room away from the evidence of my affection, your panties and your bras. What a relief to open the door and lead you out of my home, and it's a whole new world with you in it. You pause in the stairwell and point to a smudge on the wall. "Blood?" you whisper, alive and jocular, my furry nymph, and I nod in affirmation and you raise your eyebrows. "*Larry*'s blood?"

I smack your ass and you like it and you hop down my stairs and I'm the only one who knows about your dad and soon it will be time for the red ladle. You push open the door that I've been pushing open for almost fifteen years. We walk to the bodega and you're practically skipping.

"Is this the part they're trying to make into a historical district?" you ask. "I read about that somewhere."

"No," I say. "This is the other part of Bed-Stuy."

My section reminds you of "Sesame Street and Jennifer Lopez songs" and every guy in the shop wants to bang you but you're with me. You like the attention; you tell me you feel like a celebrity in here and you giggle. I pay for the Twizzlers and the Evian and you shove the Twizzlers in your back pocket, as if you need to draw more attention to your ass. So this is what it would be like if you lived here with me. It would be good, warm. Before you know it, we are back on my stoop.

We sit close and tear into the Twizzlers and share the Evian. A couple of teenage girls from the block pass by and mad-dog you with your Evian and you get sweet, defensive and assure me that you only drink Evian because Peach says it's *alkaline* and you're not wearing a bra, the way you weren't wearing a bra that first day in the shop and it really does feel like a new beginning.

You scruff my hair with your cold little hand. "You wanna go back up?"

"Yeah," I say and I wish, I wish I could have prepared for you, hidden your things and showered, and put on matching socks. But you are here now, walking up my stairs, slowly, teasing me with every deliberate, soft step.

It's a blur from then on. My shitty sofa transforms into a hammock on a desert island in a Corona commercial minus the beer. We don't need beer, we don't need anything, we have us now. I keep my arms around you and you hold me in a way that would please Eric Carmen. We suck face until we can't and then we just tell each other things. You tell me all about the Dickens festival, the fight with your father over cigarettes, your stepmonster and the shitty motel, the bratty stepsiblings, the overpriced candy apples. You want to know about me and I tell you I like you, a lot. We go back to sucking face. It goes on like that for a while and you're all worn out and cozy. When you finally fall asleep your little body is limp. I don't know if I will ever be able to sleep with you this close to me. You can't tell lies in your sleep and you smile slightly, I think, every so often, and move closer to me.

The only reason I know that I am able to sleep in such close proximity to you is that the next morning the sound of the shower turning on wakes me up and you are no longer in my arms and you are naked, wet, there.

25

IF you live alone, you'd be a fucking masochistic freak to buy an opaque shower curtain. I started thinking about this in the Silver Seahorse, where the shower curtain was white, save a few spots of mold on the bottom. It's like they were trying to make the rooms feel like *Psycho*. I thought buying a shower curtain would be the easiest fucking thing in the world but you go to Bed Bath & Beyond and they have like six hundred opaque shower curtains that are obviously not an option. And then you go online and there are thousands to choose from. I didn't buy a totally clear one because you need something to look at while you're on the can, but when you think about it, this shower curtain is something you are going to look at

Every.

Fucking.

Day.

So I started going through hundreds of options online. Most of the designs are bullshit you could never stomach every day (a map of the world, go fuck yourself, fish, a map of Brooklyn, really go fuck yourself, snowmen, the Eiffel Tower, nautical signs—I mean, I'm not some fucker who buys scarves at Urban Outfitters and rates movies on IMDB). I just wanted something funny and classic.

I finally settled on a clear shower curtain with yellow police tape marked POLICE LINE DO NOT CROSS slapped across. And when I bought this shower curtain, I never imagined that you would be on the other side of the police tape, those damn yellow stripes blocking my view of you. Next time I'm going for an all clear, Beck. Lesson learned.

And really it's all for the best because I don't have time to watch you shower. I have to take this opportunity to hide all the Beckmobilia and hope that you didn't do any snooping when you woke up. I retrace your steps. You left the bathroom closet door open (typical woman) after you got a towel. Fortunately you took the towel on top and you didn't find your bras stashed under the bottom towel. Hopefully, you didn't open the medicine cabinet in the bathroom and find your scratched-up silver hair clip (I stole it the first day I stepped into your apartment, those clips are everywhere, you'd never miss it, right?). I needed it because a few delicious strands of your hair are woven in, holding your DNA, your scent. Did you open the refrigerator door and find your leftover bottle of Nantucket Nectar diet iced tea, half-empty? Your lips touched it and I wanted to keep your lips in my refrigerator. You did pour a glass of water and there is always the possibility that you would have mistaken your iced tea bottle for my own.

The bathroom door is the one thing in here that is actually not even slightly broken and you could have closed it all the way, but you didn't. It's like you want all doors open at all times, the way your windows have no curtains in your apartment. And I can't help but feel excited that in some way, you wanted me to sneak a peek at you in there, right now, blocked by that Big Bird–colored police tape. You arch your back and let the water hit one tit and another tit and then you turn around and you like it here, in my shower, in my home and you let the water go at your neck and drip down your back and you take the bar of Ivory soap (my soap), and hold it between your breasts and move it down and let it fall and then you rub the suds on your belly, lower, lower until your hands are down there and then as soon as they're down there they're back up on your neck and you're holding back and you're so hot for me right now and I should take off my clothes and get in the shower but if I did that, you would look at the moving door and realize that your white bikini top is hanging on the doorknob. I know you didn't notice it yet. And there's a chance you will never notice it since you didn't close the door all the way. I can grab the bikini and pray that you're so wrapped up in your sopping wet—double entendre, baby—self and don't notice or I can leave it there and assume that when you do finish—cleaning, not fucking—that you will be so preoccupied with drying off and blinded by the steam that you won't notice your own bikini top.

Who am I kidding? I have to get that bikini top. I close my eyes. I pray. My hand is shaking when I reach around to the interior side of the door and pull it off the doorknob. You don't notice and everything is safe again and I really need you to get the fuck out of my apartment. I put your bikini behind the frozen Stouffer's things I buy but never eat and then you are out of the shower, out of the bathroom and you call out.

"Hey, Joe, where you going with that gun in your hand?"

For a second, I panic. You know and the bikini is a gun and I am fucked but you are in a towel, dripping and I look like a fucking lunatic against the fridge.

"I'm just kidding," you say. "I know it's a bad joke, but it's not *that* bad. Chill out."

"I guess you found the towels."

"I hope it's okay," you murmur, and my home is no place for bare feet and you keep moving around because the floors are sticky and dirty and you're looking down at my typewriters and asking too many questions and you're picking up my taxidermy miniature alligator head that I would have hidden if I knew you were coming and this is wrong, all wrong, this is not right in the morning light and you got to sleep here and shower and soap up without making love to me and in what universe can that possibly be a good thing? Your clean hands are too clinical right now and you're examining this place like it's a crime scene. Maybe that yellow tape put you on guard. You are asking when I started collecting typewriters and dead animals and jokingly asking if I'm a serial killer and pointing at the hole in the wall and saying, "Joseph, tell me again about the hole," and, yeah, you're laughing and you don't mean for me to defend it all but this is not good for us and you're too clean and I have sleep in my eyes and morning wood and no coffee and no eggs to make for you. The faucet drips (you didn't shut it off all the way) but I can't shut it off because you can't be alone in my living room. You excuse yourself to the bathroom and you wash your hands with a lot of soap (taxidermy and typewriters). When you get out of my bathroom with your freshly scrubbed hands, you're all done with me, talking about school, kissing me good-bye, no tongue.

When you leave, I sit in the wet tub and breathe you in. All of you.

"DUDE, you don't think that's a little harsh?"

Curtis is pleading his case and turning red and the little shit has never been fired before and suddenly he loves it here at Mooney's and suddenly he gives a shit and suddenly my pothead minion is never getting stoned again.

"Curtis, the right thing to do now is just say 'Okay, boss.'"

He flares and a fat little woman knocks on the counter like it's a door. "S'cuse me, guys, but do you have any Zone cookbooks?"

"Yeah," I say, and I am about to say where but suddenly Curtis actually works here and actually gives a shit and he's zipping behind me and leading the sweet little fatty to the cookbooks and talking to her about our ability to special-order any Zone book her fat little heart could desire and telling her about our return policy, so loudly you'd think she was deaf, not fat, and it's amazing, how people only shape up until they have a gun against their head and then I hear you (*Hey, Joe, where you going with that gun in your hand?*), and that morning was all his fault and he will pay. He must pay and the fat lady wants to pay part by check and part by cash and part by credit card and I have to wonder how she will afford to buy the ingredients in the Zone book recipes and suddenly Curtis is a fucking Volunteer Police Man, all about double-checking her driver's license like I taught him to do, like he never does, and running the credit card the right way, hard and tilted so that the weak old machine picks up the swipe. He's inserting a bookmark in each fucking cookbook and, man, this kid, only a nut job psychopath perfectionist mother fucker would fire this kid, so good he is, so dedicated.

The little fat lady is pleased and she whistles at me. "Yoo-hoo, hon."

I nod and I smile and she should have addressed me as *sir*.

"You should give this young man a raise," she says and she's pink all over from hustling around the store. "I tell you, I was in another little shop uptown for *two hours* before someone came to help me and this young man you have here was a wonderful and gracious host to me. And knowledgeable too."

I'd like to tell her that in both bookstores and coffee shops, it's actually *polite* to leave browsers and readers alone. When you harass people and offer to help them too much, they feel like you're nudging them out the door. This lady doesn't know anything about the world and she's still raving about this *friendly young man* and I would like to tell her that overeager Curtis (did he start doing meth or something?) has actually driven customers away today because most people don't want to be interrupted when they're reading the first few pages of a novel. Oh, I want her to know that Curtis smokes pot four times a day and steals bicycles and fences them for spare cash. I could tell her that he is late every fucking shift and that he shits in the bathroom on a regular basis (rude), and that he's cheated on every girlfriend he's ever had, and that when she exits this place, were he not getting his ass fired, he'd mock her to high hell and possibly even write down her checking account information. Yes. She pays with a check.

Instead I just smile at the gal. "You're the exact reason that we open up shop every day," I say. "We're in the business of helping people buy books."

"This is just like that Meg Ryan movie." She squeals. "You know, where the nice girl has the small shop and she falls in love with the man with the big shops?"

Curtis fucking sings, *"You've Got Mail!?"*

"You've Got Mail," she cries and she laughs. "Oh, I love that movie! Do you have that here? DVDs?"

This sloth won't use her cookbooks. She will buy a small shelf at Target and have someone nail it into the wall in her kitchen. She will line up those cookbooks and love the way they look and throw a pizza in the microwave and tear into the DVD of *You've Got Mail* that she'll truck across town to buy. She'll never come back here again.

When she goes, Curtis gets it somehow. He knows he's done.

"Dude," he says. "For what it's worth, I thought I was helping you out. That chick was hot. Bangable hot."

"You don't give out my address to strangers."

"She said she knew you. And did I say bangable? Mad bangable."

Let it be known that I only punched him once and not in the face. You better remember that, Beck. It's not like I'm some monster and it's not like I hurt him. I fired him, man to man, boss to worker. It wasn't personal and it wasn't hardcore and that fat lady was the first customer he treated well since week fucking one. Also, you're not bangable, Beck. You're beautiful. There's a difference.

26

THE day after our sleepover without sex, you asked me to meet up with you in midtown. Curtis was gone and I was alone in the shop, but the day after a woman is naked in your apartment, everyone knows the only thing to say to her is yes. We picked up your new cable box. The line was a mile long. Then you sent me home.

And it's been more of the same for the past two weeks. Today, you asked me to meet you in front of a Starbucks in Herald Square, where I stand now as you kiss me hello (on the cheek). You're not gonna sit on my lap in an overstuffed chair and lick whipped cream off my upper lip. You're in get-it-done daytime mode and Christmas shoppers walking by probably think I'm your gay best friend. My dick hurts, Beck. Where's my holiday?

"So the good news is, I know exactly what I want."

"You do?" I say and I hope you'll ask me to eat you out in the bathroom at Starbucks.

"I want to get my mom those headphones that double as earmuffs."

"Ah." Digital earmuffs are the physical opposite of oral sex.

"And the better news is, I have a coupon," you say and we are on our way into Macy's.

Now you start in about money. You're strapped for cash. I pretend that I didn't read the e-mails you exchanged with your father this morning. I know that you're waiting to see if your old man the Captain is gonna help you out.

We are in the ladies' shoes section (didn't you want earmuffs?) when you ask me about Curtis. I tell you that I caught him stealing and fired him. I do not tell you it was because he gave you my address. You sigh; he seemed *like a good kid.* Ha. We wander through jewelry (didn't you just need earmuffs?), and you want to know when I'll hire a new clerk. I tell you that the only thing more impossible than finding good help is running the store on my own. You nod and agree that most people are *unemployable* and is this really how it's going to be, small talk about résumés and shit?

"Wanna go for a ride?" you say and if you mean that you're gonna go for a ride on my dick, then yes.

But instead, you take my hand and lead me onto the escalator. It is crowded and sweaty and Christmassy and I would rather be balls deep in a trash can. There is no privacy on an escalator at Macy's in December, but you're a little performer, and here you go.

"So, my grad school adviser, the one on sabbatical who's on a grant at *Princeton.*" And you pause, as if the Mexican chick in front of you cares. "He wants pages before we break, which is obviously ridiculous."

"What's his name again?" I say even though I have never asked.

"Paul," you say and you don't offer a last name and the conversation is over, thank God. We get off at the fourth floor. It's loud and smells like pretzels and perfume. A Miley Cyrus song plays and it's too hopped up in here. Loud skanks picking fights with each other assault my senses and I ask you if the headphones are on this floor and you tell me you need to return something.

Fortunately, the line at the Young Sluts Department isn't that long because most Young Sluts can't afford to buy shit. As it turns out you weren't telling me the whole story and when it's our turn, you pull out leggings and a wrinkled receipt out of your bag and the poor girl behind the counter has never done a return and, of course, we have to wait.

"Is there a reason this is taking so long?" you snip.

"Well, you bought these more than a hundred days ago."

"So?"

And holy shit, you really *are* broke because why else would you be digging up pants from three months past? You grab the pants and the receipt and you shove them in your bag.

"I'll just come back when there's a manager."

"Fine by me."

You are stung now; you were *depending* on that refund. You take it out on everyone in the Young Sluts, plowing through rayon and neon without saying *excuse me*. A couple of bitches say they want to kick your ass, but they won't; they're in high school, they are happy just to call you a *beeatch*. I tell you to slow down and you don't listen and I almost love what a cunt you can be because one of these days you're gonna tie me to a bed and slap me and lord over me the way you lord over all the people who get in your way. You're so revved up and I want to play with you and I do.

"Beck."

"What?"

"Look, I don't know shit about girls' clothes, but those pants that you were trying to return, they look good."

"They don't look good on me."

"Can I see?"

You fight a smile but you lose. "Here?"

"Yeah," I say and you're walking more slowly now and there's nobody monitoring the dressing room because it really is Christmas and Santa knows I'm a good boy. We walk down the corridor of dressing rooms toward the handicap one on the end. You don't tell me why you're pushing that door open and you don't invite me into the room but I follow. I sit down on the bench and you stand in front of the three-panel mirror. You pull the pants out of your bag and what is wrong with you that you're still thinking about pants?

You sigh. "See, what I really want are jeggings."

But what you really need is an orgasm and I tell you to try them on. You are blushing, naughty and a door slams and someone's muttering *get a room* and we *did* get a room, we have this room and your furry boots are off and you're unzipping your jeans and they're so snug that when you pull them down your panties start to go with them.

"Come here."

"Joe. Shh."

I motion for you to come here. Because you are shy at heart, you pull your pants up and even start to zip them as you walk over to me. I look up at you and you look down on me and you start to crouch down and reach for my belt buckle but no. I grab your hand, firm.

"Stand up."

You do. And when I start to unzip your pants you step closer and wiggle and help me get you out of those pants and I get you all the way out of them and throw them at the mirror and finally, at long last, in the Young Sluts Department of Macy's in Herald Square, Christmas comes early. I taste you. I lick you. And when you cum you cum at the top of your lungs.

I love shopping.

Sex clears the mind and the orgasm agrees with you. We leave the dressing room and you decide to give the pants you were trying to return to your mother—I knew we were never getting any earmuffs. You hold my hand hard and tight and we ride the escalator four flights back down and you do not want to browse anymore. The music softens as "Have Yourself a Merry Little Christmas" begins, my favorite sad holiday song. You ask me what I'm doing for the holiday, and I tell you that I'm working, of course, and you tell me that you're going to have to get a job. You lead me into men's hats and you pick up a red and green wool monstrosity. I shake you off.

"Maybe I can work here." You smile. "You could come visit me on my breaks."

"Do you really need a job?"

Instead of answering me, you pick up a red hunting cap like the one Caulfield wore in *The Catcher in the Rye* and you look up at me. "Please? It's pretty much my favorite book of all time."

I can't say no and I love you for not mentioning the book by name. I put the hat on and you bite your lip. "Adorable."

It's hard to get you to take me seriously while wearing this ridiculous hat but I try. "Seriously, Beck, do you need a job?"

"You are too hot." You squeal and you take out your phone. "One picture, Joe. You have to let me get that for you."

"I better not see that on Facebook."

"You're not *on* Facebook, silly," you say. "Smile."

You take my picture and I give you the hat and you dig in your bag for your credit card. "Beck," I say. "You don't need to buy me a hat I'm never gonna wear. Seriously. Do you need a job?"

"I know I don't need to buy it," you say. "I want to."

It's Christmas so I let you buy me the cap and I say I'll only wear it on one condition.

"Anything," you say and you have gorgeous tunnel vision.

"Tell me you'll take a job at the bookshop."

"Yes!" You cheer and you throw your arms around me, I give you everything you want, everything you need, and you kiss my neck so softly, my lips, tenderly. You murmur my name—*Joe*—and everyone walking by probably thinks we just got engaged.

LATER in the day, Ethan shows up for an interview. I don't have the heart to tell him that the job has been taken. He looks like a gerbil and he's friendly as a puppy and he'd be better off in an animal shelter than a bookstore. He talks a lot and I check your e-mail and it's clear to me that you called Peach and told her about our shopping excursion and your new job. She writes:

> *Beckalicious, I hope you're not beating yourself up after the Target romp. Remember: Doing something trashy does not make you trashy. You're only human, little one! Just please be tender with him, probably not the best idea to work together. Maybe better to work on campus? Anywho, be well, Peach.*

The e-mail from Peach kills my Macy's buzz. What if you back out on me? What if we work together and we don't get along? What if you need to have #*girlsnight* on your nights off and I never get to go shopping with you again? Ethan would never bail on me; he brought three copies of his résumé. "You seem awfully busy, Joe," he says, perky. "If you want me to go I can come back in a little while! My day's clear!"

I buy time. I don't know if I can deal with his energy. "What are your five favorite books?"

He smiles like I just told him that Santa Claus is real and I read your response to Peach:

Oh, it was Macy's, not Target, so that's more respectable . . .
I hope. And you're right, I know I shouldn't work at the
bookstore. I am sooo bad about boundaries. Why are you
always so smart?!

Ethan is the middle of his analysis of *The Lord of the Rings* when I interrupt him.

"I'm sorry, Ethan. Just give me another minute here."

"You don't have to be sorry!" He sings, "You're the boss!"

Everything is an exclamation point with this guy, which is why it's puzzling that his favorite book of all is *American Psycho*. "I love a good scare! Don't you, Joe?"

I prefer literary fiction and he wags his tail and I refresh your inbox and open Peach's response:

I just care about you, Beckalicious. Remember: boundaries!
Also, I feel like I haven't seen you in foreverrrrr.

I put your phone away and quietly thank your mother for footing the bill. Ethan is still talking about the gerbil in *American Psycho*.

He gushes and giggles and who the fuck *is* this guy? "I just love books," he chirps. "I could talk about books until the cows come home! That's the hardest thing about losing the job and the girlfriend. I miss talking. I love talking!"

Ethan is the loneliest, most depressing man I've ever met in my life and at the same time, he's saving me. And he's perfect, just what I need. You will not be into this guy and next to him, I'm the man. I smile. "So, Ethan. Can you work weekends?"

"Of course!" he chirps, not entirely unlike a gerbil. "I can work anytime!"

When we stand I realize that he's almost a foot shorter than I am. He has dandruff and he gushes with gratitude as I walk him to the door. "You know, Joe, I always had this feeling that I'd wind up with a fun job like this! To be honest, majoring in finance was my dad's idea. Not mine!"

"Well, that's good, Ethan, this is good," I say and he is the one with boundary issues. "You go have a beer and celebrate."

"I don't really drink but maybe I'll put a little rum in my Diet Dr Pepper!" he exclaims and when I watch him walk down the street, I feel proud like a teacher. I have done a good thing today.

You write to Peach and wish her a happy holiday in the sun. You tell her you're probably going to stay in the city because it costs so much to get to Nantucket and she responds:

Sweetness, if you need a loan, you know I am here. . . .

You write back NO adamantly and Peach is leaving to meet her family in St. Barts and rub organic sun block all over her grotesque body and think about you. Maybe she'll find a native girl, fall in love, and let you be. I e-mail you that you start tomorrow and you respond right away, the right way:

☺ *Yes, Boss.*

Later that night, you call me to clarify your start date. When I tell you about Ethan, you are confused at first.

"I thought *I* got the job," you say.

"Well, it's the busiest time of the year, Beck."

"Does this mean I won't get as many hours?"

"This means we might have a night off together once in a while."

You get it and you lower your voice. "Are you sexually harassing me already?"

I don't laugh. "Yes, miss. I am."

I'm a genius, clearly, and Peach can fuck off because we keep talking, like boyfriend and girlfriend. I tell you more about Ethan and you laugh.

"He's like the anti-Blythe," you say. "She crosses out exclamation points in everyone's stories. Literally."

"Damn," I say. "I wonder what would happen if they were in the same room together."

"Omigod," you say and I can tell that you just sat up. "We have to do that."

"Beck."

"We *have* to set them up."

"This kid is so innocent," I say. "I don't think I can unleash Blythe on him."

"Honestly, Joe," you say. "Ethan might be just what Blythe needs. And vice versa. I mean, opposites attract, you know?"

"Are we opposites?"

"Well, we'll see," you say and then we move on to talking about Indian food and music and it's one of those conversations that just flows, the kind you can only have after a dressing room.

When we finally hang up, I send you Ethan's contact information for Blythe. I write:

Merry Christmas!

You write back:

It is indeed. ☺

27

I love having you at the shop. Working with you has made me fall back in love with Mooney's place. We are an adorable couple and a good match and you love it when anyone says so. There are no more dates. There is just us. You get here before your shifts start and kiss me hello. Dull, pedestrian couples get a dog to practice raising a kid, but we have a shop full of books together. We share the load and laugh at the customers and playfully argue about what kind of music to play and we are one of those 1950s couples, very sexist, because I am in charge and you like it that way. You toy with me, bending the rules on a daily basis and you live to push my buttons. We laugh easily. I bring my Holden hat to work and put it on when you're not looking and you burst out laughing when you see me.

"Omigod, Joe, you have to let me take that away."

I playfully fight you off. "You can't take my Holden Caulfield cap!"

You laugh. "No, what I can't do is let you go out into the world wearing that thing. Clearly I was not thinking straight when I picked it out."

I like the reference to our time in Young Sluts and I let you grab my hat. I never even took the tag off and you are pleased to find it there. "Now I can get you something even better."

And I can't believe how cheesy I feel, how upbeat, but it feels like the world is on my side; it's downright happy in Mooney's place! Ethan and Blythe are actually going on dates, which is amazing, and I go to bed wondering what you're gonna wear to work the next day, wondering when our chemistry will erupt into a marathon fuck session in your bed that I built. We are waiting to have sex because you say this is *special*. And it is.

Every day is Christmas and today you arrive in a slutty gray slouchy sweater that hangs off your shoulder and transforms your collarbone into a boner-inducing porno shot. You're chomping on baby carrots. I tell you to go home and change.

You talk with your mouth full. "You never said there's a dress code."

"It's implied."

"By what?" you sass. "Ethan's baggy sweatshirts?"

"Calm down."

"I am calm, Joe. I'm just asking you to tell me about this dress code."

"Think of it like school. You wouldn't go to class in this."

You toss the carrots on the counter. You cross your arms. "I came from class."

"Just cover it up," I say and I want to tell you this is why the guys in your class feel permitted to try and fuck you.

"Cover what up?" you say and now I want to bend you over and teach you a lesson. Your daddy issues are intense, Beck.

"Cover your collarbone."

"Well why don't I put on your fleece?"

I let you try on my black fleece and it drowns you and I'd like to pick you up by the collarbone and bring you to the F–K section where you went your first time here when you didn't even know what you were looking for (me), and I can do that because I'm the boss and you want me to do that and I want to do that but I won't. I like how much you want it now and it's going to stay that way and I shake my head at you and motion for you to get out of the fleece and you piss and moan and your slutty sweater goes up along with the fleece when you pull it over your head and some pervert in reference books is looking and I reach over and yank at your sweater and pull it down.

You startle and the radiator hisses and the soundtrack of *Hannah and Her Sisters* delivers instrumental old love songs and you brought me a coffee like a good girl and you hand me my fleece. I take it and sit down on the stool at the register and you bat your eyelashes at me and that perv is still looking and I have to take care of him.

"When you come back," I say, raising my voice, "you better be wearing a bra."

You blush and try not to smile and you slip into your peacoat and grab your bag of shit you dragged in here and you nod. "What color?"

It can't be long before we fuck and I shrug. "You pick."

"Red?"

"Fine."

"Black?"

"Go," I say and you go and I look at the pervert and call him out good, cold. "Did you need help, sir?"

"Uh, no, just looking."

"Well, if and when you do need help, I'm here," I say, and I turn off the *Hannah* and put on the Beastie Boys and wait for you to come back, which you will, because you love it here with me and did I mention that this was the best idea ever? Your first shift, you were an arrogant disaster and you fucked up every sale you made and overcharged and undercharged and wore your fucking *Brown University* sweatshirt as if you needed everyone to know that you're above this kind of shit and I told you no sweatshirts and you turned red because you know when you're being an asshole. The perv in References asks if we have a bathroom and I tell him, sharp, cutting, "No," and he doesn't say good-bye when he leaves and I take the opportunity to go downstairs and beat one out because working with you and waiting for you to get here so I can smell you and see you and be near you every day has me worked up like a fucking eighth-grade kid with a slutty substitute teacher.

My phone buzzes and you're fast and you have texted me:

Knock knock

And there's a photo and it's you, in a red bra, and you text again:

Is this appropriate for the workplace?

And I write back:

No

And January is the deadest month in the world and I could stay down here reviewing bras all day and you know it and you come right back:

Knock knock

I type:

Yes?

240

And here it is again, you, no face, just your tits shoved into a pink lace bra and your nipples are hard for me and I can't take it anymore and I finish and you text me again:

?

And I refuse to give my dick to you in this way and you're starting to figure that out and you text another photo of yourself. No bra. And I give you what you want. I text:

Bad girl. Come here. Now.

You text right back lightning fast:

Yes boss

No punctuation just *yes*, the universal euphemism for FUCK ME NOW, and *boss*, the universal euphemism for I SUBMIT, and I clean myself up and bound up the stairs and find the Paula Fox I'm pretending to read every time you show up and I take out the Beastie Boys and put on some Beck—it's a regular thing now, a joke we have, we are that couple with a secret vocabulary of songs and books and looks and meals—and by the time you get here it's almost time to close and I haven't even checked your e-mail in days, that's how into me you are, and you slip out of your peacoat and you're in a fucking lace, see-through tank top and you smile at me.

"Is this inappropriate?"

I close Paula Fox and the Beck song "Sexx Laws" starts to play, an ode to handcuffs and illogically great fucking. You and I will make our own fucking song and I adjust so I'm facing you and the door is not locked and the sign says open and the streets are emptying out (a Monday in January) and the *Hannah* was foreplay and the texts were first base and you move toward me, slightly, and I spread my

241

legs, slightly, and you are standing on your peacoat in your fuck-me boots and I can't take it anymore and I break.

"You're late. We're about to close."

"Sorry, boss. When do we close, boss?"

"Now."

"Uh-oh."

"Yeah," I say, and I'm a rock and you're not wearing any panties under that skirt, you whore, and you tilt your little head and twirl your little hair and it's amazing how the most generic shit in the world can be so hot: half-naked girl in a bookstore, reaching for a Twizzler, chewing on it, slowly, begging for it, silently.

"Well, maybe there's something else I can do for you," you coo and I shake my head no and motion for you to come here *now* and you have the Twizzler hanging out of your mouth and you put both of your hands on both of my knees and lean in and dangle the Twizzler at my mouth.

I bite it. Finally.

28

I have just fucked you for the first time in our lives and it was not good and it did not go on forever and you did not scream. Where was that Macy's heat when I was inside you? And who's to blame for our quick fuck? Was it because we weren't in a dressing room or in front of an open window? Or was it me? Was I too hungry? Too eager? Did I hold you too hard? Maybe I'm better at eating you out than I am at fucking you, and that's a horrible and unfair possibility. We've only done it once. Do I get to do it again? Do you want to do it again?

You don't want to do it again. You aren't revving up as we recover on the floor of the cage. You are on top of me stroking my hair and I can't see your face but I can feel the disappointment in your hands, in your touch, which is full of pity. The pads of your fingers go *pat-pat* and I can't let go of you or you might back off of me and I might have to face you and I can't do that. I lasted maybe eight seconds. Nine. I'm running over it in my head and I don't know how this happened. Maybe I jerked off too much and maybe you teased me too much and maybe I should have locked the door.

"No," you said. "It's so hot with the door open and the open sign up, right?"

I should have been honest with you and told you that the lack of security would only make me nervous. But I didn't want to disappoint you and I wanted to put your needs first. You wanted to go at it by the register, but I said no.

"Let's go downstairs."

"Really?" you said and you were lit up. You were. I'm sure of it.

We got down here (my idea, I have the key, I am the boss), and I unlocked the cage and ordered you in there and I locked it and you smiled and I told you to take your skirt off and you obeyed (I am the boss) and you weren't wearing any panties and I told you to touch yourself and you did and I willed the other Beck to shut the fuck up. You wanted the music on and so I left it alone (I am the boss and I am allowed to please you on occasion). You stood holding the cage door with one hand and working at yourself slowly with the other while I started getting undressed, and you watched me smiling one second, intent and ready the next. I told you to beg for it and you begged me to come in there and I took my pants off and you saw how badly I wanted to come in there and I told you to get down on your knees and you did and you reached for me (I am the boss, I am allowed to please you on occasion) and I unlocked the cage and entered. You took me in your hands and in your mouth and you kept looking up at me and I knew it was time to fuck you and let you know that it was time and you leapt at me, an animal, and straddled me and commanded me downward (I am the boss and I am allowed to please you on occasion), and then.

And then.

And then I was inside of you and I came. I blew it. I came so fast and so hard and you said nothing at first and you didn't act like you wanted me to help you finish, you just went smack into gentle stroking my hair mode (the wrong kind of fucking touching), and you quietly told me:

"Don't worry, Joe. I'm on the pill."

And that was the moment I was most afraid of you and what you could do to me and not do to me because that was the moment that I realized that you are the boss, not me and you can please me on occasion if you want to. When we finally stood up we were both hungry and dizzy and there was an old man upstairs standing at the register and he looked at us, me all dressed, you in your bra and he smiled.

"You kids have a good night. I'll come back another time."

There was something deathly unsexual and anticlimactic and flattening in his words, his old man eyes and his pleasure at seeing us, young and hot and alive. He had more fun in that moment than you and I had in our first fuck and there was no getting around it and I wasn't surprised when you said you should go check on Peach because she's been really depressed. I wasn't surprised that you didn't suggest we go to your bed and fuck again. I was bad and you are the boss.

But this is what surprises me. A day later—you didn't even wait a whole day—you texted me:

Hey Joe, I can't make it in today. Sorry!

And that exclamation point was the beginning of the end of us and I made a mistake by writing back:

Okay!

And then you made plans to go out with Lynn and Chana instead of seeing me.

You: *I miss you girls. I have an emergency session with Dr. Nicky, but want to get late lunch and/or happy hour?*

Chana: *Who is this? Haha. Yes. Fine.*

Lynn: *I'm already in pajamas and Housewives mode.* ☹ *Have one for me!*

So this was it, right? The true end because instead of seeing me, you were opting to see a mental health professional and a girlfriend to *talk about me.* And when a girl likes talking about you more than talking to you, well, in my experience, that's the end. So I was gonna fucking kill myself and everyone in the shop and take out the Eric Carmen CD and smash it into bits because I stopped believing in myself and our future. I wrote back to you, pathetic:

Okay!

It's a good thing you knew that I was close to losing my shit because not five seconds after I shut off the CD—sometimes silence is the best sound—and sat down on the stool and thought about castrating myself like the perv in *Little Children* you wrote back again:

But what are you doing tonight? ☺

And all was well in the universe because that smile was your gaping wet pussy that knew that I had more to give. And I was okay again. It was clear to me now that you were going to your shrink to talk about your problem, that you enjoy sex more when there's an audience. And you were going to see Chana because you've been busy with me and she's been away on vacation and you wanted to tell her all about the best head of your life in Macy's. That emoticon was your way of saying that we don't work together anymore. We fuck together. So I told you to be at my place at seven and you wrote back:

See you then!

It was 7:12 when I realized that the candles were cursed. Five little votive candles that I picked up at Pier 1 Imports because of some guy in the bookstore who stayed in my head for some reason. He seemed cool, like a guy I'd be friends with if I was on the market for friends, and he dumped a heavy bag on the counter so he could get out his credit card and he sighed. "Fucking candles. Women and candles, right?"

"Right," I said, and I didn't realize it but an imprint was made then and I would never have a woman over without candles lit because of some pussy-whipped husband buying Tom Clancy for himself and candles for his sex-withholding wife. What makes us become us? What fucks us up and why? I have no idea but I know that at 7:12 I started to resent those candles and the little pathetic scented fires in each of them. The pizza was cold and the wine I bought—I hate wine—was getting shittier by the second. You can't let wine breathe for that long—and I knew you weren't coming and that it was a matter of time before you flaked out on me and sure enough at 7:14 when I was sitting at the table—the table I dragged home and up the stairs for this very moment—when you texted:

Don't hate me but I have to bail ☹

And that smiley face is your body, closed, and your eyes averted and your resignation from all things me, from all things us, and I don't need to read your e-mail to know that I can't fully blame this on Peach because she's not the spazzing dick, that's me, and I put Twizzlers in a vase for you, Beck. I pick up the vase and throw it at the wall, at the tapestry I bought from an old lady down the street to cover the hole in the wall to make you feel more at ease in my place. The vase doesn't crack. It just bounces onto the couch and I must be the limpest limp dick in the world. I can't even break a vase and I lunge at the candles but I don't want to set this place on fire. You were in this place and still you fucked me. I cannot hold this place responsible and I cannot blame the vase or the Twizzlers or the DO NOT CROSS police tape on the shower curtains and I lower my hand onto a candle and the fire is hot and my skin aches and I'd set my dick on fire if I could but we know that I'm a limp dick pussy. I don't have the balls to do that. The smell of burnt flesh overwhelms the cold pizza and it's a good thing I didn't waste any money on flowers.

29

I'LL tell you something about suicide, Beck. If I were going to off myself with a handgun or a noose or a permanent swim, which I'm not, now would be the time to do it. You have dismissed me and it's been *five hours and eleven days* since you took your love away and all of our songs sound bad because they will never *see us standing from such great heights* and no, you will not *still love me tomorrow* because you never loved me at all. I'm not Bobby Short or (the real) Beck and you don't want to *defy the logic of all sex laws* with me and you are not *in love again* and you do not *love, love, love it*. I made it inside of you and you don't want me back. Nothing is fun anymore, not even coming up with tweaked-out Benji tweets:

Coke. Because I'll sleep when I'm dead. #cocacola #hahaha

"Excuse me but can you stop with your phone and look at me," an uppity old broad squawks. I hit TWEET and offer my assistance.

The bitch barks, "I said I don't need a bag. I brought my own."

"Good for you," I snap and crumple the paper bag and throw

it in the trash just to let her know who's boss and Ethan sighs and apologizes to her and pulls the bag out of the trash and this is what my life has come to: me, Ethan, and a bunch of book-buying assholes.

I spend day after day with Ethan and getting to know him is no easy thing especially now that I don't get to tell you about him. You complained about the loud fan in the employee restroom and pushed me to replace it as anyone would; Ethan calls it a "sound machine" and claims it doesn't bother him. He's almost like a hermaphrodite, this kid, in a CK One asexual cologne 1992 sort of way. Without asking I can tell you that he knows all the words to "Gonna Make You Sweat" and he'd be at home on a dance floor sidestepping, clapping, and counting. Out loud. He's aggressive in all the wrong ways and he was born too late and he looks tired at forty-one from years of hunting for a color-blocked, Rick Dees–narrated way of life. You can either feel bad for the guy or jump him and steal his wallet. He's a litmus test of a person and half the customers meet his smile and the other half glare at him and I tell him all the time that he should work in an old folks home and I mean it. He could deejay dance parties for people in wheelchairs, on life support. People with crooked, chamomile-scented dicks and lazy, warped vaginas would spark to his total, complete, and tragically inherent want for a time long gone.

"Have a good one, ma'am!"

"Ethan, you don't have to call everybody 'ma'am,'" I say. "Some people, some people you just wave or leave it at 'you're welcome.'"

He won't listen or learn or bend and I'm losing patience with him, with life, with humans. I have nothing left to crave and dream about anymore. I feel queasy when I look at him because he's so fucking *nice* that he doesn't mention you at all. He doesn't lord his relationship over me and he says as little as possible about Blythe, which makes me like a pity case. All I have is a shitty memory of our quick sexual congress, your eight seconds as a monkey locked to my dick. Every day, the hotness in Macy's seems cooler and the sex memories are like all memories, doomed to tarnish and weaken with time. You told Chana:

I just got too deep, too fast . . . again.

The *again* hurt and it's all perpetually downhill. My days begin with stale Frosted Flakes and newly ripped jeans I forgot to wash, won't wash; you were on them. I ride the train to work and I don't care about the books because you're not touching them. I check your e-mail ferociously. You go on with your life and you don't write to me. I pick at the scab on my burnt finger. I don't want it to heal and I want this pain and I tear at my finger that you liked so much that night in the horse-drawn carriage. My finger oozes pus and blood and pain like everything else in my life. If Ethan tells me one more fucking time that I ought to go get my finger checked out and sue the maker of the coffee pot—I had to think fast, you can't tell the new kid on the register that you lit up your finger when you got dumped—well, if Ethan doesn't shut his face he's gonna get hit in the face, pus and all.

And even though you only worked here a short while, you were a permanent marker on this place. And somehow, it feels vicious that Ethan now stands in your place. He likes new things, crisp Gap "merch"—"What a great sale!" he exclaims as if I want to know the story of how he got his discount denim—and his button-down shirts—"On Tuesdays, everything in the clearance section at the Gap is an additional forty percent off!" he informs me, as if to mark my calendar, as if I asked—and every day he's in a good fucking mood and clean shaven and tragically, pathetically hopeful that more good things are going to happen for him. Having Blythe has made him feel like a winner and he plays the lottery now. "Hey, Joe, maybe we can go in on a ticket together, you know, like you read about in the paper, those guys that work together and win together!" Every day he raves about his coffee—as if this is something that needs to be pointed out, that coffee tastes like coffee—and when it's January, the most universally reviled month of the year, and it's sleeting and the sky looks like acid washed jeans and the store has to be mopped three times a day because of slobs in their boots and slobs with their umbrellas, and he's got to fucking sing out, "Don't you love a gray day?" and when the sun does shine to mock us cuz it's thirty-two degrees he's got to sing out again, "Nothing like a winter sun, am I right?"

And the worst part is that he won't hate me, Beck. I can ignore him and bark at him and he's my dog, smiling every time I walk into the shop. He'd never kill himself either, even if he missed a 75 percent off sale at the Gap. He's too mild. One day, when he first started, he showed up with a bag from Bed Bath & Beyond. When he went to take a shit—he eats too much bran, worries about his colon—I peeked in the bag. Do you know what was in there? I'll tell you what was in there: a collapsible tray table. Is there any sadder purchase in this fucking world? Maybe a CD of C+C Music Factory's Greatest Hits, but that's about it. And I remember thinking, Ethan is gonna go home from the shop and make fiber for dinner and put the dinner on his new tray and watch network sitcoms and think about how funny *The Big Bang Theory* is. He will literally lick the plate clean and fold his tray table and put it in the place where he will put it every night for the rest of his painfully lonely, fibrous, organized life. But then he got Blythe. And I know they are together; I'm not an idiot. And now it feels like *I'm* the one with the fucking collapsible table and the world is upside down. You should be here, telling me what Blythe says about him in her stories. I need you. I need levity.

I hate Ethan. I hate him for having Blythe. When we broke up, they should have broken up and I try to be normal. I ask him what's up with them, but he feeds me bullshit: "We don't want to rush into anything and we both value our independence, so we're taking it nice and slow, you know?"

No, I don't know because I don't value my independence. I value your pussy. If I were in his Reeboks—divorced, coupon-hoarding, slow—I would have put a bullet in my head. These are the darkest days in the history of the world and I'm losing it. And as if that's not enough, he is trying to learn Spanish from listening to Enrique Iglesias songs and he asks if he can put some on right now.

"Sure," I say. I don't care anymore. I'm so dead that I'm deaf.

"I don't have to listen to it right now." He panders. "Want me to play something else? I have a ton of playlists on here. I have club music and rock music and jazz music."

"Ethan, it's not 'jazz music.' It's just 'jazz.'"

"Joe, you know so much about everything," he says and he always finds a reason to smile. If I gave him a bloody nose he'd find a reason to thank me. "I feel like I'm learning more every day!"

I go downstairs and lock the door and check your e-mail. There is a lot of junk about school, some financial bickering with your parents, your dad is helping you "a little" and you're pity-partying with Lynn and Chana about "the Januaries." You are trying to keep busy, buying all kinds of shit online, putting it on Daddy's credit card, then promising Daddy you'll return it. There's no way around it anymore. You are gone, shopping, and I peel the new skin off my burn and watch the pus ooze. I am not healing. I refuse to get over you. Then you write to Chana:

> *I am so sorry but I am not gonna be able to go to that show*
> *with you next week. It's just, well, I miss Joe.*

If I had a folding TV dinner tray I would hurl it at the window and pound my chest like a barbarian, like a thick-dicked alpha gorilla. *Yes!* You miss me! It's true! You do! The countdown to the apocalypse is canceled and you *miss* me and I blow on my finger and I love life and C+C Music Factory and maybe Ethan really *will* learn Spanish and I read on:

> *I don't know if it's him per se or what we had. But I keep*
> *thinking about him and I keep almost calling and I am going*
> *to call if I don't get out of here. So I am gonna go to Peach's*
> *place in Little Compton and just kind of decompress.*

And now I'm pacing because you love me so much you have to leave New York. It's official. You are obsessed and you go on:

> *So, again, SO sorry to bail. But Peach says you are welcome to*
> *join if you want!*

Chana's response is epic and I love her and I love the world. She is succinct:

> *? Um, ok, Beck. You miss Joe so you're running off to a deserted*
> *beach house in the dead of winter with Peach?*

You: *I need space.*

Chana: *Well, no offense but I don't think of a Peach pit as "space." See you when you're back.*

You *miss* me and you *miss* me and there's an e-mail from Peach:

> *Beckalicious, you rule. I know you were on the verge of calling Joseph last night and I am SO PROUD OF YOU for not caving. You are so talented and you're in school. Of course that has to come first. And Joseph above anyone would want you to do what's best for you. Don't be so hard on yourself, B. Anywho . . . we're going to have a blast in LC. Oh. Before I forget, it turns out that most of the bedrooms are mid-renovation. I hate to do this but can you actually not invite C&L? Thanks!*

Bedrooms are under construction but there is always room for one more. It's vacation time! And before you can vacate you need to prepare! Everyone knows that! I bolt up the stairs and tell Ethan I'm going to the Gap.

"Don't even look at anything in the front!" he advises. "Plow right on through to the back!"

"You're a good man, Ethan," I say and I mean it. "You'll be speaking Spanish in no time!"

"Thanks, Joe! Or should I say . . . *Gracias*! And remember, it's Tuesday!"

"I know," I say. "All clearance items are forty percent off."

"You know it, Joe!"

And I do. I can't wait to get new things. I like old things but you like new things and maybe there's something to be said for new things. You *miss* me and that's new, and that's good.

30

I'M back at the shop surrounded by newness, and maybe I'm more like you than I know because the new things are exciting, Beck. New bandages—clean!—new hat—wool!—new haircut—short!—and a new attitude—psyched! I let Ethan go home early and he said he was happy to see me in such high spirits. It's only a matter of time before you reach out to me—you *miss* me—and I check your e-mail again because the news has been so good. Chana's laying into you about your "LC" tweet:

Chana: *"LC"? Beck, the only way you could sound like more of an asshole is if by "LC" you mean Lauren Conrad. You can't call it "LC" if you've never been there. Which you haven't, right?*

You: *Okay, you're right. LC was a lame tweet. I just feel kind of off since Joe.*

Chana: *If you feel off, then you should be a grown-up and call him up and see him again. Running away with Princess Peach is literally the worst thing to do.*

You: *I know. It's like in* Sex and the City *when Carrie is in Paris with the Russian and she says she can't help but wonder what it would be like if she were there with Mr. Big.*

Chana: *Except that's a bullshit TV show where they have to drag things out. This is real life. Stop being a drama queen and call him up. Who knows? Maybe he'll even go to Rhode Island for a night.*

Oh Beck, I'm going to be there every night. This is it. Our new beginning. You write back:

You: *Hmm. That actually sounds kind of nice.*

Chana: *Then do it. Invite him. Fuck Peach. You can pretend he hunted you down all romantic and shit.*

You: *Maybe. Imagine if I just text him the address and say come lol.*

And I check my phone for a text from you. Nothing. But it's official, you want me and it's official, I want you. I can't sit around here and wait. I have to man up and I do. First things first, I find Peach's family's address online through a combination of an old article in *Architectual Digest* and Google Maps. Now I call Mr. Mooney and ask if it's okay to go on a road trip and close up for a few days.

"Joe, you're the boss over there now. And you know how I feel about January. It's a waste. Take a vacation. You've earned it."

And I have.

All the while, you've been e-mailing with Chana and Lynn, who is also on Team Joe, naturally:

Lynn: *So why don't you run away with him instead of Peach?*

You: *Please don't hate on Peach. She's going through a rough time.*

Chana: *Her whole life is a rough time. Ugh. Next!*

Lynn: *You know everything in that part of Rhode Island is closed, Beck.*

You: *Guys, please. It's just a weekend. It's not a big deal.*

Chana: *Tell her thanks for inviting me and Lynn. Whatever.*

You: *Chana, she* did *invite you. She asked me to invite you.*

Lynn: *That's not the same thing as a personal invitation . . .*

You: *Guys, she's depressed. You know she has a stalker, right?*

Lynn: *LOLOLOLOLOL*

Chana: *How much is she paying him?*

Lynn: *LOLOLOLOLOL*

You: *Guys . . . she means well*

Chana: *Of course $he doe$.*

Lynn: *#welldonechana*

You: ☹

I love your friends for being on my side. It means a lot to me and one day at our wedding I'll thank them for it. I would like to say the same for Peach, but she's not on Team Joe. She's on Team Beck and she doesn't understand that Team Beck and Team Joe are the same team. You've also been yapping with her:

Peach: *Almost forgot, you will DIE over our library. Tons of first editions, Beck. Spalding was a friend of the family, we have tons signed, so much amazing stuff, real rare editions that you can't get anywhere. I mean I have a signed* To the Lighthouse. *Virginia Woolf, well, it's a long story better saved for this weekend over a bottle of Pinot.*

You: *You know who would love that? Ugh, of course you know who would love that.* ☹

Peach: *I know, sweetie. I also promise that getting out of the city will be the best distraction.*

You: ☹ *Yeah. I hope so.*

I toss your phone into the plastic Gap shopping bag. It's time to stop reading your e-mail and start getting ready to see you. I can't wait until you break down and write to me. And I know you will. You'll be all alone in your bedroom in the beach house thinking about how much better it would be with me. You'll text me and I'll get there and you'll let me in and we'll sneak upstairs and have beach house sex. I am calm now that I know our fate. All I have to do is get to Little Compton and await your call.

I lock the basement doors and turn off the lights and try to remember where I parked Mr. Mooney's car and wonder if I should take 95 the whole way. Murphy's Law exists for a reason, so the front door opens and a few latecomers shuffle inside.

I call out in my friendliest tone, "I hate to do this but we're closing!"

I know the sounds of this shop and I have a bad feeling. I know what it sounds like when someone locks the front door and I know what it sounds like when the OPEN sign flips to CLOSED. My machete is in the basement and I am upstairs and I hear them charging me, whoever they are. There are three of them, faceless dudes in Barack Obama masks, two big, one smaller. The smaller one wields a crowbar and there's no time to hide in the vestibule or the basement. When you can't win, you lose and they all come at me at once.

They attack.

I take it like a man and they pound me like I'm a motherfucker, like I literally fucked their mothers. My face is mashed in blood and saliva and it's possible that my right eye is no longer functioning. Finally, the attack ends and I am not a man right now, just a collection of pulsing wounds. I open the eye that still works. The smallest Obama swipes my new Gap hat off the counter and pumps his fist. And. *And.*

Holy fuck. I recognize those sneakers because I've asked Curtis to keep his dirty feet off the counter at least a hundred times. So this is him, his revenge. Curtis and the other Obamas scramble for the door and I remain on the ground, throbbing. I will not feel sorry for myself. I did have this coming. There are things I have done, bold things; I remember Benji's red badge of courage. Of course at some point, I would have to suffer. You *miss* me and I am about to have you, at last, and this is the turning point in my life, so of course there is a time for atonement. I bleed and I swell. My left eye flutters and I have atoned and the CLOSED sign is accurate; there is closure. Finally, I am free.

31

IT'S a long, cold drive to Little Compton. The heat in Mooney's Buick is still broken. My wool hat is gone so I'm wearing Benji's Figawi hat—or rather, the hat Benji stole from Spencer Hewitt—but it's canvas, not wool. At times like this, it would be nice to be rich, to have a *new* wool hat and a brand-new SUV and I wonder what I was thinking, leaving the key card to Benji's stolen goods in the locker. All that bounty is going to rot until some scavenger buys the locker on a reality show. My tendency is always to sink and this is why I need music, but I forgot my music because I have other things on my mind like the fact that I might be fucking blind in one eye over someone as commonplace as *Curtis*. I'd sooner have my left nut chopped off in honor of Exclamation Point Ethan.

I'm stuck with the radio and there's nothing but Taylor Swift on every fucking station. She's like a famous version of you, Beck (dates too much, falls too hard, fucks too fast, flees too hard), and I keep switching stations but apparently Taylor Swift owns a mansion not far from *LC* (nowhere is far from anywhere in a state this small), and she may as well be the queen and the mayor and the princess of Rhode Island because they play her on the rock stations (*Ya know, I'd like to see the Foo Fighters cover some of Miss Swift's early stuff, or maybe Arcade Fire!*), and they play it on the country stations (*Let's check out the latest single from Rhode Island's newest treasure, y'all know who that is, right?*), and they play it on the pop stations (*We're never too old to feel twenty-two, Rhode Island!*). Well, fuck you, Taylor Swift, because I never felt further away from twenty-two in my entire adult life and why haven't they invented a solvent to stop highways from freezing? I'm skidding all over the fucking place.

I stop for gas and check your Twitter. You just tweeted from Mystic, Connecticut. Because you're a girl, you included a photo of Mystic Pizza.

Limo ride to Mystic for Mystic Pizza on the way to Little C. for winter cottage retreat? #doneanddone #pepperoni #betterthansex #beachhouse

My associations with Mystic, Connecticut, have nothing to do with the fucking Julia Roberts movie. Mystic is a bad place for me. I went there once, with my fourth-grade class, on a field trip. At the time, I had a crush on a gruff, odd misfit named Maureen Grady, "Mo" for short. Most kids are assholes, just like most adults, so yes, a lot of people called her "Ho Mo." We were with our class touring the deck of a tall ship and it was boring, so Mo and I ditched the tour and broke into the off-limits hull.

In the dark, Mo told me she was going to steal my virginity. I tried to run and she pinned me down. I punched her, escaped, and told the teachers. Mo told a story too, and she was good at crying. Who do you think got sent to the fucking psychologist, to the dean's office, to the "counselor" with the fucking show-me-who-touched-you-where doll? Not Mo Grady! But I don't dwell on the past. Mo's the fuckup now (a twice-divorced paralegal with a profile on OkCupid and a Pomeranian named *Gosling*—obviously, she'll be alone forever). I prefer to live in the moment, which is why I erase all thoughts of Mo and log on to Benji's Twitter and tweet:

There's nothing sweeter than townie —y. *#WinterinNantucket*

You officially unfollow Benji. And you send him a direct message: *You are dead to me. Dead.*

I smile. I pat myself on the back because Benji's off in heaven now and I'm dealing with a busted defroster and wet, icy snow. Living is harder than dying, Beck, and I'd give anything to eat pizza with you. I wash my hands in the bathroom at the gas station and my face is hard to look at right now. Fucking Curtis and his goons marked me. There is a large, Halloween-ish gash on my forehead and another one on my cheek. I splash cold water and I go on, just like Celine Dion's heart did back in Bridgeport.

I make relatively good time to Little Compton considering the snow and my face. My vision is blurry and I try to watch the road with my left eye. The snow is still going when I reach the outskirts of town. I'm nervous. I don't do well in seaside havens with ice cream parlors and boat people and I have to slow down. These bald tires can't handle the snow and the Buick sounds like Sloth from *The Goonies*.

The road is stronger than the Buick and the shops are all closed and the lights are out for the season. It's as if the entire population of Little Compton is holed up in Tay-Tay's mansion. But the animals are still on the loose. And by the time I notice the deer that's bolting across the road and slam on the brakes, it's too late. The Buick moans and rams the deer and we are one now, flesh and steel, a tornado car wreck spiraling across the road, into the trees and through the trees. I lose time. I lose my equilibrium and close my eyes and the smell of burnt rubber and flesh overtakes me. Everything. And then.

Nothing.

WHEN I wake up, there is only silence. The pain, then branches in my lap, blocking my view. But, miracles abound in the Buick: I am alive. My Figawi hat is on my head. And my phone is intact. I was only out for twenty minutes.

"Wow," I say because it has to be said.

All I see are glass chips and bark and leaves. It's as if a tree ate the Buick and for a second, I fear there is no escape. I bleed into my warm clothes but that is nothing new. I am blessed, again, because nothing in this car is electronic. I can unlock the dented door and fight my way out of this gloriously analog American-made beast. I fall into the red snow. Deer blood. My blood. Yet I am alive.

I check my e-mail; you haven't tried me yet, but you will. I go to Google Maps and we really are destined, Beck. I am destined to be with you because my phone confirms that I am 234 feet due west of Peach Salinger's home at 43 Plover's Way.

But it's a hard climb back up to the street. Something bad happened to every part of my body when I hit that deer. I lift my right foot and my left leg hums. I shift my weight to my right foot but then my right rib cage bites. I fall into the snow and I just let the coolness into my clothing. "Patience, Joe," I say. "Patience."

I crawl forward a few feet and notice two signs, partially obscured.

One is a simple stop sign, universally understood. The other is prissier, on a white board:

HUCKIN'S NECK BEACH CLUB INC. NO TRESPASSING. MEMBERS ONLY. KEEP OFF ROCKS. NO JUMPING OR DIVING. NO LIFEGUARDS ON DUTY. SWIM AT OWN RISK.

Nature is on my side because these rules don't apply in winter. A tiny security booth adjacent to the sign is very clearly closed for winter.

"All right," I say and I go on, stronger than Celine Dion's heart.

Like a soldier easing out of a foxhole, I stay low to the ground. My arms are not as fucked up as my legs and my midsection. I am fully sweating with teeth chattering and my right eye is a useless blob but my left eye is unscathed, functioning. But I must be there and I recalculate the distance on my phone: I am 224 feet away.

"Are you kidding me?" I say out loud. "I've only gone *ten fucking feet*?"

My mouth is dry and I stuff it with snow. At this rate, I will get to you next summer. I close my eyes. I can do anything. I can do anything, and you *miss* me and the hardest part will be this walk and you could call at any moment, you could. I dig my hands into the snowy dirt and I get some traction. I have to do a cheater's push-up from my knees and I wince and I sting but I do it, Beck. I'm up. And I find a limp that works for me, a zombie sidestep, like I'm missing a conjoined twin. I check my phone and the blue dot is on top of the red dot.

I.

Am.

Here.

Three more steps and I've reached the driveway and wow. This

265

isn't a *cottage*, Beck. This is a mansion from a storybook about an evil seaside queen who takes all the township's money and builds an unnecessarily long driveway, ensconced in shrubbery and emptying like a river into a fuck-you-world four-car garage. The house is two stories, three if you count the widow's walk. The front yard is a clean sparkling carpet of new white snow and the lights flicker from inside while stars hover above, hoping to get inside. If Thomas Kinkade, Painter of Light crossed brushstrokes with Edward Hopper, it would look a lot like this.

And the quiet! I expected to hear the sea, but the ocean sleeps too, and I can hear snowflakes melting, branches tweaking. Am I always this loud? My breathing is too raspy and what if you can hear inside that *cottage*? I step backward, instinctively. I hear a drop of my blood *plop* into the weak new snow. I can't leave tracks; Peach will think her stalker is back and call in the National Guard. I don't want to scare you, so I head east to case the house next door. We're in luck, Beck. The neighbors don't share the Salinger family's passion for landscaping. This property is lush, overgrown with trees and the snow isn't a clean sheet for me to disturb. This is a quiet most people will die never knowing.

And then a shriek, Peach yells, "Beck!"

I duck. But I can tell by her screaming that you are heeding the call, running to the west wing of the *cottage*. This is my chance and I bolt to the east-facing wall and allow myself a look inside the great room. (That's what rich people call living rooms.) It's huge. A giant nautical-blue sectional winds like a fat, loving snake. The coffee table is repurposed lobster traps welded together and topped with glass. And it's aglow thanks to the flames crackling in the fireplace.

When I hear you laugh, I am, at last, sure that I'm not dead. Smoke sails out of the chimney and no wonder Taylor Swift bought a house here. I can hear the Elton John—Peach really *is* on vacation, replacing her morose, vaguely suicidal running ballad with the slightly cheekier, self-indulgence of "Goodbye Yellow Brick Road." Oh, and I can smell the marijuana. I crouch as you breeze into the room.

The seaside suits you and God do I miss you. You stand before the fireplace with your legs apart as if you're about to be patted down— you are lit as the fire, alive—in black leggings and that gray sweater you wore to work the day we had sex. When you bend slightly to warm your hands over the fire, I have an uncontrollable urge to jump through the window and enter you.

But Peach plods into the room and ruins the scene and offers you a glass of wine—typical—and you sip it and she goes back to the kitchen. I wouldn't be surprised if there's a roofie in there.

You *miss* me. And I miss you. It hurts, seeing you at that fire, giving your hands to the heat, the way I gave my hand to fire, only different. I imagine pushing you into the red abyss and jumping in after you, with you, so we can burn together, forever, a tree of life, light, sex.

And, of course, Peach plods into the room again and tells you dinner will be ready in an hour. She wants to play gin rummy—is she eighty-five years old?—and you obey your hostess and join her on the giant sectional sofa.

My hands are numb and yet aching and it's too cold to stay here; I'm not an animal, and what is my plan? I realized that I drove here with dreams, not plans. My dream: You text me. I pretend I'm in New York and wait three hours. Then I drive down Peach's driveway.

You run outside before I even have the car in park. You bounce—joy!—you offer me dinner—steaks and potatoes—and then we go at it all night in one of the unrenovated bedrooms.

I don't have a plan or a backup plan and I didn't think things through. You're a good friend, polite and loving. Of course you need your time with Peach. And I'm a serious mess, pained and bleeding. My car is in the trees and I'm not strong enough to walk back to town and break into a B and B. I crouch and make my way back to the neighboring property.

The front door is locked (go figure), and the world is lit by moonlight on snow (God bless), so I make it around back without falling and causing a ruckus. There is a boathouse—go figure—and the door is unlocked—God bless. I sneak inside and wrap myself up in a tarp. My wounds come back to life in the warmth, as if there are invisible dogs biting me, gnashing. I hurt. But rise. You *miss* me and that thought lifts me above my pain. I settle into the far left corner where the wind can't nip me with such force.

A cop shines a flashlight in my face. I see his gun and I don't need a mirror to know that I look like and smell like a zombie. The cop is jacked with a thundering baritone. "State your name."

I cough up blood before I get my last name out. The cop pockets his piece. Progress. I sit up. Progress. He's the most American man that America ever made, dark skinned in a white town with white snow. He scans my Figawi hat that he holds in his hands as if there's a barcode in the Mount Gay Rum logo. It must have fallen off while I was sleeping. He smiles. "You raced in Figawi, Spencer?"

"A couple of times," I answer and now I know why Stephen

King can't stop writing about New England. I'm bleeding. A deer is dead. I'm squatting. My car is steaming in the woods. And this motherfucker wants to talk about *sailing*.

He hands me my hat. "Are you a friend of the Salingers? I noticed some activity there. Did you get lost?"

I will die if he says the name Salinger again and I shake my head. "No. I'm lost."

"Where are you trying to go?"

The questions unnerve me and the stress intensifies my pain. Everything is wrong and my ribs twinge. I wince. The cop is concerned (yes) and he offers a hand (thank you, RIPD). I take it and I hold on. "Officer, in all honesty, I don't even know where I am. My GPS crapped out a while back. I got lost. I'm a wreck."

"So that *is* your Buick in the woods."

"Yeah," I say. Fuck.

"Spencer, did you have anything to drink tonight?"

I'm about to ask why he's calling me Spencer but I remember the name sewn into the hat: Spencer Hewitt. Relief. "No, sir."

"Did you have anything to smoke?"

"No," I say. "But you might want to ask the deer that rammed me out of nowhere."

He smiles and I wince. He radios the station about ER wait times and we have to get out of here now. You are close, mere footsteps away. For all I know, you're already awake, rubbing sleep out of your eyes, soothing paranoid Peach. What if she saw the cop car? What if the cop used his lights? What if he called for backup? What if you are out there right now giving a statement to the police? I vomit all over the tarp.

"Let it out, Spence." He has a comforting way. "We'll get you an ambulance soon."

But ambulances are bright and loud. I have to be strong for your sake and I manage to get up. "Not necessary, Officer."

"Fine," he says. "But I'm taking you to the hospital."

I'll go anywhere to get away from you and he helps me hobble outside and toward the car. The trees obscure the view of Peach's house, so even if you were standing at the great room window, you couldn't see me. Officer Nico—cool name—didn't leave his lights on—cool dude—and his cop car is a hybrid—only in *LC*—and we are driving, relief.

Nico is a good man, friendly, distracting me with tales of his football days at URI. He loves it out here. He's from Hartford and he comes to life regaling me with stories about nut jobs who come up this way hoping to get a look at Taylor Swift. "As if she's gonna go out with some stalker, right?"

"Right," I say.

"Try and get a little shut-eye," he says. "We got a bit of a drive."

I admit that it's nice to have someone take care of me, someone who wants me to get enough sleep. I can relax in here, the doors locked, the heat on, the partition solid. Soon, I am out, cold, dreaming of you in an old, billowy Dickensian dress, *you*.

CHARLTON Memorial Hospital is in Fall River, Massachusetts, only twenty miles away. But twenty miles may as well be twenty light-years because this place is depraved, loud and smelly, the anti-*LC*. When Nico opens the car door, a wall of cigarette smoke consumes me. A dozen degenerate junkies hang around trying to score Oxy. I'm tempted to ask Officer Nico why he didn't take me to the hospital where the summer people go, but what's the point? We're here. The guy ahead of us has a bloody knife protruding from his back pocket and he's trying to tell the nurse he had an accident with a car door. A fourth grader would know that he was lying, yet he begs, "Just one Oxy'll do, Sue."

But Sue is tough. "Get a coffee, go to a meeting, and fuck off."

I'm no junkie lowlife and Nico has pull so we're ushered into a room right away. It turns out Nico used to work in this town, but he left because it's been "chewed up, swallowed, and spit out" by heroin and Oxycodone. He shakes his head and I must be glaring at the desperados in the waiting room because Sue grins at me. "Whatsa matta, kid?" she sneers. "Too much glamma fah yah?"

She cackles and her accent is so thick that I feel bad for the words coming out of her mouth. Nico chuckles. "The kid's not from around here."

Sue doesn't laugh anymore. "No, shit, Sherlock. You got a license I can give to the gals up front?"

"No," I lie. "I got mugged."

"In the paahking lawt?"

"In Manhattan," I answer in my most Whit Stillmanesque voice.

Sue rolls her eyes and I'm relieved when the doctor pulls the curtain across, then back again. Exit Sue, and my physician extends a hand. "I'm Dr. Kazikarnaski," he says. "You can call me Dr. K."

I nod, bobbing my head like a guy who sailed in Figawi would do. "Excellent," I reply. "I'm Spencer."

Dr. K prods my wounds and asks me who did this to me.

"Well," I begin. "It's been a wild twenty-four hours. I got jumped in Manhattan. I was leaving Lincoln Center and walking and the next thing you know, bam."

I'd forgotten Nico was here and then he speaks. "Who was playing at Lincoln Center?"

I shrug. "We were just passing through," I say and I wince to remind everyone that I am the patient. "Anyhow, then, I left the city and hit that storm. I had an accident. A *deer*. And, well, here we are."

"That's one old Buick you got," says Nico. "What year is it?"

I wince and signal that I need a minute to recover. Fortunately, Nico and Dr. K fall into conversation about old cars, about the warm front moving in—*gonna be like Indian summa* according to Sue, who's in and out—and they do all this instead of asking what an uppity sailor like me is doing in an ancient brown beast. Dr. K tears off his gloves and tosses them in the trash. He says my ribs aren't cracked and my body wounds will heal. But my face is another story.

"Have you ever had stitches?" he wants to know.

I shake my head no.

A pregnant nurse with heavy eye makeup shuffles in with two coffees and two Danishes. I can't believe my good fortune. I'm starving.

"Helen, you didn't have to do that," says Officer Nico as he takes the loot.

"Please," she says. "I know you don't got someone at home cooking for you. A man your size needs to eat."

So do I but Nico chews and swallows my Danish and the doctor holds a syringe and tells me to close my eyes. "This will hurt," he says and when Jude Law said that to Natalie Portman in *Closer* he wasn't kidding, and you aren't here to hold my hand.

The shot in my forehead doesn't just hurt, it kills. Nico pats me on the back. "Breathe, Spence, you got this."

The doctor jabs me again, this time on my cheek. I am told to stay put and wait for the anesthetic to kick in. The pregnant nurse dillydallies, hot for Nico. "So, Nico, how you doing over in Snotty Town?"

"Good enough." He laughs. "You?"

"Better if I had a nice tall, strapping cup of hot chocolate to keep me warm at night, right, Nico?"

Nico is amused and the pregnant nurse shakes her ass as she leaves. "Say the word, hot stuff."

Suddenly, I like it here, the way people are so blunt about what they want—Oxy, Nico's dick, coffee—and I want to be a part of things, so I whisper to Nico, "You think they got any more Danishes hanging around?"

Instead of answering me, he pulls the curtain out, creating privacy. He takes out a notepad and I wish the medicine could numb my brain. I don't like that notepad or that pen and it begins. "I know you don't have your ID, but you wanna give me your address?"

I make something up and hope we're done but we're just getting started. Nico wants to know about me. He saw the car; he saw my *blood* on the street; that's how he found me and I pray the snow is melting. I pray that you and Peach stay inside. I don't want you to see my blood.

"And what you were looking for?" Nico asks. "Did you think those people were home?"

"I was so out of it, I don't know."

"You made a beeline for that house, Spencer. Why didn't you try the gas station up the street?"

"I didn't see it," I say and why is he attacking me?

"But did you really think somebody would be *home*?"

"I don't know." I don't want to do this. I want a Danish.

"Do you know anyone in LC, Spencer?"

"I didn't even know I was in LC," I say and it's time to up my game. I know how to work a cop; I'm gonna say what I said when I got pinned for stealing candy when I was a little punk. I swallow and my lower lip trembles. I can act. And I stammer, "L-look, I don't want to get into it, and it's got nothing to do with anything, but my mom died. She just died."

He pops his pen and closes his notepad. "Spencer, I'm sorry. I had no idea."

It's easy to cry because I miss you and I still don't know how to get back to you and you still haven't called me to tell me you miss *me*. Nico gets me a Danish and I swallow it. When the doctor comes back and sews me up, I don't feel a thing.

THIRTY minutes later, Nico and I are back in the lot and he wants to drive me to the train station. The scene out here has escalated. There's a full-on tailgating party for junkies talking about which emergency facilities are loose with their Oxy. A guy in a tattered North Face jacket tries to break into a Mazda with a crowbar. Nico bellows, "Hey, Teddy. A little respect!"

Teddy salutes Officer Nico and I accept my fate. "Are you sure you don't mind?"

"No," he says. "But wait. How are you gonna pay for the train?"

Good question, Officer. I pat my lower leg. "Emergency credit card stashed."

"That's good thinking, Spence. Always be prepared."

I bob my head. "Always."

Nico assures me that "Leroy" will tow my Buick and get her back up and running. "And he won't up-charge you, either."

"You're the best, Officer Nico," and I shake his hand, firm.

He drops me off at the train station, which is almost as bad as the hospital. He helps me out of his ride and the loitering junkies scatter like roaches. I go into the station and sit. When he's gone, I walk outside. I unzip my interior jacket pocket and pull out my wallet. I can't believe they all believed my bullshit about my wallet being stolen. But then, I take another look at the poor doomed souls. Of course they believed me; look what they're up against. I walk outside and hail a cab. "LC, please."

The driver huffs and sneers at my Figawi hat. "You mean *Little Compton?*"

New England: All of the Bitterness, Most of the Boating, None of the Bullshit.

32

I wake up in a different boathouse, a good half mile down the beach from Peach's home. Nico and Sue and the doctor were right about the warm front; we're in a new world now and that storm feels like it must have been a mirage, an aberration. It really *is* like summer. It's amazing how good fifty and sunny feels after you've been bleeding in *twelve* with a wind chill of *go fuck yourself*. And then, even more important, nobody found me this time. I think Mother Nature is atoning for my accident and I walk out of the boathouse and what a relief, to not be hit with icy wind. I hunker down in the tall grass in the dunes. You and Peach are just dots on the horizon. You're both stretching; you'll go running because you're a good houseguest. My phone is dead, which is a problem, because if you wrote to me in the middle of the night begging for me to come, I wouldn't even know. I watch you girls take off down the sand and I run through the dunes so I can duck just in case. When I get to Peach's house, the cut on my face is throbbing again (fucking Curtis) but the back door is open, as I hoped. You're not afraid here, which is good news for me.

Everything in the Salinger house is nice and everything in my family's home back in the day was scuzzy and this isn't even the house they live in. This is an extra! There is a whole *drawer* full of iPhone chargers and I plug in my phone. I make a cup of coffee in the Keurig and I promptly burn my tongue. I've tracked wet sludge all over the floor and ain't that the way? It's like the house knows I'm working class and wants me to pick up a fucking mop.

I use a dishrag because of course they don't have paper towels. (I'm sure they're saving the world.) I get down and scrub and I hate Peach. She's dominant and clingy; she was rude to disinvite Lynn and Chana. I unplug my phone—10 percent charged—but still no text from you. I pocket the charger and go upstairs and find that all six bedrooms are in mint, clean, guest-ready condition. Peach is a seriously pathological sicko and I'm nothing like Peach. I always give you space. Elton John hisses low everywhere because of the state of the art sound system and I can picture Peach pleading with him in a court of fandom. She begs to be his number one fan but Sir Elton slams the gavel and sends a collections officer to seize all his music from that prissy cunt and she has to go work as a greeter at Walmart.

But, I have to say, the bedding is fucking rock star. You slept in here last night and it smells like you and I pick up the leggings you tossed on the floor and take in your scent. My face has calmed down in the warmth, thank God, and I wrap your leggings around my neck, tight, and I'm hard for you and I cum easily with you wrapped around me, tight.

There are only seventy thousand Ralph Lauren towels up in this joint so surely the Salingers won't miss the one I use to clean up and my coffee is still hot and I kick back because it's comforting in here and I deserve this. I rummage around in your duffel bag and line up your panties and bras and I have lost myself in you and now I am in trouble.

You and Peach are back in the house, downstairs in the kitchen, kicking off your sneakers, laughing or crying, I can't tell. I can't go down the back stairs and flee because the floorboards creak under my feet. I hear your voice and I hate old houses. They're big-brother-watching and a guy can't move a muscle without being found out. I take four giant steps into the hallway—coffee still in hand—and tiptoe as softly as possible into the master bedroom that's almost directly above the kitchen. I crouch in the cedar closet just in case and once again I am closeted while you and Peach are free. I am sure that you are crying, not laughing, and I have to take a leak and there's no choice. I piss in the mug.

Peach must be hugging you because I hear her kicking the wall in the *mudroom,* an architectural staple of excessively wealthy white people; they think you need a space exclusively dedicated to taking off your fucking *boots*. She kicks and grunts and drones, "No matter what I do my boots get *so* grimy. It's like the winter *wants* me or something!"

She says she's trying to make you laugh but you don't think she's funny (does anyone?) and she's telling you to stop crying and you're sobbing and I'm trying to piss quietly in a coffee cup and Peach is not very good at soothing you, Beck. I would do better, could do better. And I want to know what's wrong. If you had reached out to me like you wanted to, I would be the one hugging you. Your crying is so loud that I feel safe leaving the closet and going to the door.

"Read it again," you demand.

Peach sighs and reads, "Dear friends of Benji."

"His poor mom," you whimper.

Peach continues, "It is with great sadness that we inform you that our son Benji is presumed dead."

You interrupt, "Shouldn't they be looking for him?"

Peach is annoyed. She reads over you. "His precious Beetle Cat, *Courage*, was found wrecked just off Brant Point. As some of you know, Benji has battled addiction for some time. He recently informed friends that he was on Nantucket."

"That fucking tweet," you say.

"I know," says Peach. "I hate drugs."

Thank God for technology because honestly, I'm starting to freak out. I go to the *Nantucket Inquirer and Mirror* website and, sure enough, there's an old picture of sober Benji in a suit alongside a picture of his destroyed boat. There are no witnesses who saw Benji on Nantucket, but his parents confirm that he withdrew money in New Haven and that this wouldn't be "the first time that our son fell prey to his demons." The harbormaster confirms the boat missing. And I confirm that I had nothing to do with this. Winter on Nantucket can be violent, apparently, and Benji's mother tells the *Mirror*: "At least he died doing what he loves." I don't know if she's talking about heroin or sailing. I've never felt so lucky in my life.

Peach blows her nose and you're still crying and she says the two of you should run away to Turks and Caicos and you laugh but she's serious. "You know I've done it before. Why can't we? We pack a bag. We're gone. Even better, we *don't* pack a bag. You would love it there, I swear."

"I have school," you say and there's a clink as she pours you a drink.

"Screw school," she says, a failed attempt at being sassy. I hear a zipper and she moans. "Omigod, is there anything better than getting out of sweaty Gore-Tex?"

"Ha," you say, and you are so halfhearted and I want to hug you.

I hear more kicking as the gruesome striptease continues and Peach testifies. "I swear, it's like my spandex are glued to my legs. I literally have to peel them off because they itch so bad I'm going to explode."

I might throw up and you are quiet.

"I hope it's cool that I'm changing right here," says Peach. "Sometimes I get *so* sick of going upstairs to do the littlest things. And ugh can it *be* any hotter?"

You say it's fine and I hear her pulling the spandex off her bony body. She walks out of the room and returns and you like what you see because you say, "Wow."

"My dad is obsessed with robes," she says and thank God you were referring to the robes. "The Ritz makes the best ones. We have a zillion in every house. You want?"

You want and you take and you opt to change in the bathroom. When you return, she gushes, "How good is it in that robe?"

"It's amazing," you say and you are not one of those girls who call everything *amazing*.

Peach announces that she is making kale smoothies and she would lock you up in here and throw away the key if she could and you don't even realize it, do you? The loud blender is my savior and like a ninja I fly down the hall, down the back stairwell (just for servants) that leads to the hallway between the kitchen and the great room. Fortunately, there are saloon-style doors that block this stairway, because who the hell wants to look at a servant, right? I can see it all from here. You girls are in matching giant robes and you flop onto the couch and put a glass of scotch and the smoothie on the lobster trap coffee table. She nudges your tiny foot with her big one. "Don't be sad."

"I shouldn't be sad," you say. "He treated me like shit."

"Oh, Beckalicious, it's not your fault. Boys can't help it. They're intimidated by girls like us."

"I don't think he was ever intimidated," you say and Peach sweeps her feet off the table and plants them on the floor. She rubs her hands together, generating some heat. "You, my sweet, need a massage."

You laugh but she's serious and she moves onto the floor and kneels and rubs your pretty little feet and you moan—you like it—and you tell her she is good at this and she smiles. She likes that you like it and she continues up your legs to your calves and I can't tell if she pulls your legs apart or if you pull your legs apart but I know that your legs are apart and she is working on your lower thighs and you relax your head, back, you exhale, *mmm*, and your arms flop to your sides and she is getting in there, up there, moving up your thighs. You are moaning, you are.

She sits up and somehow gets herself between your legs. She parts your bathrobe and your body is naked under there and your nipples are popped and she rubs your hips and you say no but she tells you to be quiet and you are quiet and she kisses your left breast and holds your other breast, firm, hard. You protest but she quiets you and you obey and she is kissing your neck and moving one of her hands down you and you aren't fighting her and you aren't doing anything, you are taking it and she is wrong.

You are tipsy—whatever she gave you hits you harder in the daylight, after running—and heartsick for me and shocked over Benji and she is supposed to be your friend. Just moments ago you were a wreck, sobbing, and what kind of a friend responds to a friend in obvious emotional distress by taking advantage of her and sucking on her earlobe? You have yet to touch her but your body is open to her and I don't even think you're in there right now, you're somewhere deep in your head, away and finally, you are back and your whole body flinches and your legs snap and Peach pulls back. You are on your feet, closing your robe. "I'm sorry."

"Forget it," Peach says and she drinks old kale smoothie right out of the pitcher. "I'm gonna have a shower."

"Peach, wait. We should talk."

"Beck, please," she gripes. "Did you ever think this is possibly why guys can't deal with you? I mean just let it *be*. We don't have to analyze every stupid thing."

She marches off with her kale smoothie and I can tell you feel responsible and this is not right. You call out to her and she responds by raising the volume on the Elton John. I hear a door slam. You cry and how dare she lay this all on you? You pass into the kitchen—fortunately, you don't choose the path by the servant staircase—and you return with your phone. I am shaking. This is it. Here you come. Call me, Beck. Call me. But you dial a number and my phone doesn't vibrate.

"Chana, I know you're pissed at me but I need your help. Benji's dead and Peach is upstairs crying and I never should have come and I don't know what to do. Please call me."

You go upstairs and pound on the door and beg her to come out and say you're sorry until your voice is raspy. She ignores you and she is vile. She has you trapped and you don't even know it. I push through the saloon-style doors and leave.

33

IT'S a shame that this beach is wasted on people like Peach. All these waterfront mansions are empty, even though it's unseasonably, gloriously warm. (Knock on wood.) The beach couldn't be more pristine, yet none of these fucking second-home owners drive to *LC* to pay their respects. What idiots. I, on the other hand, am a grateful beachcomber.

Yesterday, I followed the tracks you and Peach left all the way down to the jetty that reaches into the bay. This is a great place to hide, to wait. There are scattered boulders—KEEP OFF ROCKS—and there's a weathered wooden walkway that ends in the sand. I dug out a foxhole beneath the walkway and I think it is warmer here than it was in either of the damn boathouses. Although, it's impossible to compare, given how cold it was the night of my accident.

In any case, the sun is coming up and it won't be long now. Soon, Peach will be here, alone.

Candace would love it here. The last time I saw the sun rise on a beach, I was with her. This is no time to be thinking of Candace, but how can I not? We saw the sun rise on Brighton Beach and as it got brighter, she tried harder and harder to break up with me. I asked her to walk down to the water with me. She did. She was cruel in that way; a nicer girl would have said no, and left me to cry on my own, but she wanted to see me at my worst so she stuck around.

"I *am* leaving you," she said.

Then go, bitch. Go.

It wasn't my fault that Candace followed me down to the water's edge and it wasn't my fault that I picked her up and held her down in the water and watched her pass on to the great beyond. She wanted to be there, or she wouldn't have gone down there with me. She knew she was killing me and she knew that I was not the type to go down without a fight.

I don't blame Peach for being so miserable, the same way I don't blame Candace for wanting to escape her family. What a shame to be so angered by what you *don't* have that you treat what you *do* have like it's nothing. She's not grateful to have an extra home in a place where the biggest danger is Taylor Fucking Swift. She's a lot like Candace, who wasn't grateful for her voice, her talent.

I have a little time so I walk a few feet down to the shore. I like the way the water comes and erases my steps. I think of that fucking poem from middle school where the dude walking on the beach isn't alone because Jesus is carrying him on his shoulders and I smile. For years, I thought it was the other way around, that the guy in the poem was carrying Jesus, you know, the way a Hare Krishna carries his tambourine, the way a Jewish boy carries a Torah at his bar mitzvah. I didn't think of Jesus Christ as being this guy giving piggyback rides to fuckups and I don't even leave one set of footprints, so take that, middle school poem. I admit, I *am* kind of grumpy. The last food I ate was that Danish. I cross over the walkway built by some family with something against walking on white sand and return to my foxhole and wait.

At last, I see Peach emerge on the patio, a hot red speck in the distance. She stretches and she trots down the walkway and here we go. With each passing second, I can hear her more clearly, her breathing, her feet pounding, and the Elton John blasting from her phone. She passes me, swoosh, and I leap out of my foxhole like a jack in the box and run after her. She doesn't hear me. She is fearless on this beach. I grab her by the ponytail. Before she can even scream, I ram her into the sand and straddle her back. She struggles, kicking, but her mouth is in the sand and Elton won't stop singing—*sitting like a princess perched in her electric chair*—and I pick up the rock in my pocket.

She squirms her head to the side and her eyes are more beautiful than I realized and she recognizes me and she spits, *"You."*

She might be the strongest woman I have ever known and though her last words are spoken, she's still struggling, gurgling. Her skin flares, *Nantucket red*, and all the exercise instilled her with a superhuman strength, a lung capacity that boggles my mind. I don't blame her for fighting. Because she was raised by bigoted, hateful monsters, she never celebrated her life and I think this is why she musters the strength—those legs still quiver!—to maximize her last moments on earth. Her fingertips reach for my arm; it's too late, Peach. Her eyeballs sail north, toward the top of her head, and we can all learn something from an untimely tragic death. What a danger, blaming other people for your problems. What a waste of a life. Had she disowned her cunty family and moved to one of her sunny foreign havens and been a bartender or a Pilates instructor, anything, doesn't matter, she could have settled down with a nice, like-minded girl and paid respects for all her blessings—health, brains, muscles—by being true to herself. Nonetheless, fuck her parents. Don't make a baby if you're not capable of unconditional love.

She is fading and Elton is louder than the waves *and I don't hear you anymore, we've all gone crazy lately, my friends out there rolling 'round the basement floor* and I owe her a little help. I hit her head with the rock and she is quiet, at last. I flip her over and I'm shaking. She is gone, at peace, but what about me? Elton sings *you almost had your hooks in me, didn't you dear, you nearly had me roped and tied* and I feel roped and tied out here, alone with dead, heavy Peach. Elton seems louder or is that just because Peach is quieter? I try to focus on moving her but then I hear *a slip noose in my darkest dreams* and I pause. I panic. What if you decide to go for a run? What if Officer Nico runs on this beach? I have to move fast. I load her pockets with rocks just in case she doesn't disappear. I have to collect more rocks because this jacket has a lot of pockets and Elton *would have walked head on into the deep end of the river.*

I need to calm down. I close my eyes and see Candace's open eyes in the mucky dreck of Brighton Beach and I open my eyes and I take Peach's phone out of the contraption band on her arm. It's my phone now and I cut off Elton as he swears *they're coming in the morning with a truck to take me home.* No they're not and I lift her body. Peach is so clothed and Candace was nearly naked, only wearing a little black dress over a bikini. It was summer, drunk girls drown, it happens, her family accepts that she is never coming home—and I walk toward the water. It is winter. Sad girls walk into the water to die. It happens.

I do not *keep off rocks* anymore and I carry Peach Salinger onto the jetty. The rocks are smooth and dry and I am steady. Peach is heavy because of the rocks in her pockets, because of the weight of her misery. I count to three and then I drop her into the ocean. The waves welcome her the way the water at Brighton Beach embraced Candace. I start an e-mail from Peach to you. It's so easy to know what to say:

> *Beck, I need to go away. Lately, when I run, it's like*
> *Virginia Woolf is running with me. She said, "I thought how*
> *unpleasant it is to be locked out; and I thought how it is worse,*
> *perhaps, to be locked in." She was right. It's worse to be locked*
> *in waiting for someone who isn't coming. Much worse.*
> *Enjoy the cottage. I love you, Beckalicious.*
> *Bye,*
> *Peach Is*

My body is slick with sweat and my muscles ache from the exertion and I crack a smile because I understand what Peach was talking about earlier. I'd love to peel off my clothes right now. They *do* itch.

I check on you once before leaving. It's less than an hour since I sent you the e-mail from Peach and you appear to be handling it all with aplomb. You're blasting your Bowie and trying on Peach's clothes in the great room while you dance and call Lynn and Chana and your mother and pig out. You are happy, Beck. You tell Lynn what you told your mother and what you told Chana: "This isn't my fault. Peach ran away every other month in college. Hell, who wouldn't with that kind of money? Also, I think it's for the best. She seemed almost *happy* that Benji was dead. And yes, I know how sick that sounds."

"Forget Benji," Lynn says. "It's sad, but being dead doesn't make him into a good guy. Have you talked to Joe?" *Go Lynn!*

"No," you say. "But I want to."

That is all I need. I leave.

I walk up the deserted street into town. Nico's guys at the body shop are super friendly. There's not a lot going on (no shit) and they love the *summa weathah sahprize* so my brown beast is already good to go. The repairs cost four hundred bucks, and I'm glad I came prepared. New England is not a lucky place for me, Beck, so I took an advance on my salary before I headed out. The roads are clear and Peach's phone has a lot of good music. Maybe my luck in New England is changing.

I'M almost home when I remember the mug of my DNA in the *cottage*. I hit the brakes, hard. But I don't have to worry. People with second homes get off on giving out keys to maids, carpenters, and interior designers. I'm not gonna worry about a mug of dried-up piss, not after all the good I just did.

Besides, this is about you, and your Twitter confirms that you're already on the way back to Bank Street. I know it will take time for you to open slowly *petal by petal, as spring opens.* But you will open. Peach can't drag you down anymore. You're free. She was never going to loosen her grip on you and you're gonna be a whole new person without that pressure. She can rest now. You can relax. And when that first whiff of spring hits the air you will pass a bookstore or a horse-drawn carriage and find yourself blushing, ripe with want. And you'll reach out to me, *Joe.*

34

MY phone is not broken. I have called it from the shop several times a day for the past few days. You're not off the grid. You are here in New York, living, writing, and tweeting:

Is there anything more romantic than new snow at night? #stillness #love

There is no logical or technological or *romantic* reason for the fact that you have not called me or e-mailed me since returning from LC. It's been *twenty-three minutes and thirteen days* since Peach left the picture. The wound on my face is stubborn but there is progress and I'm less of a monster every day. And that's just another reminder that precious time is passing. I can't figure you out, Beck. You're not e-mailing with any new guys and you're not e-mailing your friends about anything *romantic* but you're writing *about* guys. The last story you wrote was about a girl (you, duh, they're always you) who goes to the doctor and learns that she has a penis stuck inside of her. She calls every guy she's ever been with to see if he's still got his penis. The list of dudes is gross long (an exaggeration, it has to be) and they all still have dicks. Finally, she admits there's one dude she didn't call because he's married with children. She doesn't want to give him his dick; she wants him to leave his wife and come and get it. As Blythe said in her e-mail critique, "There's no real ending, no climax, no point. I'm not presuming that this is based on something real in your life, but if so, maybe think of putting this story in a drawer and revisiting it once you've got some distance from your emotions."

And naturally, I am concerned. You've been seeing this Dr. Nicky *twice* a week since you got back. And then you write this thinly veiled story about fucking a married guy. Of course I called to schedule an appointment with him. How else can I make sure that he's not taking advantage of you? And it's not like I'm the only one concerned.

Chana: *You just went to therapy. WTF? How do you even afford this?*

You: *New priorities. No boozing, no shopping, just writing, journaling, growing.*

Chana: *Okay, Beck. But remember Dr. Nicky is . . . Dr. Nicky.*

But today is a good day because the elevator has just hit the twelfth floor and I step into the hallway and find the door to the waiting room open, as Dr. Nicky said it would be. I'm a little early for my appointment, which is good, because I have time to review my new identity.

Name: Dan Fox (son of Paula Fox and Dan Brown!)

Occupation: Coffee shop manager

Disorder: OCD. I know a shit ton about OCD from reading.

I feel good already and I like this waiting room, the baby-blue walls and this baby-blue sofa. And the building happens to be in my favorite neighborhood, the Upper West Side. Elliot saw a shrink in *Hannah* and who knows? Maybe there's nothing going on between you and Dr. Nicky. Maybe he's just really good at what he does. It's possible. In just two weeks, you've figured out a lot about yourself.

I know because Nicky gives you homework. You have to write a letter to yourself every day. And you do:

Dear Beck, You only know how to push or pull when it comes to guys. Admit it. Own it. Fix it. Love, Beck

Dear Beck, You reel in men and you lose interest when you have them. You don't wear a bra so that guys will look at your nipples. Wear a bra. Nicky sees what you're doing. This is good. Be seen. Love, Beck

Dear Beck, Intimacy terrifies you. Why are you so afraid? You can only get off when you're role-playing. Why can't you be yourself? Nicky knows you and accepts you. So will others. Love, Beck

Dear Beck, You think you can't have love until you've outgrown your daddy issues. But maybe you won't outgrow your daddy issues until you let yourself fall in love. Nicky is right. You grow through love. You don't postpone love until you stop growing. Love, Beck

Dear Beck, It's not your fault that you were born on an island. Of course you identify as an island. But, dear girl, you're not an island. Be populated. Be welcoming of love. Love, Beck.

Dear Beck, It's okay to resent your mom. She does envy you.
Love, Beck

Dear Beck, Don't be your own worst enemy and chase after
guys who don't want you. Be your own best friend and learn
how to love guys that do want you. And remember, nobody is
perfect. Love, Beck

These e-mails have really helped me get through this dry spell.
Now I know that you didn't bail on me because of the sex. You bailed
on me because you have problems. So maybe in a month or so, when
I'm knee-deep in therapy, and I've written letters to myself, maybe
I'll be in bed with you on a late Sunday morning. Maybe by then, I'll
understand myself better and we'll share our therapy letters in bed.

The door to the office swings open and the air smells of cucumbers
and Dr. Nicky is not what I expected.

"Dan Fox?" he says.

I manage to say hello and shake his hand. I follow him into the
brutally beige office and sit down on the couch but holy shit, Beck.
Dr. Nicky Angevine is young. I assumed he'd be in his fifties but he's
for sure in his early forties. The walls are covered with framed classic
rock albums—the Rolling Stones and Bread, Led Zeppelin and
Van Morrison. He futzes around with his computer and apologizes
for needing another minute and I say it's okay. He's wearing Vans,
clinging to his youth. He's a picture of restraint with his thick, wavy
hair gelled into submission and encroaching blue eyes that look
chock-full of tears. I can't tell if he's Jewish or Italian and he finishes
up with his computer and sits in the leather chair. He picks up a glass
pitcher of water. There are cucumbers in the water, thus the smell.

"Can I offer you a drink?" he says and once again, this is not what I expected.

"Sure," I say and I take the water and holy shit, Beck. This shit is heaven.

"I should let you know right off the bat," he says. "I keep a notebook but I don't take a lot of notes. I prefer to keep everything up here."

He points to his head and grins and he could be a serial killer or the nicest guy in the world, but there is no middle ground for this dude. No wonder he went into psychology. He had to find some way to stop himself from acting on twisted, perverse thoughts of his own. When he smiles, his chemically whitened teeth pop out, entirely out of place on his drawn, sad face.

"Well, Dan Fox," he says. "Let's figure out what the fuck is wrong with you, shall we?"

I have to say, he's really easy to talk to. I expected a doctor's office, but this is like hanging out in a middle-aged dude's college dorm room. And if we were in college, he'd leave and go to class and then I could hack into his computer and dig up all the files about you. But that's not happening; we're adults and he has a job to do. He wants to know who beat me up and I tell him about the accident on my way to a ski trip (the LC crash) and I tell him about getting mugged after closing up the coffee shop (Curtis and his homeboys). And then he starts to get a little more personal and asks, "Do you have a girlfriend, Dan?"

"Yeah." I could easily have one so it's fine. I tell him I'm not here because of my girlfriend; she's terrific. I tell him I want help with my OCD.

"What's your obsession?" he says.

I know all about mirroring, Beck. One of the best ways to get someone to trust you is to focus on what you have in common. "It's actually kind of funny," I say. "All the albums you got here. I don't know how or why, but I've become psychotically obsessed with this random video by the Honeydrippers."

"I love the Honeydrippers," he says. "Tell me it's not 'Sea of Love.'"

"You know it," I say and he's my new best friend. And I'm good at this, I think. I tell him I can't stop watching the video (you) and thinking about the video (you) and wishing I could go live inside of the video (you). I tell him I've lost interest in everything because of this video (you) and I need to get some control.

"Is your lady friend losing patience with you?"

"No," I say, because if I had a lady friend, she would be too happy to be with me to lose patience. "I'm the one losing patience, Doc."

"Doctor nothing, kid." And he shakes his head no. "I'm not a doctor. I just have a master's."

I want to ask him why you call him Dr. Nicky if he's not an actual doctor but I can't do that and he says it's only fair that he tell me a bit about his own life. "What you see is what you get, Danny. I'm a forty-five-year-old pothead slash failed bass player with a master's in psych," he tells me. "I love rock 'n' roll and I got into this field originally because I'm a natural bullshit artist. But then I realized I actually like helping people, so here we are today."

"That's cool, Nicky." And the first time I say his name it sounds funny coming out of my mouth, a new word in my vocabulary. *Nicky*.

I tell him it sounds good and we talk about growing up—he's from Queens and I'm from Bed-Stuy. It turns out therapy is just talking and maybe you really are just trying to *grow*. Maybe someday

I'll even *be* a shrink. I could do this. I could frame my favorite books on a wall in a beige room and talk to people like me, like you.

Nicky says it's time to wrap things up and make a plan. Is it lame that I'm excited for homework?

"Danny, we're gonna do a lot of work in here. For starters, you're gonna learn that you live in a house."

I have never lived in a house, only apartments. But I nod.

"And there's a mouse in your house," he says. "The video. And the good news is that it's just a mouse."

And now you're a mouse, Beck.

"It's not strong like you, Danny." He's very serious now. "That mouse is tiny. You've got arms, hands. You have dexterity."

You only have a pussy and I agree with him.

"You can reach the doorknob, Dan. You can lay down traps."

Traps.

"You know, Danny, life's a bitch and sometimes it gets dark in your house."

He points to his head and I nod. It does get pretty dark in here.

"And that's when the mice come."

You came into my store and started this thing, us.

"Sometimes it gets so dark that all you can do is listen to that fucking mouse scramble around and eat your food and shit on your floor and it's so dark that you can't see the doorknob," he goes on. "You forget there *is* a doorknob and what we do in here is we turn on the lights, Danny."

"Right."

"We set the traps, Danny."

"Right," I say, louder than before.

"And we open the door and we get the broom and we shoo

that mouse out of there," he says and he punches the air. "And sometimes, we don't even need to do that because sometimes, we kill that mouse."

Not this time.

"And it doesn't happen in a heartbeat. I'm not gonna lie, Danny. But it's doable."

"You ever work in construction?" I ask. Most guys in our neighborhood did, at some point, and I like the idea of Nicky and I having stuff in common, being equals.

"Couple of summers back in the day," he answers, and I was right. "You?"

"Couple of summers back in the day," I say, too eager. What a loser and a copycat but Nicky smiles and I think of the past few weeks and the nights I spend on the floor against the wall with your panties in my hands, staring at the hole in the wall that I made because of you and covered because of you. "Yeah, Doctor . . ."

He shakes his head and I laugh. "I mean, Nicky. I need to find the doorknob."

"You're gonna find it. And if the house/mouse concept doesn't work for you, you can also think of the video as a zit. You can pop it and it's gone. Forever, no scars, if you take care of your skin."

You are not a zit, you are a mouse, and I speak. "I thought you weren't supposed to pop zits."

"That's bullshit," he says and he looks at the clock. "So. Do you like Thursdays?"

AFTERWARD, when I walk down the street, I feel like a changed person, Beck. Fifty minutes with Nicky and it's like I have a new set of eyes. The world looks different to me, like I put on 3-D glasses or smoked a joint or fucked the shit out of you. I feel high but straight and I head for the park where I watch the "Sea of Love" video for the first time in a long time. The girl in the video is kind of cute with the Bowie blond hair and therapy is working out already. I mean, watching this offbeat, trippy video makes me happy and I haven't been happy in a while. And the best part is, that I'm not afraid anymore. You're not sleeping with Nicky. You're just experiencing transference. I know about it from *The Prince of Tides*. It happens. Nicky has a master's and Nicky is the man and he'd never break the doctor-patient dynamic. It applies, even though he's not a real doctor.

I walk to the subway and then walk down the stairs. I like life, Beck. I feel all this new patience. I can wait for you to call me. I am strong enough to give you time. I forgot to check your e-mail and your phone is heavier than it was this morning. I write to myself even though he didn't tell me to:

> *Dear Joe, You have a mouse in your house and when she's ready, you will kiss her and she will turn into the girl of your dreams. Be patient. Be open. Best, Dan Fox*

I haven't felt this close to you in two weeks. I love therapy, I do.

35

AT my next session, I told Nicky about how I feel high when I leave his beige office. He said my reaction is common—I'm normal!—and it's all about a new perspective.

"I have a place upstate," he said. "I get out there into the woods every couple of weeks. Not because of the fresh air, but because of the fresh perspective."

In my third session, we talk all about the video (you) and Nicky tells me about what he calls the cat strategy. "I used to have this neighbor who rented her cat out. You know why?"

"To help depressed people?" I ask. Wrong.

"If anyone in the neighborhood had a mouse problem, Mrs. Robinson would lend her cat for a day or two," he says. "And, Danny, the thing about mice, if they so much as smell a cat, they're out of there."

"So if I started watching something else, I'd stop watching the video."

He nods. We don't talk. Sometimes that happens in here, an abrupt silence. Nicky says it's normal; you have to process things. I *process* the idea of a life without you. I'd date other girls (unimaginable) and go on walks and maybe I'd find people to play basketball with or sit in a dark bar watching the news and fall asleep in my bed without your phone in my hand and wake up without our phone pressing into my flesh. My hands hurt from obsessively checking your e-mail; maybe it would be nice to have fingers that don't sting. I don't know what it would be like to be here without you inside of me, Beck. I do know that you are a lot to handle. I am tired.

Nicky can sense when I'm done processing. He readjusts in his chair. "Give it a shot this week," he says. "Journal on it and let me know how it goes."

I like having homework and I leave his office and find that the world is full of women. So maybe I *do* want to find out about life without you. I'd almost forgotten about girls. They're everywhere, Beck, on the subway platform there are college girls in tight jeans with their heads buried in Kindles and round old chicks hanging on to reusable bags of vegetables and middle-aged housewives heaving with raggedy bags from Macy's and Forever 21, and there's a hot blond chick who's so little she makes you seem like a jolly green giant and she's in scrubs and she looks freshly scrubbed and I'm totally fucking staring and she smiles. Game on.

"Do I know you?" she says and she has a little bit of an accent, Long Island City, I think.

"No," I say and she walks toward me, not away from me and she smells like ham sandwiches and rubbing alcohol. I like her tits.

"You don't know me at all?"

"Sorry, no."

"Then why the fuck are you staring at me?"

"I don't know," I say and I wonder what Nicky would say. "I guess I must just like staring at you."

The train screeches to a stop and her electric green beady little eyes home in on me and random women go onto the subway as random women get off and the two of us lock eyes like animals in heat. She has thin eyebrows and long painted fingernails, nothing like yours, which is good. I could never love this girl. But I sure can practice on her.

She starts, "Who kicked your ass?"

"I had an accident."

"You had an accident," she sneers. "That's a good one."

"I got jumped."

"So you just fucking lie about it before you even know my name?"

"I guess I just felt like lying." And I am good at this and Nicky would be impressed.

"Well, what if I don't go out with liars?"

"Then it sucks to be you."

"What the fuck is happening right now?"

"You know, who cares?" I say and I am on like Donkey Kong. "If this conversation were happening in a dark bar and we were both shitfaced it would be perfectly normal."

Her name is Karen Minty and she bites her glossy lip and gets in my face. "And if your grandmother had balls she'd be your grandfather."

Karen Minty decides right there that she's going to have sex with me and I know it. She is so much easier to read than you are and I couldn't ask for a better cat and it starts with an obligatory drink at some fuckface bar packed with NYU kids who drink American beer out of buckets. You'd hate it here but she loves this place. This bar was her choice so now it's my choice and I take her to a hole on Houston that I know will impress her—I was right, she *is* from Long Island City—and she *is* impressed by Botanica Bar and she drinks Greyhounds and says shit you would never say like:

"Do you know how I know about this drink? Leonardo DiCaprio drinks these. It's true."

"Do you know why food in hospitals sucks my ass? Because they *do* want you to die. It's true, Joey. It's true. It's fucking cheaper and not as many people have to work doubles if you got more empty beds."

"Do you know that I had this feeling like I was gonna meet someone tonight? I shouldn't be fucking saying this, fucking Greyhounds, but, Joe, I had this fucking feeling. And then you were staring at me." She burps. "That needs to come off, Joe."

"My shirt?"

"That bandage on your hand."

I forgot it was there. Look what you did to me. It started when I burnt my hand in the candle. Then the healing was interrupted because I picked at the scab because of what you did to me. Then Curtis beat me up while I was rushing to get ready to go see *you*. And then of course I crashed my car while I was looking for *you*. I see a pattern here and Nicky says life is all about patterns and now Karen Minty grabs my hand like it belongs to her. Karen Minty is fucking *strong*, and she whispers in my ear, "Save your energy, Joey. You're gonna need it."

She yanks the bandage off my hand and before I can wince, she kisses me. As it turns out, Karen Minty's lips are strong too. My hand doesn't hurt anymore.

By the time we get on a train I don't think either of us knows which way the train is going. It's a miracle that the train is empty, not even the random bum or gangster or ho. It's a miracle that Karen Minty licks the place on my face where Curtis fucked me up and her tongue is sharper than yours and I fucking tear off her scrubs—she's wearing a thong—and she grabs at me and we go at it on the fucking subway at four in the morning and when Karen Minty cums, she screams—*yeah Joe yeah I'm yours cum now NOW*—and she digs her claws into my back and her eyes roll around in her head and when she finishes, her legs are still wrapped around me, vibrating. I hold on to her tight, wishing she were you. She sticks that pointy tongue down my throat and she takes it back and she looks at me.

"I love you," she says and what have I done and she bursts out laughing and hops off of me and wraps herself in my coat. "Your face, Joey, omigod. You should see your fucking face right now, I'm just fucking with you."

"I know," I say. And I will not worry; most girls go fucking insane for a few minutes after they fuck. That's just the way it is.

She is defensive. "Obviously, I don't even know you."

"I know," I say and she curls into me, not away from me and I look at us in the window. We come and go as the lights flicker in the tunnel and I will sleep tonight for the first time in a long time and Karen Minty will make me an egg sandwich and give me a blow job in the morning. I can just tell, something about those Greyhounds, something about that mouth. She does love me.

I am the best patient ever because already, I have found a stray cat.

THE next day, I get to the shop and I'm hungover as all fuck and full of an egg sandwich that was a bad idea. Karen Minty meant well, but Karen Minty was probably still too drunk to cook. I told her it was a nice time. She told me she'd come by the shop. I didn't encourage her, Beck. And now I have Ethan up my ass—he's early, again—and he wants to know if I'm sick.

"Do you have a cold, Joe? Or did you just have too much sauce?"

Only Ethan calls it *sauce* and I unlock the door and if I were a therapist like Nicky I wouldn't have to deal with Ethan. I send him to Fiction to find staff picks and I turn on the music. Karma is a bitch. The first song that comes on is "You Are Too Beautiful" from *Hannah and Her Sisters*. I slam it off. Suddenly it hits me. I cheated on you, I cheated on us.

My head pounds. The doorbell chimes and every noise hurts, especially the one that comes now, the girl I just banged, Karen Fucking Minty. I want to slit my wrists.

But at the same time, I'm dying for coffee and she's holding two hot cups—Starbucks, surprising—and she shrugs. "I didn't know how you guys take 'em so I just got fucking everything."

She plants a heavy paper bag on the counter. Ethan comes bounding to the front of the shop and she is scary friendly to him right off the bat. "You must be Ethan, right? Joe told me all about you."

How drunk was I last night? Ethan can't contain his joy at the idea of me telling some chick about him and he practically drools all over

Karen Minty. She wastes no time making herself at home and she looks at me. "So, how *do* you take coffee, Joe?"

I tell her I'm fine and she rolls her eyes and winks at me and calls, "Hey, Ethan?"

He trips over himself running back. Only Ethan. And he tells her that I'm black, two sugars and he's "Cream and Stevia. Or Truvía. Or Splenda. And if they don't have any of that the real sugar in the brown packets. But never Equal!"

All the while, Karen is looking deep into my eyes and she thinks she's gonna bring me coffee for the rest of her life. I love you, not her and oh fuck she's one of those girls. She smiles at me hard and winks. "Thanks, Ethan."

And there's no way around it. I didn't just pet this cat. I adopted it.

36

BEING with Karen is shockingly effective, at least in the sense that you're farther and farther away from me. I try to see the good in it: I get to practice being a boyfriend, and that's good for us. But I do feel bad when I'm caressing her ass in bed and folding her thongs at the Laundromat and sending her mother a handwritten thank-you note after Sunday dinner. It's wrong of me to betray you. But, know this, Beck: Every day I find a way to visit the pictures of you in my phone. I'm faithful. Seven weeks into life with Karen Minty and eleven weeks into therapy and Nicky thinks I'm making good progress. I'm not as depressed anymore. I read your e-mail and I know you're still doing your thing—no booze, no shopping—and now that I'm seeing Dr. Nicky, I totally get why he makes you want to focus.

"You look so much happier than you were the day you started in here, Danny."

"Thanks," I say. "I feel happier."

"And things are good with Karen?"

"Things are great with Karen," I say and they are, technically. Nicky laughed when I first told him about her. He said a girl is *a much more effective* cat than another YouTube video. He's right.

"I know that look, Danny." He grins. "After I met my wife, I don't think I stopped smiling for two years."

I blurt, "Oh, we're not gonna get married, Nicky."

He gets that know-it-all look and I go further. "I just mean, she's not it for me."

He pushes. "Now you don't look so happy. Are you afraid to get married?"

"Not at all." And it's true. I'd marry you in a heartbeat.

"So what's wrong with Karen, Danny?"

She's not you. "She's just . . . nothing."

"She's nothing," he says and he raises his eyebrows. "Ouch."

I groan. "I meant that nothing is wrong with her."

"Regardless," he says and that's how I know our time is up. "I got some homework for you. I want a list of ten things you like about Karen. The cat helps the mouse stay away. And remember. Thinking about the cat is better than thinking about the mouse."

"Okay, Doc," I say and the "Doc" thing is our running joke, you know, because he's not a doctor. I try to do my homework on the ride home, but I just keep thinking about you.

I'm still trying a few days later as I sit on the couch watching Karen Minty's favorite show, *The King of Queens*. She laughs at a joke that wouldn't make you smile and I love you because you don't laugh easily. She picks her thong out of her ass and I love you for your healthy cotton panties.

She moans. "I fucking love Kevin James."

"He's good," I lie. I love you because you don't love Kevin James and if you laughed at one of his jokes, you still wouldn't love him.

A Burger King commercial comes on—Karen Minty fucking loves commercials—and she flips the bird at the TV. "Bite me, BK. BK fries suck, right, Joe?"

I play along and laugh but I love you because we could be married a hundred years and you'd never ask me what I think about BK fries because you'd never say *BK* and if you were talking about French fries, there would be more to it than fries. They would have significance. There would be a story there. You're an onion and Karen's a Maraschino cherry and I love you because onions are more complicated than cherries. I'm doomed.

I almost forgot that Karen Minty's head is on my lap and she peers up at me. "Babe, you all right?"

"Yeah." And I run my hand through her hair the way she likes. "I'm just thinking about my homework."

Karen doesn't approve. "I swear, Joe, I think that shit's a waste of money."

"I know you do."

"At the hospital, all the fuckups are shrinks. Every one of them, they're fucking cheaters and liars and they're crazier than their patients."

"Nicky's not like that," I say.

She huffs. "Like fuck he's not. They're cheaters and liars, Joe, cheaters and liars."

You never repeat yourself because you're creative and Karen is not and she pinches my nipple. "Joe, look at me."

I look at her. "Watch it, miss."

"What do you talk about in there anyway? I mean you're perfect, Joey."

"Nobody's perfect." I sound like a teacher. "And I get a little OCD."

"Yeah." Karen Minty laughs. "You are OCD . . . on my pussy."

You would never say anything so crass and I pet Karen Minty and watch Kevin James and I miss you so much I feel sick. Suddenly, I have to go. I stand up.

"Whoa, where's the fire?" She hugs my seat cushion, she's too needy.

"I'm going to the store," I say and I grab my keys.

"You want company?" She's not mysterious.

"No," I say and I grab my coat.

"You need cash?" She sits up. She's pathetic.

"No," I say. "Stay put. I'll be back in a bit."

I run down the stairs and I stop. I could do anything to Karen Minty and she'd stay. She has her claws in me, Beck. Her mother is knitting me a *sweater* and her father wants to take me out on his boat one of these Sundays. I sit down on the stoop. Maybe now that I'm away from Karen Minty I can make a list of things that I like about her.

#1 Karen Minty grew up with three brothers so she's mellow.

And it's true. She *is* mellow. FedEx fucks up the new Nora Roberts and I can put Karen on a subway and send her uptown and she'll haul ass up there, and drag a box of books back on the subway, up the stairs, and to the shop. And if I ask her to, Karen will unload the books, price them, and stack them. She doesn't complain, Beck. She *wants* to be asked, like a little brat trying to do good on Christmas

Eve in case Santa is watching. I can even ask her to get out the Swiffer and clean up the dust she noticed while she was stacking.

#2 Karen Minty likes to clean.

"I grew up in a fucking pigsty," she likes to say. "Only way shit gets clean is if I clean it and I like shit clean, so there you go."

#3 Karen Minty likes to cook.

And she's good at it. I haven't eaten like this in I don't know how long, real family food (a lasagna that will taste good even five days later cold), and the runner's body I had going when I was tracking Peach Salinger (who would be absolutely horrified by Karen), well, I still have it for the most part because Karen likes to cook, eat, clean, and fuck. And she intends to do all these things with me forever. I found a little plastic file box of recipes that belong to her mother. I texted her about the recipes and she wrote back:

I'm cooking a helluva lot more in your kitchen than I am in mine.

Anything I want, anytime, I can ask her for it and she can make it because her mother knows how to make everything. I brought leftover lasagna for Ethan and he thinks her mother should do a cookbook. She is that good.

#4 Karen Minty is a good fuck.

The way that you like to talk shit about Blythe, the way that you like to tease—your nipples popping in the shop on Day One—well, Karen Minty just likes to ride dick. All dick; you can tell she's been *fucked* a lot and it doesn't bother me. I'm the best she's ever had; her words, not mine.

#5 Karen Minty knows Ethan is good people.

We went out with Blythe and Ethan once. It was bad. Blythe balked at Karen's greyhounds and told her that Leonardo DiCaprio drinks *a lot of beverages, Karen. Are you that naive?* Ouch. The next day, Ethan showed up at the shop apologizing—"Blythe doesn't have a lot of girlfriends! I hope Karen isn't hurt!"—and Karen popped in while he was there. Karen told Ethan that Blythe is "super smart" and "wicked pretty." When Ethan went to go take a shit, Karen told me that she thought Blythe was a cunt. "Ethan should be with a nice girl," she said. "But nice guys *always* get with bitches. They don't break up if you call 'em out on it. Give him time. He'll dump her eventually." Karen Minty truly is a *nurse.*

A couple of days ago, he asked me, in complete seriousness, if I plan to propose to Karen.

"Ethan, it's been two months."

He shrugged and told me for the fiftieth time how he proposed to his ex Shelly after six weeks.

I told him straight, "And look how that turned out."

"When you know, you know."

"Well, I don't know, Ethan."

"Well, you better start thinking about knowing," he said and for once he had a five o'clock shadow—another miracle. "Because she definitely knows."

#6 . . .

It's no use. Maybe Dan Fox loves Karen Minty, but I don't love Karen Minty. I love you. I love your depth and your letters to yourself and I am wrong to be leading her on. And honestly, she comes on too strong. Otherwise why would Ethan *and* Nicky be talking about marriage when we've been going out less than two months. And here she comes, bounding down the apartment building's stairs after me.

"Boo!" she screams.

And I flinch even though I knew she was coming.

"Oh my God, you scare so freaking easily." She laughs. She sits down next to me and leans her head on my shoulder and she sighs. "I don't scare at all. When I was a kid, my brothers tried to fuck with me so much that, I don't know. I think I just like lost all my fear or something."

It's a nice night. There are kids playing outside. It'll be spring before you know it. Karen Minty yawns. "What a night, right?"

"Yeah," I say.

She hears the timer on the oven and she pulls me close and plants one of her hard, bossy kisses on me. "You want enchiladas?"

"Do I ever not want enchiladas?" I say and I get another kiss.

"Well, come on," she says. "First enchiladas. Then you promised you'd help me with my flash cards."

I pocket my store keys and follow her back up the stairs to my place.

#7 Karen Minty has a great ass.

#8 Karen Minty makes great enchiladas.

#9 Karen Minty mixes sexual favor cards in with her nursing school flash cards so that randomly, I'll flash her a card that says TAKE MY TOP OFF.

#10 Karen Minty likes to fuck.

After we fuck, I look at my list and realize that I left off #6.

#6 Karen Minty knows what she wants. She wants to be a phlebotomist.

She doesn't complain about her homework because she knows what she wants. She wants to draw blood from people; she wants to be a phlebotomist.

"I'm a great fucking stick and when you're laid up in a bed for eight days with fucked veins and your IV jams because some dumb tramp messed up your meds, the most important thing in the world to you is a great stick. Not a great doctor, a great stick. And I want to be the stick heard 'round the fucking world."

Do you see that, Beck? It's not like she wants to tweet about being a nurse—"Fucking Twitter my ass, I prefer life," she said just the other day. There's a simplicity to it all that is really good for me and I know it because my cheeks are flushed, my belly is full, my dick is the stick heard 'round the fucking world—just ask Karen—and I wake up and I want to get out of bed and do my life. But I also wake up thinking about you.

I finish reading my list to Dr. Nicky. At first he doesn't say anything.

I am impatient. "What's up, Doc?"

"You tell me, Danny."

"I did my homework. Now it's your turn."

Dr. Nicky just stares at me and I just stare at Dr. Nicky. Does he do this to you?

"Okay, Danny. I'm gonna ask you something." He leans in. "Does Karen know that you're not in love with her?"

I can't lie to him about Karen. He can't help me unless I tell the truth. "No," I say. "She doesn't know."

"Lies don't pave the way to joy," he says and sometimes he reminds me of a rabbi and I can't believe I used to think that you had sex with him. "And, if there's anything I've learned in almost fifty years on this planet, it's this: If you don't start with crazy, crazy love, the kind of love that Van Morrison sings about, then you don't have a shot to go the distance. Love's a marathon, Danny, not a sprint."

I blurt, "What about you? Do you love your wife?"

"No," he says, super quick. "But I *did*."

On the way home from therapy, I'm depressed and I check your e-mail. You RSVPed yes to a birthday party at an upscale bowling alley for assholes. I know that you won't go; you never go anywhere anymore. You only go to *Dr. Nicky's because he's* . . . *Dr. Nicky*. But I know that Karen Minty will go with me to the bowling alley and sit there until I say it's time to go home.

She sits with me at the hipster bar near the lanes and we don't belong. We are the only people who are not a part of the party. They are all around us, talking about Lena Dunham's wardrobe—*Who's Lena Dunning?* Karen Minty wants to know—and they talk about the alpha male's vintage suspenders—Karen Minty chews on her straw and shrugs—and they talk about Campus Dance at Brown—Karen Minty plays a game with jewels on her phone. You don't show up at the party and Karen Minty is in love with me and I don't love her back, I can't. It's been so long since I've seen you and life would be easier if I could turn into a fan of *The King of Queens*. But I can't, Beck. And you of all people would understand. It's like the letter you wrote to yourself today:

> *Dear Beck, Louisa May Alcott is right. An extraordinary girl can't have an ordinary life. Don't judge yourself. Love yourself.*
> *Love, Beck*

37

I'VE read enough books and seen enough movies to know that Nicky fucked up when he told me about his wife. I'm not surprised when he tells me we need to *talk*. He accepts full responsibility for the breach, for crossing the patient-therapist boundary. I've never seen the guy look worse, Beck. And he's such a good person, like Mr. Mooney back in the day, before he got angry at me, at life. I can't stand to hear him cut himself down.

I plead, "Hey, come on, Doc. Stop beating yourself up already."

I can't tell if he's laughing or crying and he might be the only guy on earth who can do those two things at once. He's a juggler and God bless him because I could never apologize to another dude for saying *one* freaking thing about my own life.

"Danny," he says. "All I can do for you now is give you a referral. You want a referral?"

There are pit stains on his shirt and his clothes are wrinkled, as if he's been in them for too long. I know how to cheer him up and I tell him I don't need a referral because I'm better. He smiles. I go on. I tell him I don't have a mouse in my house because he's the best shrink ever.

"How's it going with Karen?"

"It's good," I say. I want him to feel accomplished. "Seriously, the mouse is dead."

"Wow," he says and somehow, he sounds jealous. Or maybe he's just sad.

I tell him that his mouse-cat theory is genius and he likes that I use that word, *genius*. Of course, I don't tell him that I want to cover myself in cheese and peanut butter in order to get the mouse to come back. He deserves better.

"I'm happy for you, Danny," he says. "You worked hard and you did your homework and this is all you, kid. Figuring out what makes you happy is a journey."

You make me happy. I nod. "You said it."

"Being obsessed didn't make you happy," Nicky continues. "And you knew that. And more important, you acted on that knowledge and decided to rise above your obsession. You're smart, Danny."

"I can't thank you enough, Doc."

"I wish we were all as smart as you," he says and he has that sad, glossy-eyed look again as he talks about how hard it is to make a mouse go away. I'm sitting and thinking about you, my beloved mouse. Nicky is right. You might never show up again—you might be gone—I know it's possible that you've moved on—you could even be seeing someone. But the most important thing I know is that I want the possibility of you more than the reality of Karen Minty.

"And what can I say, Danny? I'm also so happy your cat worked out," he says. "When you came in here, I was worried. You did not look well. You looked like a prisoner."

"I felt like one," I say. And I did. I do.

"But then you got yourself a cat," he says.

"Amen," I say. I picture Karen Minty on all fours with your little body hanging out of her mouth.

"Hey, I went on YouTube and watched that Honeydrippers video today right before you got here," he says and his eyes pop. "I can understand your obsession. That video is trippy, that guy in his Speedo, that jacket. What is that jacket doing on that hanger?"

We laugh but his sadness is like a fever that shows up in his eyes, in his mouth. I feel bad about lying and his phone buzzes. "I'm sorry," he says. "But I have to check it." He says he has to step out—"shit hitting the fan at home," now that he has broken the doctor-patient dynamic he can overshare again—and he promises to be back in five minutes. He closes the door and immediately I look at his computer. I wanted inside that computer the first time I stepped into this room. You live in there, somewhere, and the temptation to find the *Sea of Love* is overwhelming. I would swear that you are calling from inside the hard drive, luring me to your own sea, and I can't help it. I really am like the guy in the video. And this is it, my big chance. I've never been alone in here and fuck it. I run over to Danny's desk and I tap the space bar and dive in.

Looking at the screen-saver family snapshot of Nicky with his wife and his daughters makes me feel guilty. I'm violating our trust and Nicky's family is so innocent, lined up in front of Nicky's Pizza in Chestertown, NY. There's something pathetic about a grown man forcing his wife and daughters to pose on a rainy day in front of a pizza place just because it's called *Nicky's*. I feel for the guy but I want you and I minimize the Honeydrippers video—he's a good man, he really was looking at it—and I search the hard drive. Wow. Dr. Nicky doesn't write about my sessions or your sessions or anyone's sessions. He just dictates his thoughts into his iPhone and downloads the MP3 files onto his computer. There is a folder called GBeck with a bunch of audio files. I get that Van Morrison feeling that Nicky was talking about. I send myself the folder. I delete the e-mail in his sent folder. I empty the trash. I made it.

But I didn't. It's over. I fucked up.

Nicky's back with a disappointed smile and he sighs. "Danny, I'm so sorry. This is my fault. I tell you the video's here and I *leave*. I'm losing it, Danny."

I breathe. I made it after all. "No you're not, Doc," I say and I mean it.

He looks weak, and his voice is unsteady. "How about that referral?"

I take the referral and shake his hand and leave. I am sad for Nicky but nothing can touch my excitement over the files, *GBeck*. In the elevator I do something I never do. I pray for Nicky to find someone who can give him that Van Morrison feeling so that his bleached teeth won't seem so laughably out of place on his drawn, sad face.

The elevator dumps me in the lobby and Danny Fox is dead. When I step outside I stumble, a fucking crack in the sidewalk. There is a black hole in my mind: Am I nuts? I could just keep eating Karen's eggs and Karen's pussy. I could start over with Nicky's referral and try to live life without you.

I could.

But the truth is, cats bore me. I'd rather listen to tapes of Nicky talking about you than have intercourse with Karen Minty. And if Van Morrison's not crazy, then neither am I.

Dear Joe, You are not a cat person. You want a mouse. Love, Joe

38

I have to buy headphones at a fucking deli because I have to know now what Nicky has said about you and the guy takes forever and why do so many morons go into customer service and I grab the headphones and mutter, *thanks, asshole*, and I'm out of there and I tear into the package and it's sealed too tight and I scream and a few people on the street back away from me like I'm the Hulk busting out of his dress shirt and I duck into the alley and take the time to crack the plastic and get the headphones out and throw away the instructions and I can't get them into my phone fast enough as I run down the stairs and swipe my MetroCard and hit play on the first MP3 as I step onto the train and sit down across from a blind black guy who smiles for no reason.

Okay, day one, Beck. Female. Early to mid twenties. Hypersexualized. Boundary issues. Father issues. Claims to be here to resolve her issues with men but doesn't seem to realize that I have a ring on my finger. Only mode of communication is seduction. Repeatedly crosses her legs and wears a flimsy shirt without a bra. Attention seeking. Directly asks about transference, severe narcissistic disorder. Insists on calling me Dr. Nicky in spite of my repeated statements that I am not an MD. Repeatedly asks if I'm married and if I have a good sex life with my wife to avoid discussing her own life. Tells me she slept with her therapist in college. Repeatedly. I ask why she doesn't see a female clinician and she says she has one mother, doesn't need another. Possible borderline, predatory, masochistic tendencies.

The blind black guy is staring at me but he's blind and he can't see me and I can't get mad at him and I skip ahead to another segment. Maybe the next one will be better. It has to be.

Marcia was a fucking nightmare this morning. Mack overslept again and Amy has the flu and Marcia is just incompetent as a mother. I almost canceled but found myself soothed by knowing that I would see Beck. I've grown to look forward to my time with this young woman. I find myself counting down, thinking about what I'll wear that day. She makes my life bearable, damn it. Now who's asking about transference? Today, she presents in sweatpants and a formless top, with messy hair and shiny skin. I can't help but feel that she dressed down for me, which is more intimate than dressing up for me. We establish goals: She wants sexual confidence. Which I find amusing because she is sex.

I hit PAUSE and I want the black man to stop smiling. I want the world to stop smiling. I fast-forward. I hit PLAY.

She claims that I have opened her up and that she's taking a much-needed break from men, that she's realized things about her father, things about her love life, and all of this after just a few sessions because I am the most amazing doctor she has ever had. I tell her again I'm not a doctor. Is it terrible that I love it when she calls me Dr. Nicky? Don't answer that. (Sigh.) Anyway, I tell her that there is no magic cure. She shakes me off.

She says I have lit up something inside of her. She says she has never felt so in tune with herself. She says talking to me is the time of her life. She is presenting more sexually, in kneesocks and skirts. I think she knows I'm falling for her. And my God, I think she's falling for me. I think about her too much. And sometimes I worry that she knows. I should stop therapy but I can't. I am so tired of Marcia and the broken washing machine and Beck is . . . a reprieve.

I hit PAUSE. I look around. I wish there was someone I could punch in the face. I could never punch a blind man and I press PLAY.

I know I should give her a referral and send her on her way.

I hit PAUSE again because I'm going deaf from anger. He had no problem giving *me* a referral. It's fine to kick Danny Fox to the curb but *you* get to stay. I press PLAY:

Her journaling is productive. She is receptive to my suggestion that she needs to be in a relationship in order to address her issues. She repeatedly tells me that we have a connection. And I don't encourage her but this connection is all I think about. How come I am so willing to accept failure in my work? Yet I am not willing to accept it when a very intelligent patient calls me a genius. Maybe I did cure her in a matter of weeks. Has my self-esteem tumbled to the extent that I no longer think that's possible just because I bought the wrong washing machine?

He loves you and he's after you and the blind man is smiling, now standing, poking around and we're all hunters, we are, and I skip ahead:

I tell Diane that I'm starting to have dreams about Beck. And of course Diane tells me to stop treatment. That's what a good therapist would say and Diane is a good therapist. But I can't. Beck is opening up to me and she trusts me enough to tell me about this green pillow she uses to masturbate. To masturbate! The backstory is revelatory. Her father left. He then asked her mother to mail him his green neck pillow. Her passive mother agreed but Beck had already stolen the pillow. In my fantasy, we are in my office and she comes over to me and asks to sit on my lap. I say no, but she will not be stopped. She straddles me. I fantasize about her all the time now and the bad washing machine is actually good because there's a lock in the laundry room and I can jerk off in there and think about Beck without getting caught. In my mind, when I'm inside of her, she calls me a rock star and a cock star and I haven't felt this alive in years. Staying with Marcia feels more like a betrayal. Like I am cheating on Beck even though nothing is happening. Every day, I am more detached from my family. The truth is ugly: I would rather have Beck.

At some point during that recording the blind man exited the train. I missed my stop and the headphones jam my ears, pieces of dime-store junk, and I yank them out of my phone and hurl them at the window across from me. People are looking at me and people can fuck off. The train lurches to a stop and I'm the first one out the door. I can't get angrier than I am right now. I feel like a sucker and I want to tear my own head off because I can't believe that I fell for his bullshit. I can't believe I told him things I never tell anyone. I round the corner and see Karen fucking Minty sitting on my fucking stoop with a picnic basket and cats are supposed to be smarter than this, colder than this.

"Surprise," she says. "I made a picnic!"

And can you believe that Karen still exists? I want to go inside and throw typewriters at the walls until they cave in and the mice are collateral damage, falling to death, screaming and Karen Minty—*my girlfriend*—has to be here with an actual picnic basket.

I've never seen one in real life, only in cartoons, in books, and I don't want to go on a picnic. I smell garlic and rosemary and the Noxzema that Karen has rubbed all over her tight, pointy face since she was a kid. It's over. If she knew what a sucker I am, if she knew that I *paid* a married dickwad to try and *fuck* the love of my life, she wouldn't want to take me on a picnic. I need her to go away. This has nothing to do with her. This is Nicky's fault and I tell her I'm not hungry.

She *is* hungry and she reaches and I pull away. "Joe, what the fuck?"

I'm not Joe, I'm Dan Fox and I am loud. "Jesus Christ, Karen! Can you take a fucking hint?"

And that's it. She is on her feet, shivering. "Fuck you."

"That's intelligent."

"Fuck you and your intelligence," she snarls. "You think I'm some doormat piece-of-shit chick that you can bang and fuck as you please? You think I'm some fucking rag doll?"

"Yes," I say, not missing a beat. "That's exactly what you are."

And it's true. I am wrong about everyone. You are a whore and Nicky is a prick and sweet Karen, the cum Dumpster, is boiling over with repressed rage. Or is that sadness? She is quivering and the basket is making her forearm tremble and I'm a fucking asshole and she's a phlebotomist who loves me, *me*, and if Nicky wasn't in love with you then none of this would be happening. But he *does* want you and that chicken smells delicious and I'm a fool.

"Sit down," says Karen Minty and I let her help me onto the stoop. How could Nicky do this to Karen? She is a hard worker; the basket is full. She has heart; last month, she lugged a vacuum cleaner all the way here to my place. She vacuumed beneath the sofa. She wore tiny little whore shorts and a half shirt and she found dirty places I didn't know existed.

"You don't want to get mice," she had said. "Otherwise I won't wanna come here anymore."

Nobody ever made a vacuum cleaner into a dozen roses, a beating heart. And like everything bad, this too is Nicky's fault. He's the one who told me to get a *cat*. Karen would stay with me forever and pump out kids when I want kids and work doubles so we can go to Florida once a year and I have all of this here in a *picnic basket* and that rosemary smells like heaven. But the thing is, she's never heard of Paula Fox or *Magnolia* or tried to bang her married shrink. She's not *different, hot* like us. She follows the rules; she doesn't dare touch the hole in my wall because that's *for the super to fix.* She respects boundaries and fuck Nicky for wasting her time and breaking her heart.

"Why are you mad at me?" She is quivering. "I thought you'd think it was cool, a picnic. It's gorgeous out."

"Karen."

"Oh fuck," she says and she knows I'm dumping her. She leaps off the stoop and she's running, crying, gone. I will never see her again and I take the picnic basket upstairs and spread it all out in my Minty-fresh apartment. I gorge on chicken breasts and roasted potatoes and cauliflower in cream sauce and wine right out of the bottle. I eat like it's the last supper, because it is. I buried Dan Fox today and now I have to take care of Nicky. There's no way around it, Beck. I listen to his recordings all night long. He's taken advantage of you in the safest place in the world. He's in your head, *a mouse in your house* and he's clearly tricked you into thinking that you love him. We can't get together with him controlling your thoughts. *Dr. Nicky is . . . Dr. Nicky*: a greedy, married pig. And he was wrong about me. I don't have a mouse in my house. I have a fucking pig.

39

I don't remember the last time I was this close to a school. A lot's changed. PS 87 on Seventy-Eighth Street has a slogan, for fuck's sake: "One family under the sun." I spent the early morning on the steps of the American Museum of Natural History drinking coffee and learning about Nicky and waiting for the families to get out of bed and *under the sun* already. The journey to this school was shockingly easy, thanks largely to Nicky's sister-in-law, Jackie. I found her on the Yelp page for Nicky's Pizza, where she has contributed countless photographs of "our extended family gorging on our favorite 'za!" Jackie's Yelp account led me to Jackie's bountiful Facebook page, which features numerous check-ins at "the cabins upstate!" at Nicky's Pizza (duh), and, most important, to "PS 87! Best School in the City!" Best Facebook page in the world!

Really, I should sign into Yelp just to endorse her foamy, panting restaurant reviews. I owe her. I know everything about Nicky.

So, I'm dressed up like a runner today because if there's anywhere in the world you can't chill out undisturbed, it's a school. I'm fucking out of shape as all get out. I haven't run since Peach. I've been running in circles, jogging really—since four thirty in the morning, listening to Nicky's fucking perv diaries to keep me focused. I go down Columbus, bang a right onto Seventy-Seventh, pass the empty playground, turn right up Amsterdam, and then right onto Seventy-Eighth, pass PS 87, and do it again. I've made I don't know how many laps when it all pays off because I see Nicky walking down the street. He looks different to me now. I used to feel sorry for him the way he was so hunched over, his eyes hell bent on the floor. But now he just looks evil. His hunchback is a punishment for his sins. (You.) A father should be looking out for his daughter, but Nicky hangs his head.

His daughters are older now and that picture on his computer must have been taken a while ago. He's holding Amy's hand (Amy's the one they had instead of getting divorced) and calling out for Mack to slow down. Mack's the one they had to seal the deal—older, detached. It's okay for me to jog in place because I'm wearing sunglasses and headphones and if there's one dude that everyone on the Upper West Side will welcome with open arms, it's the fucking jogger.

Nicky walks these kids into the school (and what happened to this city that parents are fucking inside of the school with the kids? Nobody held my fucking hand or anybody else's for that matter back in the day), and a mother glares at me and I wave and smile (I normal-up good!), and she waves, assuming she forgot my name and knows me from the PTA or the gym or what have you and *come on, Nicky* get out of there because jogging in place is not like jogging in circles and we've got work to do, me and Nicky, and we don't have much time because you're supposed to see Nicky tomorrow afternoon at one and I've decided that that's not going to happen.

NICKY is living proof that idle hands are the horny, cheating devil's playground. The guy's so leisurely, Beck. After he dropped his girls at school, he took the long way home and talked on the phone—to you?—and then disappeared into his building. I didn't see anyone buzz his place, so it's not like he was seeing patients. He and his wife came out three hours later squawking over the washing machine— this is why marriage scares me, they've been talking about that malfunctioning machine for months—and I stay with them on their walk. If Nicky had balls, he would leave her, but he doesn't. And I'm not mad at you for falling for him. I don't blame you. The more I listen to the tapes, the more I see Nicky for what he is: a very talented, very sick manipulator. I didn't see through his bullshit so I can't very well blame you for falling under his spell. And if you think about it, it's kind of sweet that we both got swindled. We're alike. I smile.

Nicky's wife, Marcia, is nothing like you. She's boorish and loud. She teaches psychology at various local and online colleges. She's a thick-legged martyr with a yoga mat over her shoulder. I hate to sound crass, but yoga's not doing the trick. She's wearing a Stop Breast Cancer visor—you know this woman is always bellyaching about something—and her hair is tied back in a low, sad ponytail. This is not a happy woman, Beck. She's gruff. She crosses her arms when they pass by homeless people as if the homeless people would ever even try with her. I could feel sorry for Nicky but the facts are facts: At some point in his life, he proposed to Marcia.

Watching him trot alongside Marcia is depressing. She does all the talking about birthday parties and pediatricians and kiddie yoga classes—as if kids don't stretch out on their own. There are vitamins to be bought and babysitters to be fired and poor Nicky is hunched over more with every block. When I do finally kill him, I will be putting him out of his misery. You don't want him, Beck. Life does not suit him. All that power he has in the beige room with the records on the wall disappears when he exits his playroom. He wants to cross but his wife yanks his arm. She snaps, "Green light."

They cross when it's safe—*LOL*—and they enter a nondescript town house. I Google the address and naturally, they're here for couples therapy. Fifty-two minutes later they emerge, deflated. They walk in silence to a gym and they hug, family-style before she disappears into her refuge of yoga and like-minded women. I follow Nicky down the street and he is less hunched every block. He arrives at his destination, Westsider Books, and he emerges an hour later standing up straight with three new used records (and no books, tsk tsk). I follow him until we reach Urban Outfitters and he goes in with his bag of records and looks at all the clothes and tries on T-shirts and Shazams one song after another and finally he leaves, without buying a thing. Now, it's off to school, where he picks up his daughters and walks them back home. The young one is happy and talking and the old one is morose and not talking and people have to be careful or they wind up with lives they didn't want. It's lucky we found each other when we did, you and me. I hang out by his building like I'm waiting for a running buddy. Here comes Marcia with a friend whose taste in clothing is equally drab.

Marcia sighs and it's clear to me that she sighs a lot. "He said that he would sooner kill himself than leave his children."

"And what did you say?"

"I said I think that all children do better with happy parents than married parents. I said there's no stigma about divorce anymore."

The friend nods in agreement and her ring sparkles.

Marcia goes on. "And then he said it's easy for *me* to be cavalier about divorce because my parents were happily married. But you know Nicky the martyr. His children will *never* deal with a divorce."

The friend sighs. Women sigh. A lot. She lightens. "Maybe you should start a profile for him on Match."

The ladies share a laugh and the friend says she was only kidding.

There are no easy answers and they make plans to get their families together—because that sounds like fun—and Marcia plods up to the home she doesn't want to the man she doesn't love. Now I know why Nicky became a shrink, for real. He needed someone to talk to because he married the wrong woman. He knew he was giving up on his music, but he didn't know he was giving up on love. I am starting to feel sorry for him again, because I'm a pushover. I duck into the subway and watch a couple of nurses bitch about work. I think of my nurse, Karen, and how miserable she must be right now.

I can't tell you what a relief it is to arrive back in my hood. Killing Nicky is gonna be difficult. But it's necessary. You're obsessed with him; he's *a mouse in your house* and because of my current thought process, I almost freak out when I see a cop on my stoop. He blocks the front door and he is a giant and my brain freezes up on me— BenjiPeachCandacemugofurine—and it's me he's looking for. Like Ethan says, *when you know, you know.* This giant cop has his nightstick out and he's not fucking around, "Is that you, Joe?"

It takes everything I have left in me to walk toward this man when all I want to do is run.

"Get over here," he says. The sad thing about being poor is that the few little hood kids running around don't even react; this is just another day.

"Can I help you?" I say because I am innocent, I am. I wish I were Dan Fox but he's no good either, not anymore.

"Yeah, you can help me," he says as I walk up the steps. I stand directly across from him now. His pores are enormous and his forearms are bigger than mine are and his neck is veiny and I bet his dad was a cop and his granddad too. "You can tell me who the fuck you think you are."

"Um," I say and might piss my pants. "What is this, uh, what is this about?"

He mocks me. *"What is this about?"*

It happens so fast. He grabs me by the collar and yanks me close. His breath is made of onions, raw onions. He seethes. "You little fuck."

Am I going to die? I close my eyes and he tightens his grip on my shirt. I'm innocent, innocent until proven guilty. He spits at me. And then he lets go.

I don't wipe my face and I take a step back. He slams his stick into the cement.

"You know, you better respect this uniform, kid. Because if I wasn't in this uniform, I'd kick your ass and throw your bones in the Dumpster over there and see to it that nobody finds you."

"I'm s-sorry," I stammer and he probably hates me more for my yuppie running clothes and he shakes his head.

"You know, my sister . . ." He's blubbering, crackling and now I recognize his cadence, it's Minty. "My sister Karen is a fucking saint, you prick. She's as beautiful inside as she is outside and you, you little pansy, you got no right."

Sister and I can breathe again and I'm begging for his forgiveness and telling him she was too good for me and he doesn't buy it. I shut up.

"You don't fuck over Karen Elise Minty." He raises his stick and I cower and I don't want to die, I can't leave you like this. He slams his stick into the concrete by my feet. "Stand up, you fucking pussy."

He grabs me by the throat. And this too is on Nicky. He's the one who pushed me on Karen and then made me push her away. The giant Minty cop clenches my throat, lets go, and smashes the concrete one last time with his stick. He storms away and no wonder Karen Minty wants to be a phlebotomist. Her brother's got a good stick. Why shouldn't she have one too?

40

TAKING care of Nicky is going to be easier than I thought. He's a do-gooder, Beck, and once a week he takes the train out to the part of Queens that's still all about crack and crime to council druggies who are trying to get sober. But tonight, he's gonna become a cautionary tale for all the UWS assholes who think they can atone for their sins with four hours a week. Tonight, Nicky not-a-doctor-except-to-you will be mugged by drug addicts.

I take a swig of Jack and open the front page of a self-help book, *When Bad Things Happen to Good People.* Nicky Angevine's friends will give his wife that book when he's found dead in Queens. Nicky's death will be looked upon as a tragedy. His daughters will grow up without a father (until his wife bangs a replacement, which will probably happen in a matter of weeks) and there will be a simple, perverse beauty to his demise. No suspects, no confusion, no malfeasance, a straight-up mugging, wallet gone, the guy was in the wrong place at the wrong time. Marcia Angevine's friends will hover around her with coffee cakes and their own kids and bottles of wine and tell her how sorry they are for her loss. But I know that she'll be thanking the Lord for her *gain*.

It's time, Beck. Nicky emerges from the sober house and looks both ways like a good little white boy. He hangs his head and starts down the street and his wife must have laundered his Vans because they're especially bright and white tonight. He's a *mouse in your house* and I wish you didn't want him. But of course you do, Beck. He's like the father you never had and you want to break up his family. And that's natural. That's the cycle of abuse and it was Nicky's job to help you overcome that desire.

But Nicky didn't do his job. He is a pig. And there's no possible happy ending to this mess. If I let him live, you will eventually get what you think you want. He will fuck you in the beige room and cry to his wife and beg for a divorce and he will go to you—because he's right, *you are sex*—and the truth is, the second he becomes available, no ring, no more teeth whitening, you won't want him.

He is leading you down the path to hell and he was supposed to keep his distance from you and he didn't. And you were supposed to call me—*you miss me*—and you didn't. And I know you so well, Beck. You are charisma, you are sick, and for some reason you are a magnet for weak, spineless people like Peach, like Benji, like Nicky. I pick up my pace and I hold my new nightstick. (I went to the Army Navy store to cool off after that bullshit with Officer Minty; it's only fair that we *all* be armed against cops who think they're above the law.) I clench my jaw. I am gaining on him and I can do this, one fell swoop. But then I feel a vibration in my pocket. I have no choice but to duck into an alley. Nicky will turn around if he hears the phone and I can't make it stop and I can't breathe and my hands shake and I look at my phone.

It's you.

You are calling me.

You have, at last, decided to act on your feelings.

Your name looks beautiful in my phone, shining in the dark above the picture of you in your white bikini. I stare at you, aglow. I smile; I too glow. You surprise me, you delight me, and you miss me. I try to make my heart slow down and Dr. Nicky is already blocks away and I bring the phone to my head and I speak. "Well, hello, Beck."

"Joe?" you say, soft as your skin. "Can you hear me?"

I lose my voice and cough. I'm not myself because I was just about to kill Nicky with a nightstick because he was trying to have sex with you. I am dizzy and you sound tipsy when you speak again. "Joe? Can you hear me?"

"Bad signal," I say. "I'm waiting for the train."

Forward as a dictator, you make your demand. "I need you to come over. Can you come over? Can you come over right now?"

I've never been so sure of anything in my life and I answer, strongly, "Yes."

I hit END and I can't believe your timing. I need a minute to get my head right. *You called.* I ditch the nightstick in a trash heap. My hand is still sore from gripping it and my heart hurts from the whiplash. *You called.* You're back! I'm calmer now and I'm walking and it will be nice to get out of here and get to you. *You called* and I can't help but believe that for all of Nicky's idiocy, he might be good at what he does after all. Clearly, you are in a better place now; you called *me*, not him. I hop in a cab because I'm too happy to get on the subway. I wonder what you're wearing and I can't get to you fast enough. I leave *When Bad Things Happen to Good People* in the backseat of the cab. I don't need it anymore. I have you.

41

OUR IKEA pillow is still tagged and it's underneath your table on the floor. I hold you in my arms and you cry. You're drunk and I don't ask any questions. I will not let you and your pillow get me down. Besides, you feel as good as I remember, better. Your place is a mess, which makes me believe you really have been *growing*. There are curtains now—that's progress—and you're almost out of tears. I stroke your head and stare at our pillow and breathe you in, your scent, your apples rotting on the counter. I can't stop smiling and the harder you cry the broader I grin and finally, you have nothing left and you stop, you whisper, "Sorry."

"Oh it's okay," I say. "I can send you a dry-cleaning bill."

If you were Karen Minty you'd laugh too hard but you're *you* and all you do is smile. "I don't remember the last time I laughed."

"Just about two seconds ago, Beck."

You stretch your arms above your head and twist, to the left, to the right and then your arms flop and you look at me. "You must think I'm nuts."

"Not at all," I say and I don't.

"Oh, come on, Joe. I see you and we get together and then I just disappear off the radar."

I make a joke: "Actually, I was in the south of France on a top secret mission for the FBI."

You don't laugh and you're not in the mood for dumb jokes and I love you for being so honest, so present and all the hard work was worth it because all of it was leading up to this moment.

You speak. "I kind of do wish you were in the FBI."

"Seriously?" I say and I don't like where this is going.

You quiver. I don't.

"Peach is dead, Joe." And you sound exasperated and this isn't supposed to happen. *Peach is in Turks and Caicos, goddamn it.*

"Are you kidding?"

"They found her body in Rhode Island."

"No."

"Yes," you say.

No. Impossible. I put a *ton* of rocks in her pockets. When I walked her onto that jetty, she must have been a buck fifty. This is bullshit. I did my job. Did I zip her pockets? Fuck yes I zipped her pockets. Nothing is made well anymore. The zippers were plastic, now that I think about it, and they probably disintegrated. Fuck those zippers.

"I just can't believe it," you say. There are so many horrible things you could say right now and what if you led me here under false pretenses and what if the FBI is here, spying.

"Rhode Island?"

"Yep," you say. "Rhode Island."

I talked to too many people in that state. I was sloppy and friendly and there's Officer Nico and Dr. K and all those junkies and the guy at the garage. What if they all got together? What if they know? The mug of piss flashes through my mind's eye and what have I done?

"Her family has a place there," you say. "We were there and I thought she took off. I mean she sent me a melodramatic e-mail, but that's Peach. I didn't think she was, you know, serious."

"Jesus," I say and would you visit me in prison or would you be afraid?

"I figured she took off because she does that sometimes!" You pick up your bottle of diet root beer and you take a swig and I wish you would just keep going. "And for the past few months, I haven't heard from her, but you know those old friends that you can go ages without talking to and then you talk, and everything's fine? Hang on."

You bury your head in your phone and I don't know what you mean because if I go more than a month without seeing Mr. Mooney, it's super awkward, but how can I think about Mr. Fucking Mooney right now? Are you wearing a wire, Beck? Are you trying to get me to confess? Is that why you got *curtains*? I look at my watch. 10:43.

"Sorry," you say. "It was just school stuff. Anyway, where was I?"

"She disappeared."

"She didn't disappear. She committed suicide."

"Oh, Jesus." *Praise Jesus!*

"I know," you say and you finish your root beer. "How did I not see it?"

You're heading to the kitchen, getting the vodka out of the freezer, the glasses out of the sink—Karen Minty doesn't leave glasses in the sink but Karen Minty doesn't have the capacity to cry like you do—

and you're gonna tell me a story and Karen Minty can't tell a story. "I don't know where to begin."

"At the beginning."

You sit down next to me and we won't kiss for a long time but God did I miss the nearness of you, the anticipation of your words, your voice. "So we were in Little Compton, it's this beach community in Rhode Island. She was pretty depressed but me too. Remember that guy Benji, my druggie ex?"

"I think so."

"Well, he died. I mean that was always possible because he's crazy. But still," you say and you bite your lower lip. You are pretty. "He dies and then she dies. I'm Death Girl."

I love you for making this all about you, for giving yourself a name. You are so flagrantly *you*. I tell you what you want to hear: "Beck, you're not Death Girl. It just sounds like you know some troubled people."

You cut me off. "That's *two* of my friends dead in a matter of months. And you know what I think, Joe? I think this is the universe punishing me for being a fucking liar. I lie and say my dad is dead and now my friends are dying. I mean obviously that's what's happening."

"Let it out," I say because I know when you're drunk there's no point in arguing the benefits of life without Peach and Benji. "But it's not your fault."

You huff. "Like hell it isn't."

"So talk to me," I say. "I'm here."

It's fun to watch you try and decide whether to tell me about the massage session with Peach and you decide against it. "Peach left to go running, which she did every morning. But apparently, this time she filled her pockets with rocks. And it *is* my fault, Joe. I was the last one to see her alive. I should have known."

I was the last one to see her alive, but never mind that. "Beck," I say. "You can't blame yourself for what she did. She was depressed. You knew that. You were a damn good friend and this has nothing to do with you."

You motion for me to stop talking and I pour vodka into the dirty glasses and you dig around for your phone, which has fallen into the sofa with a lot of other junk and you scroll and find the e-mail that Peach wrote to you, the one that *I* wrote. I know I'm not a suspect anymore and I can't help but think that it's kind of hot, hearing my words come out of your mouth. You finish reading and look at me. "Virginia Woolf. I should have known. And I did nothing."

"You can't save someone who doesn't want to be saved."

"But she did want to be saved," you say and you pull your hair up into a high bun. "I just couldn't do it."

"Couldn't do what?"

You gulp and I remember you naked and I want my turn and take a hefty sip. "This has to stay right here for obvious reasons, but you have to know. She tried to fuck me, Joe."

"Oh man." Yes, you're opening up, *petal by petal*, it's happening.

"I pushed her off, of course. Right away," you say and again you can't resist lying, from stealing a little cash from the Monopoly board when the other players are out of the room. You are a cheater, to the bone, a renovator and I admire you, Beck. You never stop making improvements on life. You have charisma. You have vision. Someday, maybe we'll have some beat-up farmhouse and you'll paint the walls until you find the right shade of yellow and I'll tease you but I'll love the way you look with paint on your face. This is where you do your real art and this is where your magic happens. You need an audience, alive—me—not a shrink, not a computer.

"How'd she take it?"

"Not well."

"Fuck," I say.

"And the saddest thing is, it's not the first time this happened."

"Fuck."

You take a sip and you're too embarrassed to look at me. Or maybe you're just too drunk. "Are you horrified?"

"Beck," I say and I rest my hand on your knee. "I'm not horrified that your best friend was in love with you. I don't blame her."

You come at me hard and whole, sloppy and groping. You tear your top off and your hot hands are underneath my shirt—my shirt marked by your tears—and your kiss is wet and hungry and you bite my lip and there is blood, a sweetness, a saltiness, a touch. You have my belt off in no time, a professional under the influence. This time when I fuck you I am the mouse in your house and you can't get rid of me and you want to get rid of me because you hate how much you want me, how I own you when I'm inside of you, how you'll never want anything but me—Nicky who?—and at some point your emotions all turn into one, your tears for Peach, your cunt throbbing for me, your tits humming because of me, all of you exists solely because of me and I fuck the Peach out of you, I fuck the Benji out of you, and the Nicky out of you, and I am the only man in the world and this time, I wake up first. I go into your bathroom, into your tub and I piss all over the floor of the shower and mark my place, my home, you. I take the IKEA pillow out from under the table and rip off the tag and bring it back to bed. You're half asleep when I slip the pillow under your chin and you purr. "Mmm. Joe."

When we get out of bed, we know that we're together now. It's not about whether we'll go out to breakfast; it's just a matter of deciding where to go. We sit across from each other at a diner and we're there six hours because we can't get enough of each other. I finally manage to pull myself away and take a leak and when I'm gone, you e-mail Lynn and Chana:

Holy fuck. Joe. JOE.

When I get back to the table, we start all over again.

42

OUR first eight days together are the best days of my life. You have these plush giant robes from the Ritz-Carlton. You tell me this elaborate story about stealing them while on spring break with Lynn and Chana. I love that you love to tell stories. You couldn't possibly know that I know that you stole them from Peach's place and I don't tell! We live in these robes and you like to entertain me and you do.

Day Two of us, we're lounging around in our robes and you declare the Rule of the Robes: "When you are in my apartment, you are allowed to be naked or in a robe."

"And what if I don't comply with the Rule of the Robes?"

You saunter up to me and growl. "You don't wanna know, buster."

I promise to abide by the rule and I like you all charged up, adult. Your therapy worked because your daddy issues are gone and with me, you're a woman, not a little girl. You're not sending e-mails to yourself anymore, and why would you? You have me to talk to and oh, do we talk. Van Morrison doesn't know shit about love because you and I are inventing love in our Ritz-Carlton robes, with our all night conversations, with our moments of silence that are, as you say, "the opposite of awkward."

We're living on each other and we don't need sleep and by Day Five we have more private jokes than Ethan and Blythe do. We watch *Pitch Perfect* on Netflix—you call it your favorite movie but you don't own the DVD; you are fascinating—and you press PAUSE. You curl up into me and tell me I'm the best and I tease you about loving this movie and you giggle and snort and we wrestle and by the time they go to their championship or whatever, we're in bed, fucking. You love me more than anything and you tell me I'm smarter than the guys in your grad program and the guys you knew in college and we read one of Blythe's stories together and I call it solipsistic and you agree.

The next morning, I wake up first—who can sleep with you in the world?—and I notice that you were up earlier. You're like a child in the best way and you leave a trail of bread crumbs wherever you go and your trail leads me into the kitchen, where the dictionary is open and the word *solipsistic* is smeared with chocolate icing from the half-eaten chocolate cake on the counter. I love you for listening, unabashedly.

You don't want me to leave but I *have* to go to work.

"But I want you to stay," you argue and even your aggression is sweet. "Can't Ethan cover?"

"I hate to break it to you, Beck, but you should have thought of this when you were fixing him up with Blythe."

You groan and you block the door and you let your robe fall open. "You're breaking the Rule of the Robe, Joe."

"Fuck," I say and you maul me and eventually I do leave and the day goes by so slowly and we text so much my thumbs are falling off. I want to bring you all the books in the world, but I settle on one of my favorites that you've never read, *In the Lake of the Woods* by Tim O'Brien.

You let me into your place and you take it with tender hands and you kiss me with your sweet, soft Guiniverean lips. "I knew I was waiting to read this book for a reason," you say. "It's like I knew someday there'd be someone who gave it to me or something."

"Well, I'm glad you waited."

On Day Seven we invent a game: Fake Scrabble. The rule is no real words allowed. You come up with *calibrat* and I spell out *punklassical* and you beat me and you brag and I love you all hopped up on the win. You love to win and I'm not a sore loser and we'll be as good in forty years as we are now.

On Day Nine, I catch you using my toothbrush and you blush. At first you rinse your mouth and claim it was a mistake but I see through you and I know your eyes and you bite your lip and cover your eyes. "I'm just going to say this and I can't look at you when I say this. I like using your toothbrush because I like having you inside of me and I'm sorry I know that's weird and gross." I don't say a word. I clap a hand over your hand and pull your panties off and give it to you right here, in my bathroom.

On Day Ten you tell me that you've never felt less single in your life.

On Day Eleven I tell you that I found myself singing a song from *Pitch Perfect* in the shop and didn't stop even when people started laughing. "You're inside of me," I say and like that, you're on your knees, hungry.

On Day Fourteen I realize that I have lost track of time because I'm not sure if it's Day Fourteen or Day Fifteen and you squeeze my hand as we walk down the street. "That's because every day is the only day," you say. "I've never been so present in my life."

I kiss the top of your head and you're my articulate little bunny. "I never lose track of time, Beck. I think I might be into you."

On Day Seventeen it rains and we're in our robes in your bed and you highlight your favorite parts of *In the Lake of the Woods* and read them to me. When I go to work, I barely get anything done because you can't leave me alone for five minutes without texting. Sometimes you want to talk about nothing:

Did you ever notice that the fingers on my right hand are crooked? Yep. You can tell I'm getting a lot done over here. Anyway . . . how's work?

And sometimes, there are no words, just pictures, intense close-ups of my favorite places on your body, of which there are so many. You never make me wonder and you write back to me while I'm writing back to you and we never run out of things to say. Nobody's ever known me this well. Nobody has ever cared. When I tell you a story, you have questions. You are rapt.

How old were you? Oh come on, I won't get jealous if you tell me about your first time. Joe, please. Tell me tell me tell me!

And I *tell you, tell you, tell you*! Ethan says the first few days of any relationship are intense but Ethan doesn't understand that this is not a *relationship*. You say it's an *everythingship*. And what do I do with that adorable word after you come up with it? I buy a box of cake mix and a disposable silver pan and a can of frosting and three tubes of icing. I bake a cake for you and I write on the top of it:

Everythingship (n): a meeting of the minds, bodies, and souls.

And I carry that cake down the block and down into the subway and on the subway and up the stairs and up the street and up to your door and you squeal and you take about a million pictures of the cake and then we get into bed and eat the cake and have sex and watch old home movies of your family on Nantucket and eat more cake and have more sex and this is the only *everythingship* I've ever had.

I am on the ladder at work and Ethan is passing me unpopular books to hide in the high shelves and he says I can't expect for it to stay this good and I am quick to respond, confident, bold. "I know it's not gonna stay this good."

"Phew," he says.

"It's only gonna get *better*."

He goes to help a customer and the what-ifs crawl into my ear, right out of Shell Silverstein in Poetry. I text you:

Hi

And I tremble and sweat. What if Ethan is right? What if you don't write back? What if you don't miss me anymore? But you text me immediately:

I love you.

I could fall off the ladder and crack open my skull and it wouldn't matter. Like Elliot says in *Hannah*, "I have my answer."

My answer is you.

43

IT'S a good thing that I took a screenshot of your *I love you* text. Something changes after that night and it's like I'm standing so close to a pointillism painting that I only see the dots, not the picture. You are still my girlfriend—you are. But . . .

You don't e-mail me back right away, which would be fine if you weren't making excuses:

> *Sorry, I was in class.*
> *Sorry, I was on the phone with Chana. . . .*
> *Sorry, do you hate me?*

I try every kind of response:

> *No worries, B. Did you want to get dinner?*
> *No sorries allowed. Unless, of course you're not wearing your robe . . .*
> *Hate you? B. I love you.*

But no response is the right response because as soon as I hit SEND, the wait begins again. My thoughts turn dark and my mind wanders into Nicky's beige den of rock 'n' roll and lust. But you're not seeing him. Were that the case, you'd tell someone or write to him and you don't. I still have your old phone and I still check your e-mail and your Facebook. You love me. And one of these days, I'll find a way to get you to admit that your mother still foots the bill for a phone you lost months ago. We're getting there. But I love you so much that I can't willfully close down my portal to your communications. When I worry that you're drifting—and I do worry—I hold your phone and will you back. It sounds crazy, but I think it works. We need all the help we can get right now. Relationships get like this; I know that. But I'm allowed to be frustrated. Your word is *sorry* and my word is *no* and what happened to the time when our word was *everythingship*? Ethan says not to worry.

"She's nuts about you, Joe! Blythe says she's practically writing pornos in class, you know."

Only Ethan would call it *porno* and Ethan doesn't have to wonder where he's eating dinner or when; Blythe is in it with him and since when did that *relationship* seem stronger than our *everythingship*?

My toothbrush is dry. You're not using it anymore and I can pinpoint the moment you stopped. When I want to watch *Pitch Perfect* you are tired or you just watched part of it on the train. When I want to go out for pizza you had pizza for lunch—once upon a time, I knew your lunch at lunchtime—and when I want to have sex you want to wait just a little while longer.

"Just let me finish writing this paragraph. I am so late. So bad, I know."

"Just give me a few minutes. I ate falafel and I think it was not a good idea."

"Just wait a little while. I put our robes in the washer at the Laundromat and I should go back sooner rather than later."

I bring you *A River Runs Through It* and *The Things They Carried* because you never knew that both books have more than the title stories. I write inscriptions in each and I don't tell you. Four days go by and both books are still on the counter. There are no loving chocolate smudges, no highlighted paragraphs, no pages marked. You don't love them, you don't know them and at times I feel like an intruder.

Me: *I was just looking at that picture of that place on your thigh.*

You: *Ack, hang on. Bad signal.*

Me: *Do your thing. I'll catch you later.*

And then you don't write back to me and I slowly descend into insanity because

What

The

Fuck?

You're not talking smack about me to Lynn and Chana. You're not cheating on me; you'd never be able to pull that off with my access to your e-mail. I know. I know that you don't have a lot of work at school and setting Ethan up with Blythe really *was* a bad idea because he comes into work telling me about the fun they had last night at the golfing range—I shit you not—and I can't even get a response from you when I write to discuss the odd coupling of Ethan and Blythe.

It hurts, Beck. I don't know what to do with your absence. You're not mad at me. I know you well enough to know when your tail starts pounding the floor, and you're not *happy* at me, either. I ask you if you want to get into our robes and you kiss me and tell me we're beyond robes. You wrap yourself in me and hold on to me but what does that mean exactly?

Beyond robes.

We still have an *everythingship* because you still do things. I wake up with my dick in your mouth at least once a week. You still let me know when I'm on your mind for no reason:

Solipsistic (n) ☺ thinking of you and your hot bod

And you rave about me when you write to your mother:

> *This is different, Mom. He's on my level. And yet he shouldn't be technically because our lives are so different. But when it works . . . it works. You know?*

Your mother can't wait to meet me and I close my eyes and see us in Nantucket, in love. I even ask you about it one night when you're laid up with cramps.

"So you think this summer we'll hang out in Nantucket?"

You giggle and I burn. It wasn't supposed to be funny and you feel bad. "Joe, baby, no, no. I wasn't laughing at that. Of course we can go to Nantucket. It's just that you don't say *in* Nantucket. You say *on* Nantucket."

I can't think of a witty comeback and I used to be so good with you but maybe Ethan was right and you ask me to run up to the store and get you Advil and I do. The curtains are open and I see you open up your computer and start replying to an e-mail. I know that I shouldn't look at your e-mail as much now that we're together but it's a cold night and a long walk so I refresh your outbox.

Nothing.

I look in drafts.

Nothing.

And that's not possible because I saw you writing an e-mail with my own eyes. I buy the Advil and start home and decide to confront you but when I let myself in—you gave me a key a couple weeks ago—you aren't in the apartment. I call your name but you're gone and I panic. But then I hear the water turn on and I walk into the bathroom and you're wet hot, mine.

"Well, get in here already," you say. And I do. You fuck me like an animal and we get into our robes and I don't think about the e-mail and maybe I was wrong, maybe you deleted it. We are close that night and the next day I wake up and you're already gone and I text you.

Me: *That was fantastic. I woke up thinking about you in the shower.*

You: *Good good.*

Me: *Let me know when to come over. I have a feeling you're gonna need another one.*

And then it happens, the most dreaded response in the world, more terse than any word, more withholding than a *no*, and strictly verboten for someone as in love with language and me as you claim to be.

You: *K*

I get the dreaded *K* and I ask Ethan to fill in for me for the rest of the day but he can't. The day doesn't go by and I'm losing it and I'm looking at pictures of you and losing my patience with customers and I close early and call you but I get voice mail and I leave you a message asking when you can come over. I'm home when you finally respond and as it turns out, there is something worse than the dreaded *K*.

You: *Long story, honey but I gotta bail. Call you tomorrow xoxo*

I cry and watch *Pitch Perfect* and sing along with the Barden Bellas. I don't want to be a person who knows the name of a fictional a cappella group in a chick flick but that's what love has done to me. When it's over, I jerk off in the shower like a lot of unhappily married men in this world. But I cry harder because I'm not even married to you. Yet.

44

THERE are only so many times you can tell a person that you're happy for them. I have been happy for Ethan a lot lately and it's starting to get a little old. Every day he has good news of some kind and today is no different.

"You're not gonna believe this, Joe."

"Try me."

"Blythe wants to move in together!"

He beams and I smile. "That's great, E."

He's gonna miss Murray Hill. He's the only person on earth who would feel an attachment to Murray Fucking Hill and I say my line: "I'm happy for you, kid." And I mean it.

But I think your competitive streak is starting to rub off on me, Beck, because suddenly, I feel like life is a race I'm losing to Ethan and Blythe. I want life to be like Chutes and Ladders. I want us to climb a ladder as they slip into a chute. I'm starting to be kind of a dick and I throw a dart at his balloon. "Are you sure you want to move all the way to Carroll Gardens?"

"Blythe doesn't like Murray Hill." He shrugs. "It's a no-brainer."

"I hear you," I say and I can't help but try and one-up. "I don't remember the last time I spent the night in my place. It's all West Village, all the time."

It's a dangerous thing to put out in the universe, because naturally, you e-mail me a few minutes later:

> *Can we do your place instead of mine tonight? I've had a crazy*
> *day and my apartment is a disaster.*

I tell Ethan I have to go outside. I call you up. You don't answer. You never answer anymore. I pace. I panic. There are pieces of you that I collected along the way, souvenirs from my journey. I call you again. Voice mail. I lean against the glass front and it hits me: I'm scared for us, Beck. When we move in together, which we will, I am gonna have to choose between you and the pieces of you currently stored in a box, in the hole in the wall I made because of you. The walls in the building are terrible (surprise, surprise) and the plaster is cracking and the hole is bigger and I keep meaning to tell the super but I don't want to tell the super because I want your things in my hole. I'm being a lunatic. You'd have to climb into the wall to get at the box and no girl in the world would do that. Breathe, Joe.

My phone buzzes. I answer. "Hi."

"Joe, listen, I really can't talk because I'm so late."

"Where are you?"

"Here," you say and I turn and there you are and you smile. I like it when you surprise me at the shop. There's nothing like throwing my arms around you when I least expect it. I reward you with a kiss. You kiss me back, no tongue. You're in school mode.

"I can't stay."

"You sure? I got Ethan in there. We can grab coffee."

You put your hand out, palm open. "Can I grab your keys?"

This is an *everythingship*. I shouldn't hesitate but I do.

"Joe, think about it. I'm gonna get home before you do."

You called my place *home* and I give you my keys. You kiss me. Again, no tongue.

"Don't you have class soon?"

"Yes," you say and you hug me and it's good-bye. "See you later!"

You're gone, along with my keys and Ethan is chuckling when I get back into the shop. "So should we flip a coin?"

"What do you mean?"

"Well, Blythe just called and told me about how the girls have the day off from school because of the bomb threat."

"Yeah," I say but this is news to me.

"So should we draw straws?"

"No need," I say. "Beck's got a friend in town. Get outta here, have fun."

He's gone and I text you:

Hey. You got a second?

Ten minutes go by; still no response. I put up a sign in the window: BACK IN TEN. I go down to the cage. I pace. Why didn't you tell me class was canceled? Why didn't the bomb threat bring *us* together? I've never been so scared in my life and I wish Nicky wasn't a bad guy because I could really use a talk right now. I plod up the stairs, broken, uneducated, sad. I tear the sign off the window and unlock the door. Still no response from you and I'm losing my mind. I slump into the chair at the register and my head is a bomb that might explode. But that's when she walks through the door. A girl.

A customer. Her eyes are giant chestnuts and she's wearing a SUNY Purchase sweatshirt, a short skirt and kneesocks and sneakers; frisky. I check my phone; still no response.

She waves hello and I do the right thing and respond. I check my phone; still no response. I put on some tunes, Robert Plant and Alison Krauss. In no time, she's singing along, *somebody said they saw me swinging the world by the tail, bouncing over a white cloud, killing the blues* and I check my phone; still no response. I lower the volume and she responds by singing even louder. She's as good as any of the Barden Bellas, if not better. She pokes her head out from behind the stacks and I hit PAUSE.

"Was I singing out loud?"

"You're fine."

"Were you about to close up?" she says.

"Nope."

She smiles. "Thanks."

She disappears and I check my phone; still no response. I walk around to the other side of the counter so I can get a better look at those legs and Justin Timberlake's "Señorita" starts. Fucking Ethan, fucking shuffle. I scramble to get back behind the counter and change the music.

She laughs. "Leave it."

She crosses the aisle holding a Bukowski and I swallow. I check my phone; still no response. She approaches the register with a stack of books, as casual as someone popping into the corner store for milk. I can't check my phone; she's a customer, she deserves my full attention. She sets her novels on the counter. Charles Bukowski is right on top, *The Captain Is Out to Lunch and the Sailors Have Taken Over the Ship.*

"I'm not one of those girls who buys Bukowski so I can be a girl who buys Bukowski. You know what I mean?"

"Oddly, yes," I say. "But you can relax. I don't ever judge anyone."

"Then all my hard work was for nothing," she says, and who's the flirt now?

I scan the Bukowski and look at her. "Pardon my French, but this is one of the fucking best."

She agrees. "I lost my copy in a move. And I know it's stupid but I can't sleep or function unless I have that fucking book in my possession, you know?"

"Oddly enough, I do," I say and since when do I say *oddly* so fucking much? I lower the volume on Ethan's dance party and I scan *Old School* by Tobias Wolff. I've never read this book and I tell her so.

She doesn't miss a beat. "Well, after I finish maybe I'll come back and tell you about it."

"I'll be here," I say.

You still haven't touched *The Things They Carried* and she claps as I ring up her final purchase: *Great Expectations*.

The universe has a sense of humor and I have to share. "You should know, there's a Dickens festival in Port Jefferson every year, in December."

"What goes on at a Dickens Festival?" she asks and her eyes are as open as Karen Minty's pussy.

Oh no. I am flirting. I smile. "Just what you would expect. Face painting and flutes, costumes and cupcakes."

She gets me, she agrees. "That's why the terrorists hate us."

I am not editing myself. I am blunt. "And that's why God made terrorists."

"Do you think there's a God?" She too is *different, hot.* She is decisive. "There has to be a God. Only God would create something as awesome as Marky Mark and the Funky Bunch."

I don't even hear "Good Vibrations" and she reaches into her wallet and hands me a Visa covered in puppies. I run the pad of my finger over the elevated plastic letters. You would hate me right now. "So your name is . . . John Haviland?"

Her cheeks turn red. "I hope you don't need my ID because I lost it. Misplaced it, I mean."

I run the card. She exhales. "You rock."

I shouldn't care; I have you. But I pry. "So what year are you at Purchase?"

She shakes her head, no. "I hunt thrift stores and buy random college shirts," she says, proud. "It's sort of an ongoing social experiment. You know, I see how the world treats me based on what school I'm representing."

I tear off the slip and she signs, fast, messy. I've never bagged books so slowly in my life and I blurt, "I'm Joe."

She swallows. "I'm, um, I'm Amy Adam."

"Amy Adams."

"No *s!*" She grabs the bag and flies. "Thanks, Joe. Have a good one!"

I want to run outside and take her home to you. I want you to know that she came onto me, that she talked to me about God. I run to the door but she's gone. The phone rings. I answer. Is it her? No. It's a bank. They want to know about a recent transaction. The card she used was stolen, apparently. I don't rat her out but the phone call kills my buzz; that's what I get for flirting. I check my phone;

still no response from you. And somehow the absence of a response from you is a signed permission slip to be bad. I search the Internet for Amy Adam, almost as a dare for you to get back to me.

It's virtually impossible to find anything because of the actress, Amy Adams, and Ethan texts me a photo of him and Blythe on Coney Island. I don't respond. I take my time getting home and I don't need to check my phone for a response from you, because if you were responding to me, your response would interrupt one of my fruitless searches:

"Amy Adam New York"

"Amy Adam not an actress"

"Amy Adam sweatshirt"

"Amy Adam Facebook"

"Amy Adam SUNY Purchase" (You never know. . . .)

I walk home and plod up the stairs and I check my phone; still no response. I hear something from inside my apartment; you're here. I smell pumpkin wafting from my apartment; you've been baking. I hear singing come from my apartment and I smile. You're no Amy Adam. I love you for being off-key. I was wrong to doubt you and I knock twice on the door. There is a response, you cry out for me to wait.

You open the door and wow. This must be your second home because you brought the robes. You're in yours (naked underneath) and you baked a pie (pumpkin underneath). You tell me I have twenty-five seconds to get naked or get into my robe. I pick you up, my impish little wonder, and you kiss me; you respond. You are so proud of your spontaneous surprise. You admit that your building was off-limits because of roaches and resultant exterminators. You decided to turn a bad thing into a good thing, a surprise. I eat your pie and I eat your pussy and when I get up in the middle of the night to brush my teeth, my toothbrush is wet with your saliva.

"I'm sorry," I say quietly. And I am.

45

I don't know what you put in that pumpkin pie and you laugh that it was right out of a can. But the pie and the robes did something to us, for us. The next morning, I wake you up with a kiss and you embrace me. You beam. "Remember when I baked you a pie?"

"I remember when I baked you a pie," I say and you love it when I mimic you. You kiss me and we take our time with each other and you are full of new ideas for my hands. I love how you're not shy. I love how you tell me what you want. Your imagination should be bottled and stored and studied and I've never had you like this. You're so upright and your legs are intertwined with mine. Good God, what a fit, what a fuck and we collapse. "Wow," I say.

"Yeah," you say and you roll over to me and ask me if I want leftover pie and I ask you where you learned to fuck like that. You blush. You are shy, perfect. You pull a T-shirt over your head and when you're halfway out the bedroom door you run back to me and smother me with kisses and touches.

I am the luckiest man in the world and while you're putting pie in the microwave I'm erasing my search history in my phone. You'd never snoop in my phone; you respect my privacy and you trust me. But I don't want my phone tarnished with Amy Adam or Amy Adams or any other girl in the world. You sing out from the kitchen, "I keep forgetting. I started one of those stories in *A River Runs Through It*."

And you're reading my books after all and I like the sound of you in my kitchen so much that I can't wait for you to come back. I get out of bed, naked. I walk into the kitchen and pick you up and set you on the counter and spread your legs and nothing stops you from extolling the virtues of my tongue, my lips, not the noise from the street, not the hum of the microwave, not the fighting upstairs, not the beep from the microwave. When I have you in my mouth, you are mine and mine alone. You have never cum this hard in your life; I know it, I feel it. Something ferocious and far away inside of you has let me in at last. You stroke my ears with your fingers and thank me and I pull you off the counter and we settle onto the couch with our pie and *A River Runs Through It*. You read me a sentence you like and I interrupt you.

"You want to stay here again tonight?"

You hesitate, but only for a second. And then you smile. "Sure!"

We shower together behind the yellow police tape and I wash your hair and you kiss my chest. We get dressed together and the future is now, here.

"Hey, Beck."

"Hey, Joe."

"What do you think about moving in here?"

You smile at me. You stop buttoning your silk blouse and you walk across the room and the sun follows you because all plants lean toward the sun, *you*. You gaze up at me and I kiss you and you whisper, "It's only my first year, Joe. Let me get my MFA, you know? I need that to be my focus."

It's not the answer I wanted but it's good enough for me. We finish getting dressed and go into my kitchen and if Karen Minty were here, she would know how to make us egg sandwiches but if Karen Minty were here, I wouldn't have you. You slip into your coat. I tell you that I understand that you're not ready to move in but you're welcome to bring your computer here and write any time you want.

You are moved. You hug me. "That's so sweet, Joe. But my computer is so old and clunky."

"I wish I could get you a new one," I say. "One of those MacBook Airs."

"You don't need to get me anything," you say. You are not greedy. You are content. "And those MacBook Airs are crazy expensive, Joe. And besides, when I'm here the last thing in the world I want to do is write, so it all works out with my clunky, old computer."

I kiss you. I know to let you walk out on your own and you turn back and blow me a kiss. Twice. When you're gone I flop onto the couch and fuck around on my computer. I look at MacBook Airs and college courses. Let's face it. You are a writer. That's your life. I love the bookstore, but business will never be what it was. I want to buy you a MacBook Air and I am overwhelmed in the good way. I e-mail you. I feel close to you.

Is it time for you to come back yet?

You don't reply, but I'm not worried or scared anymore. I know you too well. I know that you're jotting ideas down in the notepad application on your phone. I know that you're not ignoring me. You're writing because you're inspired, because you're content, because of me.

IT'S a slow day in the shop, which is fine by me. I have time to make plans, to plant seeds. I sign up for a Q&A at NYU about part-time student life. I don't know what I'll study—Books? Business?—but I want to work hard for you, for us. I call Bemelmans and make a reservation for us next week. You probably don't realize it, but it's almost six months since we first met, and I'm gonna go for broke. We're gonna start off right here. I'm gonna set up a table in the cage and have a candlelit dinner. We're gonna fuck in there and do it right and then you're gonna get your present—a dress I just bought online at Victoria's Secret. They keep e-mailing you reminders about your shopping cart and I was able to find the item number and search the online inventory. It's hot; you showed it to Chana and Lynn, you think it's too hot.

Chana: *Get it. Why not?*

Lynn: *Just don't get it in red. Also, wear tights.*

Chana: *Are you kidding? The whole point of a slutty dress is that it's slutty.*

You: *Ladies, ladies. Calm down. I know I could never pull this off.*

But you can and you will and the dress is going to arrive tomorrow. It's going to be hard to hide it from you, to wait, because I know you're gonna look great in it, Beck. But if you're too shy to wear it to Bemelmans then I'll understand, of course.

FedEx arrives and there's a new James Patterson—gonna get busy in here tomorrow—and there's a little something for me too.

I'd almost forgotten that I ordered a DVD of *Pitch Perfect*; you only watch the download, but you should own what you love, it's that simple. I should wait to give it to you until it's our anniversary, but at the same time, you're coming over tonight and you made me a pie. There's no way I'm waiting and I stash the DVD in my bag and tear into the box of Pattersons. I put on some tunes—for once, I'm in the mood for Ethan's music and maybe this is what it means to be happy—and I make adjustments in Popular Fiction to make room for Patterson, the same way I'm gonna make room for you when you move in with me. I'm happy, Beck, and the juices are flowing and I just got another idea for our anniversary! Before we go to Bemelmans, we'll go to Macy's in midtown and head back to our dressing room. You're not gonna believe the way I went out of my way for you and maybe after Bemelmans we'll go to a tattoo parlor and get tattoos that only we can see. *Everythingship* would look hot in small black letters high up on your inner thigh and I better calm down or I'm gonna have to hang a sign and take five in the cage downstairs.

The day soars into night and I can't believe it when it's time to close up shop. My senses are alive; you do that to me now, not fucking Nicky. I walk this block every day but today it looks different, freshly washed, even though it's not; street cleaning happens on Tuesdays and it's Friday. Teenagers abound, talking about plans for the weekend and I was lonely in high school, but not anymore. I can't resist and I text you:

Be home soon.

You get back to me right away:

K

And even the dreaded *K* doesn't bum me out. There's nothing to worry about anymore. I've never felt so at peace with where I am, right now, on a train, tunneling toward my home, toward you. I take my time walking up the stairs and onto the street. I want life to move slowly because I want to anticipate you with all my heart, greet you with all my heart, fuck you with all my heart and miss you with all my heart. I have to laugh because I sound like a greeting card but I deserve this, you, joy.

My whole life, I've never felt at home, my whole life I've wondered why other people seem to be able to set themselves up with a job, with family, with friends. Every year, my dad would bring a Christmas tree home and my mom would get angry and drag it onto the sidewalk. Everyone at school knew; we were the weirdos who toss our tree on the street before Christmas. I'd plan on Hanukkah, but my dad would yell at my mother, *You don't even own a menorah! Since when are you so Jewish?* I've survived winters without presents in red and green or blue and silver. I've known Thanksgivings without turkey; my dad prefers beef. I've waited, Beck. I reach my stoop. The wait is over. I unlock the front door and the key sticks because I gave you my keys and this spare I'm using is rusty. I get the mail, just bills and coupons for J. Goldberg. The usual. I climb the steps and I remember what it was like climbing these steps when they led to Karen Minty and I think of something I love about you with each step and I do my homework even though I don't need therapy anymore:

#1 Beck sees beyond my background and knows that you don't have to go to college to be smart.

#2 Beck loves me in her own way, with a toothbrush, a robe.

#3 Beck isn't afraid to tell me how much she loves being with me.

#4 Beck wakes up happy when she wakes up with me.

#5 Beck can't cook and neither can I and she says that's good because it means we get to learn, together.

#6 Beck looked up solipsistic *in the dictionary that night. And now her dictionary is marked with all kinds of words that came out of my mouth and into her world.*

#7 When she orgasms, she clings on to me with her entire body. Her tits respond to my touch. Respond. Her whole body is a response.

#8 She has the capacity to be genuinely happy for other people. She takes pride in the fact that she put Ethan and Blythe together. She is sweet.

#9 She remembers everything I said or nothing I said and it's always good either way. She says sometimes that she's so crazy about me that she goes deaf when I talk.

I can't wait anymore. I want you now and I run up the last few steps and swing open the door and I'm hard as a rock and I've got *Pitch Perfect* in my hand but it doesn't matter. Nothing matters. The tapestry that covers the hole is on the floor. And you look at me with new eyes when you see me. You are holding a pair of your panties. You quiver with fear, like I am a horror movie, like I am a Rottweiler or a rejection letter and I am none of those things and I take a step toward you. "Beck," I try.

"No," you say. "No."

46

YOU'RE the one who snooped in *my* wall yet you're acting like I'm
the only one in this apartment with problems. You want to leave me,
of course. You are afraid of the Box of Beck. You are judgmental,
nasty. You stand in front of the hole in the wall behind my sofa—
my special and private place—and my box is on my sofa, partially
shredded because you tore into it like a sewer rat. There is only one
good thing about any of this. In your haste to snoop through my
things, you left your phone on the coffee table. I grab it while you're
burrowing through the box.

"This is a *used tampon*."

"It's in plastic."

"Don't you fucking move," you order.

A lot of guys would be pissed, but not me. I know you're out of
your mind right now, Beck. Hell, you're angry that I "stole" your
Mardi Gras beads but you didn't even know they were missing until
now. You're mad that I helped you scour your apartment for your

Chanel sunglasses last week when I "clearly" knew they were in this box. But honestly, you're better off without those fucking obnoxious glasses. They're for people like Peach; you look silly in them and you change the subject.

"Well, what about this?" you vent. "This is *my yearbook*, Joe."

"And it's perfectly fine."

"It's *mine*, you sicko. You didn't go to Nantucket High School. This is *my* book from *my* life and *my* friends and *my* home."

"Beck." You have never sounded more selfish but I will be patient. You point at me. *"No."*

You can't be held responsible for your actions. You keep looking at the fire escape like that's a possibility for you. You're talking crazy, like you'd leave me after all that pie, all that talk about moving in together. I try to reach you: "Beck, calm down. You're not climbing out the window and you're not gonna run down the stairs when you're out of your mind like this."

Round and round we go, one minute you are afraid, one minute you are going to kill me, one minute you think I am going to kill you, one minute you are the victim of my evildoing (LOL) and one minute *I* am the victim because you are going to kill me (LOL). You snarl and call me a *fucking sicko*. I know you don't mean it. If you were truly afraid, you would make a serious attempt to "escape." But the fact is that I know you. I know you are pleased with your discovery. You like attention and devotion and that box is proof that I am attentive, devoted. If that box contained Candace's things, you would have broken your neck trying to get out of my home. You will get on my side, but I have to be patient. You're in shock. You scream again. My head is starting to pound and I worry about the neighbors and I snap.

"Would you please shut the fuck up already? Do you hear me calling you names? How do you think I feel when I walk in here and find you in my *wall*? Do you think that feels good? Do you think I like to be *spied* on?"

"You have a *box* of my shit," you sneer. "I'm leaving."

"Nobody's making any decisions right now," I say. "And let's be honest, Beck. I could just as easily say I'm done with you for snooping around in my stuff."

"I—I can't believe this," you stammer. "You're crazy. You're crazy." And here you go again, with the chattering teeth and you're pulling at your hair. "I can't believe this is happening to me." Don't you get tired of your dramatics?

"Calm down, Beck," I plead. "Why don't you sit down on the sofa?"

Your cheeks get red and you get up on your tippy toes and you call me names—*psycholoonnutjobfreakassholesickocreep*—and it's fine. I know you don't mean it.

"Oh I mean it, Joe." You gawk and you brandish my Figawi hat. "I don't even want to know where *this* comes from."

"It's a long story."

"I'm sure," you say. "Fucking sicko."

I remember last month around this time, you got violent and screamed at me for throwing away a three-day-old burrito that was stinking up your fridge. The next day, you got your period and you kissed me on the cheek.

"I'm not crazy," you said. "I'm sorry."

"I know, Beck."

"I promise," you said. "When I get nasty like that, it's like I'm standing outside of myself and I know I'm being terrible and irrational but there's nothing I can do about it. I have serious PMS issues sometimes."

I forgave you and I haven't thought about that moment until now because I know how to be in an *everythingship*. Anyone who walked in here right now would think you're nuts, Beck. Anyone would try and protect me and ask you to lower your voice as you assault me with accusations. I'm a *pervert* and a *sicko* and a *stalker* and a *hoarder* and a *psycho* and I don't respond.

"Are you deaf, Joe?"

"You know I'm not deaf."

You're screaming again and do I scream at you? Never. When I text you and you don't respond right away, I let it go. And now it's your turn to let it go. It's not like I stole anything that you need. Who looks at their high school yearbook? You're moving on with your life; I never *once* saw you look at that thing. You don't miss those people. And a lot of girls would apologize for invading my privacy. You're ungrateful right now. You're still calling me names: *depraved, twisted panty-hoarding creep*.

You will settle down and I will get through this and I pretend you are a lion at the zoo. I am the zookeeper and I guard the door and I pray that I don't have to use my fist on you but if I do, you will recover, probably. For now, my job as the zookeeper is to stand by and wait. You'll wear yourself out soon enough, the same way you wear yourself out on my dick.

"How long has this been going on?"

"There's no need to raise your voice."

"How long?" you say and you obey. You use an indoor voice.

"As you know, I was quite taken with you when we met," I say and maybe there is hope. "You flirted with me and we had a connection and I didn't want to spring myself on you, you know, ask you right there. So I waited."

"Uh-huh," you say and you cross your arms and tap your foot.

"And then I learned about you, Beck," and I feel like the guy in *The Princess Bride* and you are as stubborn as Buttercup. "I was enchanted, Beck. I still am. There's nothing in that box for you to be afraid of."

You look at the box and you look at me. I don't know what to do and I feel inadequately prepared for my job as a zookeeper. I want you to see it all, I want you to know the depth of my passion, the power of my grasp, and the certainty of my love. But then again, you're PMSing, you're probably still scared from being in the wall, and every once in a while you mumble something about missing that asshole Peach.

"Go ahead," I say, because there's no turning back. You can't put your panties back in the box. Literally and figuratively, the box is scratched and torn; you've wrecked it. This is not what I imagined. I want to lead you away from the splayed box, but as a zookeeper, I know I need to keep a safe distance from the animal for the animal's sake and my own. You burrow through my things that you think of as your things and now you find my *pièce de résistance*, *The Book of Beck*. It's beautiful. You should be flattered that a stand-up guy like me who's *smarter than most guys* is creating a tribute to you.

"It's not done," I say. "I'm going to have it bound."

"My stories," you say and you are you again.

"They're all there," I say. We are fine, now, we are.

Any second now, you will run across the room and hug me. I am wrong. Your mouth contorts. You bark, "This is my *e-mail.*"

"Beck, please," I say. "It's a tribute."

"You hacked my fucking e-mail."

"I didn't *hack* anything," I snap, because again, you let me down. And you could have told your mother to cancel your fucking phone. That's on you.

You close the book and drop it in the box. The sun is setting and it's almost time to turn on the lights. I step toward you. You flinch and you are hateful and here we go again. Now you have new mean names for me like *murderer* and *killer* and *liar.* I remain tough, focused like a zookeeper must when the animals turn violent.

"You don't mean that," I say, calm.

"You're a twisted fucking stalker and you don't know what I mean."

"No I'm not," I say. "No I'm not."

I chase you. I deflect your barbs and I block you when you come at me. It's so easy to grab both of your wrists because you're so little and I'm so strong and I have no trouble forcing you onto the sofa. You can't fight and when you promise to be good, which you always do, I let go of you and return to my post at the door.

You are panting. "What's wrong with you?"

"I love you."

"This isn't love. This is *sick.*"

"This is our everythingship," I say. Our word.

"You need help," you say. You are deaf. "You're a sicko."

I would like to be a bigger person, but you call me names and then I think about *your* crimes.

"You should be locked up, Joe. Okay? Do you understand that? This is all bad."

You don't close the refrigerator all the way and twice in your place we've had to toss out all the food.

"You're a sick person and sick people need help, Joe."

I am healthy and you are a trollop; you threw yourself at Nicky. You're incapable of admitting that you're jealous of Blythe.

"Joe, let me call the doctors. Please, let me help you."

I don't need *doctors* and you lie, even now you are looking around for a weapon. You try to return clothes you've already worn and even though you're my girlfriend, you let me go to voice mail when I call you sometimes. You're not always attentive with your razor and sometimes I think the lady who waxes you doesn't have a license to wax anyone because your thighs are often coated in little red dots that don't feel good against my nice, clean legs.

"Joe, you need to let me go now."

And you need to stop judging me. You're a slob, and not in the way you think you are. You leave used tampons in your trash and you don't take the garbage out frequently enough and for a week last month, your apartment reeked of moon-blood. You still masturbate even though you have the honor of access to my cock. That silk blouse you're wearing? You look slutty, Beck. I thought so this morning, but in an *everythingship* you have to let things roll off of you and focus on the positive.

"I'm leaving," you say. Ha.

"You don't want to do that right now." I remain calm because someone has to remain calm. "People always regret what they do in emotional moments like this."

You don't even bother trying to get past me. You respect my strength. But I see you looking around. You are an animal and you run into my bedroom. *Mine.* You reach onto my shelf. *Mine.* You pick up the Italian Dan Brown. You throw it at me.

"Where's my phone, Joe?"

"In good hands," I promise. And I pull it out of my pocket. "You left it on the table."

You call me a *sick fuck* and you groan and you're a slob and slobs suffer.

"Stop imagining things, Beck." I would be a great zookeeper. I am good at this, slowly closing in on the animal as it works itself into a tizzy.

"I'll scream. You don't know how I can scream. Your neighbors will come. They'll know."

I don't mean it but I say it: "I'll kill you if you scream."

And it's over. You begin to yelp and spring at me and I don't like you right now. You make me do terrible things like hold you down and clap my hand over your mouth. You make me twist your arms and bear down on you, and this is our *bed*. You kick.

"You scream and it's over."

You just kick.

"Beck, stop fighting me."

You squirm but I'm stronger. You're a danger to yourself, to the world. You don't know what you're saying and you need me now more than ever and eventually, your anger transforms into sadness. Again. Your muffled blubbering heats the palm of my hand and I don't loosen my grip. "You're gonna wind up with nodes like your friend in *Pitch Perfect* if you keep yelling like that."

You stop, finally. I make a proposal. "Beck, blink your eyes if you promise not to scream anymore. If you promise, I'll take my hand away."

You blink. I am a man of my word and I take my hand off your mouth.

"I'm sorry," you say. You are hoarse and you flash your eyes at me. "Joe, we can talk about this."

I can't help but laugh. Ha! You think we're gonna *talk* while you're in the middle of a PMS explosion? We can't talk now! Your mood swings are psychotic! My goodness, Beck, do you think I'm that stupid? But you beg.

Please, Joe, please.

I love the sound of your voice and that would have been my *#10:*
Beck has a beautiful voice.

Unfortunately, you were lying and you kick once more, trying to escape. The worst part of being a zookeeper is the moment when I have to save the animal from its emotions, from its wild, illogical nature. You kick and scream. You bite. But your Portman-sized body is no match for mine, Beck. I count to three. I give you the chance to shut up. But you don't shut up and after three, I take your little head in my hand—sorry—and smash it against the wall—sorry. You are going to be so sorry too when you calm down and realize what you made me do.

I am lonely in the silence and I kiss your forehead. Clearly, you have problems and your menstrual cycle issues are just the tip of the iceberg. What kind of a girl climbs into a *wall*? You can't accept my love when you're this messed up. And you've got one hell of a way of asking for help. I move fast. You won't be asleep for long. I pack supplies and sling my messenger bag over my shoulder and lift you up and carry you down the stairs and hail a cab.

The driver sizes you up and wants to know which hospital. But we're not going to the hospital, Beck. We're going to my shop. This is New York. The driver doesn't ask questions. Animals know you don't fuck with a zookeeper.

47

YOU won't be happy when you wake up alone in the cage. But I have done my best. I left you a plastic bottle of root beer, a plastic bottle of water, a bag of pretzels, some crayons I found in a drawer, and a notepad. It's not like you can ever say I starved you or deprived you. You're safe. I even brought the shop's laptop downstairs and put the *Pitch Perfect* DVD on with speakers on a chair outside of the cage. You've seen the movie enough to know that Beca does some terrible things to Jesse. She rebuffs his advances, she mocks his interests, she bites his head off, and she won't let him get close. But in the end, she makes a bold public proclamation of love in the form of a song and he forgives her for all the terrible things she did. And I am going to forgive you, Beck. I kiss you good-bye and I lock the basement doors and text Ethan:

Hey buddy, no need to come in tomorrow. Pipe burst. Gonna be a few days!

The miracle about love is that I'm still not angry with you. I feel sorry for you. It must be so hard to carry all that anger around. I don't have that kind of anger in me. You were so vicious and I wish I could reach inside of you and suck the venom out.

I unlock the door to your place and I prove my forgiveness: I take out the trash. It reeks of bananas and womanhood. All of this might be your way of punishing me for the mistakes I've made, for my hands on Karen Minty, for my thoughts of Amy Adam.

I flop onto the couch in your living room. Something jabs my ass and I stand up and jam my hand between the cushions and it's my copy of *Love Story*. I don't remember you asking to borrow it. It's soiled with milky coffee, shards of tobacco from the cigarettes you smoke for no reason, a gum wrapper, ink stains, sand. How the fuck did sand get in there? *Sand*.

And I'm still not angry with you. I love you, my little piggy. I flip through *Love Story* and wonder why you stole it from me, why you tarnished it with an 800 number for a rice cooker you'll never buy. I would have given my *Love Story* to you. I would have given you anything. I look at the blank television set and wonder if this is my fault too? Was I stingy with you? Did I miss a hint you dropped about *Love Story*? I can't sit here anymore and I go into the kitchen to clean my book. But of course you're all out of paper towels and I remember one of my favorite nights in this kitchen, a few weeks ago, a few eons ago.

We'd had a great day together even though you'd been tied up with school and I'd been slammed at the shop. I joked that I'd be arriving at your place at seven sharp and that I expected dinner to be on the table, the joke being the fact that you can't cook. But when I hopped up those steps that lead to you, you saw me coming from out the window and I didn't have to buzz. You ran to the door and grabbed my hand and told me to close my eyes. And I did.

You led me into your apartment and guided me to the sofa and I didn't peek and you told me to open my eyes and I did. There you were, in your robe, holding a paper plate with a sweet potato you had sliced down the middle and molded into the shape of a heart. I looked up at you and smiled and you teased, "Welcome home, honey."

I fucked you like the glorious animal that you are and you told me the long-winded story of how you bought a sweet potato—the first one was rotten and you had to go back!—and poked holes in it and gutted it and splayed the skin, the way a high school sophomore splays a frog's abdomen in biology.

I laughed at the still untouched sweet potato. "Now all I see is a frog."

You were serious and soft. "No, Joe. That's my *heart*."

Then we ordered Chinese because one sweet potato was never going to be enough and I love you. But now I am here alone.

I use one of your little tank tops to wipe down *Love Story* and you won't be knocked out for that long and it's time to get to work. I'm gonna need your computer so I go back to your bedroom and take it off the nightstand where it lives and I go to the end of the bed I built and I sit and immediately, I am on my feet. Under the tangled sheets there is something hard and flat: a MacBook Air. You don't have a MacBook Air and I don't like the MacBook Air and I take it out of your room because I don't want that thing in the bed that I built.

I need a drink and I open the freezer and there's our vodka but there's something else in here, *gin*. Since when do you drink gin and own a MacBook Air? I take the vodka into the living room and sit on your filthy couch. I take a swig. Maybe your father got it for you. Maybe your mother got it for you. Maybe Chana left it here and maybe there was an intruder and maybe I should grow a set and open it. How bad can it be?

I'm an imaginative guy and I picture a lot of scenarios, but what I find in the MacBook Air blows my mind: a screensaver shot of you and *Dr. Nicky* taking one of those motherfucking pictures they call a *selfie*. You're both naked in my bed, the one I brought back on the ferry, the bed I built for you, for us. He's in our fucking *bed* and I go into the kitchen and take the gin out of the freezer and pour it into the sink over all the dirty dishes. Fuck you, computer. Fuck you, Nicky.

But when I reenter your living room, the MacBook asshole is still on the coffee table and if computers could smirk, this flimsy piece of shit computer would be smirking at me. I have to calm down and who knows? Maybe I'm jumping to conclusions. Maybe this MacBook asshole is actually old and you made a mistake a long time ago. But the homepage of this MacBook Asshole is a Gmail account for Beckalicious1027@gmail.com. You opened the account a couple of weeks ago, right before I met Amy Adam, when you started to get quiet on me, when I started to get suspicious. You opened it for Nicky. You are a bitch and you told him that you thought I might be reading your e-mail. *Cunt.* I read.

Nicky: *Wasn't I right? Your boyfriend can't read what he doesn't know exists.*

You: *You're terrible but you're also right.*

Nicky: *You like your new toy?*

You: *It's too much a whole computer ahahahha*
Nicky: *Stop.*
You: *Make me*

That's all I need to see. There are over 437 e-mails between you and Nicky and I'm not crazy. That middle-aged hunchback has been defiling you and taking advantage of you and letting you *pay him to fuck you.* When I felt like you were pulling away, you *were* in fact pulling away. You've been reduced to secret e-mail where it's all about Nicky. All those times you apologized to me for being late/tired/overwhelmed with work/busy/in class/full, you were either sleeping with Nicky, talking about sleeping with Nicky, or writing to Nicky. I open the photos and there's one thumbnail of particular interest. Nicky stands over my bed holding your naked calf. He's laughing and he's wearing my Holden Caulfield hat you were going to bring back to Macy's.

I'll admit it, Beck. That hurts. But I can't put all the blame on you. I'm the one who fucked up and let you down. I *knew* something was wrong. I have instincts and I ignored them and now you're locked in a cage because of me. I had the opportunity to take the mouse out of your house and I didn't. No wonder you couldn't stop screaming at me. You have every right to be mad at me for failing to protect you from this lecherous, Vans-clad semi*doctor.* I send Lynn and Chana a note from your secret account:

> *Things got ugly with Nicky. I'm so afraid Joe is going to find out and I am sooo behind on writing. I'm running away from it all to write for a few days. Love you girlies xo Beck*

We can't have your classmates worrying about your whereabouts, so I switch to your legitimate e-mail account and reach out to Blythe in a way that ensures she won't be trying to track you down:

Blythe, omigod big secret, you know my maid story? Your notes were incredible and I sent it to you-know-where and . . . they want it! I have so much writing to do (they're brilliant with notes, you should be interning there). Good luck with your workshop and I want us all to get dinner when I'm done writing. Your choice, it's on me. ☺ xo B

I take out your phone and open your Twitter app:

#SocialMediaVacation starts now. Xo B

48

I think I have memorized the treacherous e-mails between you and *Dr. Nicky*. I had to know them because I had to prepare an exam for you. I am cold, calm; I put us before my own selfish rage and I write the questions on a yellow legal pad that I bought at the deli on the way to the shop. I am ready and I carry my heavy messenger bag of computers to the bottom of the stairs and try to calm you down. You are shrieking. You should preserve your energy. "Okay, Beck, that's enough."

You look like hell, you poor thing. Your hair is a wreck and you've been crying. "What are you trying to do to me, Joe?"

"I'm here, it's okay."

You look at the computer I set up and you shriek again and clap your hands over your ears. I don't understand because *Pitch Perfect* is your favorite but I fucked up and forgot to hit PLAY. The intro screen has been repeating since you woke up, which appears to have been a long time ago. I hit the MUTE button. "There now. How's that, Beck?" *Alicious1027.*

You blubber and whimper and you're a mess but you nod, I think, and I tell you to walk over to the sliding drawer where I deposit two flashcards.

You look around. "What the fuck is this?"

"The drawer, Beck."

I tap the drawer where Mr. Mooney gave me pizza, where I gave Benji club soda. Sometimes people do change and I want you to pick up the cards.

I explain. "You need to take the two cards. Then we'll begin. One reads 'yes' and one reads 'no.'"

"Joe," you say and you're not walking, you're not listening.

I point to the drawer in the cage and you obey and you plead, "Joe, look, I overreacted."

"Beck, take the cards," I say and you look at me like I'm crazy. "Pick them up. The sooner we get started, the sooner you get fed."

You pick them up and you do love a test. You sit down on the bench and you face me. I see that you ate some of the pretzels and drank most of the water. Good girl.

"This is an oral exam," I begin and you laugh. I'm rooting for you to succeed so I look the other way. "Each question is true or false. And after each question, you'll have the opportunity to back up your answer."

"You're kidding, right?"

I ignore you and you're blubbering. I can't get mad. If I had to watch and listen to the DVD menu for *Pitch Perfect* for more than five hours, I too would be a mess. I look down at my yellow legal pad and begin. "True or false? You're having an affair with your therapist, Nick Angevine."

"False," you snap.

I want you to pass this test, so I press. "Again. True or false? You are having an affair with your therapist, Nicholas Angevine."

I deliberately left out the world *doctor* and you hang your head. "False."

I sigh. "You sure about that?"

Finally, you open up to me *petal by petal, as spring opens.* You pull your hair behind your ear. "It's complicated."

"This isn't Facebook, Beck. Nothing is complicated. It is or it isn't."

You are on your feet rattling, pulling at your hair, growling, screaming for help, afraid for your life, your poor vocal cords, what a waste. I drop my legal pad. I walk to the cage. "I love you, Beck. The last thing in the world I want to do is kill you."

"Then let me out."

"Soon," I say and I return to my station and pick up my legal pad. "True or false? You are having an affair with Nick Angevine."

You groan and kick but you stab the air with the YES card. Yes!

"Correct," I say and I make a check mark next to the question.

"Joe," you say and you're on your feet again, then falling to your knees, like an orphan. You beg, you supplicate. "Please don't lose it over Dr. Nicky. It was a mistake, okay? I was crazy and it's over. I mean we slept together once, Joe. It was nothing. One stupid night."

It wasn't *one stupid night* and it's time to move on. "Next question," I announce and this is hard, Beck. This is hard for me. "True or false? Joe Goldberg has a lot going for him."

You guffaw and you answer, sure and fast. "True. Are you kidding? You have a *ton* going for you. I'm always telling you how smart you are, how much smarter you are than everyone I know. You're amazing and you're funny and smart and *real*."

I was afraid you'd say something like that. I reach into my messenger bag for the MacBook Asshole. You see it and you growl. You kick and stomp and pound your fists. You're acting like a five-year-old and I wait for the tantrum to end. I know you love me and I know you didn't mean these things but we can't move forward without full disclosure. You're the one who went into *my* wall. I had no choice but to go into *yours*.

I read an e-mail you sent yesterday to Nicky from Beckalicious1027:

"Nicky, honey, I'm trying to end things with Joe, but he has so little going for him and I'm definitely the best thing that ever happened to him and it's hard. And honestly, Nicky, sometimes, in the middle of the night I wake up and I think I don't want to be a stepmother. Oh! Can you bring back The Things They Carried? *Thanks!"*

I close the MacBook Asshole. I don't show you any emotion. As the test administrator, I must maintain my professional emotional distance. There is a dense quiet. It feels like the rare books are listening to us, breathing, waiting.

"Okay," you say and we are in a new place. "I am a *shit*, Joe. Textbook damaged goods. And you always look at me like I'm so amazing and I don't know. I don't know why you do that because I'm not. And I was gonna get your book back, I was."

I want to kiss you and tell you I love you and hold you but I don't. I speak. "True or false? You don't want to be with Nicky anymore."

"True, Joe," and you sit down in the chair and spread your legs and hang your head in between. You lift your head. "One hundred percent totally, finally true."

I open the MacBook Asshole and take a deep breath. "We're moving on to reading comprehension. I'm going to read you something that Nicky wrote to you. And then you're going to tell me what it means."

You stare at me. You say nothing. I take your silence as understanding and I cough. And I read aloud from Nicky's e-mail to you:

"Is that what you think, Beck? Well, I think I just told my wife about you. It's a little late for you to say that you're reluctant to be a stepmother. This isn't a game, Beck. This is life. I'm coming over. I have nowhere to go. She wants me out, Beck. All this is happening and you ask me about a book."

I close the MacBook Asshole. "You have two minutes to tell me what this letter means to you."

I want to tell you the answer bad but I can't. I start the stopwatch on my phone. The answer is so obvious, Beck. You're supposed to tell me that you want to report Nicky to the authorities so they take away his license. You are supposed to tell me that you want his wife to kick him out and that you want him to die homeless, alone with a suitcase of scratched records and nowhere to play them. And then you are supposed to realize that you don't really want that to happen. You should realize by now that you feel nothing for him. You should know that all you want is *me* but fifty-nine seconds of your allotted time have passed by and you haven't said a word. You clap your hands.

"All right, Joe. The jig is up," you say, too singsongy. "I fell hard for a married guy. I'm a horrible person. I'm not gonna sit here and blame my parents or whatever, because I'm twenty-four years old. A lot of girls have shitty dads. There's no excuse."

You gave the wrong answer. Nicky really did a number on you and it's physically and emotionally exhausting to climb your way out of the trap he set for you, a pig in his rig. You are trying. I see that. I open the MacBook Asshole and announce, "Next question. Reading comprehension of the last exchange between you and Nicky. You wrote: *I'm soooo sorry. Nicky, I really believe that I will never love anyone the way I love you.*"

You leap up, you object. "Joe, stop. Please."

I raise a hand. STOP. I read what you wrote:

"*I get wet just thinking about you and that's never happened for me.*"

You interject aloud, "I've said that to every guy ever, Joe. That's what guys like to hear. You can't think that's the truth."

I lose focus and I react. "Well, you never said that to me."

"Because you're different," you say, *different, hot.* "You wouldn't buy into my bullshit."

You are charming but I have a test to administer. Besides, you don't want to get by on your good looks, your sexy cadence. You want to pass the test with your wits. I look down at the MacBook Asshole and continue reading your letter to Nicky:

"*I feel like you love your wife more than you know. I feel like I might love Joe.*"

You interrupt again. "I *do* love you, Joe. I *do.*"

I ignore you. It is still my turn to speak. "Now I'll read Nicky's response: *You want to know how I feel, Beck? I feel like you're a selfish fucking cunt. Good luck to you, Beck. You're gonna need it seeing that you haven't any morals.*"

I close the MacBook Asshole and return it to my messenger bag. I pick up my yellow pad. "You have three minutes to convey the meaning of your last communication with Nicky."

I give you extra time because you're a good listener and you've been through hell. Nicky should fry for what he did to you. And I failed you when I let him go. He abused you in that sacred "safe" haven of beige pillows, classic rock, and bullshit. I feel sorry for you, Beck. It's no surprise that you were so demented that you lied and told me your place was being "exterminated." You needed to get away from your MacBook Asshole and the asshole that gave you the MacBook Asshole. Of course you were climbing into the walls in my home, literally, you poor thing.

You are still thinking, pacing, and I am praying. I want you to give the correct answer. I want you to tell me that you don't recognize your voice in those e-mails. I want you to tell me that after less than eight hours in the cage you feel born again. I want you to say that you *never* got wet upon seeing that hunchbacked megalomaniac and tell me you love me and beg for my forgiveness. All I want to do is forgive you.

It's been *thirty-four seconds and two minutes* since I started the stopwatch and you look up at me and answer, "The funny thing is, the first time I ever went to see Nicky, he wanted to know what was wrong with me. He was like, 'Well, Beck, let's figure out what the fuck is wrong with you.'"

You laugh lightly and Nicky used the same line on me. Bastard.

You go on. "And I told him that I felt like my head was a house. He didn't get it but I said that my head is like a house and there's this mouse in there. And that's why I'm so anxious all the time."

You came up with that and he is a thief, low.

"Oh," I say and I should have killed Nicky the first day I walked into his office.

"He didn't get it until I told him that the only thing that made me forget about the mouse was hooking up."

I look at the *Pitch Perfect* menu on mute. You are nothing like Beca.

"Anyway," you say and you continue to break my heart. "I told him that I love to be wanted. I told him I love new things. And I told you that too, Joe."

"I thought you meant crap from IKEA," I say and you look away.

You try to explain yourself and you talk about your problems like you're talking about a movie you watched in the middle of the night. You are clinical, detached and you've been this way for a while, long before we met. You call yourself a *stalker*. You say that you've pictured the same wedding—the song is "My Sweet Lord"—with a million different guys, "including you, Joe."

"So you did want to marry me," I say. You are my love, *my sweet lord*.

You growl. "You don't get it, Joe. I'm not like that."

I think you are wrong and you say that therapy is a joke. You continue. "You *can't* get a mouse out of a house. Not unless you blow up the fucking house."

You are exhausted and hungry and incoherent and I slide the legal pad into my messenger bag and put two cherry pie Lärabars in the drawer for you. You do love to talk about yourself, even in a cage. I play *Pitch Perfect* and I walk up the stairs and ignore your calls for me to stay. I can't stay. I have to prepare the second segment of the test.

I hustle over to Popular Fiction and pick up two copies of *The Da Vinci Code*. I jog down the stairs and find you tearing into a Lärabar with your eyes glued to the Treblemakers "making music with their mouths." I did good! I pull the drawer out and toss a *Da Vinci Code* inside.

"Are you kidding?" you say, your mouth gorging with cherry pie woman food.

I point to my copy. "I'm gonna read it too."

"Why?"

"Because it's the only book I can think of that you and I have both never read."

We need to share an experience together in order to move forward. You flip through the book and you have a deep confidence, a sexual prowess, a bullheaded pride in the soft, hungry magnet that heaves between your legs. You're not afraid of me, of anyone. Men love you. You know it. No man can ever be a mouse in your house because you'll always have someone—a hot clerk in a bookstore, a horny shrink, a closeted rich girl. Someone will always watch over you and you believe that you are special. In the cage, you feel loved, not trapped. Just like me.

49

THERE is a mouse in our house and his name is Dan Brown, lord of our manor, creator of Professor Robert Langdon and keen, mesmerizing cryptologist Sophie Neveu. We are hooked almost immediately and we travel well together. We go to the Louvre and we follow the clues and you lie on your belly and you kick up and down when something exciting happens, which is often. I am on my side, on the other side of the cage, just as hooked as you are.

We take breaks to talk about the Opus Dei and the Priory of Sion and we both wish Robert Langdon were real and I find clips of the film adaptation online for both of us to devour when we need to rest our eyes and our fingers. You have never felt so compelled to read and I admit the same is true for me.

"I mean, I love Stephen King books," you say. "But that's different because his work is so well crafted. *The Shining* is fucking literature, you know?"

I do know and I remember Benji and his refusal to admit that he loved *Doctor Sleep*. We read late into the night and you wake me up the next day by sliding the drawer back and forth and back and forth. "Come on!" you squeal. "I'm dying over here."

We start to read but we need coffee and I bolt up the stairs and through the shop and down the street and you aren't just passing the test. You're acing it. There is a long line at Starbucks but you deserve that salted caramel stuff you drink every so often and our book club is the best.

"Is it twisted that I can relate to Silas?" you asked me last night. "This will sound sick, but when I found out Peach was dead, I was more angry for myself than I was sad for her. She was the best friend in the world because I was the world to her. She was obsessed with me and I couldn't even remember the exact date of her birthday."

"You were the church," I said.

"And she was the Silas," you said.

I reminded you of the first conversation we ever had in the bookstore, when you teased me that I was a preacher and I said I was a church.

"Wow," you said. "Wow."

I smile at nothing and everything as I walk back to the shop, carrying your salted caramel. We are a dream couple, we are what happens after Meg Ryan and Tom Hanks finally kiss, after cancer-free Joe Gordon-Levitt and sweet shrink-in-training Anna Kendrick eat their pizza in *50/50*. We are Winona Ryder and Ethan Hawke after U2 finishes singing "All I Want Is You." When I reach the bottom of the stairs, you clap but you are puzzled.

"Joe," you say. "That tall cup is too tall for the drawer."

"I know," I say and I love you for living in here, for not fighting.

"So how are you going to get that to me?"

I smile and show you the low, wide mug I bought for that specific purpose and you say it again, "Wow."

You've said that word more in the past twenty-four hours than you have in the past twenty-four weeks and you call me a *genius* and ask me to tell you again about how I got Benji to go to the shop. We have our coffee together on opposite sides of the cage and when I finish telling you the story you shake your head and here it comes again, "Wow."

"Nah," I say.

"One thing though," you say and you set your coffee on the ground. "That last Benji tweet, you said *in* Nantucket. And I remember reading that tweet and thinking he must be *seriously* fucked up because he knows that it's *on* Nantucket and not *in* Nantucket."

"Nice work, Sophie," and I grin and there is no mourning and there is no war because we are united, we are Unicef. We give.

"Thanks, Professor." You glimmer and you wink.

"Break?" I say.

"Perfect," you reply and we are so good in here and I play "We Are the World" and you laugh and ask why I chose that song and I tell you about how I feel like we improve upon the world in this basement and you are serious and you know what I mean and you agree and I have never been this connected to another human being in my life. You know the way my senses work, the way my brain works. You like it in there, in here.

The hours fly by and something in *The Da Vinci Code* leads into a conversation about the Dickens Festival and costumes leads to hats and I blush and you realize that I know about the Holden Caulfield hat. You close your *Da Vinci Code*. You hug your knees the way you do when you are truly, totally sad.

"That must have been horrible for you," you say.

"It doesn't look good on him either," I say and I am as stealthy as Robert Langdon. But you still feel bad.

"I'm a phony."

"Beck, no you're not."

"You're like this nobleman of the Priory of Sion running around figuring me out and I'm so inept I can't even properly hide a hunting cap, let alone a disgusting and cheap and shitty fling."

Disgusting! Cheap! Shitty! Fling! It is a relief to hear you talk this way and I smile. "You give it your all, Beck. You just have to be more careful about who you give it to."

"You're right," you say. "Nobody is more dedicated, more *intense* than you, Joe."

"Except for you," I say and you smile. You wink.

We read. When we are both in it we are quiet. We get sucked into a book in the same kind of way and at some point we both fall asleep. I wake up first—Yay!—and I let you rest. I go up into the shop and stretch. Ethan has texted me:

Joey my man! Congrats to Beck. Blythe tells me she is getting published in The New Yorker! That's amazing! Let's meet up for a drink next week! On me! Or housewarming, moving to Blythe's as we speak!!!!!!

Exclamation Point Ethan finally has reason to use exclamation points and I feel happy for him. I go to Fiction A–D and find *Great Expectations* by Charles Dickens and I am dizzy. I anticipate our future, the day I tell you about following you to Bridgeport, to the Dickens Festival in Port Jeff. You will say *wow*. Again.

And less than an hour later, my predictions prove accurate. You leaf through *Great Expectations.* "Wow," you say. "So you really did know what my half siblings look like."

"Yep," I say. "I bought a beard, you know, just in case."

You toss *Great Expectations* in the drawer. "I think you're a genius."

I pull the drawer and take Dickens out. "You ready?"

You grin. "I thought you'd never ask."

We settle into our spots and it feels like we're holding hands and running off the dock, holding our breath as we jump back into the deep, consuming water that is *The Da Vinci Code.* These are the happiest moments of my life, looking up at you and waiting for you to feel my eyes as you give me what I want. "Two forty-three. You?"

"I'm on two fifty-one."

"Well, take a break and let me catch up," you say and you remark once again that I am both a fast reader and a thorough reader which is special because most people, men especially, are just one or the other.

We cry when Robert and Sophie make it to the chalice. We know what's to come as they cross the landscape and enter the church. You put your hand on the drawer and I put my hand on the drawer and the drawer is designed to keep our hands apart, but I feel your pulse, I do. You sniffle. "I don't want it to end."

"This is like the end of *The Corrections,*" I say and the problem with books is that they end. They seduce you. They spread their legs to you and pull you inside. And you go deep and leave your possessions and your ties to the world at the door and you like it inside and you don't want for your possessions or your ties and then, the book evaporates. You turn the page and there is nothing and we are both crying. We are happy for Sophie and Robert and we are jet lagged from travel. We journeyed. At times we were so in the book that you *were* Sophie, descendant of Christ, and I *was* Langdon, savior of Sophie, and we are easing back into our bodies, our minds. You yawn and I yawn and your back cracks. We laugh. You ask me how long it's been.

"Three days, almost four."

"Wow," you say.

"I know," I say.

"We should celebrate."

"How so?"

"I don't know," you lie, you nymph. "I could go for some ice cream."

The Da Vinci Code is the greatest book in the world and someday, when we live together, we will have a shelf—brand-new, not used, I know you and your *new things*—and there will be nothing on the shelf except our *Da Vinci Codes*, nestled together, merged forever by the supernatural force that is our love.

50

I run out to buy you ice cream and I hear Bobby Short singing in my head—I am your prince—and I am on air on the way to the deli and on the way back. I bound down the stairs, can't get to you fast enough, with the ice cream you wanted, vanilla. You are simple again; three weeks ago you would have wanted some fucking gelato you read about in the *Sunday Styles*. I want to tell you about the funny dude in the line at the deli but when I reach the bottom of the stairs you are different. You are naked. I am still. "Beck."

"Come over here," you command, low. "Bring the ice cream."

I do as I am told and your right hand moves over your collarbone and onto your breast and you have another demand. "Give me my dessert."

I tear at the bag and the spoon falls on the floor but fuck it and I tear off the lid as well as the plastic lining. The ice cream is soft and my dick is hard and I know why Bobby Short felt like a racehorse; I am a racehorse.

"One second," I say.

"Ticktock," you say, you purr.

I play the song on the computer. You like it. You command, "Put it on repeat."

I obey and I return to the drawer and you kneel before the cage, your nipples hard. You want to know if I can pull the drawer out and *make an open window*. I can. You tell me to take off my pants. I do. You reach both hands through the new open space where the drawer used to be and I pick up the ice cream and approach the cage. You touch yourself and your finger emerges wet, glistening and I know to bring the pint closer. The ice cream is hotter because of our heat, melting. You immerse your other hand in the magnet between your legs and you don't let go of my eyes. Both of your hands are covered in your juices and you dip those wet fingers into the melting vanilla. You tease me. You tell me you want my mouth and I give you my mouth and your fingers fill my mouth and your other fingers are *touching skillfully, mysteriously, her first rose*. My dick. Your hands are *The Da Vinci Code* and my body is yours. I suck the life out of your fingers and you pry them from my mouth. I look down at you and you are in the vanilla. You dig, deep. Your vanilla hand joins your other hand on my hard cock, and I am cool and hot and hard to your soft. Your hands can dance and they lead me to your mouth and you swallow me and I moan and *we are the world* and there is barely room for the three of us, my cock and your hands. I belong in your mouth, and when I open my eyes you are staring at me, wide, whole. I need you, all of you. You want all of me. You know all my secrets and your mouth has teeth. You take me out of your mouth and hold me in your hands. You look up at me, pleading, "Fuck me."

I don't consciously decide to trust you. My body takes over and I can't unlock the cage fast enough. You rub your hands over your body and you wait. I jam the key into the lock and I miss your touch and I enter your space, *you*. You do not run away; you run at me, lust. I lock my hand around your neck and inject my tongue into your mouth and you take it. You scratch me. I could kill you and you know it and your nipples are harder than ever and your pussy never felt this sweet, this tight—*just vanilla*—and we could go on like this forever. You orgasm truly, you're exploding and it's an exorcism and an exclamation point. You're speaking in tongues and I own you and I'm in you and I loosen my grip and explode and you own me, you do. Your back arches, *wow*. I have taken you places better than the Upper West Side, superior to Turks and Caicos and Nicky's beige room. I have taken you to France, to the chalice, to the moon, and you cease to move and a smile rolls over your entire body and you're a lily pad, sun stroked and floating, rooted to the floor of the lake, me, dark, above you.

The cage door is wide open and I'm half naked and I'd never be able to catch you if you ran up the stairs. If you grabbed my empty dick and kicked and tried to make a run for it, you would make it. The basement doors are unlocked so you could, theoretically, escape upstairs. But the front door is locked; you didn't work here long enough to learn where I stash the key. Still, if you wanted to, you could risk it all to run naked into the shop and scream for help. Someone would help you and someone would come for me but none of that is happening. Your body can't tell lies and your goose bumps tell the truth. You lick your lips and look up at me. You purr. "Joe. Wow."

51

AT some point I stop pretending to be asleep and allow myself to watch you sleep. We live in a new world and I kiss you and I stretch. I need to wash up and I walk out of the cage. I don't lock you in; we don't lock doors in this new world. I leave the cage door ajar and I do the same for the soundproof basement door as well as the vestibule door that opens into the shop. We are free and I carry the *Da Vinci Codes* with me, like a kid with a new toy. When I make it upstairs I am genuinely surprised to find the books are where they were before we started reading. They survived the earthquake of our orgasm and the closed sign is where it was when we traveled into *The Da Vinci Code* and the bathroom is just as it was earlier today, before I fucked you to life.

I flip on the switch and the tiny bathroom fills with halogen light and the loud, shitty fan that you nagged me to replace. Even the fan makes me smile because of you and I will replace it, Beck. You're right; it's too noisy. And it's so old that it can't possibly serve any function. It's also a safety hazard when I'm in the shop alone because one switch controls the light and the fan. You can't have light without noise and you can't hear anything above the whir of the fan. And you're right, Beck. It's dangerous.

I flush the toilet and turn on the water and look at myself in the mirror. I look good, happy, and I wonder if I should join Facebook so that you can link your profile to mine. I should get on that now before you have to nag me and I add it to the list in my head. I let the water run hot over my hands and I don't know if I can really join Facebook for you. I read somewhere that kids now are so dishonest that there's an actual game they play called "Truth." You go to someone's *wall*—such bullshit, the language—and you write, "Truth is . . ." and then reveal something both surprising and true. It's a sad and grotesque thing that you and your friends have become so accustomed to lies that the truth has to be prefaced because it's inherently surprising, a startling departure from the lies that comprise your lives.

But you're done with that now and maybe before you delete your Facebook profile you'll make one last status update:

Truth is, I fucking love The Da Vinci Code.

We've got big decisions to make, Beck. Will you move in with me? Will I move in with you? Will we stay in New York? Granted, I have this great job, but I think you'd do well in California—you don't know enough to be around New York writers—and now that we have each other, we can roam. I look at my *Da Vinci Code* on top of yours. They look good together, Beck. This is right.

I pick up the bar of soap and get a good lather going. I am sad to wash off you and the vanilla ice cream. But then again, I am excited to soil myself anew with your sweat and your cum, your juices and your saliva. The fan is loud and my dick is hard and I know what I'm gonna do now. I'm gonna wake you up with my mouth, I'm gonna eat you alive. It's a good thing I keep a toothbrush handy and it's dry and I smile because the next time I brush my teeth, the brush will be wet because you will have used it. I feel holy and dedicated as Silas while I brush my teeth and dampen my pits and spray the cologne I bought to smell like the bartender. God, I *know* you. I splash some water in my hair. I would shave but I miss you too much. I need to eat you and I need to eat you now.

I flick the switch. The lights go out and the fan slows and I do not open the door. Something is wrong. The silence is cracked by terrible sounds, feet pounding on the floorboards, your distressed vocal cords—*Help!*—and the front door resisting you as you tug. I grab our books and creep out of the bathroom and you are still up front and pounding and it is, fortunately, four o'clock in the morning and there is nobody around to hear you. Whoever called New York the city that never sleeps didn't work at Mooney Rare and Used. I walk to the center of the shop and see you at the front, your crazy hair, crazy limbs, in my mother's Nirvana T-shirt, pulling on the door with both hands, so lost in your mission that you don't hear me coming. I am quiet as a cat. I take soft, meaningful steps and I set our *Da Vinci Code*s on the counter. You do not sense me and you are so close to the glass door that you don't see my reflection. I was right; you couldn't find the key. I wrap my arms around you and you kick.

"No! Let go of me you sick fuck!"

I have a solid grip on you and it's a shame that you're in a rage because I could really give it to you right now. But you are an animal—kick, kick—and a handicapped monster. Why do you waste time flailing your arms, little one? You can't reach me. I carry you down the aisle and drag you onto the floor behind the counter. I slide us to the floor and stretch my legs and hold you on my lap. Even if someone were to pass by, we would go unnoticed, protected as we are by the counter. You fight to get away, but I can hold you for the rest of my life if I have to.

As always, your anger eventually cools. Your muscles relax and you are my new doll: Sad Beck. You don't talk. You just cry. You don't fight me and there is hope. I kiss your neck; you don't like it. It's not a time for kisses, I understand. This is a lot to take in, a lot of change and the sun isn't coming up for a while and I rock you and look at your naked legs on top of mine. This is what love looks like. I know it. You don't try to claw me anymore. We sit in silence for so long that you must be ready to be good. I begin, I test you. "So, what are we going to do with you?"

The correct answer: You should beg for my forgiveness, admit that you freaked out when you woke up alone. You thought I had abandoned you, the way your father abandoned you, the way all the men in your life abandon you. And then I promise to stay with you forever and you caress my hands and I forgive you and let you guide my hands to your center, your magnet. I killed for you. I deserve you. I wish I could see your face and you haven't answered so I rephrase the question, "What happens now, Beck?"

The correct answer: love.

You answer, with a voice so flat I almost don't recognize you. "I disappear."

"No." No.

"Listen to me, Joe," you say as you press your hands into mine in a manner that is entirely devoid of sex, of passion. "I don't care about what you did to Benji or Peach. I get it. Benji really *did* have a drug problem. And Peach really *did* have issues."

"She was a liar, Beck. She even made up bullshit about her *bladder*."

"I know," you say and you forgive too easily. "I just loved that she loved me."

"And what do you want now?"

The correct answer: me!

You sigh. You tell me that you don't want to be a writer. You want to go to Los Angeles and be an actress. "And maybe if I don't get any jobs, well, maybe I'll write something for myself, you know?"

It gets worse. You tell me that you are basically a "very lazy girl." I hold you and you elaborate on your flaws. "Blythe is right. Half the time my stories really *are* just diary entries. Half the time I have to search and replace the names in order to turn the pages into fiction. That's how bad I am."

"Uh-huh," I say and I am not letting go and these are the wrong answers.

"You don't want me, Joe," and I look at your feet, the toes that Peach molested in Little Compton. "You think I'm this dreamy writer girl but I'm not. Nicky has every right to hate me. I fully admit it. I didn't really want him. I just wanted him to leave his wife for me. I wanted to fuck up his kids, and yes, Joe. I do know how sick that sounds."

No. "You're not sick."

You blurt, "I saw you at my reading that night in Brooklyn. I knew you followed me."

I hold on to you and kiss your head because we really are the same and we are the house and the mouse and you know it. You do. "I thought so," I say. "I hoped so."

You squish your toes into my pants. "Then you know I'd never turn you in, Joe. I'm the connector in all this. I'm the toxic one. I know this mess is my fault and I would never go to the police, Joe. You let me out of here, and I'm gone. Forever."

I give you another chance. "I don't want you to be gone, forever."

"Oh come *on*," you say like a friend, no sex between us. "I think you can find another girl to read *The Da Vinci Code* with you."

"Beck, stop." Tell me you want me.

"I will walk out of this store and never look back. I swear to God, Joe."

"Beck, stop."

But you don't stop. "Joe, listen to me. I swear to you. I will disappear and it will be like I don't even exist anymore. Let me go and I promise that you will never, ever see me again. I swear. Joe?"

You failed and you do not get a gold star and I squeeze your neck to make the wrong answers go away. They fester in your bulging eyes and they turn your cheeks *Nantucket red* and I squeeze, harder. The wrong answers must be choked out through the bubbles of saliva that ooze from the corners of your gnarled mouth. You are a fucking idiot for thinking I want you out of my life, after all I've done for you and this is not *Reality Bites* and you don't want me over the other douche bags in your life and I was wrong about you.

You gasp. "Joe."

I will not be fooled. "No, Beck."

You whisper, "Help."

And I *am* helping because you need an exorcism, a rebirth. You have sinned and you *did* manipulate Nicky and you *did* lead Peach on and you *did* stalk Benji. You are a monster, deathly, *solipsistic* to the bone and you're blasphemous because *all* you *want is*

You.

I squeezed too hard. You've gone quiet. I let go.

"Beck," I say.

I want to hear your voice. I call again. "Beck. BECK."

Nothing comes from you and *fuck*. What have I done? I shake your body and I can't hear you breathing and I need to hear you breathing because *Reality Bites* is a stupid movie and you *did* push Peach away and Benji *did* lead you on and Nicky *did* break the rules. So you said some stupid things—I do too sometimes and I forgive you. I slide you off of my lap and onto the floor. You are so still and all the good in you is in you, beneath those eyelids, latent. I love you for being so lovable. I am sorry, Beck. I can't hold you responsible for the fact that people go crazy over you and you have to wake up because I want to give you *love love love love crazy love.*

I push my hands into your tiny chest. You are breathing, I think. You must be breathing. There cannot be *nothing* inside of someone as lovely and lit as you; we had an *everythingship.* You are too robust and full of life and bathrobe rules and orgasms and pies and bitter caramel apples to be gone. I hate myself and I love you and I kiss you and you don't kiss me back and I beg you to come back and I hold your little hands and I look into your little eyes and at the end of the play *Closer* upon which the movie is based, the Natalie Portman character gets hit by a car. She dies. In the movie you don't see Natalie Portman die and I like it better that way and you cannot be dead, Beck. You're not even twenty-five and you don't do drugs and you are safe and sweet and studious and I lean over you so that my ear touches your lips. When you breathe I want to hear it and taste it and I wait. I wait for *sixteen centuries and eight light-years* and I pull away.

You are gone.

I stand up and grab my hair and I want to pull it out because you can't run your fingers through it anymore and maybe I am wrong and I get back down on the ground and mash my head into your hand and wait for you to touch me. *Please, Beck, please.* But your fingers don't move and when I lift my head up the silence feels official. It's hateful and personal unlike the peaceful silence of the basement. You don't rise up to forgive me and ward off the evil silence that weighs me down more every second that you are mute.

I look at you. You don't look at me. Your body is just parts now. You can't help me because you left me because you wanted to be *gone, forever.* Your crimes are many and you stole my *Love Story* and I pick up your *Da Vinci Code.* I am stunned because some of the pages have never been turned; I know my way around a book. I think you skipped entire passages, you brainless phony. When you asked me where I was in the book, you were cheating. The most romantic time of my life was a hoax and I am so preoccupied with exploring your *Da Vinci Code* that I don't see you come back to life.

But you do.

You tricked me, you cunt. You latch on to my ankle and pull and I fall over and I drop your *Da Vinci Code* and land on my side and it hurts *goddamn it* and you kick me in the dick and that hurts *goddamn it.* You are not *gone, forever* and you are possessed and out of words

411

and my groin aches and my side pounds and you are not my savior,
you make things *worse*. You are alive, underhanded, kicking me
when I'm down and I scream in agony and you are *toxic* and Satanic
because just a minute ago:

"You were dead, you fucking bitch."

You say nothing. You kick. But I'm nontoxic and I'm bigger and
braver and God gives *me* the strength to recover from your nasty
blows. I swat your legs and now *you* collapse, flat on your back. I
mount you. You try to bite me but you can't and you try to kick me
but you can't and you try to claw me but your wrists are locked in my
hands. You can't do anything with me pinning you down. You spit at
my face; you are a *Masshole*. And you are weaker now and I let go of
your arms and wrap my hands around your neck for real this time.
You try to hit me but your little fists aren't what they once were. The
bad in you outweighs the good and your cheeks turn white and my
cock throbs in pain and my hipbone pulsates and your eyes bulge.
You're disgusting. My mother's Nirvana T-shirt that I was wearing
the day you *stalked* me to my house, the one I've held on to my whole
life, it's a mess of cum and vanilla. You have torn it beyond repair,
you bitch.

"You were right, Beck," I say to you. "You kill people. You do."

I squeeze your neck and I thank you for kicking me in the dick, and
I try to blink your saliva out of my eyelashes. I thank you for proving
beyond a reasonable doubt that you *are* bad. You do not want love
or life and we never had a chance and you are commonplace and
raw, gasping and gurgling. *Solipsistic* with your fudgy inconsiderate
fingerprints ruining my books, my heart, my *life*.

"What's that, Beck?"

You have one word left in you: "Help."

And I do help you. I take my right hand and reach for your *Da Vinci Code*. I shove the book into my mouth and bite a few pages. I yank the book away and I toss it and grab the torn pages out of my mouth, wet with my saliva that you wanted so badly.

My last words to you: "Open up, Guinevere."

I shove the pages into your mouth and your pupils slip around and your back arches. This is the sound of you dying. There are bones cracking—where, I do not know—and tear ducts in emergency mode—the tear of death seeps out of your left eye and onto your porcelain cheek and your eyes are fixated on *somewhere I have never traveled, gladly beyond any experience; your eyes have their silence*. You are no better than a doll now and you do not react as the pages in your mouth take the blood that rises from your gullet.

And all at once I *miss* you and you *missed* me and I call to you and I seize your tiny shoulders.

You don't respond. You are as flawed as all the books in the store; you have ended and left me and you are *gone, forever*. You will never leave me in the dark ever again and I will never wait for a response from you ever again. Your light is out for good now and I take you in my arms.

No.

I want to throw myself in front of *engine engine number nine*. How could I have done this? I never made you pancakes. What the fuck is wrong with me? I can't breathe and you are *my sweet lord*, Beck, *different, hot*. You are. Were.

I cry.

52

AT the end of your days, you claimed that you weren't a writer. But I think you would appreciate the poetic symmetry regarding your burial. It was a long, lonely drive upstate, more than four hours outside of the city. It was tough going in the Buick, with you in the trunk with your green pillow, silent as Little Compton in the winter. I drove past Nicky's Pizza and I kept going and I found this diner. Nicky's and his brother's extra homes are nestled in nearby Forrest Lake, a private area just outside of Chestertown. This is a pure township, Beck, old-fashioned and pleasantly anchored to an antiquated way of life. I eat a grilled cheese sandwich because I have to, because burying you in the cold forest will be demanding, even though everyone who comes into the diner can't resist remarking on the mild winter. So mild, I wouldn't need a red Holden Caulfield hunting cap from Macy's even if I still had one. I will not cry. Not here.

Most in the diner are local, and those who aren't local have driven in for a car show. The waitress asks me if I'm here for the car show and I say that I am and I check my phone and I have to go to the bathroom again, because every time I check my phone, it's like you die all over again. *Nobody, not even the rain, has such small hands* and I cry, quietly, so as not to attract attention. Your death is a song on repeat and I splash cold water on my face and try not to think about the fact that I will never hear from you ever again. I won't, Beck. You are dead.

I know that Nicky is not stupid. He wouldn't bury you on his own property. But he would drive into the nearby woods off Forrest Lake Drive, as I do now an hour after sunset. I see a pink-and-white sign. There is an event, "Chet and Rose's Wedding" is happening *tonight* at the camp at the end of the road. But I will not be deterred. I veer off-road into the blackness that's purer than the beaches of *LC* and darker than the depths of your *solipsistic* soul. There is no ocean here to soften the starless blow of eternity. I brake, slowly. Chet and Rose are the ones with bad timing, not me, damn it.

The night is so empty that I can hear the wedding when I shut off the Buick. I strap on my night vision goggles and grab my shovel and step out into the darkness. I try not to listen to the wedding as I shovel. But it's hard. Chet and Rose take their first dance—Clapton's "Wonderful Tonight"—as their friends and family clap. I wonder what our wedding song would have been and I ask you but you don't answer. You are dead.

I dig. I have never been and will never be as alone as I am while I dig. Upstate New York clings to the cold like no other place. Only here would I have to listen to Eric Clapton shut off lights and praise his loyal, beautiful, girlfriend as I, alone, sweat and shiver and prepare to put you into the dirt. Life goes on, so literally, and I stab my shovel in the bitter earth. I bend over to catch my breath. I look over at you, wrapped up in a wooly blanket from Bed Bath & Beyond, silenced in the open trunk. I am breathing normally now and the revelers are doing the Electric Slide and would we have had a wedding like this? I suppose it would have been on Nantucket because you're the one with a family. I would have invited Ethan and Blythe and Mr. Mooney. Mr. Mooney wouldn't have come. But he would have transferred the title of the shop to you and me. I know it. I want the wedding to stop and I would like to scream at the top of my lungs but I don't want to alarm you. But I can't alarm you. You are dead.

I dig and the party goes on. There are toasts and cheers and Stevie Wonder sings about his precious daughter—*Isn't she lovely made from love?*—and we'll never have a daughter and I lose my temper and throw my shovel. I crawl into the earth and let the music beat the living fuck out of me. I can't fight it anymore and joy at the far end of the woods has become monotonous—I'm not one of those people who ever thought "Get Lucky" was so fucking special. I can almost taste their vodka and I am the uninvited guest, out of sight, alone. What soothes me, what allows me to keep digging, is the likelihood that Chet and Rose have a website, a registry. Knowing that I will be able to find them, to see them, is a comfort somehow. Neil Young sings for Chet and Rose—"Harvest Moon" that hurts—and Neil Young will never play for you and me on our wedding day and you don't hear him now. You are dead.

I lift your body out of the trunk and unravel the area rug that encapsulates you. You are still beautiful and I rest my head on your chest and tell you about Chet and Rose. I will probably die alone, under an insignificant moon and you won't be there to mourn. You soar on to heaven and I have to summon the strength to set your precious corpse in the ground. Chet and Rose are surrounded by friends and family but I, alone, lift your petite body and *maketh you to lie down in green pastures.* It would be nice to have a moment of silence; Chet and Rose are rude to be so loud. But I can't blame them; they can't see me, can't hear me. They're in their own world, where good things happen, a quarter mile and a million light years away. I kneel on the ground and recite the 23rd Psalm. I memorized it for this occasion. You are dead.

There is no way to know what happens to us after the wedding we won't have, after life. I walk in the woods and look at the world with inhuman night vision and see all that man was not built to see. I don't know if you will *dwell in the house of the lord forever* but I lie on my back and listen to the party for Chet and Rose grow as quiet as the night, as death. They will get tired and their party will end and if anyone was ever going to live eternally in the light, I think it would be you.

I cover you with dirt and rocks and branches and leaves and you are so much more than a body. The walk back to my car is a short one. The drive away from Chet and Rose and your body is a long one in the dark of night. I don't know that I'll ever make it home, and even when I do make it into my apartment, I remain unsure of whether or not I will ever have a true home. I will never have you. You are buried by Forrest Lake, near Chet and Rose, *somewhere I have never traveled, gladly beyond any experience.*

I don't open the shop the next day. I can't. You are dead.

53

THE mail I typically receive is boring and financial, bills, coupons, crap. But today, almost three months after your passing, I receive the first wedding invitation of my life, via the United States Postal Service. The envelope is so big the postman had to walk it upstairs and lean it against my door. I know I'm not an expert, but it's a beauty, Beck, and I have it with me here at the shop. I'm enamored with the triumphant romance of the thick, embossed cardstock juxtaposed with the delicate, gold, italicized cursive. Who knew Ethan and Blythe were royalty? A lot happens in three months. Exclamation Point Ethan and Blythe have gotten engaged and invited me to their wedding in Austin, Texas. A lot doesn't happen in three months. The HELP WANTED sign is still in the window; Ethan got a corporate job, marriage is expensive.

But, this invitation has altered my perspective. I haven't felt this hopeful since exiting Dr. Nicky's office, since entering you. The future exists again because of this invitation. This invitation necessitates that

I mark dates on my calendar. And it feels good to flip ahead through the calendar in my phone. Before this invitation arrived—addressed to *Mr. Joe Goldberg and Guest*!—I was only flipping through months gone by, inventing anniversaries for our life that's gone. You above all others know the importance of moving on; you like new things, you *liked* new things. Life is not a Dan Brown book; you are dead and you are not coming back. But life is better than a Dan Brown book because at long last, I have something to look forward to, a *wedding*. I have to decide between steak and fish and I am genuinely torn about the decision and I have to make this decision within the next forty-one days, according to the rules on the reply card.

The bell chimes on this slow day that's neither summer nor fall. An unremarkable man in shorts asks about *Doctor Sleep*. I point him to Fiction G–K and I think of the time I saw you in Fiction F–K and what a fool I was in the days after. I have rearranged the shop; I couldn't look at F–K anymore. I genuinely believed that reshaping the shelves would make it easier to live in the world without you, the world I built with my own two hands, the world that won't allow me to tell you that I know you stole your Ritz robes from Peach. I still get flashbacks. I still cringe. I am eating again, but only because I hate fainting. Everything has been an exercise until now. I will always feel indebted to the United States Postal Service, to Ethan, to Blythe. And I will never again underestimate the power of anticipation. There is no better boost in the present than an invitation to the future.

The loner buys the King and leaves with the King and I am going to need to buy a suit. It's wonderful to have a project and I celebrate by visiting Chet and Rose's online love nest. I feel like I've gotten to know them so well since that dreadful night in the woods. I want to tell them about the invitation. I've become obsessed with Chet and Rose, but how could I not? They gathered in the woods to be married so that I could still believe in love. I love them. I've watched their honeymoon slideshow hundreds of times. They were there for me. What timing. I used to play the slideshow and pretend that we're the ones on a honeymoon in Cabo San Lucas. But these days I'm less bitter. I know that we all don't get to be Chet and Rose. It is an indisputable fact: Some people on this earth receive love, get married, and honeymoon in Cabo. Others do not. Some people read alone on the sofa and some people read together, in bed. That's life.

I will probably die alone. Karen Minty will probably die married; lots of people love *The King of Queens.* And I am fine with my fate. It was my decision to spare you the pain of life. I let go of you. I forgive you. It's not your fault that you carried your demons awkwardly in that big Prada bag, in those giant used robes from Peach's Ritz. You were toxic, not vicious and the men who did leave you are thriving; that Hesher guy has a television show that doesn't suck. An online registry at Babies "R" Us shows that your father is about to become a father, again. Some people get it all, they do.

I think you would be happy to know that your voice carries. I am the sole reader of *The Book of Beck.* I had your short stories bound at FedEx. But millions of people have devoured the story of your life. Everyone knows about the twisted psychologist who murdered you. You never were published in the *New Yorker* but you did make the *New York Post.*

You changed me, Beck. I will not grow lonely like Mr. Mooney. I have Ethan and Blythe. I have the girls they periodically foist upon me. The girls are always terrible, wan and patronizing or shallow and simple. I am like Hugh Grant in *Love Actually* minus the love, which isn't so bad when you realize that in real life, Hugh Grant is single, like me. Once again, not all animals are destined to pair off. Yes, I understand that we are built for companionship; God gave us vocabularies. We need to speak. We need to listen. I fuck occasionally, girls from the Internet, girls from the shop. But mostly I keep to myself. No longer do I open *petal by petal* and you were right, Beck. You were not the girl I thought you were and Barbara Hershey wasn't the one for Elliot in *Hannah and Her Sisters*. The doorbell chimes and I look up from a photo of Chet and Rose on paddleboards and see a girl, a girl I know, sort of. She wears a University of Pittsburgh tank top and jeans. She squirms. She waves. I wish there was music playing right now. She liked my music last time.

"I saw the sign in the window." She swallows. "Are you still hiring? Sometimes they forget to take down the sign. Sometimes it's bullshit. I'm sorry. I'm swearing."

I forgot about the sign but I did not forget about Amy Adam and her stolen credit card and her fraudulent academic attire and her large chestnut eyes. We are still hiring. She comes over. She glances at my wedding invitation and nods. "I love Austin."

"So, how have you been?" I ask and it's a silken maneuver on my part. I am the gentleman, assuming the role of the one who remembers so that she may be the lady, remembered. She fawns, almost curtsies. She is flattered and happy. She is staring at me and it feels good in her eyes and she hands me a résumé.

"I *used* to work at a little bookstore in Williamsburg, but let's just say that it didn't work out because of their shortsighted policies about what they call *stealing*." She grunts. "Like I *shouldn't* bring books home and read them. And exactly how do you even read a book without marking it up?" She is loud. "Excuse me if I'm not one of these ultramodern Kindle people, but I like *pens, paper*, real pages I can rip and touch." She shakes her head. "And if you bought a book and found notes in the margins, I mean who *wouldn't* love that? It's a bonus." She doesn't want me to answer. She blinks. "I'm sorry. I'm going off. But it has to be said."

She needs my acceptance. I smile. "No apology necessary."

Now it's her turn and she complies, playful. "I probably sound like a lunatic. Do you guys hire lunatics?"

I tell her that we *only* hire lunatics and she thinks I am funny. She has a lilting laugh and she likes it here with me. She will be my cashier and my girlfriend and the next time I'm invited to a wedding, it will be addressed to *Joe Goldberg & Amy Adam* and I won't have to worry about finding a *Guest*. You are *gone, forever* and she is here, now.

ACKNOWLEDGMENTS

I want to thank Joe Goldberg for demanding to be heard. Well done, Joe.

And now, for the real people who brought this book to life. Thank you to everyone at Emily Bestler Books, Atria, and Simon & Schuster. I hit the editorial jackpot with Emily Bestler. Emily, I am so grateful for your enthusiasm, intelligence, and acute sensibilities. Also, don't get stalked. Judith Curr, Ben Lee, Paul Olsewski, David Brown, Mellony Torres, Hillary Tisman, LeeAnna Woodcock, Jeanne Lee, Kristen Lemire, and Kate Cetrulo—thank you for making me feel so at home. Megan Reid, thank you for the world's greatest valentines. Alloy, oh Alloy. Josh Bank, Lanie Davis, and Sara Shandler, your brains and hearts are perfect. Joe agrees. Josh, your voice is more potent than Karen Minty's stick. Lanie, you always know best and I am so grateful for your direction (and your ladle!). Sara, you are so freaking articulate and you draw the best hearts. Thank you all for caring so deeply about the world in this book. Jennifer Rudolph Walsh, Claudia Ballard, and Laura Bonner at WME, thank you for believing in *You* and knowing what to do with it. Natalie Sousa, you read my mind when you designed this cover. Thanks for that.

Countless Barnstable High School students would agree that we had the greatest teachers in the world. Mick Carlon and Ed O'Toole, your encouragement had profound impact on me. Linda Friedman, Meredith Steinbach, thank you for being a wonderful mentors. Matt DiGangi, thanks for masterminding Thieves Jargon. Lauren Acampora Doyle, you are a wonderful, wise pollo, and I thank you for introducing me to Alloy goddess Sara Shepard. Thank you, cousin Tommi Hurme for picklebacks, and thank you, cousin

Kristiina Hurme for your support. These things help when you are writing a stalker book.

I started *You* after losing my father to cancer. My friends, I owe you: Amy Sanborn, I am so lucky to have known you since I was in the womb. Lauren Heller, you are a gift. Sarah Tatting-Kinzy, you are a true listener, an incredible friend. Matt Donnelly (and Corky and Pinky), I am so grateful for our inspiring times in Splendorea. June Hurme, Kathleen Kelly, thank you for wanting to know what happens next. Lorena David Esguerra, George Esguerra, Dylan's Roald Dahl guest suite was divine. Lia and Todd Haberman, thank you for the donuts. Crispin Struthers, thanks for being there. Nicholas Fonseca, you lift me up. Sharon and Paul Swartz, I'm grateful for my writer's retreat (and pancakes!) at the Cape Point Hotel. Sophia Macheras, it meant so much to me when you loved "Owen." Michael Wyman, you are the best; love ya babe, don't change. Thanks and love to Eric Scott Cooper, Frank Medrano, Beverly Leiberman, Karen and Howie Onik, Erin Penner, Jen and Jon Sackett, Korbi Ghosh, Josh Wyman, Auntie Carole and Uncle Den. Macherases, Swartzes, Wymans, cousins, family, I love you. I could fill a book with more names, and then another book. I'm lucky to know so many splendid souls.

Love and hugs to my brave brother, Alex, my Xanadu sister, Beth, and my awesome nephews, Jonathan and Joshua. And now, my parents, Monica and Harold Kepnes, thank you for creating a home where Led Zeppelin and laughter dominated. Dad, I wish you were here to celebrate. You and Mom have believed in me since I started writing about stolen axes in my Hello Kitty diary and hoarding Sweet Valley High books. That means everything. You inspire me, always.

Finally, thank you to the artists whose works are referenced in this book. You rock.

Permissions

THE CHARMINGLY MURDEROUS JOE
HAS FALLEN IN LOVE AGAIN, AND HIS
NEW OBSESSION IS EVERY BIT AS
TERRIFYING . . .

THE CHILLING NEW NOVEL

BY CAROLINE KEPNES,

COMING SOON . . .